The Wedding Party

Tammy Cohen

BLACK SWAN

TRANSWORLD PUBLISHERS

Penguin Random House, One Embassy Gardens,
8 Viaduct Gardens, London SW11 7BW
www.penguin.co.uk

Transworld is part of the Penguin Random House group of companies
whose addresses can be found at global.penguinrandomhouse.com

First published in Great Britain in 2021 by Black Swan
an imprint of Transworld Publishers

A CIP catalogue record for this book
is available from the British Library.

ISBN 9781784162481

Typeset in 10.57/14.45 pt Sabon LT Pro
by Integra Software Services Pvt. Ltd, Pondicherry

Printed and bound in Great Britain by Clays Ltd, Elcograf S.p.A.

The authorized representative in the EEA is Penguin Random House
Ireland, Morrison Chambers, 32 Nassau Street, Dublin D02 YH68

Penguin Random House is committed to a sustainable
future for our business, our readers and our planet. This book
is made from Forest Stewardship Council® certified paper.

For Tom and Niko,
and all the Aunties,
and the entire Kazoo Chorus

Prologue

From up here the body resembled a swastika. He'd watched it materialize gradually in the grainy grey pre-dawn light, lying on the beach below with its limbs splayed out at right angles.

A faint buzzing noise like a stupored fly on a window made Panos look out at the sea, where, in the soft rose-gold glow of early morning, the pointed grey bow of the coastguard launch was carving a straight line through the still, pale pink water of the bay. It cut its engine suddenly as it approached the jetty so that the silence fell with a thud, reverberating around the cliff faces that enclosed it.

Panos stretched. It had been impossible to sleep in the folding chair they'd brought him from the hotel and his back ached where a draught had penetrated the canvas sides. He heard sounds further up the hill behind him, the hotel coming to life, and wished his colleagues on board the launch would hurry up and retrieve the body before anyone came. Last night it had been impossible, the tiny bay inaccessible except by clambering over rocks from the bigger bay next to it, with its steep steps leading up to the hotel, but now time was of the essence. It was early, but the coastal path was popular with walkers, and who knew whether the strip of police tape he'd tried to tie across it further down in both directions would have survived the night intact.

Now the men were disembarking. Six of them. Half – like Panos – wearing the dark blue uniform of the Greek police. Two carried a stretcher between them. As they progressed along the jetty their voices floated up to where Panos stood guard, making sure no one disturbed the section of the clifftop from where the body had fallen. They seemed in high spirits. One of them laughed as he mistimed his step at the other end of the jetty and had to bend his knee to absorb the impact. But they fell quiet as they arrived at the back of the beach, where the body lay. Panos watched them bend their heads, each paying his own wordless respects. One of them said something and the others turned their faces up to where Panos stood at the top of the cliff. He waved and they all raised their hands in salute.

Two of the men were carrying rucksacks and now they knelt on the fine pebbles to open them. One proceeded to erect a rudimentary white tent over the body while the other assembled his camera. Panos's aching muscles unfurled with relief. At least now no one could happen across the sight by accident. Already there were voices coming from the hotel up the hill behind him. Probably early-rising guests helping themselves to breakfast on the terrace.

His colleagues had been there late last night asking questions. And today it would all start again.

He lit a cigarette. Ahead of him, a seagull soared high above the glassy surface of the sea, turned golden now in the ripening morning sun, and its loud caw mixed in the already warm air with the smell of wild thyme and laurel and sage and the fresh scent of the cypress trees further inland and the cigarette smoke, making him momentarily giddy.

A small lizard, perhaps drawn by the insects already buzzing around the heady white pittosporum buds, shot across the path towards the gorse that lined the cliff edge, startling him.

Panos threw down his cigarette butt and ground it into the dirt under his shoe. Then he folded up his chair and picked up the Thermos that had kept him company during his lonely vigil.

Before he left, he cast one final look down to where the men on the little beach were now moving around with purpose, taking photographs, measuring angles, their shadows dancing across the white canvas tent that formed the flimsy barrier between the living and the dead.

Chapter One

Shelly

The woman washing her breasts in the sink of the ladies' toilets at Kefalonia airport had one of those faces older white women get from spending too many years abroad in climes unsuited to their skin, as if a brown paper bag had shrink-wrapped itself around her bones. The breasts themselves were large and hung to her waist, and she heaved them individually into the basin, which she had half filled with soapy water. She looked over at the small queue of female passengers who were determinedly staring at their phones or at the tiled floor or at the door behind which the toilet attendant had disappeared, quite as if they hadn't noticed the half-naked woman in their midst. Unable to resist, Shelly glanced up, and immediately the woman latched on to her. 'Needs must, eh, sweetheart?' Her laugh was startling, a sudden, spontaneous volley of applause, but the smile that followed was small and tight as a purse zip.

The woman had a silk turquoise scarf tied like a headband around her stringy brown hair, which was streaked with blonde and grey. The scarf was fringed with tiny silver discs, and on her tanned, leathery wrists she had matching turquoise and silver bangles. Her eyes, which were sunk deeply into the brown paper of her face, were a bright, marble-hard blue and they fixed greedily on to Shelly, giving her the unpleasant sensation that it was she who was naked rather than the other way around. A cubicle came free and as she hurried in Shelly stored up the woman's details in her head, already anticipating how the others – Lucy – would laugh when she recounted the scene. Funny how we always think the people who will do us most harm will enter our lives with a fanfare or a cacophony of alarm bells ringing. But sometimes they're just washing their breasts in a tiny sink and we haven't a clue.

Jess

Something had woken her up.

But if she was awake, why weren't her eyes open? Jess experimented with first prising one eyelid open, then the next. Which is when she realized she wasn't in bed. She was lying on a prickly blue blanket. No. A rug. She was lying on the bedroom rug. What had she taken last night? Images came back to her in snapshots: cocktails, two-for-one, rude not to. Tequila shots lined up on a bar. Crammed into a toilet cubicle, kneeling, supplicant, in front of a long line of white powder.

Now she became aware of a buzzing under her left hip. Her phone. That's what had woken her up.

She brought the cracked screen level with her eyes without raising her head.

Lucy. FaceTime.

The last thing she felt like doing was talking to her sister, but in her groggy state she lacked the wherewithal to decline, jabbing at the screen ineffectually, intent only on silencing that infernal buzzing.

Her sister's face appeared on the screen, frozen there silently, her mouth slightly ajar, as if suspended in the act of formulating her words, then the signal jogged into gear. And her sister started screaming.

'What?' Jess rolled over on to her front and heaved herself into a sitting position, holding the phone with the image of her still-shrieking sister about six inches away. Her hand was unsteady and the picture wobbled, rendering her own tiny image a small dark blur in the uppermost right corner. '*What?*'

Now that she was upright, she became aware of a crushing pressure in her head, as if her skull had shrunk until it was several sizes too small for all it contained inside. There was a hard ball of anxiety in her stomach that had something to do with her sister's very obvious horror and a sour smell that she suspected was coming from her.

'Fukssake. WHAT?'

Lucy stopped screaming and pointed to the place on her screen where Jess imagined her own image must be.

'Your face,' she whispered. 'What have you done to your face? WHAT HAVE YOU DONE?'

Jess rolled her eyes, assuming she was talking about the hungover state of her, but still her hands crept up to her cheeks. And came away wet with blood.

Suddenly horribly sober, she scrambled to her feet and made her way to the chest of drawers, on which rested a tarnished junk-shop mirror with photos and postcards tucked into the frame and strings of beads draped across the top.

She stared at her reflection. And her reflection stared back. One eye almost buried beneath swollen, discoloured lids, a gash over one brow from which blood had gushed at some point, only to dry in rusty streaks across her face, fresh blood trickling from a cut to her upper lip that she must have ripped open when she spoke. She felt gripped suddenly by nausea, and by fear, an awareness of being on a path that could only lead somewhere really, really bad.

Lucy was right. What the absolute fuck had she done?

Lucy

'Don't cry, babe. I can't bear it when you cry.'

'I'm sorry, Jase. It's just so disappointing. She knows how much I've put into this and how important it is to me. Couldn't she just once let me have something for myself without making it all about her?'

'That's just Jess, though. She's not about to change now. Isn't that why we love her?'

'Easy for you to say. She's not your sister.'

'She will be soon. Sister-in-law, anyway. And she really can't remember what happened?'

'No! Face pouring with blood and no idea how it got there.'

'Legend.'

'*Jase!*'

'Sorry.'

'I'm just tired of it. I'm tired of her non-stop drama. This is my wedding. I've lived and breathed it for a whole year.'

From the lounger next to the one where the soon-to-be-wed couple lay squashed up together, Shelly dipped her head so she could peer at Lucy over the top of her dark shades, her huge eyes soft with concern.

'Please try not to let it get to you, Luce. It's not fair. You don't deserve this.' When Shelly was stretched out like that Lucy could see the individual ridges of her ribs pressing against the Lycra of her one-piece swimsuit.

'I've planned every single last detail, Shelly. You know I have. How long did I spend sweating over those canapés, back and forth, making sure there'd be something for everyone? Vegetarian. Gluten fucking free. I just want everything to be perfect. And now my own sister is going to show up looking like she's literally gone ten rounds with Tyson Fury. And don't even get me started on the dress fiasco.'

Shelly winced in sympathy. She'd been there for every painful step of the bridesmaid-dress nightmare. Sometimes Lucy didn't know how she would have coped without Shelly. In the two years they'd been working together Shelly had become like family – particularly as the poor girl had such a rubbish excuse for a family herself. After Jason, Shelly was the first person Lucy turned to in a crisis. Like when Jess refused point-blank to wear the colour Lucy had picked out for the bridesmaids.

'It's blush-pink,' Lucy had told her. 'No, it's urine-infection pink and I'm not wearing it.' And as usual it'd been Lucy who'd ended up compromising, though she'd drawn the line at the fuchsia, which was Jess's suggestion. 'So tacky,' Shelly had shuddered. And seeing as Shelly would have to wear it, too, with her pale, ethereal complexion, that almost translucent skin of hers, that'd been the end of that discussion, thank God. In the end they'd gone for a dusky rose colour that Lucy had persuaded Jess was 'retro'. But – surprise, surprise – Jess had left it until the last minute to find a dress, with the result that Lucy still hadn't seen it. She'd FaceTimed that morning specifically to vet the garment, which, after all, would be featuring in most of her wedding photographs, but then had come the drama of the unexplained blood and Jess had been so obviously freaked out it had felt wrong to bring up the dress. And now Jess was in transit (hopefully – Lucy didn't take anything for granted when it came to her sister) and it was all too late.

'At least your mum and dad will be here soon. They can help deal with her.'

'Right.'

Shelly's voice sounded small and strangled, and Lucy's heart constricted. Shelly put on a brave face, but it couldn't be easy for her to be around other people's families. Other people's parents.

'Tell me the truth, Shelly. Am I being too bridezilla about everything? That's what Jess calls me. Sometimes I feel so stressed out with the whole thing. I know I overreact, and it probably seems petty. But we've spent so much money . . .'

'Bridezilla? Are you joking? You're the nicest, most generous person I know, and Jess should learn to shut her . . . Look, you just want your wedding to be perfect. That's completely normal. Come on, talk me through the itinerary again.' Shelly swung her long, skinny, pale legs over the side and adjusted the wide-brimmed hat she always wore in the sun. Lucy found herself softening, tension leaking from her as if someone had opened up a valve. Shelly had that effect on her, with her freckles and her lopsided smile and the way she just understood things without having to be told.

'Right, well, tonight at seven there's the welcome reception with the selection of warm canapés, then tomorrow it's the fishing trip . . .' Instantly, Lucy was calmer. This was her wedding. It would be the best day of her life.

It had to be.

Therapy Journal, Week 1

For the record, I never expected you to set me homework! This feels so weird, I'm not going to lie. I've spent so many years hiding my true self and now you want me to lay it all out. Be honest, you said. As if that was something I knew how to be.

Where to start? That's a rhetorical question, of course.

Everything starts with the mother, like Freud said. Everyone knows that.

Chapter Two

Hazel

By the time she flung open the door of their Nissan Juke hire car – which they never would have rented if she'd been the one booking it – Hazel and her husband, Dom, hadn't exchanged a word in eighteen minutes. In fact, the only voice either of them had heard was the sat-nav woman, who took them at one stage into a dusty supermarket loading bay, and Hazel had had to bite back the words 'I did say,' having advised Dom right at the start that a paper map would be a better bet in a place like this. They were on the tip of her tongue, but she contented herself with an eye-roll and a small shake of the head. Was it normal, she wondered, not to have anything to talk about after thirty years together? What made a silence companionable, as opposed to just habitual?

'That wasn't bad, was it?'

Dom beamed at her over the bonnet of the awful car – red, of all things! – and Hazel allowed herself to relax.

This was a happy occasion, she reminded herself. How often did the whole family get together these days?

'No. Not too bad. Can't wait for a drink, though.'

'Not for me. Fast day, don't forget.'

Hazel took a deep breath in. 'Please tell me you're not going to do the bloody 5:2 on our daughter's wedding day.'

'Of course. I intend to save all my permitted calories for my toast . . . Joking, darling! This is the only day, I promise.'

Dom was so pleased with himself, and with her and with everything, standing there in his straw pork-pie hat and crumpled linen shirt the exact same blue as his eyes, that Hazel forgot about the silence in the car and the wretched diet and all the worries of the last few weeks and smiled back. It was all fine. Everything would be fine.

'This is nice.'

Hazel followed her husband's gaze as it swept across the hotel's crisp white facade, all tasteful blue shutters and exotic cacti and a bamboo pergola on the roof under which one could stand, cocktail in hand, and watch the sun setting over the navy-blue Ionian sea. Of course, she'd seen it in the brochures. Oh Lord had she seen it. Well, they were paying for most of it, weren't they, her and Dom? Lucy's fairy-tale bikini wedding. The nuts and bolts of it, anyway. Along with half the cost of the huge party Lucy had organized for their friends at home once they got back. Sometimes when Hazel totted up how much the whole thing was costing, she worried she might be sick.

Dom hoisted the bags out of the boot with a flourish. He was in good shape for a man approaching sixty, she acknowledged as she followed his lean, rangy figure into the hotel entrance. All that running was paying off. Those Saturday-morning 10k fun runs. Fun? Oh, dear God. Hazel remembered what fun used to look like – hung-over mornings in bed with the papers, fry-ups followed by long Sunday afternoons in the pub. When did everything change?

At the threshold of the hotel, Dom paused for her to catch up. Together they surveyed the sleekly tasteful lobby with its white walls and the porcelain tiles made to look exactly like pale oak floorboards, the abstract oil painting on the wall in Mediterranean colours – cobalt blue, turquoise and gleaming white to match the gleaming white smile of the beautiful blonde receptionist – the enormous blue glass vase at one end of the bespoke white reception desk that contained an even more enormous bouquet of exotic flowers, all purples and blues and violets, offset by extravagant green foliage. They took in the soft jazz music piped in from an unseen source, and the smell of eucalyptus wafting from a fat clotted-cream-coloured scented candle in which tiny flowers – blue, naturally – were embalmed in the wax.

For the first time, Dom looked uncertain. 'We should tell her,' he said, taking in the sheer opulence of the place.

'No. We agreed. Not until after the honeymoon. Let her have her wedding. She's wanted it so long.'

'But we—'

'No.'

Hazel's raised voice was jarring in the rarefied atmosphere of the hotel lobby and the receptionist looked up, aiming her bright smile in their direction like a laser.

They were taken up to their room. No, not a room, Hazel reminded herself. This hotel didn't have rooms, only suites of varying degrees of luxuriousness. The Comfort Suite was the basic, then the Senior Suite, then the Superior and, finally, the De Luxe. Dom and Hazel were in a Superior Suite. Hazel had tried to insist they'd be just as happy in a Comfort, but Lucy wouldn't hear of it. 'How do you think I'd feel,' she'd asked, 'knowing I was in the De Luxe while the two of you were slumming it in Comfort? How would it look to the other guests?' It worried Hazel how concerned Lucy was about how things looked to other people. You thought you'd done a good job bringing up two strong, independent women, but it was only in a crisis that you truly saw their hidden neuroses and vulnerabilities. And now she had to remind herself sternly that this was a wedding, and not a crisis.

The Superior Suite had white flooring and huge sliding glass doors that opened on to a private terrace with a circular whirlpool and a glass balustrade giving a clear view of the two pristine, curving swimming pools below, divided by a central bridge, and beyond that, the clifftop path that curved around the base of the hotel wall and, just visible, the tiny white shingle cove, accessible by a set of terrifyingly steep stone steps. 'It will keep you fit, no?' the receptionist had said.

Hazel started unpacking, carefully hanging up the dress she'd brought for the wedding. Lucy had been horrified when Hazel had told her she wasn't buying a new outfit for the wedding. 'But I love this dress and I've only had one chance to wear it,' Hazel had protested. It was perfectly true. She did love the dress she'd bought for her niece's wedding the previous year. Obviously, that didn't mean she wouldn't have loved to get something new and special for this occasion, too, but in the circumstances . . .

'Oh my God, you're actually here. Can you believe this place? Isn't it amazing?'

Lucy burst in through the door in a sensory explosion of golden flesh and multicoloured floral sarong and coconut-scented suntan oil. A pair of aviator sunglasses held back her highlighted blonde hair, which was wet at the ends, as if she had been trying to keep her head out of the water while swimming.

Dom put his arms around her and they hugged for a long time. She had always been such a daddy's girl. With Hazel, there was always that little bit more restraint. Not that there was any dearth of warmth and love. Oh dear God, there had been times when Hazel had thought there was something deranged about how fiercely she felt about her daughters. But privately she worried that there was a disconnect between her and her older daughter, a point at which, while they loved each other, they didn't always quite get each other. As a child, Lucy had been so greedy for her attention, so physically demanding, that Hazel, by nature someone who was used to tightly patrolling her own boundaries and who found unbridled displays of affection as difficult as surprise parties and – another of Lucy's favourite things – spontaneous FaceTiming, had struggled to reciprocate. Even as an adult, Lucy would quite often fling herself down on to Hazel's lap without warning or lay her head on her shoulder while watching TV, and Hazel would submit to it stiffly and, she often worried, gracelessly, as she had done the few times she'd given in to pressure and gone for a massage, tensing under the masseur's hands. 'Let yourself go for once,' Lucy had urged her at the Pampering Day she'd organized for Mother's Day at a posh Bath hotel a couple of months before. 'You don't have to do a photo shoot on it, just enjoy it.'

It was an old family joke. How Hazel couldn't leave her work persona behind when she came home. 'Er, hello, living human being here,' one or other of the girls would say, drawing an imaginary circle around her own face when Hazel looked at her in a certain way. They were people, they'd remind her impatiently, not *subjects*.

Seeing her husband and daughter together loosened the band that had been tightening around Hazel's chest over the last few weeks. They were so similar, the two of them. Both rangy and long-limbed, short on patience and ruled by emotion. So often she and Dom would be watching something on the television and Hazel would be shocked when she turned to Dom as the credits rolled to see fat tears rolling down his cheeks. But they were kind, the two of them. It was another thing they shared – that soft heart that beat inside them both. Hazel had actually banned Dom from answering the door in their Bristol house because he couldn't resist a sob story. The number of monthly direct debits to this charity or that one, a fiver here, a tenner there. The number of bloody dishcloths and tea towels he'd bought from ex-cons or young lads claiming to be homeless. 'You know they're not really, don't you?' Jess had said once. 'You know they're all working for Romanian gangsters who take all the cash and give them peanuts?' 'I'd rather be a mug than a misanthrope,' was Dom's unruffled response.

As so often, Hazel felt a swell of gratitude for her family. So many of their friends had divorced over the years – her own sister, too – getting together with other people to form new units with varying degrees of success. But Hazel was glad their little unit had made it through intact. Not that she and Dom hadn't had their wobbles over the years. Too many to count. Only a couple of years back they'd discussed seeing a counsellor. She'd even found one who lived conveniently near, although Dom had seen that as a drawback. 'Imagine standing in the queue at the Tesco Express next to a woman who knows when and how you last had sex.'

'You don't know how glad I am you're both here. Now you can take over on Jess-Watch.'

'Has she arrived?' asked Dom, ruffling his daughter's hair.

'Not yet. I gave her a wake-up FaceTime call really early this morning. I had to set an alarm and everything. She asked me to, so that she wouldn't miss her plane. Though, obviously, I was also hoping to see her dress. And anyway, she was . . .'

Hazel didn't like the look on Lucy's face.

'She was what?'

'Oh, never mind. Just please promise me you'll make her show you what she's going to wear. I've sent Nina, my wedding planner, my Pinterest mood board of what look I'm going for and I don't want there to be any nasty surprises.'

'She won't want to spoil your wedding, sweetheart,' said Hazel, with as much conviction as she could muster.

'I know she wouldn't do it deliberately, it's just . . . I want this one day, this one week, to be mine, without it becoming the Jessica Show. That's not too much to ask, is it?'

Lucy's eyes filled with the tears that were never far away and Dom put his arm around her. 'Don't worry, chicken. We will keep your sister under house arrest for the duration.'

It was very quiet in their suite after Lucy left. Dom came and stood behind Hazel and put his arms around her. 'Aren't we lucky?' he whispered into her ear. For a moment the two of them stood looking at the huge kingsize bed with its pristine white sheets and the plump pillows with chocolate hearts resting in the dimple in the middle. Hazel thought about the days, years even, when the two of them would have been beside themselves with delight at all they could do in a room like this, hardly able to wait until the door was shut before falling on to the bed, when she would have worn her best underwear just for this reason.

As if he could read her mind, Dom's hands slid down to her hips and he pressed into her back, making his intentions very clear. 'We could always . . .' he murmured. Hazel laughed and pulled away. 'Not until you've had a shower. You're minging.'

She tried to hold on to her good mood, but as Dom moved off to continue his unpacking and she took in the corner bath in the bathroom and the top-end toiletries by the sink and the whirlpool on the terrace, screened from view from neighbouring rooms, all she could think was how much it was costing and what a terrible waste it all was.

Chapter Three

Shelly

Shelly was buzzing. It was such a novelty, this feeling of being in the right place at the right time with the right people.

'Can you believe how fast everything is happening?' said Lucy, grabbing on to Shelly's arm. 'It's so unfair. All these last months in England, time has been d-r-a-g-g-i-n-g.' She drew the word out dramatically. 'And now the wedding's here, it's galloping along like someone has pressed fast forward.'

They were in the lobby of the hotel, awaiting the next tranche of guests, who had texted them from the airport to say they were on their way. Lucy had sorted it so that Jason's mum, Cora, had travelled over on the same flight as his best mate, Gil, and his wife so that they could all save on the taxi fare. Shelly had stored away that detail when she found out. It was the kind of thing that was second nature to Lucy – thinking ahead to see if there was anything she could do to make her loved ones' lives easier. The kind of thing Shelly needed to learn.

Shelly squeezed her friend's tanned, perfectly manicured hand where it rested on her own pale, freckled arm. 'Isn't there some law of physics that says time goes a million times faster when you're enjoying yourself?'

'Too right. Remember all those Christmases when you were a kid when the lead-up would take for ever, and then Christmas Day itself went by so fast you could blink and miss it?'

Lucy glanced up at Shelly and her eyes widened. 'Oh God, Shell, I'm sorry. I should have . . .'

Shelly smiled, even though her chest felt tight. 'Relax, Luce, it's fine. Anyway, I had some really good Christmases.'

This wasn't a total lie. There had been one or two Christmases where nothing had gone wrong, where there was food in the cupboards and Shelly had opened presents that actually seemed like they'd been bought with her in mind, and no one had got drunk or taken offence at some imagined slight or gone to bed in the middle of the afternoon and not got up again and the basement had been just another unused space in their house. But when she looked back on those occasions, all Shelly remembered was the knot in her stomach as she waited for something to happen, not daring to believe she would be allowed one perfect, normal day.

'I suppose Christmases with your uncle and aunt must have been fun,' added Lucy hopefully.

Shelly nodded, because she didn't want Lucy to feel worse than she did already. Besides, Lucy would never have understood all the different ways good people can inadvertently make you feel bad. She changed the subject.

'Have you told Jason yet, about your Davina McCall mission?'

'You are funny, calling it that. But no, I haven't told him yet. I wanted to surprise him and Cora with a fait accompli.'

'And still no response?'

'Not so far.'

Lucy looked momentarily crestfallen and Shelly was sorry she'd ever suggested that Lucy try to track down Jason's late dad's relatives. It had seemed such a good idea at the time. They'd been at work and Lucy was saying how sorry she felt for Jason having so few relations coming to the wedding party. After his dad died, they'd drifted apart from his dad's family and now it was just Jason and Cora. Of course, as soon as Shelly had planted the possibility of Lucy looking for them herself, Lucy had set her heart on it. She'd rushed off to google the Beazant family tree, finally coming up with a cousin somewhere in Exeter she'd been trying to contact ever since.

'And how about your parents?' Shelly asked, hoping Lucy couldn't hear the catch in her voice. 'Are they settled in OK? Did they freak when they saw the place?'

'They *loved* it. As if anyone wouldn't. I looked for you to come say hello, but you'd disappeared.'

'I just wanted to give you some alone time.'

'No need. I've told you, you're part of the . . . Oh, they're here!'

Through the lobby doors came handsome, charming Gil and his wife, Zoe, who still, three years on, no one could quite believe he was married to. Shelly experienced the usual confusing mix of emotions on seeing Zoe. Frustration that they now had to put up with her particular brand of snark and superiority but, worse than that, the clawing feeling of recognition, the troubling awareness that in many ways they were the same, she and Zoe. Both outsiders who had to earn their place here.

'Oh, wow! This place is incredible.' Gil's wide smile threatened to burst clear through the smooth caramel skin of his face. Sharpened cheekbones and soft hazel eyes. Only the hardest-hearted wouldn't melt.

And now here came Zoe, trailing behind with a sour expression as if she'd just smelled something she couldn't quite identify but didn't much like.

Why did he marry her? Shelly and Lucy had discussed it so many times in their forensic post-mortems after various parties and nights out. She was attractive enough. Lots of dark, curly hair that she pinned up with a variety of quirky clips and pencils or, as now, just wound around itself until it sort of held itself up by its own weight. Not like Shelly's own hair, fine and poker straight. Shelly used to hate her hair – all those ginger jokes at school – but since Lucy told her how she'd kill to be a redhead, she was starting to come around to it.

Zoe had an interesting enough job in market research, though she was inclined to bore on about it. And sometimes she could be funny – Shelly remembered her doing an impression of her boss that had had them all in stitches. There was something murky in her past, too, which ought to have forged some sense of solidarity. Even without the hints Gil dropped from time to time about Zoe 'working through some stuff', Shelly would have guessed she was hiding something. When you grew up like Shelly had, you learned to sniff out other people's dysfunctions like truffles.

So yes, there were redeeming features and mitigating factors, but the fact was Zoe wound everyone up the wrong way. Shelly tried to give her the benefit of the doubt, for Lucy's sake, but there was a level where she knew her to be a threat. Being on the outskirts of a group puts one in a precarious position, like balancing on the very lip of a cliff.

One person's weight can cause cracks to form. Two people will send it crashing to the ground.

15/6/19, 23.05. Original English-language transcript of police interview with Mr Gilberto Victor Rodriguez. Police officers: Demitri Iraklidis and Tomaso Diakos. Interpreter: Eulalia Scala.

I wouldn't use the word 'hostility'. That's not right. It was a big group, yeah, and everyone liked a drink, so you're gonna get a few flare-ups, but it was just banter really. On the whole, everyone was chilled. We were here to celebrate Jason and Lucy, you know. This beautiful, beautiful couple. We were here to show love. That's why I can't believe what's gone on. It was supposed to be about love.

Oh man, this is so messed up.

Hand on heart, I love the Collinses same as if they're my own family, my own blood, you know what I'm saying? That's why I just can't even . . . I can't even . . .

Including Jess. Absolutely. The thing with me and her was over and done with years ago. My life has completely turned around since then. I've got my baby – my whole world, my Anastasia – and my incredible wife.

Difficult? Zoe? Who have you been talking to? Look, man, my wife is complicated, that's the truth. She doesn't let everyone in. But when she does let you in, she lets you in completely.

Mr Collins? Dom? He's cool. He's a big guy, but he wears his heart on display, do you get me? All his emotions are written on his face, whereas Hazel, well, you have to work harder to find out what she's thinking. But it's always worth it. Deep waters, you know?

I'm still so confused about what's gone on. I keep hearing the word 'dead', but that can't be right, can it? Come on, guys, I'm being straight with you, can't one of you just be straight with me? Come on, throw me a bone here.

Chapter Four

Lucy

Lucy was determined not to let Zoe cast a shadow over her day. She'd always believed in that old adage that everyone was fighting a battle you couldn't see, and she tried to see the best in people. She just wished Zoe's best was a bit . . . better.

Jason had once let slip that he thought there might be some weird sex thing between Gil and Zoe that kept them together, but when she'd pressed him for details he'd clammed up. He was infuriatingly loyal like that. For ages, Lucy had secretly hoped that whatever it was that held them together would wear itself out and she could set him up with someone far more compatible. Not Jess, of course. That had never been going to work, and Lucy was relieved when their brief affair had burned itself out after just a few weeks. But there were others who'd be perfect. Then Zoe had got pregnant and now Anastasia was two and a half years old and no one talked about them splitting up any more.

And that was another thing that had caused problems. Lucy, who normally bent over backwards to accommodate everyone, was adamant about her wedding being a child-free zone. Non-negotiable. When she'd spent so long making sure everything was perfect, arranging every last detail, why would she risk adding the unpredictable factor of children with their weird nap times and their e-number overloads and their wild, random shrieking? Why would she go to the trouble of colour-coordinating bridesmaids' dresses when some four-year-old was liable to turn up in clashing trousers and a jumper because they just weed the clothes they were supposed to be wearing? It wasn't that she had anything against little Anastasia, who was adorable, really, with a round face topped by a mass of black curls, and fat little fingers behind which she pretended to hide whenever Lucy was around, but it was her wedding and she wanted it to be calm and chic. Grown-up.

Anyway, the Paradise View luxury hotel and spa was adults only and while, whatever Zoe might think, that wasn't the reason Lucy had chosen it, it had certainly made it easier to enforce the ban.

While Lucy and Jason hugged Gil, Zoe was already on her phone, checking in with her parents, who were on childcare duty, her voice rising in volume and pitch. 'What do you mean, she had two Petit Filous? Do you know how much sugar there is in those? I specifically said, "occasional treat". For God's sake, Mum, didn't you read the instructions?'

Gil shrugged apologetically. 'Annie can be a bit of a nightmare if she has too much sugar. Zoe is only thinking of her mum and dad. Is Jess here yet?' Gil's voice was studiedly casual. Or maybe genuinely casual. To this day, Lucy hadn't been able to work out if he was still holding a torch for her younger sister, despite it being nearly four years since they broke up. He had been heartbroken for a while, even though Lucy had warned him what Jess was like with men, how quickly she got bored of them. And by the time Jess had second thoughts, which she quite often did, being the contrary person she was, Zoe was pregnant, and that had been that.

'Not yet. She sent a text saying she'd arrived, though.'

Lucy didn't mention the perturbing thing about the text, which was that Jess hadn't said 'I've' arrived, but 'we', which had given her a tight, sick feeling in the pit of her stomach, though she'd told herself she must be referring to the other passengers.

And now, while Gil was still checking in, the receptionist's bright, white smile brighter and whiter than ever as she handed him back his passport, her eyes with their extravagantly curled lashes travelling over the intricate black floral tattoos on his muscular arms, there came another commotion in the doorway behind.

'Well, this beats the A2 on a rainy Monday afternoon.'

As ever, Lucy felt a little knot of tension forming at the sight of Cora Beazant, in wide white linen pants and a simple spaghetti-strap vest. Not that Cora was ever anything but lovely, but she was just so lithe and so *unassailable*, all those yoga classes, all that downward dog, so socially word perfect in all situations, knowing exactly how to adapt her conversation to each new person. Lucy was too busy being intimidated by Cora to relax around her.

'This is heaven,' said Cora, pushing her tortoise-shell sunglasses up on to her head to hold back her honey-streaked hair, and gazing around. Lucy basked in her soon-to-be mother-in-law's approval. It had been like this since the minute the two had met, with Cora gracious and friendly but Lucy recognizing it instantly as her stock manner and craving more, desperate to be singled out as special. Wasn't she the girl her son loved? Didn't that merit a different kind of bond, distinct from all the others? If she was absolutely honest, Lucy decided to marry Jason when she met his mother. And since then she had done everything she could to impress. Spent hours choosing her clothes before a casual meeting for Sunday lunch in the pub, fresh flowers and expensive candles before Cora dropped round for a cup of tea, snuffed out the second she left. Even this wedding had been planned with half a mind on Cora's reaction. See, Lucy wanted to say, pointing out the natural beauty and the understated luxury, how lucky you are that your son chose me?

Yet still she hadn't quite broken through to the inner sanctum of Cora, even though Jason kept telling her there was no inner sanctum and she didn't have to do anything to impress his mum apart from just be herself. He didn't get it. Cora was one of those women who had much more straightforward relationships with men than with members of her own sex, Lucy thought. She had brought Jason up single-handedly after his dad had died and now the two of them were so close you couldn't slide a hair between them. Too close, perhaps, Lucy sometimes thought. But that would all change once they were married. Wives came first, didn't they? Anyway, when the two of them found out how much effort Lucy had gone to to track down Jason's long-lost cousin, Cora would surely be won over.

It wasn't anything to do with money, this worry about being found wanting by her soon-to-be mother-in-law. Cora had a good but not particularly glamorous job as an arts administrator for the local council. She had a nice, modest cottage in the Kent countryside where everything was restful – muted colours, pale green and biscuit, comfortable sofas with soft woollen throws draped over the arms. Every time Lucy went to stay, there were plump pillows on the beds and thick, fluffy towels laid out ready for use. Not like in her parents' rambling, draughty Georgian house in Bristol, where the sheets were the same ones they'd been using for decades, including the tell-tale florals of Lucy and Jess's pre-teen bedrooms, and the towels were like sandpaper because her mum refused to put them in the dryer.

Lucy's mum favoured splashes of bright colour to cheer herself up, so there were vivid rugs in red and purple stripes and gay Mexican cushions and a squishy corner sofa in dusky orange which sagged mournfully in the middle. Assorted knick-knacks – misshapen clay animals she and Jess had made at school, carvings from the far-flung places her parents had travelled to pre-children – gathered dust on the windowsills.

The house itself was lovely, bought in the early 1990s with the proceeds of her dad's one big success. At school, Lucy had been mortified when her friends had discovered her father was responsible for the monstrously successful *Wrong Position of the Week.* (The 'wrong' was scrawled in red pen at the top with one of those little inverted v's underneath, as if it was a late add-on.) The book was a pisstake of the infamous 'Position of the Week', a popular sex column that had run for years in a women's magazine. The illustrations, all completed on Dom's angled drawing table, which he refused to replace out of superstition, were basically just the things that could go awry when two people got over-adventurous in bed (or on the floor or the washing machine or up a tree). It had spawned various spin-offs, each less successful than the last, and a ton of merchandise. They were still using *Wrong Position* tea towels, though they were so old and faded they ought to have been chucked out years ago.

These days, no one under thirty remembered the *Wrong Position* books, thank God. And it had been years since Lucy's dad had earned any proper money. It was accepted in her family that her mum was the breadwinner, even though she complained all the time about how precarious print media had become in recent years, with magazines and newspapers closing left, right and centre or whittling down their staff to the bare bones. 'Journalism schools call it *legacy* media,' she'd exclaimed recently. 'Like we're *dinosaurs*!'

After her first visit to Cora's cottage, Lucy had offered to go around to her parents' house to help them declutter, and her mother had looked at her as if she was insane. 'It's not clutter to me.' 'Yes, but does it spark joy?' The utter blankness with which her question was greeted had made Lucy despair. She was only trying to help. It's not as if she wanted to spend her free time sorting out her father's old comic collection or getting rid of the cupboards full of plastic bags they'd collected over the years and now couldn't throw away. 'Think of that poor sea lion with her cub!' her mother had said, the last time she'd tried to dispose of them. Well, yes, obviously Lucy had cried at that David Attenborough documentary, just like the rest of the country, but that didn't help when there was no room to keep the smoothie-maker she'd bought her parents for Christmas because every cupboard was stuffed with plastic bags.

At the reception desk, Zoe and Gil were having a furious whispered conversation. Lucy caught the word 'Comfort', and grimaced, realizing Zoe had cottoned on to the fact they were in the lowest-graded suite. 'You're the bloody best man,' she heard Zoe hiss. While all the guests had paid their own airfares, Lucy's parents were footing the bill for the accommodation and food and drinks, plus all the extra excursions, while Lucy and Jason were paying for the wedding itself. Lucy and Nina, the Kefalonia-based wedding planner who had been with her every step of the way, had been charged with allocating who got what suite. One of the hotel's USPs was that no two rooms were the same, so it wouldn't have been possible for everyone to be completely equal. But in truth, Lucy liked the fact that there was a hierarchy. This was *her* moment, her one chance to design an unforgettable experience, not just for her and Jason, but hopefully for all their guests, too. She liked the fact that you could look at the hotel and immediately know which was their suite – theirs had the biggest terrace, complete with its own small private pool and whirlpool, and the best view. And that's how it should be. Lucy had never begrudged any of her friends their moment in the spotlight and she didn't expect anyone to judge her for wanting to be a princess for just one day of her life.

'Nina will be here later to answer any questions,' she said, smiling sweetly.

Jason, who had been standing behind her, put a hand on her waist and squeezed. He knew Zoe could wind her up if she was in one of her moods. He claimed to have perfected the art of tuning her out when she was like that. Imagine you're under water, he told Lucy, and her voice is just burbling away there on the surface but the sounds don't make any sense, they're just background noise.

Except she didn't want background noise at her wedding. She wanted the music she'd picked out herself and the speeches she'd asked for and guests saying nice things about her dress and her hair and the beautiful surroundings. And that was all.

'Just as long as we're not above the restaurant,' Zoe said. 'It's just that I'm very noise-sensitive. And seeing as we've had to leave our baby behind, the least we deserve is a lie-in.'

She said the last sentence with a smile, as if she was joking, but Lucy knew she wasn't.

Chapter Five

Lucy

An hour or so later, out by the main pool, Zoe was showing signs of mellowing. Well, who wouldn't, with the sky that perfect shade of blue and the wide, cushioned beds and the sun sparkling off the pool and the smell of jasmine and thyme wafting up from the clifftop path? She was stretched out, with her mass of hair cascading over the top of a visor – who on earth wore a visor these days? – wearing a white bikini that looked as if it was crocheted, for heaven's sake. Irritation snapped like an elastic band against Lucy's skin. Wasn't it disrespectful, to dress like that at someone else's wedding?

Zoe raised a leg high into the air in order to apply sun lotion, spending an unnecessary length of time rubbing the oil into the soft skin of her thigh, and Shelly nudged Lucy and raised an eyebrow conspiratorially behind her sunglasses. Instantly, Lucy relaxed a notch or two. No matter what, Shelly always had her back.

But now Shelly was sitting up and staring over to the far side of the pool.

'Oh my God!'

'What?'

'Over there. On that lounger nearest the shower.'

Lucy followed her gaze, already frowning. Even though there was no way they could possibly have afforded to hire out the whole hotel, it still irked her that there were other guests here. Who she hadn't invited. She'd already issued clear instructions to Nina to make sure they didn't find their way into any pictures.

'What am I looking for?'

'It's her. The woman who was washing her boobs in the sink in the airport loo. Remember, I told you.'

'Oh my *God*!'

The two of them stared at the woman, who was sitting up on the lounger, sipping a clear drink through a straw and reading a thick paperback novel. Unlike most of the other guests, she was in full sun, her darkly tanned skin glistening with perspiration. She had on a pair of mirror-lensed aviator glasses and her stringy grey-blonde hair was mostly wrapped in a turquoise scarf. She must have been getting on for seventy, judging by the creases on her arms and décolletage, yet her ample body was squished into a rather skimpy bikini, also in turquoise. Lucy never liked to judge. She was all in favour of older women wearing exactly what they pleased. But all the same.

'Are you sure it's the same woman?'

'Positive. Bang goes the neighbourhood.'

The two giggled with the detached superiority of young people who are secretly convinced they will never get old. The woman looked over sharply, the reflection of the pool dazzling in the lenses of her glasses.

The doors that led to the lobby and then up to the rooms opened and Lucy's parents stepped out, looking self-conscious in their unfamiliar poolside gear. Her heart softened at the sight of their impossibly pale legs and arms. Her father, tall and still handsome in his new Hawaiian-style swimming shorts, would tan within minutes, but her mum would go pink first – at least the parts of her she allowed to come into contact with the sun. Her mum had a capacious bag over one shoulder that Lucy was certain would contain her laptop so she could book photographers or check invoices while she was supposed to be relaxing. So many childhood holiday memories centred around trying to drag her mother's attention away from whatever she was working on. 'Look at me, Mum!' she'd cry, wobbling on the edge of the pool, waiting to perform a dive. '*Look at me!*' And her mum would look up startled, as if surprised to find herself wherever they were.

'Mum and Dad are here,' Lucy said to Shelly, getting up to make introductions. Though Shelly had met her mum before, it was the first time she'd be meeting Lucy's dad. They hadn't discussed it, but Lucy knew her friend would be finding this bit hard. Family. Parents. All the things she'd missed out on. True enough, Shelly's fingers gripped tight on the arm of the lounger, though her expression was impossible to read behind her dark glasses.

But as they came near Lucy's parents stopped and Lucy saw her mum turn to her dad and ask him something. He gestured towards her bag and shrugged, then turned back, disappearing through the doors of the lobby.

'Idiot,' said Hazel, dropping her bag down on to the lounger next to them. 'I told him to bring his book, but he wouldn't have it, and now the minute we set foot outside he gets book FOMO.'

Cora was also out on the terrace. She'd changed into a loose cotton shift dress that was practically see-through when she stood in the sun, Lucy couldn't help noticing. She was already lightly tanned and Lucy wondered whether it was fake tan and, if so, whether she'd tell her the name of the brand.

'I think I'll explore the little beach down there,' Cora said cheerfully, and Lucy's smile grew hard and tight when Jason practically flew off his lounger to join her, the two of them exiting through a bougainvillea-framed archway where there were steps down to the clifftop. On their first day here, Lucy and Jason had taken the path which skirted the bottom of the hotel, following the line of the coast, past the three little coves that made up the small bay over which their hotel presided from its isolated hillside position. Lucy wasn't great with heights, but she hadn't minded the path, which was bordered on both sides with thickets of wildflowers and herbs that flavoured the air with intoxicating aromas. They'd used Jason's phone to look up what they were – wild fennel, mountain sage, orange blossom. Even the names had made Lucy feel languid and heady, as if she'd had a full glass of wine in the sunshine.

But Jason and Cora would be crossing the path to take the stone steps which were carved into the cliff, descending to the little beach below. This was the middle and biggest of the three coves. The others were accessible only by clambering over the rocks at either end of the beach. Lucy imagined the pair walking together along the shoreline, or finding a shady patch under one of the trees at the back of the beach to sit and chat.

It was lovely that they had such a good relationship, Lucy told herself firmly. She lay back on her sunbed, determined not to stress about her soon-to-be mother-in-law or where her errant sister had got to or why her dad still hadn't returned from his suite. And she was definitely not going to start worrying about whether the last payment to Nina had cleared the joint account or when she was going to tell Jason exactly how much money she'd – they'd – spent on this week. Everyone overspent on their wedding, didn't they? It was practically tradition. And, somehow, it always worked out in the end. No one would begrudge her wanting it to be perfect, from the speedboat she and her dad would arrive on, her filmy antique lace veil fluttering behind her in the gentle breeze, to the rose petals on the steps, to the string quartet who'd be playing on the beach as she walked down the makeshift aisle. Lucy wasn't a particularly ambitious or selfish person, but she wanted people to be talking about her wedding for a long time to come.

How was she to know, as she positioned herself under the umbrella so that her face remained in the shadow – the sun was so ageing – while the rest of her body basted in the heat, that she would get her desire and that, when she did, she would wish with her whole heart that she had not?

Therapy Journal, Week 2

My parents got married in Marylebone Town Hall on a Thursday lunchtime on a whim, less than two months after they first met. I've only ever seen one photograph taken as they stepped out of the building into the sunlight. Daddy is twisted away from the camera, as if already looking for the exit door out of the marriage, while Mummy's lovely eyes are wide and startled. That's kind of how it was with Mummy. Everything in her life, even the things she'd actively chosen, seemed to come as a surprise to her, as if they'd been foisted on her without her knowledge.

You've asked me to describe her. Well, she'd done a little modelling in the past and was the kind of beautiful that made men queuing with their wives at supermarket tills look away sharply, as if caught out doing something wrong. She wore jeans that sat so low her hip bones jutted over the waistband, or baby doll-style dresses that ended mid-thigh. 'It's disgusting how men stare,' she'd say. Her hair was thick and wavy and reached halfway down her back. When we were out I was proud she was my mum. But at home she was a different person every day. Sometimes loving, sometimes resentful, but the worst was indifferent. I spent my childhood trying to adapt myself to fit around her moods. Shapeshifting, you could say. I was always exhausted.

When your first experience of love is someone who is never the same from one day to the next, you learn that love requires you to be watchful at all times and to never relax your guard. Harry said that being with me felt like being a laboratory mouse, always under observation. Harry said a lot of things.

Chapter Six

Nina

Nina had the perfect life. Living in a villa with a pool on a gorgeous Greek island where the sun shone eleven months of the year, working alongside her husband to make other couples' dreams come true. She really was blessed. At least, that's what she regularly wrote on Facebook, usually alongside a photograph of a beach or a sunset or a cocktail laden with sliced fruit and miniature umbrellas. Sometimes even an inspirational quote in a slanted handwriting font.

It was the image she needed to project for her business – selling the dream of the beach wedding to would-be brides surreptitiously browsing in the office on a rainy Wednesday lunchtime.

And it wasn't *entirely* a lie.

Driving up the steep windy road to the Paradise View, she sent up the usual prayer that the clutch on her eleven-year-old Fiat Panda, which had been making ominous noises for months now, wouldn't choose today to pack in completely. The tyres had so little tread they struggled to get purchase on the bends and she was already dreading the trip back down again, knowing that the brake pads should have been replaced a year ago.

Still, she was careful not to let any of that show as she went into the lobby to meet Lucy Collins, having parked her Fiat in the furthest corner of the car park, hidden from the sleek hire cars of the guests.

As always, the hard knot of anxiety in Nina's stomach magically unravelled as soon as she spotted the smiling, nervous faces of the soon-to-be-married couple. No matter what was going on in her own relationship, there was something about the sheer hopefulness of the decision couples like this had made, in the face of everything everyone knew to be true, all the divorce statistics and the headlines about affairs and marriage breakdowns, something about their unshakeable belief in their own ability to buck the trend and prove that love was always, *always*, worth it, that melted Nina's heart.

They were an attractive couple, Lucy and Jason. Lucy was tall and lithe but at the same time soft around the edges, with her clear grey-blue eyes, and her endless lists in her childish loopy writing – pre-wedding playlist, order of speeches, list of likes and dislikes for the hair and make-up girl. Her concern that everything be 'classy', above all. Nina had seen a lot of women like Lucy and they always touched her, in their blind faith that the perfect wedding day would paint a glossy protective varnish over the rest of their lives, making them shinier, their marriages invulnerable. She had been one of those women herself.

Jason was tall and broad-shouldered with a mass of very curly strawberry-blond hair and a complexion that was just beginning to tip from pink to reddish-brown after two days in the sun. His blue eyes were so deep-set they appeared to sit on top of his cheekbones as if displayed on a broad shelf. While Lucy was nervy and animated, always in motion, Jason had a still, solid presence, always with one hand touching his bride-to-be – resting on her arm, her knee, the small of her back – not in a possessive way but as if to reassure her, to ground her, if you like. Nina remembered when Mark had played that role with her. Her rock, she used to call him. How ironic that seemed now.

Lucy insisted on taking Nina to the pool area to introduce her to the rest of the wedding party.

'This is Nina. She's my wedding planner.'

Lucy was one of those people who stressed the possessive pronoun – 'My bathroom is painted a really calming pale green'; 'My manicurist told me'; and her all-time favourite 'My fiancé' – at all times. She took strength from the things she could lay claim to. Nina couldn't blame her for that.

Nina and Lucy sat down in the shaded bar area at the far end of the pool, settling themselves back among the deep calico cushions. Nina breathed a sigh of satisfaction as she surveyed the view. This was her favourite of the hotels she used, but she hadn't had a wedding here since the previous year. Mostly, her couples seemed to favour the more established resorts on the island, rather than the Paradise View, which, though stunning, occupied an isolated position on its own on this vertiginous headland, its base ringed by tall cliffs. A waiter in a crisp white T-shirt came to offer them a drink, greeting Nina by name. After five years and more than thirty weddings, she knew most of the staff in the area. It was only after he'd returned from the bar with their smoothies that she realized who he was. Instantly, the drink turned sour in her mouth.

'Do you think that's naff?'

Lucy's pretty heart-shaped face was turned in her direction and Nina berated herself for allowing her attention to wander. It was her golden rule that the bride was always top priority. 'This is going to be the most special day in your life,' she told her clients. 'Be as selfish as you like.'

'The path of rose petals leading down to the beach. Is it naff?'

'How could something so beautiful as a rose petal ever be naff?'

'That's exactly what—'

Lucy broke off as a young woman burst out of the hotel lobby through the glass doors at the other end of the pool area. She had pink hair tied up to reveal closely shaved sides and back and was wearing a billowing white sleeveless dress knotted at the hem and complicated leather gladiator-type sandals with a thick platform sole. One of her arms was almost entirely covered in black tattoos, stark against her pale skin, and the other sported a thick black leather and silver cuff.

'Oh,' said Lucy, sitting up. 'My sister, Jess, is here.' There was something very endearing about her expression – half hopeful, half nervous. Nina recognized it from how she used to be with Mark when things first started to go wrong but she still thought she could fix them.

Nina followed Lucy around the side of the pool towards the new arrival, who was already surrounded by a small throng of other guests who had roused themselves from their loungers to say hello. Up close, Jess was daintier than she'd first appeared, with a small, delicate face that would have been pretty if not for the puffy purple bruising surrounding one eye and the cuts on her lip and eyebrow.

'Long story,' she was saying to her mother. 'I'll tell you over a couple of gins.'

She looked over at them and the diamond stud in her nose glinted when it caught the sun. 'Here comes the bride,' she sang before flinging her arms around Lucy and lifting her off the ground.

'I was about to send out a search party,' said her sister when they finally pulled apart. 'Especially after you said "we" on the phone. I had visions of you picking up one of your randoms on the way and being abducted.'

'Ha! Ye of little faith! No, when I said "we", I meant me and Gabriel.'

The smile died on Lucy's face. 'Gabriel?'

'Yeah, I'm sure I told you on the phone this morning.'

'No. You didn't.'

'What? Oh my God, that's hilarious, that means I must have met him right afterwards. Yes, that's right, I remember.

I put the phone down to you and then wandered into my kitchen and there he was. Poaching *eggs*!' She somehow made it sound as if it were this last, the poaching of the eggs, that was the more extraordinary thing, rather than the fact of finding a strange man in her home.

'Oh, Mum, don't look so disapproving. He's an absolute doll. The *sweetest* guy. He was walking past my block of flats late last night and saw me falling out of a taxi and then trying to fish the keys out of my bag at the top of the steps and then forgetting I'd put my backpack down behind me and flying backwards down the steps, faceplanting the post at the bottom. I *know* – classy, right? Anyway, he brought me home and then slept on the sofa because he was worried I'd given myself delayed concussion or something.'

Lucy had turned pale under her tan. 'And you brought him here? To my wedding? This complete stranger?'

Jess rolled her eyes. 'Oh, please. What, everyone else is allowed to have a plus-one except me?'

'I cannot believe this. I just can't. All the work I've put into today and you've just . . . Mum, *Mum*?'

Hazel, who had listened to her younger daughter's tale with a deepening frown, now stirred into life.

'It's very inconsiderate of you, Jess. Not even to ask.'

There was something very measured, almost detached, about Hazel's response, Nina thought, as if she were behind a thick pane of glass.

'There wasn't time. It was really spontaneous. I thought it'd be good to have some fresh blood around here, rather than the same old, boring faces. I thought you'd all . . .'

But whatever else Jess thought was lost when the door behind her opened and a man stepped out. Definitely not dressed for the weather, in black jeans and a black T-shirt, he had one of those bland baby-faces that could have been thirty or fifty, faded blue eyes and thin pale hair that was worn long but receding at the temples.

He gazed around beatifically at the wedding party in their bikinis and their flip-flops and their Hawaiian flowered shorts and their shades on the top of their heads as if he were perfectly comfortable being here among all these scantily dressed strangers.

'Well, this wasn't how I expected my day to pan out when I woke up this morning,' he said. When he smiled, a small dent appeared in the apple of his cheek, like a tiny, puckered mouth.

Chapter Seven

Hazel

Putting on make-up in the frankly ridiculous bathroom of the Superior Suite was proving a sobering experience. The lighting had clearly been conceived to help perfectionist brides and bridesmaids ensure there was not a stray eyebrow hair or blackhead in sight. For a fifty-seven-year-old woman used to grooming in the flattering light of an en suite in which half the downlighter bulbs no longer worked, it was bruising, and not helped by Hazel's secret and unbecoming jealousy of Cora Beazant. No, not jealousy, that was the wrong word. She wasn't jealous of Cora, she just wanted to know her secret. They must be about the same age, so how come Jason's mother always looked so trim and healthy and glowing, while Hazel's own skin was dull and sallow, her eyes mired in dark shadows?

Botox or fillers. It had to be. Everyone was at it these days. Even Lucy, her beautiful, beautiful girl, had had injections around her eyes and in her forehead. Hazel had almost cried when she found out, but Lucy said all her friends were doing it and it wasn't a big deal. Anyway, she said, it had been proven to stop wrinkles forming, so she'd be mad to be the only one not to do it. Privately, Hazel worried it was a sign of insecurity. Lucy always came across as so comfortable in herself, but Hazel knew she sometimes grappled with low self-esteem. In her lowest moments she worried it was her fault – Hazel had always found schoolwork so easy, so it had come as a shock when her elder daughter struggled with exams and coursework. Had Hazel's expectations been too high? At least Lucy hadn't had those pillow lips done, like so many young women. Hazel couldn't imagine why that look had caught on so much, but she did find herself increasingly wondering whether she herself might not be a fool for insisting on growing old naturally when everyone around her was frozen at a time five or ten years before. Once she had weakened and booked a consultation with a local GP who did 'procedures' on the side, only to leave, humiliated, when he told her she'd left it so late that only surgery could help. 'Don't be upset,' he'd said comfortingly. 'You have a perfectly ordinary middle-aged face.'

'Do you think Cora has had work done?' she asked Dom, trailing back into the bedroom in one of the hotel's crisp cotton gowns. It was too warm, but she couldn't find the sarong she'd brought with her, which was irritating, because it was one of her favourites, in a cherry-coloured silk, that one of her photographers had brought back from a shoot in India. She must have left it by the pool. Hazel made a mental note to ask the receptionist.

Dom was lying on the bed with a towel wrapped around his waist, reading a biography of some jazz musician Hazel had never heard of. He looked drained, even after his epic nap.

'Are you sure you're feeling OK?'

'Yes, fine. Just tired. What kind of work has Cora had done? On the house?'

'Not on the house, you plonker, on her face. She always looks so immaculate. I bet she's got the perfect outfit for the wedding. Speaking of which, do you need to get your suit pressed before Saturday?'

'No. Look, do I really have to wear a suit? Couldn't I just get away with a shirt and those linen trousers?'

'Are you serious? Lucy would disown you. Besides, you look good in that suit. Plus, it cost a fortune and you've only worn it a handful of times.'

The suit had been a bone of contention when Dom bought it for a function three years before. She'd expected him to pick up something from TK Maxx, one of the usual unstructured Don Johnson circa 1988 styles he favoured, so she'd been taken aback when he'd returned from a trip to London with a fancy carrier bag containing a beautifully cut suit in the palest pearl grey, with narrow lapels and ivory silk lining and a receipt for over £500.

Still, it was flattering, she had to give him that.

'What do you think of this latest stunt of Jess's?' he asked, peering over the top of his glasses. 'Poor Lu-lu. I thought she was going to cry.'

'Nothing Jess does should surprise us by now.'

'Yes, but we don't know anything about this guy. He could be an axe murderer.'

'I doubt he'd have got his axe through customs. He only had that tiny bag with him.'

'Ha ha. But didn't there seem something of the night about him?'

'Something of the night? You're a pompous git sometimes.'

'And you're infuriatingly reasonable, as always. Seriously, though, it feels weird that Jess is shacked up just a few feet away with some random chap she literally picked up on the street. What if he does something to her?'

'Jess can look after herself. Anyway, if we say anything, she'll just do the opposite on principle.'

'It pisses me off, though. To be picking up the tab for some complete stranger.'

'Just as well it's me who's picking up the tab then, not you.'

As soon as they were out, Hazel wished she could reel the words back in.

'I only meant . . .' she began.

'I know what you meant.'

After that they dressed for dinner in virtual silence and, by the time they went out, Hazel felt like crying. All the money it was costing to feel this miserable. She could honestly weep.

Chapter Eight

Lucy

'She's always done this, our entire lives. Hogged the limelight. I don't think she even does it on purpose any more. It's just second nature.'

'But it's your wedding.'

'Oh, Jess doesn't believe in anything as conventional as marriage.' Even to her own ears, Lucy sounded bitter and mean, but she couldn't help it. Every single time she promised herself she wasn't going to let her sister get to her, she found herself blindsided again by Jess's utter inability to consider anyone but herself.

Shelly shook her head. She looked lovely this evening, Lucy thought. After two days of sunshine her pale skin had lost its usual translucency and, while a long way from tanned, it had a healthy glow. Her red hair flamed in the reflection of the setting sun. Shelly had huge eyes – almost too big for her face, really, which was fine-boned and delicate – and they changed colour according to the light. This evening, they seemed green and luminous.

'You deserve better than this, Luce. You're the kindest, most loyal person I know, and you've been dreaming of this wedding for so long. The least she could have done was ask you first. She's so selfish.'

Clearly, Shelly saw something in Lucy's face because she backtracked.

'OK, not selfish. But self-absorbed.'

They were sitting on the terrace of the hotel's restaurant, a cool grey-and-chrome space with a glass balustrade and polished slate flooring on the upper level above the bar. Their table, with its pristine white cloth and elegant glass vase containing one single white dahlia stem, looked out across the pool area below to the dramatic cliffs that fell away into the ocean, where the sun was pooling on the surface of the water like liquid honey. Lucy had specifically chosen the rugged north-western tip of Kefalonia over the more chi-chi resort of Fiskardo on the north-eastern side because of the sunsets. Normally, she'd be busy instagramming the stunning view, but her heart wasn't in it. Already she felt as if a little of the shine had been rubbed off this week.

'And are you OK?' Lucy asked Shelly, in a low voice so the others couldn't hear. 'I've hardly checked in with you at all, have I? I've turned into such a diva. You haven't seemed quite yourself today. Is it the whole family thing? Is it too much?'

Lucy couldn't imagine how it must feel to be around someone else's relatives when you weren't close to any of your own. 'We're your family now. Jason and me,' Lucy had told Shelly just a few weeks ago as they shared a bottle of wine in a pub after work on a Friday night. But obviously, it wasn't the same.

'I'm fine,' Shelly said, her face cracking into that wide, slightly crooked smile. 'Honestly. I'm loving it. But thank you for asking.'

Cora and Jason and Lucy's parents were sharing their table, while Zoe and Gil were on a nearby table for two. Jess hadn't yet shown her face. Always one for the late entrance. Well, the joke would be on her, because this table only seated six and all the other tables were full. Looking around, Lucy again felt a flicker of resentment that there were other guests here, outside of her little party. Especially that creepy old woman from the airport loo, who was eating alone at a table in the far corner. At least Lucy was the only bride here, thank God.

When Jess finally made an appearance, she had changed into what could best be described as a kind of pink cotton romper suit with straps that tied on her already burned shoulders. Gabriel was dressed as before, in black T-shirt and jeans. Please let him have brought some other clothes with him. For a moment they hovered in the doorway of the restaurant and Lucy wasn't proud of the stab of satisfaction that shot through her when Jess saw there wasn't any space for them.

Jess and Gabriel conferred for a moment, before beginning to thread their way, hand in hand, through the restaurant.

'Oh God, I don't believe it,' said Lucy as she and Shelly watched them come to a halt next to the table where the woman from the airport loo was spearing salad into her mouth. Jess said something to her and the woman nodded, and within seconds the latecomers were sitting down and seemingly deep in conversation with their new friend.

'She keeps looking over here,' Shelly complained after a few moments.

Lucy looked over and saw that the older woman's glittering blue eyes were indeed fixed on them. No, not on them. On Shelly.

The food was delicious, as always, and it almost killed Lucy to pick at a dressing-less house salad while everyone else was tucking into big plates of chicken marinaded in red wine, or grilled sea bream with roasted new potatoes, or perfectly tender steak served with a stack of triple-fried chips.

At one point after the main course, but before the desserts, Zoe got up from the next table to go to the loo and Gil reached out and grabbed her wrist to detain her, hissing under his breath: 'Please don't do this.'

'Let go of me. I just need a wee. What's your *problem*?'

Zoe shrugged off his hand and headed for the Ladies, while Gil bent his head, pretending to be lost in his phone.

Lucy nudged Shelly under the table.

After the last of the desserts had been cleared away – not for Lucy, of course, whose wedding dress would accommodate not one single extra ounce – and the last drops of after-dinner coffee drained, Lucy finally caved in and beckoned Jess and Gabriel over. There were plenty of empty seats around them now, so they could pull a couple over and join them.

'Fun dinner?' she asked sarcastically.

'It was, actually. Vivian is a total legend.'

'Vivian?'

'That's right, over there.' To Lucy's mortification, Jess pointed at the woman in the corner and waved.

'She's totally jokes. Full of stories. Do you know, she's been to almost every Greek island? Some of the things she got up to. Made me feel like an actual nun. I fucking love her. She's one of us.'

Lucy bit her lip. She would not rise to it.

On the other side of her, her mother gamely tried to engage Gabriel in conversation, perhaps to make up for her father, who'd been virtually silent all night – so unlike him. Lucy wondered if her parents had had a row and her eyes flicked anxiously from one to the other.

'So what exactly do you do?'

Jess groaned theatrically at her mother's question, but Gabriel seemed unperturbed.

'I have a little start-up. It's early days.'

He had one of those soft voices that made you have to mentally repeat what he said, thought Lucy, as if you were translating a foreign language in your head.

'Right.' Lucy's mum clearly didn't have a clue what he was on about. 'And where are you from?'

'Oh, you know. In and around London.'

'Gabe used to live in West Sussex, didn't you, Gabe? Isn't that what you said when we were in the Uber to Gatwick?'

'Really? Which part?' Lucy's mum was on firmer ground here.

'Around Littlehampton. Arundel. That kind of area. But I wasn't there long. I'm a Londoner in my marrow, you know? I need that big-city energy.'

Really, Lucy wondered, was that smile literally glued into place?

Now Gabriel was asking her mum about her work and Hazel was having to explain once again that a picture editor didn't actually take photos. 'We organize shoots. Or we used to, in the days when local papers had any money. Now it's more like quality control. Scrolling through stock images from libraries or from people's iPhones, looking for the one that best fits the story, checking for flaws.'

'In the old days she used to have this fantastic eyepiece like a plastic tube with a huge magnifying glass on one end like some kind of cyborg,' said Jess.

'That was pre-computers, when photographers would send over contact sheets with hundreds of tiny images,' laughed Hazel. 'No wonder my eyesight is shot!'

'When Jess's primary-school teacher asked what Mum did for a living, she told her she was a looker,' said Lucy, always happy to rehash the well-worn family myths. 'She meant someone who looks, but it caused much hilarity.'

'That explains it,' Gabriel said to Hazel. 'Why you sit there, observing us all.'

Lucy looked at him with new interest. That was exactly it. Her mother *did* sometimes seem to be studying them all like she was weighing them up, checking for flaws, as she'd just said.

But now her attention was snagged by Jess, who had leapt to her feet and was waving over to the woman she'd been sitting with before.

'Vivian! Get your arse over here. Meet the fam.'

'What are you doing?' Lucy hissed. But it was too late. Gabriel had gallantly gone to fetch a spare chair and now Vivian was sitting down with them, wearing a heavy floral perfume that hung over the table like a thick blanket.

'I've been dying to meet you all,' she said in a deep, theatrical voice. Her eyes, those ice-blue mosaic chips, darted around the table like a greedy bird, coming to rest on Shelly.

'Tell them about that time you went skinny-dipping with the Stones,' said Jess.

Vivian, who had taken out a vape without even bothering to ask if anyone objected, let out a deep bark of laughter that sent out a cloud of steam into Lucy's face. The smell, sickly-sweet strawberry, mingled with the heady perfume, making Lucy feel like she couldn't breathe.

When Vivian half-heartedly flapped at the air with her hand to disperse the steam, the silver bangles on her wrists clanked together like manacles.

16/6/19, 10.30. Original English-language transcript of police interview with Mrs Vivian Cassandra Kaffel. Police officers: Theodoros Christakis and Kostas Stephanides. Interpreter: Xanthe Liourdis.

What you have to understand is I have complex health needs. This chair is no good because I require lumbar support. Do you see? And I can't be directly under the air-conditioning unit because of migraines. Can you tell them that, please? It's very important.

Well, it's not ideal, but it will have to do. It would have been more convenient to do this at the hotel. More comfortable, too. But I suppose it's more official, being here at the station. And better to be away from them all. All those Collinses.

The thing is, I was better placed than anyone to observe what was going on in that hotel. Nothing much gets past me. You know, most people are either doers or watchers. Me, I'm both, and that's a useful life skill to have.

Are you a Scorpio? I'm afraid I don't have a good chemistry with Scorpios.

Libra? Could be worse, though I can't be doing with all that wishy-washy fence-sitting. I call a spade a spade. Or is that another thing we're not allowed to say any more? I've lost track. I always holiday in the Greek islands. I've been doing it since I was eighteen. Oh, the things I used to get up to. The unsuitable men. If these islands could talk, hey?

And yes, I always holiday alone. I like to be spontaneous. Compromise is the enemy of creativity. I love meeting new people and tagging along with them for a while. You have to be open to everything in this life.

What's that? Did I think she was dangerous? Well, isn't everyone, when pushed?

The Collinses? Well, they were a typical middle-class family. You know the type I mean. Two cases of wine every month via their online wine club, mid-budget Airbnb holidays in Cornwall. I hate to use the word 'cliché' about people, but . . . I've lost them, haven't I? Good God, these two aren't the sharpest knives in the dishwasher, are they? Ha!

Jess, the younger daughter, was the only one who had anything about her, any oomph. How are you translating 'oomph', by the way? Gumption? Really? Well, you're the expert, I suppose. She was a bit of a mess personally – always trying to shock – but at least she had some pizzazz. Not like the rest of them.

People like to believe that weddings are all about fun and nice clothes and everyone loving each other. But let me tell you, that couldn't be further from the truth. Weddings are pagan rituals full of ordinary people trying to make themselves extraordinary for a day. That's what makes them so exciting. And so deadly.

Was I upset by what happened? For heaven's sake, what do you take me for? Someone died. That's a very upsetting thing. Was I shocked, though? Now that's a different question entirely.

Chapter Nine

Hazel

The woman was quite impossible. At first, Hazel had felt sorry for her, being on her own, and was proud of Jess for including her, but after listening to her interminable stories for half an hour, told in that raspy, booming voice, she had had quite enough. Vivian seemed to believe no sentence was complete without a famous name dropped somewhere into it. And everything was about her. All the time she'd sat there talking, she hadn't once asked a question about anyone else. Hazel had been surprised to see that Jess, who didn't usually like to share the spotlight, had listened, rapt, to the whole performance, even though she'd already heard some of the stories earlier. And all that disgusting-smelling vape stuff blowing about.

Finally, Hazel had excused herself, saying she was going back to her room to fetch a pashmina, even though the air was the temperature of warm soup. Her plan was not to come back and to claim if challenged that she'd sat down for a moment on the bed and fallen asleep, just as Dom had done earlier. He owed her for that, in fact. But as she slid out behind her husband's chair, Jess called over to her.

'If you're going back inside, can you please fetch my phone from my room? I left it on the charger by my bed.'

Damn. Hazel pressed her lips together, trying to think of an excuse, but Jess was already holding out her room key.

'Please, my lovely mummy,' she said in a grating baby voice.

So now Hazel had no option but to return. It was so annoying. Jess's suite was next door to their own, although one grade less expensive. Jess wouldn't mind. She'd never been bothered about material stuff.

Inside, it was all chaos, even though Jess had only been there a couple of hours. There were clothes strewn around the bed, and the once-clean white dressing-table surface was already smudged with make-up and littered with screwed-up tissues and crumpled boarding passes, empty gum wrappers and hair scrunchies with pink hairs clinging to them as if they'd been ripped out at speed. Glancing through the doorway into the sweet, light-filled living room, Hazel saw that Gabriel's few possessions had been plonked down on the sofa. A leather jacket. A nylon backpack. A few crumpled euros and pounds. A set of keys. A passport.

Jess's phone sat charging on the bedside drawers, balanced on top of the small, battered notebook Jess carried everywhere. She claimed to be writing a book – part fantasy and part philosophy – which is why she was working in a bar, long after most of her friends had found 'proper' jobs. As Hazel detached the phone from the charger the heavily cracked screen was illuminated, showing an endless list of texts and social media messages. *Omg you were TRASHED last night* read the first one, before the screen went dark again.

Something pinched at Hazel's heart. She'd always felt it important to let her daughters be their own people, which meant not stepping in to offer judgement or advice or trying to impose her own moral framework on them. But that didn't stop her worrying about them. Jess was so dangerously unmoored sometimes.

Take this man, for example. Gabriel. He could be anybody. He'd been so vague at dinner in response to her questions. What even was a start-up, anyway? Dom's implied criticism earlier had stung. *Infuriatingly reasonable.* As if being reasonable were a flaw. Still, she felt guilty about what she'd said afterwards. The trouble was that money had become the elephant in the room of their marriage as the income from Dom's one big success had dried up, meaning she shouldered more and more of the burden of keeping the house – and the girls – going. It wasn't that she'd resented it, exactly – after all, it was mostly thanks to him they'd been able to buy their house in the first place – but more and more, it was there, bubbling under the surface, coming out through any crack or fissure in their relationship. And she had to admit that in the last few weeks, since everything went to shit and she'd been lying awake night after night in a cold sweat while Dom snored gently beside her, the inequality of it all had been getting to her. It was so long since he'd been responsible for any of the bills or expenses that funded their lifestyle that he'd got out of the habit of worrying about them. He hadn't deserved what she'd said, though.

She stepped into the living room, where Gabriel's passport lay on the white sofa cushion. She knew that Dom wouldn't hesitate to pick it up. She could hear him in her head: 'Any concerned parent would want to know who their daughter was shacked up with.' Her own instinct, as always, was to leave things as they were. Not to interfere in her daughter's life. But it wasn't technically snooping, was it, if it was just lying there?

Guiltily, she flicked through the passport, noting the various visas tucked inside – India, Thailand. A Russian visa boasted a photograph of a younger Gabriel, his hairline a good inch further forwards towards his eyes. There was a US visa, too, dated three years before, with a red line scored through it and the word CANCELLED stamped across it. Hazel studied it. In the photo, Gabriel's face was less round, the features more defined. His birthdate put him at thirty-nine. Far too old for Jess. But she didn't have time to worry about that because now her eye was drawn to something that drove all the other thoughts from her head.

Earlier, he'd introduced himself as Gabriel Kidd, yet the boxes marked 'Name' and 'Surname' were filled in as Vince Harris.

Her younger daughter had brought a complete stranger to her sister's wedding – and none of them had the faintest idea who he really was. Or why he was lying about it.

Chapter Ten

Nina

There was a moment when she accelerated up that last, steep hairpin turn when Nina thought the car would give up the ghost. The loose stones had flown out under the wheels but the car felt like it had lost power. This is it, Nina thought. Finally. Yet somehow she had made it to the hotel. It was the first thing to have gone right that day.

Nina was still upset about the atmosphere at home, where she and Mark had eaten breakfast in a loaded silence that was broken only by him swearing loudly when he opened the fridge and found it devoid of orange juice. The trouble had started the night before when Nina had arrived home, exhausted, and found Mark in ebullient mood. At first, she'd been relieved. He'd been so flat and down since she'd told him their relationship was over, addressing her only in a dull monotone. Unless he'd been at the beers, in which case he'd alternate between wheedling and belligerence until Nina couldn't wait for the return of the flatness. He'd stopped pulling his weight at work, too. The original deal had been that Nina did all the people-facing aspects of the business while Mark sorted out the logistics – applying for wedding licences, setting up lighting, lugging around DJ equipment, as well as the book-keeping and the invoicing. But recently she'd been more or less running things single-handedly.

Last night, though, he'd greeted her with a smile and a bottle of French wine that had immediately got Nina's hackles up because she knew how expensive it was.

'What's all this in aid of?' she'd asked, trying to sound upbeat so as not to puncture his high mood.

'It's our wedding anniversary.'

Nina had completely forgotten. Or rather, there hadn't seemed much point in remembering, not now they weren't, technically, together any more.

'Oh, right. I haven't . . .'

'Don't worry. This is all about you. You've been working so hard. You deserve to be spoiled a little bit. Which is why I got you this.'

He'd produced an envelope from the kitchen drawer, and Nina had found herself exhaling. A card, then. She could cope with a card. He was looking so pleased with himself, and so full of anticipation, Nina felt some hardened part of her melting. This was her big, clumsy, huge-hearted Mark. The man she'd loved for nearly ten years. And who loved her still, which was something she'd never doubted, despite everything.

The picture on the front of the card was the usual pastel-coloured illustration of flowers with curly pink writing, the only design available at the village shop. There was a folded A4 sheet tucked inside.

'Open it, then.' Mark was always like this, childlike in his eagerness to see her reaction.

Nina stared down at the printout of the confirmation email from EasyJet. Two return flights back to the UK in October.

'We haven't got any more weddings after the end of September, and I know how much you want to see your mum. I've arranged everything. Your sister is organizing a big party.'

'Where did the money come from?'

'Don't be like that, doll. You need this break. You've been working so hard. *We* need it.'

'Where?'

Mark's smile had slipped down his face.

'When did you get like this, Nina? Such a killjoy? I remember when we used to have a laugh. Now, it's like you're scared to enjoy yourself.'

Well. That had been that. Nina had run to their ancient laptop, holding her breath watching the wheel of death go round and round as it attempted to power up. When she logged into internet banking, she already knew what she'd find. The emergency fund bank account held a balance of twenty-three euros and fifty-five cents.

'But it was all for you,' said Mark, as if that might make it all right. 'I just wanted to make you happy. I can't do anything right.'

She'd taken herself off to bed early, and all night she'd tossed and turned while Mark slept in the spare room. If you lay in bed in the master bedroom, you looked up at a brown stain that looked vaguely like Africa, a legacy of the storm a few months ago that had sent water pouring in through the asphalt of the roof. Funny to think how she'd adored this house when they first saw it, and now the pool was green with algae since they'd had to let the pool boy go, and the back terrace smelled of drains, and they were locked into a battle with the solicitor who'd overseen the sale without noticing that a small section of the land on which the villa stood – the site of the downstairs bathroom – was actually owned by a distant cousin of the woman they'd bought it from, rendering it all but unsellable.

Setting off across the car park of the Paradise View, Nina tried to slow her breathing down, as she'd learned in the Pilates classes she'd loved back home in England. *In through the nose, out through the mouth. In through the nose, out through the mouth.* The car park was surrounded by vegetation – fig trees, their shy fruits hiding in green clusters under flat, shiny leaves; ancient olives with gnarled, twisted trunks. The pink blooms on the spreading oleander bush gave off a sweet, bubblegum smell.

If you had to be trapped in your dream life, Nina thought, you could do a lot worse than be trapped here.

She drew her shoulders back, arranged her features into a smile.

Approaching the entrance to the hotel, her path was blocked. Automatically, she switched her smile up a notch in anticipation of an encounter with a guest, her heart sinking when she saw it was the waiter she'd recognized the previous day. The nephew of their neighbour, Mr Angelis.

Nina hated that Mark had gone to Mr Angelis for money behind her back a couple of months before, when they were in danger of defaulting on their mortgage. By that time, the business was in big trouble, the down payment for each new wedding going to pay off the outstanding debts on the last one, every time just a hair's breadth from bankruptcy.

But Mr Angelis, though outwardly charming, had a reputation locally for being someone you wanted to keep at arm's length. And Nina had worked so hard to make sure they were on good terms with their Greek neighbours. God knew the poor sods hadn't had an easy time of it over the years of austerity. On the whole, they'd been very welcoming to the English newcomers and the boost to local tourism Nina's wedding-planning business brought. Though there were plenty of British expats living on Kefalonia, Nina and Mark had deliberately chosen to settle in a village that was exclusively Greek. Why move all this way to meet the same sort of people she could have met at home? She had made friends with a couple of the younger Greek women and met up with them occasionally for a walk or a coffee. They were kind and looked on her as a novelty, gently making fun of the tins of Heinz beans she made visitors bring over in their luggage and the smelly wild rabbit Mark had found injured in the hills who now lived in a home-made wooden hutch on the back terrace and was named, predictably, Bugs.

Borrowing money had muddied everything. Everyone on the island seemed to be related to Mr Angelis in some complicated way – like this waiter, and the man lurking a few steps behind him, thickset and wearing the black-and-white checked trousers and white jacket of a kitchen chef, who the waiter introduced as his cousin.

'My uncle asks with respect when you will have money for him,' the waiter said in broken English, which Nina, who could manage the basics in Greek, took as a snub. 'You know things still very difficult here in Greece.'

'Very soon. Next week, in fact.' Nina's fake smile made her cheeks ache.

The young waiter, who had a couple of tiny nicks on his chin, as if he'd been shaving with a blunt razor, stepped forward so there were only a few inches between them.

'Next week is too late,' he said. 'My uncle says to tell you how much he respect you and how pity will be if anything bad happen for you.'

The threat was so unexpected it took Nina a few seconds to recognize it as such and, by the time she did, sucking in air sharply through her teeth, the two men had melted off around the side of the hotel and only the hammering of her heart in her chest told her they had ever been there at all.

15/6/19, 23.36. Original English-language transcript of police interview with Mrs Nina Caroline Foster. Police officers: Demitri Iraklidis and Tomaso Diakos. Interpreter: Eulalia Scala.

I'm embarrassed needing an interpreter after living here for five and a half years. It's so depressingly English, isn't it, to expect everyone else to speak our language? I was so determined to slot in here when we first arrived, not to be a typical expat. And just look at me!

I'm sorry, do I know you? It's just you look familiar . . .

First impressions of the Collinses? Well, they were just a nice, ordinary family. I mean, Lucy was a little highly strung, but then all brides are, aren't they? There's so much pressure on this one day to be perfect.

I really liked them, though. Jason was just a genuinely good bloke. Kind and steady. Big, strong hands, you know? I don't know why I said that. Sorry. His mum seemed lovely, too. Really well turned out. I didn't have much to do with the others – the best man and his wife, Lucy's friend, her sister and that man she brought. Now that was a bit odd. Springing some stranger on everyone without any warning. He seemed all right, quite quiet, but like I say, I hardly spoke to him.

The rest of them, though, were just thoroughly nice people. I'm so devastated about what's happened to them.

Tension? Between me and the Collinses? Why ever would you think that? We had a very amicable working relationship. Look, when there's a lot at stake, sometimes there are . . . differences of opinion. The Collinses were spending a lot of money. Weddings are expensive. Ha! Yes, I suppose it is lucky for me, but then I work very hard for my fee. I'm good at my job and I take it very seriously. As a wedding planner, you're only as happy as your least happy bride.

There were no arguments, though. No. Absolutely not. Look, I don't mean to be rude, but where exactly are you getting your information from?

Chapter Eleven

Lucy

Lucy was taking photographs of her breakfast. Or rather, she was taking photographs of the breakfast she could have had if she hadn't been too scared to eat in case she looked fat in the wedding pictures or didn't fit into her dress. She'd piled a bowl high with fresh fruit: slices of perfectly ripe orange-fleshed melon, peaches, apricots, plums that were squishy with juice – and behind it a plate of flaky mini croissants dusted with icing sugar. A dish containing fat chunks of white feta drizzled with honey was set next to a purple-coloured smoothie. Behind it was a steaming cup of coffee topped with a milky froth. All were arranged on a blue-and-white checked cloth, and Lucy was crouched at one end of the table, trying to capture all of it, complete with fresh white flower, against the backdrop of the ridiculously blue sky and sea and the dramatic rocky cliffs.

When she was satisfied she'd got the perfect picture she sat back down in her seat next to Jason and started posting to her various social media accounts with different witty hashtags and plenty of exclamation marks!!!

'Don't you think that's cheating, when you're not actually going to eat any of it?' Jason teased her, stretching out to pick a mini croissant from her plate.

'Life's tough when you're an influencer.'

Jason laughed, and Lucy leaned over to give him a kiss. How lucky was she? This beautiful place. This beautiful man. Until she met Jason, she hadn't understood the depth of contentment that came from loving someone who loved you back completely and utterly. In the past, she'd gone for trophy boyfriends – men who chatted her up with complete conviction, as if it were impossible their attentions might not be welcome, and drove flash cars and told her she was gorgeous. But they were like hologram relationships, everything on the surface, and when she tried to probe deeper she'd find there was nothing there, no context, no depth.

She'd met Jason through work. Lucy was assistant manager of a high-end leisurewear outlet and Jason was the regional sales manager for one of the store's biggest suppliers. She hadn't fancied him immediately. In fact, she couldn't even remember the first time they met – although he claimed to have every second imprinted on his memory. But they'd established a good working relationship and then a friendship, and gradually she found she was looking forward to his visits more and more and, in the end, it had been her who'd asked him out. He always claimed he had been working up to it but, privately, she doubted he'd have had the bottle.

And, instantly, it had been as if she'd kicked off the uncomfortable high-heeled shoes she'd been staggering around in and was barefoot and free and entirely herself. Jason didn't just tell her she was beautiful, he told her why. All the little things about her that made her irresistible to him. And he listened to her. Really listened. In a way those other men with their slick patter and their self-absorption never had. With Jason, she never felt like she had to be anything other than what she was. She was enough. She was *more* than enough.

Her hours of online sleuthing into his family tree were her way of showing him how much he meant to her, reuniting him with the relatives he'd lost touch with when his dad died. Lucy had visions of being able to announce to a dumbstruck Jason – and Cora, of course – that he would have family of his own at the wedding party back in the UK, after all. If only this cousin, this Connor Kerswell, would get back to her. It was an ongoing source of frustration to Lucy that Jason had so few memories of the dad who'd died of cancer when he was twelve. 'But everyone remembers their childhood, right?' Lucy'd asked Shelly, remembering too late that her friend probably wished to God that she didn't.

Once, soon after she and Jason got engaged, Lucy had tried to press Cora for a photo of her late husband, on the grounds that she'd most likely be producing this mystery man's grandchildren, and Cora had finally come up with a small, blurry picture of a fair-haired man with faded features and a smile that creased his whole face holding a young Jason on his shoulders, his big hands gripping the child's scrawny shins. 'There,' she'd said firmly, as if that drew a line under the matter.

Lucy laced her hands through her fiancé's under the table and gazed dreamily around the hotel terrace. Zoe and Gil were on a corner table, Zoe talking loudly enough into her phone to carry across the restaurant, reciting to her poor parents the litany of tasks they were expected to perform in her absence, including, it seemed, teaching her toddler French. 'There's a vocabulary book on the table in her room. You introduce her to a new word every day. But make sure you put it into a sentence so she can remember what it means. And then test her tomorrow. OK? But don't forget to make it *fun*!'

Lucy's eyes scanned the other guests. There was a group of six on the next table who'd arrived overnight and were admiring the view with exhausted, stunned expressions. Lucy watched them benignly until she overheard the woman facing her, who looked to be in her early thirties and had newly plumped-up lips and eyelash extensions that were just a little bit too long, talking to one of the two older women about whether her hair would get messed up when she arrived by speedboat and the penny dropped with a huge clang.

'There's another bride here,' she said, in a choked voice as Nina sat down to join them. 'I thought I'd be the only one.'

Nina, who was looking pale and strained and unlike her usual self, pressed her lips together.

'Oh, Lucy. I'm sorry about that. I know it was important to you. But I did say I couldn't guarantee there wouldn't be another wedding booking. And at least you know she can't be getting married on Saturday, because you've got the beach for the entire day, so it shouldn't make any difference to you.'

'No, I know. I just . . .' Lucy felt Jason's hand come to rest on her thigh and stopped herself. Really, what was the point in making a fuss? This other woman was here now. And probably, like her, had been planning for this for the last God knows how long.

And yet some of the joy had gone from the day, and when she looked out at the glorious view the sky seemed ever so slightly less blue.

'Now I've got you two, I wondered if I could ask you something a little, um, delicate.' Nina picked up a starched napkin and started smoothing it out on to the table. 'It's just, your second payment is overdue now . . .'

'No. That's not right. We paid it, didn't we? From the joint account?' Jason removed his hand from Lucy's leg and sat back so that he could see her properly.

'Yes. Of course. I mean, I'm pretty sure I transferred the money, but you know how distracted I've been, Jase. Maybe it slipped my mind.'

'Do you think you could check?' Nina's smile was pinched.

'Absolutely. As soon as I get back to the room.'

'Great. Thanks.'

Nina started talking about arrangements for the fishing-boat trip they were going on that day. She seemed more relaxed now she'd got Lucy's assurance that the money was on its way. But as Lucy sat there listening and studiously ignoring the Other Bride at the next table, she felt as if someone had threaded a drawstring across her chest and was pulling it tighter and tighter.

Therapy Journal, Week 3

I know we have to go here, but it's hard. I'm on my sofa with my computer on my lap and it feels like there's a cricket ball sitting in my stomach. OK. Deep breath. My first memory of that room. I must have been around three or four. I know people say that's too young to remember properly, but some things you don't forget. Mummy had put the old red plastic potty in there that I'd used when I was younger and I was upset because I wasn't a baby any more. 'It's just a few hours,' she whispered. 'Until she's *gone.' All right, she might not have said those actual words. But I do remember the door closing. I remember that. Sitting looking at that door and crying. Or maybe I'm getting mixed up with all the other times. Even now I hate to be in a room where the door is closed.*

Chapter Twelve

Jess

Jess was feeling restless. Inviting Gabriel along to the wedding had seemed like such an inspired idea at the time. Shake things up a bit. Put a rocket up the usual dull family dynamics. He wasn't her type, but he'd do for a brief foreign fling. He'd seemed cool at first. Enigmatic. But now she'd been with him twenty-four hours she was starting to realize he was a little bit bland. Oh, why not just say it? Boring. That's what she meant. He never gave a direct answer to a question. Either smiled that infuriating smile or else replied with a question of his own. Plus, he'd called her 'high maintenance' the previous evening. She'd been telling him about Lucy and how much she wished her sister would drag herself out of the conventional rut she'd fallen into. First coupling up with Jason, who was one hundred per cent lovely but didn't exactly set the world on fire, and now sleepwalking into marriage. It'd be children next and then, *bam*, her whole life would be over just like that.

Jess had snapped her fingers in front of Gabriel's face to demonstrate. They had been out on the terrace of their suite – although, really, it was Jess's suite and Gabriel was just crashing, which he would do well to remember. Jess was rolling a cigarette and Gabriel was gazing out at the view and drinking a glass of wine from the minibar, without even asking her if that was OK, which was just rude if you wanted to know the truth, and when she'd paused in her dissection of her sister's life choices in order to take a long drag of her ciggie, he'd just come out with it. Apropos of nothing.

'I get the sense you're pretty high maintenance, Jessica.'

As if he knew the first thing about her! She was the least high-maintenance woman she knew. Other women had complicated skincare regimes that required endless toiletries – serums, primers, concealers, *skin-blurrers* – that took up all the space on the bathroom shelves. Not her. Soap and water – and that's if she remembered. No expensive designer clothes. No flash cars or five-star luxury hotels (well, apart from this one, and it certainly wouldn't have been her choice). Hadn't he noticed how she'd crammed all her packing into her army-surplus canvas backpack? High maintenance? Don't make her laugh.

Now, she looked around the restaurant terrace. There were Lucy and Jason, deep in conversation with that wedding planner Lucy had insisted on hiring. A wedding planner! If Jess ever got married – which, obviously, she never would because why would you need the state to sanction your private emotional life? – it would be a totally spontaneous celebration and she'd be wearing a tuxedo, like she'd seen a woman do in a very sexy French film, or else something vintage, teamed with her pink Doc Martens. Not that she'd thought about it.

Next to her, Gabriel was tucking into bread, which he'd topped with cheese and dollops of clear honey and rolls of fat pink ham and – *oh, please* – slices of ripe tomato which dripped seeds down his chin. And did he have to make such a noise when he ate?

She saw Vivian approaching and waved her over. She'd seen the others judging her last night and it had got on her tits. She loved her family, but fuck, they could be narrow-minded. Not like her. She'd talk to anyone, give anyone a chance. Didn't matter what age or culture, rich or poor. It was all the same to her. And yes, Vivian was a bit domineering. But then she herself had had that criticism levelled at her in the past. All it meant was that you had something to say and weren't afraid to say it. Some people found that a threat.

'What are your plans for today?' she asked the older woman, who was wearing a turquoise kaftan with a fringe at the bottom from which hung tiny silver baubles.

'A bit of meditation, I expect. I need to rebalance my energies. Then just lie around the pool. Self-care is so important.'

'We're all going on a trip.' Jess made quote marks in the air around the word 'trip' to emphasize how little she cared for organized group outings. 'A day out on a fishing boat. Hey, do you want to come, too? We're all just going to be sitting around all day, swigging wine and jumping in and out of the water, while Captain Spiros, or whatever his name is, catches fish for the lunch poor downtrodden Mrs Spiros will then have to prepare. More the merrier.'

'Don't you think you should check with your sister?' asked Gabriel in that grating pretend-mild manner he had.

'Oh, for fuck's sake. This is my holiday, you know, as well as her wedding. I've had to take a week's leave from the bar to be here. But all right then, if it will make you feel happy.'

She stomped over to Lucy's table. The wedding planner had gone now, replaced by Shelly. Jess had never really seen the appeal of Shelly. She preferred people to be upfront. No game-playing or 'look at me, how deep and interesting I am because I'm not giving anything away'. For fuck's sake. If you're angry about something, say so. If you're sad or fed up or disappointed or whatever. Just say it. Don't sit there looking like you've a fucking bollard up your arse. Plus, she was such a suck-up where Lucy was concerned.

'So I've invited Vivian to come with us today on the boat. That's cool, isn't it?'

Lucy stared at her. Blinked.

'I don't know if that's a good idea, Lucy,' said Shelly. 'If she comes along today, we'll be stuck with her for the rest of the week.'

Jess bristled. Had she even been talking to Shelly? No, she had not.

'Shell's right. I'd planned this as a kind of group bonding thing.'

'Oh, all right then, so you'd rather she sat here on her own all day?'

'No, of course not, but . . .'

Jess could tell Lucy was bending. She'd always been a soft touch. Couldn't bear to leave anyone out.

'Come on. There'll be other strangers there. Captain Georgiopolopopolos and his missus.'

The ghost of a smile played at the corners of Lucy's mouth.

'Oh, maybe I should. What do you think, Shell?'

Shelly glanced across to the table where Vivian and Gabriel sat unspeaking. As if she sensed them all looking, Vivian's piercing gaze swung towards them.

'I'll be honest, Luce, she gives me the creeps. She's always *staring*.'

Lucy nodded. 'That decides it, then. Sorry, Jess. Not today.'

Jess turned away crossly and returned to her table, ignoring Shelly's parting smile. She knew it was childish, but she couldn't help feeling as if Lucy had chosen her best friend over her own sister. Resentment scorched a path through her gut like heartburn.

Chapter Thirteen

Shelly

Shelly knew she'd given Jess one more reason to dislike her. Usually that would have made her uncomfortable, so programmed was she to try to fit in with her surroundings, but right now, she didn't care. There was something about the way Vivian looked at her that made Shelly feel *invaded*. She'd been burgled the year before and the way the older woman made her feel was how she'd felt then, knowing the unknown thief had rifled through her underwear drawer.

Shelly had come up against people like Jess before. Utterly convinced that their view was the only view and, if the rest of the world didn't share it, that was because the rest of the world was wrong. What was theirs by luck – family, money – they took for granted, as if it was theirs by right.

Lucy deserved so much better.

Hazel and Dom deserved so much better.

No sooner had she allowed Lucy's parents into her thoughts than Shelly felt the heat rushing to her face, her palms slick with sweat. She stood up abruptly from the breakfast table and, with a volley of 'sorry's, made her way to the loo opposite the bar. She'd been doing so well up until then. She'd mostly avoided Lucy's parents, and on the few occasions that hadn't been possible she'd retreated to that blissfully blank area she'd created in her mind where she could escape when things got too fraught.

If compartmentalizing were an academic subject, Shelly would be an A-star student.

The acrid smell hit her as soon as she walked into the toilets, but by the time she recognized it as vomit, the door of the only cubicle was opening and it was too late to make a quick exit.

'Oh, it's you,' said Zoe flatly, wiping her mouth.

'Have you been sick?'

'Dodgy tummy.'

Shelly held Zoe's pink-rimmed gaze in the mirror until Zoe looked away, and something softened inside her, despite everything.

'Sometimes sharing a bathroom isn't easy, even with your husband. Everyone needs their privacy.'

It was an overture, an invitation to unburden. For a moment it looked as if Zoe might take advantage of it. She opened her mouth as if to speak, but something, maybe the sour smell of her own breath, closed her up again.

Fair enough. Shelly tried a new tack.

'Did you hear Jess out there, asking Lucy if that awful woman could come along on the boat today? Not even asking, actually, telling her she was coming.'

Something passed over Zoe's flushed face and was gone before Shelly could work out if it was relief or disappointment.

'*Quelle surprise*. Not. Jess is totally self-centred. It wouldn't cross her mind to run it by Lucy first. I mean, it's only her wedding, for God's sake. It's not as if she's been planning it for years or anything. I'm sure she's totally fine with Jess inviting random creeps along.'

'Do you think Gabriel is a creep? He seemed all right to me. It must be a little intimidating for him being here with all of us, don't you think?'

'Nobody forced him to come. Or to go around picking up wasted women out of gutters.'

'Jess told Lucy she's already gone off him.'

'Well, colour me shocked. 'Course she has. She only brought him along to get a reaction from her family. And now she hasn't any use for him any more it's *Sayonara, Gabriel*.'

After Zoe had gone, Shelly remained by the basin, reluctant to enter the cubicle, although the smell had more or less gone. She felt sorry for Zoe, but whatever she'd been doing in there was really no concern of Shelly's. Thinking about it, it was just as well the other woman hadn't taken her into her confidence. Even if she did have some *issues* – and who didn't? – the last thing Shelly needed was to be allied in any way with Zoe, not when Lucy had made her feelings about Gil's wife so clear, and not with Jess looking to take advantage of any weakness in Shelly and Lucy's friendship.

Now that Gabriel was here, too, that narrow ledge on the group periphery had just got a whole lot more crowded.

Therapy Journal, Week 4

You were right about me having problems opening up. Those years attuned to Mummy's feelings meant I stopped listening to my own. But I know we have to push on. What's that phrase you used? We can't put the toothpaste back in the tube?

I knew Mummy was getting worse. She'd stay in bed for days and I'd eat whatever I could find. One time I opened a can of soup by stabbing it with the kitchen scissors because the tin opener was broken, and one of the blades rebounded into my arm. I still have a scar. Or else she'd have too much energy and fly around the house opening cupboards and pulling out the contents, piling them all up in the middle of the room ready to have a 'good sort-out', and then lose interest, so the pile would sit there for weeks, until I bundled the clothes back into the cupboards. We lived in a nice red-brick house on a hill in North London, courtesy of my mother's divorce settlement from my American financier father, who'd fled back to the States when I was still a baby, but inside, the place was a pigsty. I tried my best to keep things clean, but Mummy never bought things like Hoover bags or washing-up liquid and the mophead was hard and brittle with age. I've since read accounts from people who were brought up in chaotic households where no one bothered to tidy up and they've framed it as bohemian and fun, but all I remember is gnawing anxiety looking at the pots piled in the sink or the grease around the cooker. At night we could hear the rustling of mice behind the fridge.

I had a few friends at school – quiet, watchful children like me – but I never invited them around. From early on, I knew in that way children do that the way we lived, Mummy and I, wasn't right.

It's 4 a.m. and I've got up to write this down because I need to get my thoughts out of my head so I can sleep. Talking to you about Mummy has made me realize she was like a child herself, but when I was young I thought all grown-ups were like her. Mercurial creatures who slipped through your fingers if you tried to grab them. I remember being struck the first time I saw that bumper sticker: 'Don't follow me, I'm lost too.' That was me and Mummy. I followed her because she was the adult, but all the time she was just wandering aimlessly, waiting for someone to show her the way.

Chapter Fourteen

Hazel

Hazel closed the door of her suite with relief. She'd left Dom behind on the terrace to deal with Jess, who had a bee in her bonnet about something to do with that odd woman she'd befriended. 'I'll come with you, darling,' Dom had said when he realized Hazel was leaving, but she'd insisted she wanted to be on her own. He was so needy this holiday since that little spat about the money, following her around the place like a little dog.

It was still early so she opened up the doors to the terrace to allow what slight breeze there was to circulate before the heat became too fierce. Sitting back on the bed, she opened up her laptop. While it was still whirring into life, she reflected further on her younger daughter. Last night she'd taken her aside as soon as she could to tell her what she'd found in Gabriel's passport, only for Jess to roll her eyes as if she'd said something monumentally dull. 'Loads of people call themselves different names to what's on their passport. Not everyone wants to be defined by a piece of paper their parents signed when they were born. It's called free will, Mother.'

Dom's reaction to the news had also been uncharacteristically lacklustre. Normally, he adored a mystery and it was Hazel's job to rein in his propensity for creating drama where none existed but, while he'd agreed it was odd that Gabriel should have a passport in a completely different name, he'd seemed reluctant to engage in wild speculation. 'Why don't we just ask him?' But then Hazel would have to admit she'd looked through his things. 'Look, there's no point making things awkward now, after everything Lucy has put into this week. We'll investigate properly when we get back to England – assuming this thing between him and Jess hasn't already burned itself out. You know what she's like.' He had a point. Lucy already had so much on her plate and, besides, there was already friction between the girls over Jess bringing this man. The last thing Hazel wanted was to fan the flames, especially since, as Dom said, Jess would undoubtedly have got tired of him by the time they got back to the UK.

Hazel and her own sister weren't close, swapping birthday and Christmas cards with the same 'Can't believe another year has gone by without seeing you. Next year, for sure' messages. So she hadn't been prepared for the intricate latticework of Lucy and Jess's relationship. The historic resentments and decades-old slights that were stored close to the surface ready to be whipped out at the first sign of an altercation. The rivalries, the jealously hoarded occasions when they'd felt overlooked or sidelined by their parents in favour of their sibling. The raucous bursts of love or laughter that could be punctured by a careless remark or an imagined criticism. Or, conversely, the bitter arguments that turned unfathomably into helpless giggles by dint of a single word that had become shorthand over the years for some funny story they'd both mostly forgotten. Hazel envied their dynamic and was exhausted by it in equal measure. And while they both periodically tried to co-opt her to their 'side' of whatever disagreement they were having, she was most comfortable standing well back, spectator rather than umpire.

Turning her attention back to her emails, Hazel automatically clenched all the muscles in her abdomen one by one, as she'd got into the habit of doing over these last three terrible months, literally girding herself against whatever was to come. Her eyes skimmed her inbox, her chest tightening as she saw the name Melanie Alderman, HR director of the media group that owned the *Bristol Mail*. 'P45 attached' read the subject line. Hazel slammed down the lid fast.

How could her life have tipped so completely from one reality to another in just a few weeks? From respected if long-in-the-tooth journalist enjoying her final years of work before retirement at sixty, to this? Unemployed at fifty-seven. Minuscule private pension still three years off. Humiliated.

And this bloody wedding to pay for.

She lay on the bed and gazed out through the glass windows at the cerulean sky, where an aeroplane was scoring a line across as straight and sharp as a scalpel. How bizarre it was, she thought, as she always did when she came abroad, to choose to live in grey, cloudy England when there was so much beauty in the world and places where the sun shone eleven months of the year. She could run away! Come to live somewhere like this. Living the dream, like Nina. For a few short, sweet moments she allowed herself to give in to this fantasy in which she lived a simple life, growing her own vegetables, bartering English lessons in return for meat. No internet. No mobile phone, even. No students, no mortgage. She would grow lean, with actual visible muscles in the tops of her arms, which would be nut brown and . . .

A ringtone broke her reverie. The Clash playing 'London Calling'. Jess had put it on Dom's phone as a joke but, like many things in their lives, it had just been left until no one noticed it any more, what was once ironic becoming merely commonplace. Once Lucy had left a Post-it on Hazel's home office door saying 'CLEAN ME' in thick felt pen, and had been outraged to return a few weeks later to find it still in place. 'I forgot it was there,' Hazel said. But that wasn't it, really. It was more about agency, she supposed. Or, more specifically, lack of it. The idea that once something was in place it became an accepted part of the landscape.

The song went into a second chorus. Damn. She'd forgotten she still had Dom's phone in her bag. Though it was his own bloody fault. Men and their 'Can I just pop this one thing in your bag as it won't fit in my pockets?'

thing. Phones, books, sun cream. Sometimes Hazel felt like a Sherpa.

The number showing on the screen had a UK code but was clearly not recognized in Dom's contact list.

Hazel dithered about whether to answer, and by the time she decided to do so the caller had hung up.

As she was returning the phone to her bag, a text lit up the home screen from the same UK number: *Call me. I can explain.*

Well, that was odd. Hazel frowned, trying to work out what the cryptic message could be about.

Back out by the pool area, where they were all gathering before heading down to the jetty for the fishing-boat trip, Dom's face broke into a smile as she approached.

'Darling, thank God you're here. I thought I'd have to go without you.'

'I'm sure you'd have managed. By the way, your phone was ringing.' She reached into her bag and tossed him his phone. 'Anything interesting?'

Dom's smile didn't slip as he looked at the screen, but she watched the little tic in the side of his jaw, just where it angled up towards his ear.

'Just a missed call from a number I don't recognize. Probably someone wanting to tell me I've been in a car accident or something.'

He thrust his phone in his pocket just as, way overhead, a single white cloud crossed over the sun, causing the back of Hazel's neck to come up in tiny icy bumps.

Chapter Fifteen

Lucy

Up in the De Luxe, a.k.a. honeymoon suite, Lucy's chest felt unpleasantly tight. After Nina had gone, Jason had gently chided her for not being more careful about making sure Nina had been paid. 'She's such a sound woman and I'd hate her to get any grief from her bank because of us.' What could Lucy do except agree and repeat her excuse about forgetting to put the payment through because she was distracted. But, all the time, she'd known full well she hadn't made the transfer because of the queasy suspicion that they didn't have enough funds, not even in their overdraft. And she wasn't sure the bank would let them go more overdrawn than they already were.

The truth was, she hadn't dared look at her bank statements for weeks now. She'd known her spending was getting out of control, but she couldn't seem to stop. Jasmine, one of the Saturday sales executives at the shop, was also getting married in a couple of months and she was having the full monty – £4,000 dress, big church wedding, stately-home reception for three hundred guests. Lucy knew she shouldn't compare herself; after all, Jasmine's fiancé worked in the City and didn't care how much anything cost as long as he didn't have to lift a finger to help with any of it. But, somehow, Lucy had allowed herself to get swept along in Jasmine's extravagance.

The two of them had had endless discussions about table pieces and corsages (Jasmine was in favour, Lucy not so much) and bridesmaid presents and wedding favours and the correct wording on the invitations. Lucy had been so upset by Jasmine's open-mouthed reaction when she'd found out how few people were coming to this Kefalonian wedding, she'd found herself explaining that smaller numbers made for a more exclusive event and meant they could spend more on spoiling the guests they had. After that, Jasmine had made it her mission to help Lucy pick out the most luxurious hotel, the finest shoes, dress, veil, flowers. And the same for the big party they were having when they got home – the pricier venue, because when you were already paying so much money, what difference did another £500 make? Champagne rather than Prosecco, because Jasmine said people always noticed that kind of thing.

It wasn't that Lucy envied Jasmine her City trader, who was already balding even though he hadn't reached thirty and who called his fiancée Lard Arse and claimed it was a term of affection. But still she found herself being swayed. The dress had cost £650 more than she'd let on to Jason, but she knew as soon as he saw her in it he'd forgive her the extra. Shelly had been with her when she tried it on, the last one out of a whole pile of dresses, and the most expensive, and as soon as she'd seen it she'd gasped, 'Yes. That's it. That's the one.' It was hanging in the wardrobe under a cover so that there was no chance of Jason seeing it before the big day, but Lucy quite often took it out when she was on her own, just to feel the beautiful raw-silk tulle skirt and trace the appliqué fleur-de-lis on the chiffon bodice. It fitted her as if it had been designed purely with her in mind. Lucy already knew she'd have her hair loose and wavy, just as Jason preferred it, with a beaded headband from which would trail a wisp of a veil. She had imagined it so many times, how all the people she loved would be waiting expectantly on the beach and she'd arrive, at that golden hour when the sinking sun painted everything amber, appearing from the distance with her skin glowing and the blonde streaks in her hair burnished. At first she'd imagined herself walking barefoot with her dress draped over her arm and her veil billowing in the (very slight) sea breeze, but then Jasmine had discovered the speedboat option, and instantly Lucy could see how perfect that would be, her glorious dress fanned out to its full advantage – no worries about getting salt stains on the hem from the surf or feeling disappointed that she couldn't wear the silver sandals she'd bought because the heels would get stuck in the shingle.

Lucy reluctantly tore her mind away from this vision of herself as bride and back to the matter in hand. Her iPad home screen was so crowded with photos of dresses and floral bouquets and inspirational quotes about marriage to remind her what it was all about – 'A good marriage is one where each partner secretly suspects they got the better deal' – that it took her a while to locate the banking icon. And even when she had located it, she still hesitated before pressing. Maybe it wouldn't be as bad as she feared.

It wasn't.

It was worse.

Lucy gasped aloud when she saw the figure that came after that minus sign. There was a flashing message icon in one corner of the screen and she knew, without having to click on it, that it would be a letter informing her that they'd gone way beyond their agreed overdraft limit. Surely there'd been a mistake, though. She started to run her eye down the list of transactions – the matching luggage from Selfridges she'd bought to transport her beautiful dress, the eye-wateringly expensive moisturizer to keep her skin hydrated despite the heat, last weekend's visit to that country spa, an all-over body wax, a touch-up of Botox and a couple of fillers that she could never tell Jason about, highlights from the salon Jasmine used, shapewear to go under the dress. *Shapewear*, for fuck's sake.

The upshot was, last month's salary had been swallowed up by the overdraft on her personal account, meaning there was no money left to transfer her share of the amount she and Jason had agreed into the joint account. She'd hoped she could get away with stringing Nina along until next payday.

Lucy felt sick when she thought of the money she'd overspent. And guilty knowing how hard Jason had been working to afford his share. But then, was it really fair of Nina to be putting pressure on her just four days before the wedding? Wasn't it Nina's job to make sure her week was entirely stress-free? Lucy bet Jasmine wouldn't have a care in the world when she floated down the aisle towards her minted fiancé in her £4,000 dress. And of course it wasn't Jason's fault that he didn't earn enough to give her the wedding of her dreams and she'd marry him in a heartbeat even if it was just the two of them at a registry office on a rainy Monday afternoon. But she'd already compromised so much just by having such a pared-down guest list. Couldn't she enjoy just this one week with the people she loved most in the world and the really relatively modest ceremony she'd spent so long planning?

She considered going to her parents for a loan, even though her mum had been so weird about money recently, asking the cost of even the tiniest little things. Her dad was a pushover and, in the past, he'd always slipped her money if he knew she was short. But she knew Jason would be angry. He had very definite views about being independent. 'I want this marriage to be about you and me. Sacrosanct. Much as I love your parents, I don't want to feel as if anyone else has a stake in our relationship. This is purely about us.' She'd persuaded him to accept some financial help, framing it as her parents' wedding present to them. But only on the understanding that strict parameters were put in place.

There was nothing for it. She'd have to make the payment from the joint account and pray the bank would let it go through. And once she'd done that, it was out of her hands and she'd go on the boat trip and wouldn't think about it again.

Lucy only intended to get married once in her life, and this was it. She was determined to savour every moment of this week, storing the memories away, just as she'd store away her dress in tissue paper, to be taken out every now and then in a wave of nostalgia.

Surely no one could begrudge her that?

Therapy Journal, Week 5

Memory is a funny thing, isn't it? Visceral. Right now, the cricket ball is back in my belly because I'm about to revisit that basement room. At first Mummy would make sure I had crayons and paper and snacks and comics in there with me, but over time it became more hit and miss. 'It's for your own good,' she'd tell me, smothering me in kisses. 'So you won't suffer like I did.' But I did suffer. Sometimes when I close my eyes I see that striped green wallpaper on the backs of my eyelids. There was a light in the room and a mattress with blankets, but no window, and it was so damp that even when I was wrapped up in the blankets I still felt cold.

The first time she left me in the basement overnight I thought I'd die from crying, but when Mummy appeared the next day she was so apologetic – 'I'm so sorry, my darling. I thought she'd never leave' – and so loving and kind, it almost made up for the terror of the night before. After that it happened over and over and I developed a place in my head, the Grey Space, where I could send my thoughts so I wouldn't be so frightened. Occasionally, it worked. Sometimes, when Mummy unlocked the door she was kind and loving, like she'd been at the beginning, but other times she was cold and told me it had been far worse for her – being left on her own with the monster *(that's what she called her) – and I should be thankful she loved me enough to want to protect me. Even now I believe inconsistency is the very worst trait, worse than cruelty even, because inconsistency involves the constant dashing of hope, and that's the worst cruelty of all. You know, I think part of what drew me to Harry was that he seemed to be always the same. And he didn't send mixed messages. Not at first, anyway.*

Chapter Sixteen

Jess

Oh my God, is she actually serious right now?

Jess sat back against the bare wooden bench with her knee up, picking at the peeling green varnish on her toenail where it emerged from its silver toe ring and staring open-mouthed as Zoe carried on shouting into her phone as if she were somewhere private and not on a fishing boat with at least ten other people. Behind her, the Ionian Sea rippled gently in the wake of the creaking stern, while above, a grubby canvas canopy shielded them from the worst of the sun. Directly ahead, a squat wooden structure contained the boat's cramped kitchen and toilet and all across the peeling deck were piles of yellow netting threaded with thin rope and small orange circular floats.

'She's never done that with me. Are you sure you've been sticking to the schedule? Put her on. No, I don't care if she's shaking her head. Put her on now, please.' And then, in a different voice, dripping with sugar, '*Anastasia, chérie, c'est Maman.*'

'Did she really just talk to her toddler in French?' Jess whispered to Gabriel.

'*Chérie*, you know you have to go pee pee in the toilet, like a big girl? . . . Well, that's not what *ta grand-mère* told me. She said you went pee pee in the laundry basket. You know there won't be any *petit chat* if you carry on. That was the deal.'

When she put the phone down, Jess didn't bother to hide her derision. 'Did your daughter have a little shat in the wrong place?'

'Not shat. *Chat*. It's French for cat. We promised her a kitten. As you know very well.'

Gil reached out and put a hand over Zoe's, as if telling her to stay calm, and Jess, who suspected they'd discussed her beforehand and agreed on the best tactics to deal with her, found the gesture infuriating.

'Everything OK?' Gil asked his wife.

'Except that they only went and forgot it was World Book Day. How much time did I spend sourcing that adorable Hungry Caterpillar costume?'

'Oh, that's a bugger. But Ana didn't sound too cut up about it.'

'That isn't really the point, Gil. She had to dress up as a mouse. Just a pair of cardboard ears and a newspaper tail, and that was it. Imagine what Chloe Blandford thought. Her Hugo is going as Inspector Javert from *Les Misérables*.'

'But they're only toddlers. They haven't got a clue about *Les Misérables*.'

'Oh, don't be insane. *Les Mis*. Hugh Jackman. Everyone knows about it.'

Jess didn't even know where to start. With the fact that kids were being dressed up essentially as film characters for Book Day, or that the book the film was based on was too adult for even the adults to have read? Or the fact that Zoe was only really concerned about what the other parents thought and not what made her kid feel happy? Or that Gil, who had brought Jess a hot-water bottle in bed when she had period pain and then gone willingly to the corner shop to buy tampons, even taking the first box back and swapping it when she'd yelled at him for getting normal instead of extra absorbent, had chosen this awful, shallow woman to be her replacement?

Jess knew she should hold back. She'd promised Lucy she'd make an effort with Zoe and, despite their many arguments, Jess adored her older sister and wanted to make her happy. Yet she just couldn't resist.

'Your parents must spend more time talking to you than looking after their actual granddaughter,' she said, smiling to show it was just banter and nothing to get het up about – just in case Lucy happened to overhear, although she seemed to be deep in conversation with the wife of the boat's captain. Jess had heard the word 'lobster' and seen Lucy making claws out of her hands by tapping the third finger of each hand on the thumb.

Zoe glared at her, and Jess saw Gil rest his hand warningly on his wife's thigh, which only wound her up more. Couldn't he see what she was like? Was he completely blind?

The thing was, Jess was struggling to remember now why she'd ever split up with Gil. Oh, she knew she'd persuaded herself he was too conventional for her, too passive, but here in Kefalonia, where she got to see him walking around all day without a shirt and where there were no other potential men – what had she even been thinking, bringing Gabriel? – she found herself thinking how attractive he was, how decent. Maybe it was something to do with her recent bruising experiences with a series of wankers who seemed, on the surface, to have everything she wanted but turned out to be emotional black holes, unable to comprehend the basics of a give-and-take relationship, maybe that's why her mind kept replaying scenes of them in bed and remembering how considerate he'd been, how attentive to her needs.

Gil's new-found hotness was definitely nothing to do with the fact that he was unavailable. Absolutely not. Jess had always prided herself on being part of the sisterhood. No way would she do the dirty on another woman.

Unless that woman was Zoe.

'You ought to get trying for a baby asap,' Zoe was saying to Lucy. She pronounced 'asap' as a word, rather than a string of letters, which made Jess feel stabby. 'I know you all' – here she swept her eyes around to include Shelly and Jess in her address – 'think you've got loads of time to get pregnant but – *newsflash!* – actually your most fecund time' – yes, she did actually use the word 'fecund', and not in an ironic way – 'is already behind you. I don't want to freak you out or anything, but I'd hate for you all to miss out on being parents. It changes you as a person in ways you couldn't even imagine. Doesn't it, hun?' She looked up at Gil; Jess guessed he was torn between supporting his wife and acknowledging what a completely twattish thing she had just said.

'Yeah, changes you into a cunt,' Jess muttered to Gabriel under her breath.

Well, was it her fault that an unexpected gust of breeze blew the words right back in Zoe's face?

Jess tried to explain that to her mum a few minutes later, when Hazel sought her out by the stinky fishing nets, to remonstrate with her, tried to tell her she hadn't meant Zoe to hear, but Hazel just sighed.

'Please play nice just for a few days. Don't ruin it for your sister.'

Jess's eyes stung with the unfairness of that. As if Zoe hadn't been the one goading them. Would it really kill her mum to be on her side, just once in a while? Sometimes it seemed to Jess as if she'd spent her whole life trying to please her mother. Only lately had she accepted that nothing was ever really going to make her mother happy, not in the 'shrieking for joy' way Jess craved, like she'd seen some of her friends' mothers react when they had big news. Her dad was usually the one for a grandiose response, although even he'd been a bit shit since they'd been here. But Hazel? Uh-uh. Not going to happen.

'You know,' she said, taken aback that her voice sounded thick with tears, 'maybe I wouldn't act like such a fuck-up if you didn't treat me like one the whole time.'

Behind her, Zoe screeched with laughter, but her mother's habitually perplexed expression barely changed. Well, really, what had she expected?

Chapter Seventeen

Hazel

'Please talk to her, Mum. I mean, I know Zoe can be a bit much, but this is my wedding. I've worked really hard to make things lovely for everyone, and then my sister goes and calls one of my guests a cunt.'

'Well, she didn't exactly—'

'Oh my God. You're actually defending her.'

'I'm not . . .' But it was too late. Lucy had already stalked off. Well, as much as anyone could stalk on a medium-sized fishing boat with all the equipment and nets piled up in the middle of the deck.

Hazel sighed. She should have been more sympathetic. Lucy was bound to be extra sensitive this week. She just wanted everything to be perfect. That was natural. And Jess was always dangerous when she was bored. She'd clearly already tired of Gabriel. Or Vince, or whatever he was really called.

She supposed Jess was right. Just because someone chose to use a different name to the one on their passport, it didn't mean they had anything to hide. But try as she might to convince herself to give Gabriel the benefit of the doubt, she kept coming up against her innate suspicion of the man. He was just so aggressively bland. And yes, she did realize that was a contradiction in terms.

At this moment, he was leaning back against the wooden bench that wrapped around the back of the boat, his arms stretched out along the back of the seat, talking to Cora, who looked, as ever, immaculate in a white linen T-shirt and chino shorts that emphasized her trim hips and flat stomach. Yet again, Hazel swore to herself that as soon as they got back to England she would take up yoga. It's not as if she didn't have all the time in the world now. If she went three times a week, she could have a figure like Cora Beazant's inside of six months. How hard could it be?

Regret rippled through her then as she remembered they couldn't afford yoga three times a week. Not now she had no job. What if she never worked again? Picture editor positions were almost obsolete now that so many publications had closed down, and reporters were increasingly responsible for sourcing their own images. She couldn't start drawing her meagre pension until sixty, not without taking a massive hit. How were they supposed to survive in the meantime?

'Isn't this blissful? Oh my God, I'm sorry, I didn't mean to make you jump. I'm always doing that.' Hazel hadn't noticed Shelly approach and must have visibly started.

'Don't worry at all.' Hazel smiled. Shelly was such a sweet thing, really, with those big eyes and that lopsided smile. Devoted to Lucy, of course, to the extent that Jess sometimes referred to her as Lucy's girlfriend, and touchingly eager to please. And yet Hazel never completely relaxed around her. It was something about the way Shelly studied her face, as if anxious not to miss any flicker of a change of expression. It wasn't surprising, given her background, that she'd cling to any kind of parental figure, but understanding where the impulse came from didn't help Hazel feel more comfortable. She looked around for Dom for back-up, but he was deep in conversation with the boat's captain on the far side of the deck. Hazel had noticed that Shelly tended to hang back until he was gone before approaching, as if she wanted to get Hazel on her own. Which was flattering, obviously, but . . .

'I wanted to let you know how grateful I am to be here with you guys. I know this is costing you a fortune.'

Hazel hoped her face didn't betray the stab of sheer, brutal panic that shot through her at the mention of money.

'Honestly, Shelly, it's our pleasure. You've been a great support to Lucy these last couple of years.'

How stiff she sounded, like some dusty old headteacher at prize-giving day.

Lucy called over to Shelly and for a moment the girl hesitated, as if torn between her friend and her friend's mother, but eventually she smiled in apology and hurried over to Lucy, and Hazel once again turned her attention back to the mismatched couple nearest to her on the wooden bench.

Cora said something and Gabriel leaned his head towards her. She turned her face up to his as she repeated herself. Good grief, was she flirting with him? Surely she had to be at least fifteen years older than him, maybe more? Hazel glanced over to her younger daughter. It was second nature in their family to gauge Jess's reaction before deciding on one's own. Sometimes Hazel worried she had failed as a mother by too often sacrificing points of principle on the altar of an easy life, sending out into the world a young woman who was impulsive to the point of self-destruction and regarded fulfilment as a right rather than an ideal.

Jess was squatting on the deck, where the captain's young daughter had produced a bucket of sea creatures she'd picked out of the most recent catch. The girl held up a kite-shaped fish that looked disturbingly like a stingray though was most likely a skate, and moved it backwards and forwards so that its tiny little mouth opened and shut with each movement as if it was speaking.

'Gross!' Jess threw up her hands, pretending to be horrified, and the little girl giggled.

Hazel softened. She had so many redeeming qualities, this headstrong daughter of hers. If she could only channel them into something creative, like this book she was supposed to be writing . . . Anyway, at least she didn't seem too bothered about what Gabriel, or whatever his name was, was up to. She'd never own up to having made a mistake, but Hazel guessed she was already regretting her spontaneous invitation. Not that Gabriel was entirely unattractive. He had that quality that was rare in men in her experience of not taking up too much space in a group. Her eyes swung to Dom, all six foot two of him, who seemed to have recovered a little of his usual exuberance and was conversing with the captain of the boat in a kind of pidgin English with a lot of wild gesticulating and booming laughter.

Mind you, Jason didn't seem to be too impressed with his mother's new friend. Hazel adored her soon-to-be son-in-law. He was just the kind of man she had hoped Lucy would end up with. Steady, reliable and utterly devoted to her. True, Dom worried he might lack ambition and had more than once voiced his concern that Jason didn't have enough drive for Lucy and that she'd grow frustrated with him. But Hazel had seen how Lucy was with those other men she'd dated who'd wanted a nice-looking girlfriend who'd be just another covetable accessory, like their Apple watch and Bose headphones, not someone who lived and breathed and had opinions and dreams and insecurities. Hazel had hated watching her daughter lose sight of herself in relationship after relationship. Only with Jason did she seem free to be herself. In fact, if anything, he brought out the very best version of her.

He was very protective of his mum. Well, it was natural, with the two of them such a tight little unit for so long. But Hazel knew Lucy sometimes struggled with how close-knit they were. And watching him scowling over at Gabriel, Hazel got a glimpse of why it might bother her. There was something intense about it, something at odds with Jason's usual laid-back persona.

For a moment, Hazel wondered if she should take Jason aside and tell him about the name in Gabriel's passport not matching up. But really, what good would it do to worry him when all his attention ought to be on his new bride?

Conscious of being watched, Hazel glanced around to see Dom gazing at her over the captain's shoulder on the far side of the deck. When their eyes met, he smiled and gave a small, eager wave. What on earth had got into him this holiday? It was like he was attached to her by some invisible thread, like those little mittens on strings the girls had had when they were tiny, hanging out of their coat sleeves.

From the wooden bench came the distinctive sound of Gabriel's high-pitched laugh and Hazel turned in time to see him lay his hand briefly on Cora's arm. When Hazel checked to see if Jason had noticed, she saw that his own hand was clenched into a fist in his lap.

She'd keep watch on Gabriel, she decided. She wouldn't make a fuss, wouldn't spoil the atmosphere. But he was hiding something. And she intended to find out what.

16/6/19, 00.35. Original English-language transcript of police interview with Mr Dominic Edward Collins. Police officers: Demitri Iraklidis and Tomaso Diakos. Interpreter: Eulalia Scala.

Why are they staring at me like that? Have they never seen a man cry before? Perhaps they find it pathetic. Sod them.

Don't translate that, for Christ's sake. Oh God. Oh Jesus. This is all my fault, isn't it? Because I'm a terrible person? You know what's ironic? I used to think I was quite decent. I mean, sure I did things I regretted, just like everyone else, but fundamentally, I tried to make people's lives better. The people I cared about, anyway. And now we've ended up in this nightmare.

Sorry. Ignore that. I'm all over the place. Deep breath. What would you like to know?

We've always loved both our daughters equally, even though Jess was ten times as much work as Lucy. A hundred times. Have you got kids, either of you? Then you'll know that being a parent isn't the same as being the boss of a company, where you reward people according to efficiency and results. Being a parent means you pay out just the same to the child who turns your hair white as to the one who never gives you a moment's worry. And you keep paying, regardless. Maybe 'paying' is the wrong word.

No, I don't think they were jealous of each other. Why ever would they be?

Of course we worried about Jess. Act first, think later. That's been her motto all her life. Her turning up with Gabriel in tow was typical. I knew there was something off about him right from the start. He never gave a straight answer. Of course, now we know why. And he couldn't look you in the eye. I know this is going to sound weird, but he had a strange smell about him, a kind of musty smell, like something that has been left in a damp cellar. I always think smell is so important, don't you?

You know, I think we'd got so used to Jess putting herself in dangerous situations that when she really was in danger it took a while to recognize it. Does that make sense?

No, I wouldn't describe her as vengeful. Not at all. What are they getting at? You know, we have a bloody shit-hot lawyer at home if it comes to it. Can you tell them that, please?

Chapter Eighteen

Jess

It was too fucking hot on the boat. Jess had that restless feeling where it felt as if every nerve and muscle in her body was twitching independently of one another. It was too much, all of it. Being trapped on this boat – which anyone could see was just geared up for tourists, not authentic at all; and if there was one thing Jess couldn't stand, it was things being unauthentic – with all these people, including her own family, who she loved to bits, but in small doses.

She watched Gabriel chatting to Cora and felt aggrieved that he'd turned out to be such a crushing disappointment. The night before, she'd been quite sure that they were going to have sex, had been almost looking forward to it. He wasn't bad-looking and she liked older men, especially ones with a story to tell. She knew her mother had meant her to be put off by telling her he had a different name on his passport, but in actual fact that just made him seem more attractive to her. Mysterious. Everything had seemed promising. Gabriel had gone back to the suite first and she'd followed just a few moments later, pleasantly buzzing with an anticipation which had disappeared instantly when she found him in the bathroom *using her toothbrush*. 'I forgot mine,' he'd said mildly when she demanded to know what the fuck he thought he was doing. 'It's not a big deal, is it? I mean, you had your tongue halfway down my throat earlier, I didn't think you'd mind.' 'That's completely different.' 'Why?' She hadn't been able to answer that or explain why, having been up for it, she was suddenly so completely and utterly turned off.

He'd got annoyed then, his mouth twisting unpleasantly, and she'd been reminded how little she knew about him and what he might be capable of. He'd stepped towards her and for a mad second she'd been *frightened* – really, truly afraid – frantically scanning the bathroom counter for something she could seize as a weapon, but in the end he'd just barged past, tossing her toothbrush into the sink from the doorway. Afterwards, she'd locked herself in the bathroom, her breath fast and uneven. While she was brushing her teeth with her finger – because no way would she touch her toothbrush now – she'd rehearsed telling him to sleep on the sofa. But, in the event, it wasn't necessary, because by the time she came out he'd moved all his stuff out of the bedroom and closed the adjoining door. Jess hated to leave anything unsaid and had considered going through to the living room to clear the air, but the memory of his thin lips, twisted in anger, stopped her. Scared her. And this morning, everything looked different. They'd been at cross purposes, she'd put him right, end of story. No harm done. She'd use it as a story to make her mates laugh – how she'd picked up a guy off the street, dragged him to Greece and then refused to sleep with him because of a toothbrush. *U heard bout Jess?* they'd text each other. Sometimes Jess wondered if half the things she did were done to entertain her friends. Very occasionally she worried how far she'd go and where it would stop.

Sitting on the wooden bench, she rolled herself another ciggie, ignoring her sister's glare. Yes, Lucy had made her promise to smoke on the other side of the boat, away from them all, but there was a hatch to the tiny kitchen on that side and it smelled of petrol and, well, fish.

'Would you mind?' said Zoe when Jess lit up. 'Only, since I've had a baby, I'm super-sensitive to that kind of thing, super-aware of the poison we're putting out into the planet. That's the thing about having children. It gives you an investment in the future.'

Honestly, the fucking *nerve* of the woman.

'You don't need to get knocked up to care about the future, you know. I demonstrated with Extinction Rebellion. Where were you when we were occupying Oxford Street? Drinking skinny lattes in Starbucks with all the other yummy mummies?'

'Enough, Jess.'

Hazel was standing in front of her, with her back to Zoe, wearing that weary expression that said she'd gone too far, that it was Lucy's wedding, that she should be the bigger person. Jess knew that there was something up with her parents at the moment. Her mum hadn't been going into work, for a start, and she was the biggest workaholic Jess knew, sitting in front of the telly in the evenings with a glass of wine, her laptop balanced on her knee, emailing picture libraries and photographic studios with one eye on *MasterChef*. Now she lurked around the house reading novels or teaching herself Italian or baking determinedly flat cakes in that self-conscious kind of way of people who are unused to leisure. When Jess had quizzed her about it, she'd said she had negotiated some extra time off work to prepare for the wedding, but there had been something weird about the way she'd said it.

'All right, all right,' Jess muttered, getting to her feet. 'I'll go around the side so that my toxic fumes can't sully the lungs of a child who is currently thousands of miles away in one of the most polluted cities in the world.'

She stomped off with her rollie hanging from her mouth and her hands wedged into the pockets of her cut-off dungarees. Around the other side, hidden from view, she found a spot as far from the kitchen hatch as possible and leaned over the railing, staring moodily out to sea.

Not that it wasn't beautiful here. Sun glinting off water that looked turquoise in some directions and, in others, the deep navy of her hated school blazer. Crests of white foam on the waves far out towards the horizon. And if you looked straight down you could see all the way to the seabed, where shoals of small fish threaded in and out of the speckled rocks. The sky was that unblemished blue that seemed almost too perfect, too vast. Like it was showing off. A speedboat passed them, creating a swell that made the fishing boat rise steeply then fall again, causing Jess's stomach to lurch unpleasantly. There were two women lying on towels on the polished wood bow of the boat, wearing tiny bikinis and huge sunglasses, who didn't even bother to look up.

'Cunts,' she said out loud.

'That's not very nice.'

Gil was standing a couple of metres away, his back to the rail, smiling in that way he had that made you feel like his whole being was focused only on you, like you were the centre of the entire world. He was wearing faded pink swimming shorts, and his body, which Jess knew so well, was toned and bronzed, the muscles more defined than when they'd been together. Zoe probably insisted on an expensive gym membership. She was that type.

Yet again Jess wondered why she'd ever broken up with him. She'd always been too quick to give in to boredom. She and Gil had been good together, she realized belatedly.

'You been banished?' he asked.

'Apparently, I'm single-handedly responsible for global warming. Don't tell Greta Thunberg.'

He made a face that she recognized from their few months together when she'd say something bitchy and he'd try to rein her in. 'Be kind,' that face said. At the time, it used to get on her nerves, but now she wondered whether perhaps she could do with someone making her question her behaviour and her shitty decisions. Like bringing Gabriel here.

'I'm not with him, you know,' she said now. 'Gabriel, I mean. We're not a "couple".' She made quote marks in the air.

'It wouldn't be any of my business if you were. You're a free agent, Jess.'

'Yes, but I care what you think of me. And I don't want you to think I'm a twat.'

She scowled down at her feet with their chipped green-painted toenails. What she wanted was for him to tell her how glad he was that she still cared what he thought. When Jess thought about her carelessly discarded beaux – *if* she thought of them – she imagined them frozen in time at the point at which they were discarded. Distraught. Pleading. Begging. In love. Gil's silence after her very obvious fishing remark about being a twat forced her to consider the possibility that whatever candle he'd once carried for her might have been well and truly snuffed out.

Suddenly, it seemed essential that Gil looked at her that way again – as if she was the best thing that had happened to him.

She moved closer to him along the rail, stopping with her arm just a few inches from his, and held his gaze so that he couldn't look away.

'Look, I know it sounds cheesy, but the truth is I miss you.'

As she spoke, she had an uncomfortable flashback to the ending of their relationship, sitting outside a pub in Camden at the tail end of a messy Sunday afternoon. 'You're a lovely bloke – but I don't really do lovely,' she'd said.

She drove the memory from her mind, focusing on how he looked now, the wide curve of his shoulder, the deep V of his torso. She put out a finger to stroke his upper arm, where skin stretched taut over muscle – until he put his own hand over hers to stop her.

'Jess. I know you, don't forget. You're just saying that because you're bored. Anyway, I'm married now.'

Jess blinked in surprise.

'Please give Zoe a chance,' Gil went on. 'I know she can wind people up, but it's only because she's nervous. She's got a big, beautiful heart underneath all the bluster, it's just that she's been through some stuff. You know?'

Why was he banging on about Zoe? This was about them. Her and Gil. As Gil guided her hand away from his arm, Jess caught a movement over his shoulder, a shape that was there one minute around the curved middle of the boat, then gone. Her breath caught. Was it Gabriel? She hadn't forgotten that look he'd given her in the bathroom the night before. His twisted mouth. Her fear.

When Gil went back to rejoin his wife Jess felt an empty space open up behind her ribs and she took a long drag on her cigarette to fill it up with smoke.

Therapy Journal, Week 6

We all have our regrets, don't we? Things we shouldn't have said or done. I wish now I could have reached out to Mummy in some way, but I was only a child.

I knew she was losing it. More and more, she seemed to be listening to conversations taking place inside her own head. She'd stop whatever it was she was doing and shake her head, as if refuting some point or refusing an instruction. Or she'd mutter under her breath and I'd catch snatches of phrases or words. Once she yelled out, 'You're a monster, that's what', while she was eating toast on her own in the kitchen and I knew then she was talking to her *and my eyes filled with tears because it must have been so terrible to have the monster from your nightmares living inside you, talking to you from the inside. I know we've talked about me putting Mummy's feelings ahead of my own, but I still find it painful to imagine what it might have been like to live inside Mummy's head.*

My attendance at school grew patchy and, when I did make it, my appearance raised eyebrows from the teachers. No matter how hard I scrubbed my shirts with soap in the upstairs sink, they never lost that grubby grey tinge. Neglect clings to children like head lice. When we stood in the line for lunch in the school dining hall my cheeks burned in case the children standing behind me could smell it. Nowadays, I have a standing order with the NSPCC. Harry was shocked when I told him how much I pay a month and tried to persuade me, gently, because he always was gentle then, to keep it in proportion to my modest salary, but Harry didn't grow up the way I did. Sorry, I know I'm not supposed to keep mentioning Harry, but it's hard when he's always there in the back of my mind.

The periods when I was shut up in the basement room got longer and I was scared Mummy would forget about me altogether. One of the strips of wallpaper was loose and I'd roll it up and write on the wall in crayon, just to prove I was still alive. But I always covered it up again. I didn't want to upset her. I loved her so much. I used to dream up scenarios where she was in danger and I was the one who saved her. Or sometimes I'd fantasize about her coming in and finding me ill, at death's door in fact, and how she'd be flooded with regret. Sitting on the mattress with my arms wrapped around my knees, I'd mouth the words she'd say as she swept me up into her arms. 'I'm so sorry. I love you so much. Please don't leave me.'

Chapter Nineteen

Lucy

'Sorry, Luce. I just thought you should know.'

In the bright white light of midday, Shelly's huge eyes appeared grey, flecked with amber, and Lucy could make out every one of the freckles across her nose and cheeks.

'But why would Jess make a pass at Gil? She was the one who chucked him. It doesn't make sense.'

But of course it did make a sick kind of sense. Her sister had always been dangerous when she was bored. Oh, not dangerous consciously, just careless, which usually amounted to the same thing.

'Probably gets off on the drama. You know how she is.'

Lucy felt a stirring of protest. Families were like that, weren't they? They could rip each other to shreds in private, but heaven help the outsider who dared voice the slightest criticism. Poor Shelly didn't know about families. That was the problem. At least not about functional families. Lucy could tell she'd been struggling the previous day. She'd caught her looking at her mum and dad with such a wistful expression and she'd just known Shelly's mind was full of 'what if's. What if she'd had two parents who loved her? What if she'd had a stable home life? What if? What if?

'She doesn't do it on purpose, you know, Shell. That's just how Jess is wired. She needs things to be happening all the time.'

Shelly looked as if she was about to say something more, but thought better of it.

They were lounging on the wooden seats that lined the bow of the fishing boat. The cushions underneath them were thin, and Lucy, who had slimmed down by half a stone to get into her wedding dress, felt her bones pressing uncomfortably on the hard surface.

Had the fishing trip been a bad idea? It was Jason who'd chosen it, out of all the outings Nina had suggested to them. He'd been excited by the idea of being on a working fishing boat, watching the catches coming in, diving off the deck into a glorious clear sea while the captain and his wife cooked the freshly caught lobsters ready for lunch.

And it was lovely, obviously. But she hadn't really thought through the logistics of all of them being cooped up together all day with no way of getting away from each other. Zoe was doing her head in. Lucy tried with her, she really did. For Gil's sake and Jason's. But all this stuff about babies was too much. Lucy and Jason had a five-year plan, and babies came into that around year four. After buying their own flat and going on safari to Namibia. What gave Zoe the right to push her own agenda on to everyone else?

And now Lucy was struck by another uncomfortable thought. Was that what she was doing by bringing everyone here to Kefalonia to live out her fantasy of a fairy-tale beach wedding? Imposing her agenda on to them? They'd all had to use up annual leave to be here, and for the first time it occurred to her that they might resent that.

'Jase?' She turned to Jason, only to see that he was standing with Gil at the top of the boat's ladder, looking down into the water. They had dropped anchor now and were floating in a perfectly calm sea. In every direction, the sun sparkled off the surface like freshly cleaned glass. Far in the distance, Kefalonia's hilly, pine-clad coastline rose steeply, the occasional white building dotted along the top like cake frosting, while clumps of rock emerged here and there from the water like the humps of enormous whales.

Lucy closed her eyes and soaked in the smells – the tang of the fishing nets, the cut of the salt, the coconut sun oil coming off her own skin. Immediately, she felt calmed. Who wouldn't want to be in this gorgeous place? She was giving people a gift, not forcing something on them.

There was a huge splash, and her eyes flew open as the two men dived off the side in tandem.

'Dickheads,' remarked Jess, who had wandered over to join her. 'Dared each other to swim under the boat, didn't they? Easier to have a dick-swinging contest and have done with it.'

'Oi, that's my future husband you're dissing.'

But Lucy was grinning as she said it. Jason was usually the least competitive person she knew, so she always felt a little thrill whenever he did rise to a challenge like this. She caught her mother's eye, and Hazel smiled back, shaking her head in mock disapproval.

'Idiots,' she said.

Everyone rushed to the opposite side of the boat to watch. Gil was the first up, his dark head shattering the sea's calm surface.

'Yes!' He pumped his fist in the air. 'I claim it.'

Now they all scanned the water, watching for where Jason would emerge, anticipating his disappointment at finding Gil there before him. The surface remained as smooth as if it had been varnished. Lucy felt a tiny worm of worry thread its way into the pit of her stomach. Had the captain already dropped the nets underneath the boat?

'He won't come up because he's a sore loser.' Gil laughed, shaking the water from his hair.

Lucy laughed along, but soon her gaze returned to the sea, satin-sheet flat. As she waited for the first sign of those familiar, beloved strawberry curls an icy feather trailed down her spine. What if this was payback time? What if it had all been too perfect? Falling in love with Jason, planning the wedding, this cloudless blue sky, this heart-lifting gathering of all the people she loved most. Didn't it always happen that way in films, that the moment a character was truly happy they were struck by tragedy?

'Where is he? Where's Jason?'

'Don't panic. He'll be up any moment.' But Lucy noticed that Hazel's smile had vanished.

Cora materialized by Lucy's side.

'Why did you let him do something so stupid?'

'I didn't know anything about it.' Outrage brought tears to Lucy's eyes.

'I was talking to Gil.'

Cora hadn't been anywhere near Gil. But there was no time to think about that now. Jason was still unaccounted for. Even Gil was starting to look anxious. 'Throw me my goggles,' he called to Zoe. When he'd strapped them on, he dived down and Lucy held her breath along with him, releasing it only when he'd broken the surface once more.

'No sign.' When Gil shook his head, droplets sprayed out in all directions. Lucy started making bargains with the God she only really ever believed in during moments of crisis like this one. If Jason was safe and not tangled up in the net under the boat, she'd never be uncharitable to Zoe again. She'd be more patient with Jess. She'd stop being so uptight about this wedding, because now she could see how meaningless it all was, in the scheme of things. Who cared if the creases had been steamed out of her veil? What did it matter if the tiny bump she'd felt on the side of her nose that morning erupted into a fully-fledged spot that would glare out in the photos? Let it rain on the day, if it came to that. A tight knot formed in Lucy's chest at the thought of this last, most dreaded possibility.

Gil dived down again. As the water closed over his head, Cora inhaled deeply and Lucy saw that her hand was gripping the rail so tightly the knuckles pressed against the skin, white like teeth.

The water broke again. Gil. Even before the goggles came off Lucy could tell the news was bad. Gil's mouth, which was normally stretched into a wide smile, was set into a tight thin line. *Oh my God, oh my God, oh my God.*

By now the captain of the fishing boat and his wife were both standing by the railing, conferring in urgent whispers, and Lucy had closed her eyes, not able to bear that awful expanse of calm, uninterrupted water. So when she heard Jason's voice behind her, saying: 'Looking for something?' she thought at first she might be dreaming it. Then she whirled around and there he was. Broad and very much alive and utterly, utterly lovely. As she looked, she saw him become aware of the tension in the group, the air of palpable worry. Their eyes met, and he rushed towards her. She held out her hands, only to watch him veer to the side at the very last minute and throw his arms around Cora.

'Oh God, I'm so sorry, Mum. I'm such a dick. I was just messing around, playing a trick on Gil. I should have known you'd all be freaking out.'

Cora hugged him fiercely and then pushed him away, pretending to slap him. Everyone laughed except Lucy, woodenly reliving the moment when her reaching hands encountered only empty air.

Suddenly, it felt imperative for her to win him back to her – even though, of course, it wasn't a competition; Cora was his mother, for Chrissakes. But the snub had felt so public.

As they sat down to a mouth-watering lunch of freshly caught and cooked lobster and a huge bowl of salad made from glistening chunks of tomato and pepper, strips of red onions and bunches of fresh green basil, drizzled with olive oil and vinegar, and rosé served in plastic glasses, Lucy tapped the side of her plate.

'I wasn't going to say anything until I had something concrete, but I can't hold it in any longer – you know what I'm like.' She was addressing Jason, who sat across from her with Cora by his side.

Jason smiled, as she'd known he would.

'Considering you gave me my Christmas present on 10 December last year because you couldn't wait, I'd say I do know what you're like, yes. Come on then, spit it out.'

Lucy felt warm with happiness. It wasn't about scoring points over Cora any more, it was about doing something nice for this man – this good, fine man – whom she loved more than anyone in the world.

'Well. I couldn't bear that we're having this big party when we get back and, apart from your mum, none of your family will be there. So I started doing some digging and' – she paused for dramatic effect – 'I found one of your cousins, Connor Kerswell, and invited him to our wedding!'

Her eyes flicked between Jason and Cora, desperate not to miss the moment when realization dawned, but all she saw there was shock, Cora frozen with her fork halfway to her mouth.

'I haven't heard back from him yet,' she said, to fill in the growing silence. 'But it's exciting, isn't it?'

Why didn't Jason respond? She'd been imagining this moment ever since she sent the email, how grateful he'd be, how his eyes would soften in that way they did only for her. Not this stony blankness. Finally, he seemed to recover himself.

'Wow, yeah, I don't know what to say.' He rubbed the back of his neck, not meeting her eyes. 'Thanks, babe.'

Next to him, Cora pushed her chair back and got to her feet. Her face, normally so calm, was dark and pinched.

'I know you mean well, Lucy, but I wish you wouldn't meddle,' she said, her voice shaking, then she stalked off in the direction of the toilet.

After a moment's hesitation, Jason shrugged a weak apology and got up to follow her. Shocked and wretched, that word 'meddle' echoing around her head, Lucy watched them disappear around the side of the boat through a thick blur of tears.

16/6/19, 00.04. Original English-language transcript of police interview with Mr Jason Matthew Beazant. Police officers: Demitri Iraklidis and Tomaso Diakos. Interpreter: Eulalia Scala.

Can you give me a minute to pull myself together, please? This is fucking hard, you know? My head is all over the place.

Right. Sorry. From the minute I first met her, Lucy was my world. I remember walking into that shop, and she came out of the back and she just shone. Some people do. They shine. I loved that she was close to her family. They're good as gold, Dom and Hazel. I felt like a lucky, lucky guy. But, at the same time, what you have to understand is that being around this perfect family isn't always easy, especially when you don't have that yourself. Growing up, it was just me and my mum. So yeah, in answer to your question, I guess I was maybe overprotective of Mum, though I still don't see what that's got to do with anything. I knew she'd be feeling wobbly this week. Don't get me wrong, she was happy we were getting married, but she felt guilty

I'd missed out on that family stuff. She loved the Collinses, though, just like me.

Yeah, OK. I didn't much like Gabriel. I'll put my hands up to that. But not because of Mum. The truth is, I just didn't trust the guy from the moment we met. He had the kind of eyes that slide right off you so he never looks you full on, do you know what I mean? I thought he was shifty. And I was right, as it happens.

But it wasn't a big deal. I know you're looking for some kind of big, explosive secret, but we're not *Jeremy Kyle* type of people, you know? *Jeremy Kyle* . . . it's a TV . . . oh, never mind. What I mean is, we're just ordinary, all of us – the Collinses, me, Mum, Shelly, Zoe, Gil. Which is why all this is so fucking unbelievable.

What do you mean, there's no such thing as ordinary?

Chapter Twenty

Nina

Outside the hotel, Nina leaned against the crisp, white-rendered wall and rested her hands on her thighs as she stared down at the ground. She hadn't slept more than a couple of hours and her chest felt flattened, as if something heavy were pressing down on it, so her breath came out in shallow pants.

When they first decided to move to Kefalonia she'd told people proudly that she was after a slower, simpler pace of life. She'd imagined starting her days with gentle exercises on the terrace overlooking the sea, followed by a few lengths of their little pool. Her skin would be clear of make-up and glowing, her body effortlessly slim and toned. When the weather's so warm, who wants to eat anything except fruit and salads?

The reality was very different. There was always so much to do. When she wasn't meeting with clients or restaurant owners or local musicians and photographers, or shuttling to and from the ferry port to pick up or deposit guests, there were websites to be updated, not to mention the relentless tyranny of keeping up the social media accounts, all those perky, upbeat posts and aspirational photographs. And that's before she'd even started on all the things that needed doing at home – the endless problems with the plumbing, the washing, the shopping, the bills to be paid. Her rolled-up exercise mat sat unused in the corner of the downstairs loo and the back terrace smelled of drains and of the rabbit hutch that badly needed cleaning out.

Nina's skin was blotchy with stress and not much more tanned than the guests she met from the ferry – there was simply not enough time in the day for sunbathing. These days, she found she wore more make-up than she used to in England, just to smooth out her ragged complexion. And though she managed to keep herself just about in shape through a combination of stress and skipping meals altogether, she comfort-ate through the winters, when the wind whistled through the unheated house and the resorts, with their empty shuttered bars and restaurants, were depressing and gloomy.

Today, she was conscious that she looked a mess. Not surprising, really. Lucy Collins's payment still hadn't made it into her account, despite all Lucy's assurances, which meant they still had nothing for Mr Angelis. Nina had cried when she told Mark about the waiter's threats the previous day. She hadn't meant to. She'd intended to be controlled and succinct, making it crystal clear what she needed from him, but instead she'd drunk most of a bottle of wine and her voice had wobbled and Mark had put his arms around her, and for a brief moment he'd just been her Mark again, and despite the fact that it was the last thing she needed, one thing had led to another and somehow they'd ended up having sex. Afterwards, he'd told her he was going to deal with everything, and she just had to trust him, and then he'd got dressed and gone out. And this morning when she got up he'd been in the kitchen already, humming to himself and making scrambled eggs. 'Everything's going to be fine,' he'd said, planting a kiss on her forehead.

Since then she'd been cursing herself for muddying the waters again. It had taken all her emotional courage to tell Mark she wanted a separation in the first place. She'd built up to it for weeks before finally blurting out one tearful Sunday afternoon that their marriage was over. He'd gone through all the predictable stages – anger, denial, bargaining, depression – and she had hoped he might finally be moving on to acceptance, but now a moment of weakness had set things right back again. 'I knew you still loved me,' he'd said to her the night before, and she'd kept her eyes closed, pretended to be asleep. Because, of course, the truth was so much more complicated than that. You could love someone and still want to leave them. You could *not* love someone and still want them to hold you when you were feeling scared and alone. Feelings didn't follow a nice, neatly plotted graph, they zigzagged all over the place until you wished you didn't feel anything at all.

She straightened up. This wouldn't do. There was a wedding to organize. Lucy was a bride, full of pre-wedding nerves. It wasn't any wonder she was getting her bank accounts in a muddle. Jason would sort it out. And if not Jason, then her parents would step in. They were such a nice family.

Today was the spa day of the wedding package, where guests got to make use of all the hotel's spa facilities and Nina arranged for masseuses and beauty therapists to come and pamper everyone ahead of the big day on Saturday. She always loved this day. There weren't as many possibilities for things to go wrong as on the excursion days, and the guests were usually more relaxed, knowing they didn't have to go anywhere for the whole day.

She found Lucy and Jason sitting on the terrace of the restaurant finishing up a breakfast that seemed to have consisted entirely of fruit.

'Jason's on a diet. So he doesn't split his suit trousers on Saturday,' Lucy said. She was laughing, but Nina suspected it was probably true. Lots of her couples complained that they didn't get to enjoy the hotel food properly until after the wedding was over. She always suggested at the start that they made sure their wedding clothes were comfortable, what with the heat and the sea and the pebbled beach to contend with, but so many of them couldn't think beyond the wedding photographs and wanting to see an idealized version of themselves, buying outfits a size smaller than they really were as an 'incentive' to lose weight. As if anyone cared.

'How was the fishing trip yesterday?'

'It was so cool,' said Jason quickly. 'Top day out.' But Nina saw the look that passed between the two of them and something told her that wasn't the whole story.

While Lucy described the lobster salad the Greek captain and his wife had prepared from the day's fresh catch, Nina rehearsed how she would bring up the subject of the non-appearing funds. Even after years of doing this, she still hated the financial side of things. She wished fairy-tale weddings came with a fairy godmother who waved her wand and covered all the costs but, unfortunately, that wasn't the case. And while she always tried to organize the payments so that the subject of money didn't have to come up during the wedding week itself, inevitably things sometimes went awry. Like with Lucy and Jason.

When Jason got up to go to the loo, she seized her chance.

'I really hate to bother you again, Lucy, but did you make the bank transfer yesterday? Only it still hasn't shown up in my account.'

Lucy's pretty face flushed dusty pink.

'Oh God. I'm so sorry. I don't know what happened. Maybe I sent it from the wrong account. My brain is all over the place. Please don't tell Jason.'

'No, of course . . .'

Nina stopped mid-sentence as the waiter appeared to clear away the plates. It was Mr Angelis's nephew, but he didn't look her way or smile at Lucy, as he had that first day. Instead, he stacked the plates and cutlery in silence while Nina turned her head towards the view so that she didn't have to see the livid bruised flesh around his blood-speckled brown eye.

Chapter Twenty-one

Jess

Hanging out in what was basically just a huge tub of warm water with a group of women, some of whom she'd cross the street to avoid, was not sitting well with Jess. She had promised herself before coming to Greece that she would try to be more accommodating, for Lucy's sake. But there were limits. The night before, she'd struggled to get to sleep, unable to shake off the empty feeling that had descended after her encounter with Gil on the boat, and all too aware of Gabriel's heavy, brooding presence through the adjoining door, with the result that she felt tired and out of sorts.

Across the sea of bubbles, Lucy was deep in conversation with Zoe and Shelly about tomatoes, of all things. 'People always say they taste better abroad but, as far as I'm concerned, a tomato is a tomato,' Lucy was saying.

At least she seemed to have got over that weird scene at lunch the day before when Jason's mum had told her not to meddle and she'd cried. *Awkward.* Afterwards,

Cora had been apologetic and had explained she'd never really got on with her husband's family so Lucy tracking them down had come as a bit of an unwelcome shock, which, if you asked Jess, was a lame excuse for throwing a hissy fit.

'How are things going with . . . Gabriel?' Her mother was next to Jess, leaning back against a jet of bubbles so that the old red swimming costume she wore swelled and popped with each new injection of air.

'Why did you say it like that?'

'Like what?'

'You know. Like he's something nasty on the bottom of your shoe?'

'You're being ridiculous.'

'Am I? Anyway, I'm not sleeping with him, if that's what you think.'

Hazel looked visibly relieved in the greenish light of the hotel's indoor spa, which really only consisted of this jacuzzi, plus a cold plunge pool filled with lemons, and another one that stank of eucalyptus, like being in a pool of liquid Vicks vapour, and a steam room and a sauna, neither of which Jess could contemplate going inside while the temperature outside was nudging thirty-five degrees. There were also a couple of 'pampering suites' where various of the women guests had booked in for facials or massages or other treatments that Jess privately regarded as a load of old bollocks. From time to time, Cora's voice could be heard chatting with the young woman who was giving her a hot-stone pedicure, whatever that was.

'And even if I was sleeping with him, I don't see why you have to be so judgemental.'

'The man is travelling under a different name. Have you even asked him about that?'

'What, so I'm just going to say, "My mother was snooping in your things and she went through your passport and now she has questions?"'

'I didn't snoop. It was just there.'

'Yes. There with the rest of his private things. Did you go through his pants, too?'

Jess ran a hand through her hair to check the pink dye wasn't coming out in this damp heat. She didn't even know why she was defending Gabriel so vigorously when he was starting to give her the creeps. It was just how things were with her and her mother. In her more self-aware moments Jess worried about how many of her fiercely held opinions were actually just a reaction against the opinions of her mother.

'Have you asked him about his background? Do you know where he works or where he grew up or who his family are?'

'Who his family are! We're not living in a Jane Austen novel, you know, Mum.'

The truth was Jess had asked Gabriel very little about himself. The first day they'd met had been taken up with hangovers and travelling and then, after the toothbrush thing, she'd been avoiding him as much as possible.

'What about his job, then?'

'He's freelance. Something to do with banking. Or maybe tech. Something boring, anyway. Look, Mum, if it makes you happy, I'll admit it wasn't my best idea to invite him, but he's here now, so just let up on the guy.'

Jess glanced across to Lucy, who had stopped talking about tomatoes and was leaning back against the padded cushions opposite. She seemed very subdued for someone supposedly living the best week of her life.

'You OK, Lu-lu?' she asked, the old family nickname coming out without thinking.

Lucy looked startled.

'I'm fine. Of course. Everything's perfect.'

Next to Lucy, Zoe – voluptuous in a gold-coloured bikini – also looked deep in thought. Jess remembered what Gil had said about her having been through some 'stuff' and wondered what he'd meant. As far as Jess could tell, Zoe had grown up being treated like a princess, with her parents bending over backwards to help her and lavish her with whatever she wanted, and now Gil was expected to do the same. No hardship there.

'How's . . . er . . . your daughter getting on?' Jess asked Zoe, hoping it wasn't obvious that she'd forgotten the girl's name.

'Crying for her mummy and daddy, last I heard. So thanks for that.'

'What's that supposed to mean? It's nothing to do with me that kids are banned from this wedding.'

'Not banned,' frowned Lucy. 'The hotel has an adults-only policy.'

'Yeah, and it's not like there are any other hotels in Greece you could have used instead.' Jess had meant it as a joke, but now she had both Zoe and Lucy glaring at her.

'You know what I reckon?' said Zoe, undoing the clip that held up her mass of curly hair, only to redo it more tightly, stretching back her cheeks into a temporary face-lift. 'I reckon you thought if you persuaded Lucy to make it no-kids-allowed I'd have to stay home and then you'd have Gil to yourself. Well – *newsflash* – he wasn't interested then and he's not interested now.'

'What? Are you actually insane?'

Jess was shocked at the blade of hurt that sliced through her. It had never occurred to her that Gil might tell Zoe about what had happened the day before on the deck. Although the truth was, nothing *had* happened.

'FYI, it was me who dumped your "husband",' she said, making curly quote marks in the air to emphasize her disdain for the word. 'He was so cut up about it I had to block him from calling me in the end. So, really, it's him you should be worrying about, not me.'

'Enough, Jess.' Hazel's voice was sharp.

'Fine.' Jess hauled herself out of the jacuzzi, noting how pink and mottled her skin looked after all that time slow-boiling in the lightly frothing water. 'I'm off for a swim in the sea, where there aren't particles of warm wee floating around.'

Wrapping a towel around her, she walked to the door, the soles of her unbuckled sandals squeaking on the wet tiles. But, as so often, her anger burned itself out almost immediately and by the time she reached the door she was already regretting the things she'd said. Zoe was a bitch, but this week wasn't about her, it was about Lucy and Jason. They were so well-meaning, the pair of them. So *good*, really. What was wrong with her, that she couldn't just rise above all this shit, for their sakes? Was she a bad person? It was this last thought that most bothered her, seizing hold of her brain in the early hours when, after reviewing some altercation or protest that had occurred during the day, which at the time she felt she'd dealt with in a righteous way, a tiny crack of self-doubt would open up. Was it her? Had she caused this?

For a moment she dithered on the threshold, torn between going back inside to make things all right with her sister and the desire to escape into the fresh air.

She heard Lucy's plaintive voice behind her, appealing to their mother.

'She always does this. Makes a scene and then runs away.'

Jess stepped outside, letting the door slam behind her.

Therapy Journal, Week 7

Thanks for what you said on Tuesday about me not being a bad person. Sometimes it's so hard to see your own self objectively. I hope you won't change your mind after getting to know me better.

If this was a book, I'd be starting a new chapter around now. A new volume, even! Mummy went away when I'd just turned eleven and I went to live with my uncle Adrian and his wife, Julie, and their eight-year-old twins Alex and Carl. Adrian had cut himself off from the monster – Grandma, I suppose I should call her – early on. One time he said she was so toxic battery fluid ran through her veins. He was always good with words. He tried not to say anything bad about Mummy so as not to upset me, but I know he thought her weak. 'When you have a cancer inside you,' he told me, 'you have to cut it right out or it will destroy you from the inside out.'

I tried to learn family life like a new language, studying the way Uncle Adrian and the others interacted, the things they said to each other, but it never came naturally. 'Just be yourself, Michelle,' Julie would tell me. She was a nice woman with a soft Scottish burr who wore floral blouses and trousers with elasticated waists to accommodate the 'baby weight' she was always vowing to lose. But why would I want to be myself when look where it had got me? Instead I tried to mirror Alex and Carl, mimicking the way they acted together, the things they said. But it didn't work. It was a question of expectations, I realized. To put it bluntly, they had none. They needed none. They started from a foundation of unconditional acceptance so they never worried about how something they said or did might be received or interpreted, whereas I was constantly observing and testing responses so I could adjust my behaviour accordingly. 'Why does she have to live here?' Alex asked his parents one time when he thought I wasn't listening. 'She's always watching.'

Chapter Twenty-two

Hazel

She was being ridiculous, Hazel told herself. There was absolutely no reason anyone should have gone through her bag, which she'd left casually in the changing room of the spa. It's not as if it had anything valuable in it. Her phone and money were back in the room. The only thing missing was a pair of cheap plastic reading glasses with jazzy purple frames, those off-the-peg ones you buy in packs of three in high-street shops, but, obviously, that made no sense. She must have forgotten to put them in. Even though she could swear she remembered doing just that.

But it wasn't only the missing glasses, it was also a more general sense of unease. A couple of times for no reason she'd had that prickling feeling as if she were being watched. Mind you, usually these days it was more likely to be her own husband scrutinizing her every move. Hazel didn't know what had got into Dom. Normally, he would have taken over an occasion like this. Regaling them all with stories in the bar late at night about his Groucho Club days in the 1990s, leading games and expeditions, charming the staff by chatting to them in a mixture of charades and pidgin English plus a few Greek words he'd picked up along the way. But he seemed so *diminished* here.

Case in point, here he was in the room when she got back from the spa, lying reading on the bed in his swim shorts. Instead of out by the pool with the other men.

'What are you doing here?' She didn't mean to sound so irritated, but she'd been looking forward to being on her own.

'Just chilling, as the young folk say. How was your pamperfest?'

'I made an excuse to come back early but, actually, it was fine.' Hazel kicked off her sandals and dropped down on to the mattress beside him. 'Apart from Jess throwing one of her strops.'

'Ah.' He didn't bother asking what it was about. Both of them knew by now there didn't have to be any reason behind their younger daughter's mood swings.

Dom's hand reached out across the sheet and took hold of hers.

'Darling?' He stroked the inside of her wrist, just where her skin was at its most sensitive. 'You know I love you, don't you – and this crazy little family we've made?'

She turned her face to his.

'Blimey. Are you about to cry?'

'I just feel so lucky to have you all. I don't know whether I say it enough.'

The truth was Dom *did* say it quite regularly. It was she who held back, meeting his shows of emotion with a detachment she knew sometimes drove him mad. But there was something about his mood now that was more intense than normal. She thought back to that text message he'd had the day before: *I can explain.* The missed call he'd dismissed as a cold caller. Yesterday, she'd been inclined to believe it had been something to do with work. It was such a sensitive subject between them, especially since she'd lost her job and money was so tight. She knew he dreamed of another chart-topping book, but after so many rejections from the same publishers who'd once fought to wine and dine him, and disappointing phone calls from his agent-turned-friend, he'd stopped telling her about his new projects and she'd stopped asking. Marriage was a bit like making bread, she always thought. Overworking the dough made everything flat and stodgy. Better to throw a tea towel over and allow it to prove in the dark. Now she wondered if she should have probed a little more.

But Dom's hand had moved from her wrist to her breast, and Hazel, still feeling languid and opened up after her seaweed massage, felt her body respond in that automatic way it had learned to over these last thirty years, turning to face him so that he could untie the halterneck of her swimming costume.

'I've always liked this old red thing,' he said, peeling it from her body.

Afterwards, he was in a good mood, far more like his usual self, especially when she promised to skip the rest of the spa session in favour of joining him for a swim downstairs.

'I'll go down and nab the best loungers. Anyone tries to get near yours, I'll beat them off with my Factor 50.' He lunged at the air with his bottle of sun cream.

But after he'd gone Hazel's misgivings returned. He'd left his phone charging by the bed and she lay on her side, looking at it.

She'd never checked up on him. Not once. Not even when things were really rocky a couple of years ago, classic mid-life crisis. It would be a gross violation of trust. Once, Lucy had blithely admitted that she went through Jason's phone regularly. He didn't mind, she'd insisted. It was a demonstration of how much she cared. She'd never be one of those people who allowed themselves to be blindsided by events. Hazel had been shocked. She'd hate for Dom to go through her things, even though she had nothing to hide. It seemed to her that a successful marriage was just as much about privacy as togetherness.

And yet. His weird mood. That strange text.

She sat up and grabbed her proper reading glasses from the side of the bed before unplugging the phone from its charger. She'd just key in the passcode, she decided. She knew Dom had always used the same one – Lucy's birthday backwards – although God forbid Jess should ever find out. If it let her in, she'd know he had nothing to hide.

The passcode worked. Hazel felt a brief surge of relief. Nothing to see here. But even as she was thinking that her fingers were moving as if of their own accord and double-clicking on the text-message icon, looking for the *I can explain* message. Nothing.

She must have missed it. She went back through, more slowly this time. It wasn't there. So he'd deleted it. Even though the one immediately before – from Dom's friend Jack: *Still on for next Wed, dude?* – was still there.

Hazel went to the call list, looking for the missed call, and located it immediately.

There was a smart faux-leather wallet on the white desk in the living room which held a pad of writing paper, each page emblazoned with the hotel's address and logo in a Mediterranean blue, and a pen which also boasted the hotel's name. Hazel tore off the top sheet of paper before returning to the bedroom to jot down the number. Then she returned the phone to its original place.

There would be an explanation, she was sure of it.

She stood up with resolve, folding the paper and slipping it inside the pages of her novel, which she then packed into her tote bag to take down to the pool. She collected her straw hat and the sarong she'd had to borrow from Lucy when her cherry-red one failed to turn up. A search for her missing spare specs proved fruitless so she took her prescription glasses instead.

Everything was fine, she told herself. She'd just had lovely sex with her husband of thirty years. Her daughter was marrying a good man whom she was blissfully in love with. All Hazel had to do was step back and let things sort themselves out, as they always did.

Still, when she unpacked her bag out there by the pool where Dom had, as he'd promised, nabbed the best-positioned loungers, she tried not to look at where the sharp corner of folded paper protruded from the pages of her book.

Chapter Twenty-three

Shelly

When the door of the steam room opened, admitting a tantalizingly brief gust of merciful, cool air, all eyes swung towards the human shape just about visible through the clouds.

Probably Jess, coming back pretending nothing had happened, Shelly decided. She pressed her back firmly against the hard tiles until her spine protested. If only Lucy and her parents weren't so blinkered. If they could just see what Jess was really like. Manipulative. Egocentric. Focused entirely on her own wants and needs. Of course, Shelly knew by now that this was how families operated – with blind spots and bottomless stores of get-out-of-jail-free cards. She'd learned that living with Adrian and Julie and the twins. But sometimes the unfairness of it all grabbed her around the throat until she couldn't breathe.

Shelly tried so hard to be a good person, to do right by the people she loved. Not to expect anything, which meant you were grateful for everything. And yet people like Jess took everything as their due and gave so little in return. Trampled over other people's feelings in order to validate their own. Surely there had to be a point where even the most loving sister or parent might say enough is enough?

'Greetings,' came a voice booming through the damp mist.

Shelly's heart sank as she recognized the woman from the airport toilets. By now, she'd retold that story of the breasts in the sink many times, fashioning it into a comedy sketch, but she never mentioned how uncomfortable she'd felt, or how, since they'd arrived here at the hotel, the woman always seemed to be staring at her, to the extent that Shelly had started checking for her before she stepped out on to the swimming-pool terrace or into the corridor. There was something about the way she looked at you, as if she might suddenly flick out her tongue and suck you up whole, that sent Shelly's mind free-wheeling back in time to that place she could not bear to go.

Shelly shivered despite the heat that made the pores on her skin open up like sinkholes. The woman gave her the creeps. She peered more closely through the mist. Oh God. Please don't let her be completely naked.

'You all look very cosy in here. Mind if I join you?'

Vivian didn't wait for a response before settling herself down on the tiled bench next to Shelly, who shrank away towards Lucy on her left. Oblivious, Vivian leaned across her.

'Did you know there's another bride in the hotel? She's absolutely gorgeous. And such a sweetheart.'

Shelly sensed Lucy stiffen and prickled with indignation on her behalf. It was as if the woman went out of her way to home right in on the very thing that made someone most insecure.

'Her wedding's going to be adorable. Very informal and low key. She's invited me to go. Don't you think that's lovely of her?'

The statement hung in the fuggy air like a bad smell. Vivian, who Shelly had now ascertained was definitely naked – ugh – was still staring at poor Lucy, those hard blue eyes glinting through the fog. When there was no response forthcoming, she ploughed on, her mouth a dark cave in the wet haze.

'I expect you and she are thick as thieves, Lucy. You have so much in common.'

'Actually, this week was all about being with my family and friends, so I haven't really got time for meeting new people. And I'm sure our weddings are going to be very different. I've really worked hard to make sure mine reflects my personality, and I'm sure she has, too.' Lucy's voice had been rising dangerously during this speech and now she stopped to check herself. 'Obviously, I wish her all the best,' she added lamely.

'Well, I think you've done a fantastic job of organizing this week, Lucy,' said Cora, from the opposite bench.

Cora was trying hard to make amends for her outburst at the lobster lunch. Well, so she should. Lucy had been subdued all that afternoon, even after Cora's apology. Shelly couldn't understand why Lucy tied herself up in such knots trying to impress Jason's mother when, as far as Shelly was concerned, Cora ought to be jumping for joy at her son's choice of fiancée.

She leaned back, finding the clammy heat oppressive. She had always hated confined spaces, growing panicky if she couldn't mentally plot her escape route. She knew approximately where the door was, but not being able to make out the handle was causing her to feel faint, as if gravity had sucked all her blood towards her feet, leaving her body heavy while her head felt flimsy and light. She'd been through all this with her therapist, painstakingly working out coping strategies, but the heat seemed to have wiped her mind blank.

Though her eyes were shut, Shelly was acutely conscious of the physical presence of Vivian just inches to her right. Was it her imagination, or had the woman moved closer to her?

Shelly glanced to the side and saw that Vivian's gimlet eyes were now focused on Cora.

'You're the mother of the groom, aren't you? You must be *bursting* with pride. He seems just *fabulous*. If I was twenty years younger.' Her bark of laughter set Shelly's nerves jangling. 'Is Daddy not on the scene?'

For a moment Shelly's steam-fuddled brain thought she was asking after Cora's father. Only when Lucy nudged her did the meaning become clear. Shelly sat very still, wondering how Cora would react. Would they get a repeat of the previous day?

'No, it's just me,' Cora replied. By this time, Vivian was leaning back against the bench with her arms spread out on either side, so that Shelly had to hold her whole body tense to avoid touching her. The idea of accidentally coming into contact with Vivian's flesh made her want to crawl out of her own skin.

The tone of Cora's response invited no further comment. But still Vivian stared at her, expectant.

'Families,' she said eventually, projecting her words into the wet heat. 'When they're good, they're good. But when they're bad, they'll eat you alive. Am I right?'

16/6/19, 11.25. Original English-language transcript of police interview with Mrs Vivian Cassandra Kaffel. Police officers: Theodoros Christakis and Kostas Stephanides. Interpreter: Xanthe Liourdis.

Can you tell him I take exception to his tone? Can you say that, please? I never tried to mislead anyone. I've always answered honestly. They just haven't been asking the right questions.

No, I didn't know her. We met here for the first time. And I was genuinely in Greece on holiday. I always holiday in Greece, like I told you. But yes, all right, I did come here to this particular hotel on this particular island because of her. I'd only just found her, you see. So when I tracked her down and saw she was coming here, it seemed a perfect opportunity to meet her finally in a neutral space. And to keep an eye on her, too, I suppose. You see, she has form.

I did wonder if she had some inkling who I was. Her mother and I don't look so dissimilar, although I'm afraid to say her mother's looks did not stand the test of time.

But I didn't want to force anything. I have an inbuilt antenna for other people's feelings. And yes, I suppose there was also an element of me scoping her out. *Scoping*. Weighing up.

I knew where she'd come from. And I knew what she'd done. And either of those things on its own would send alarm bells ringing, but both? So yes, I suppose I wanted to get the measure of her before I came clean. I had to consider my own safety.

I *am* answering the question. Listen, every unhappy family is unhappy in its own way. Oh, look at them, looking so blank. Do they not read Tolstoy in Greece? What I mean is that, yes, you could say there was some dysfunction, but no worse than most families.

Actually, as this is official, I'd like to set the record straight. Michelle's mother was a paranoid schizophrenic. She'd always been odd. When she was little she had a red anorak with a hood, and the first time her father and I saw that film *Don't Look Now* – you know, the one set in Venice with the murderous dwarf in the red coat – we laughed ourselves silly because it was so like her. Oh, I know you're not supposed to say 'dwarf' nowadays. Everyone is so easily offended.

By the time she was a teenager she was in and out of psychiatrists' offices and seeing various alternative therapists I found. Her father was long gone by then, couldn't cope with her. Adrian took over the role of Man Who Knows Best and tried to stop me getting her the treatments she needed. I'm sorry to say he turned into a thoroughly unpleasant young man. You know, when I heard what Michelle did to Adrian and his family, I was horrified, obviously, but I also knew it was karma. He has always been so pompous. So much like his father. When Adrian severed all ties with me it was the first time he'd done anything to earn my respect. Michelle's mother, on the other hand, lacked the spine.

You know, she tried to keep Michelle secret. As if I wouldn't know! Didn't she think I might wonder why the 'spare room' – can you make sure that goes in quote marks – was painted pink and full of cuddly toys? But I want the record to show once and for all that I had no idea she was hiding the girl in the cellar. I believed she was off at a friend's house. I didn't challenge my daughter because I thought it was kinder to let her have her secrets.

No, it wasn't me who reported my daughter. That's not my style at all. It was a neighbour who said she was concerned because she hadn't seen the child around, and when the police came around they found her in that dreadful room. I would have taken her in myself, only I had a flight booked already to Sri Lanka. It's so important to keep expanding your mind. By the time I came back the child was already at Adrian's. But I want it to be known that I would have stepped in. That's what family is for.

Chapter Twenty-four

Hazel

Hazel hadn't lasted long out there on the lounger. Dom could lie there all day probably, drinking vodka and tonics – it was not a fast day, after all – and basting himself, while befriending the people around him just by dint of appearing interested in what they had to say. It was a gift, Hazel had realized. That easy forging of intimacy. Lucy had it, too. The truth was, most people craved connection. Having someone ask you how you were, *who* you were, as if they genuinely wanted to know. That meant something to people.

Hazel herself had never been able to manage it. Once, coming away from one social gathering or another, she'd asked Dom why people didn't respond to her in the same way they did him. 'Don't take this the wrong way, but you sometimes come over as quite removed,' he'd said, adding hastily: 'Which is probably why you're so brilliant at your job.' At the time, she'd been irritated, but now she thought she understood. It was nothing to do with the quality of the questions you asked. What counted was the quality of how you listened to the responses, how invested you appeared in the answers.

She told him she was going to sit at the bar and read in the shade. But picking up her book, she'd felt that splinter of worry, seeing the crisp white folded paper which she knew held that scrawled telephone number.

There had been a moment back there on the loungers when she'd almost confronted him about it. He'd stretched out his hand to stroke her shoulder, and when she turned to look, he was smiling at her in that way he always did after they'd had sex, and it had reminded her who he was. Not some stranger harbouring secrets, but the man she'd shared her life with for nearly thirty years. *Oh, but it's Dom*, she'd thought in surprise. And it had seemed like the most natural thing in the world to open her mouth and say, 'What's with the text you deleted?' Then he'd have told her the perfectly reasonable explanation. 'Oh, that,' he might say. 'It's the funniest thing . . .' And just like that it would be wiped from her mind, so inconsequential as to not be worth thinking about.

So what had stopped her?

Her feet in their suede Birkenstocks made a slapping noise as she walked. The toenails she'd had painted a gay orange in her annual pedicure struck her suddenly as rather garish. She'd originally chosen a muted plum colour, but the young Polish beautician had frowned and asked her whether she didn't think a wedding on a beautiful Greek island wasn't deserving of 'happy feet'. So here she was.

The others were still in the spa, and Hazel knew Lucy would be wondering where she was, but she couldn't face going back in. All that bad-tempered heat.

She'd assumed the bar would be empty at this time, but she saw there was already one other guest. Gabriel.

Just her luck. Should she turn around? Would it be too obvious?

She stopped herself short. This was the perfect opportunity for a discreet word with the man who'd all but invited himself into their lives, without Jess around complicating matters. Jess had a thing for the underdog, no matter what the circumstances or how undeserving. If she thought Hazel and the others were ganging up on Gabriel, it would make him instantly more attractive to her. This was a chance for Hazel to put him on the spot, out of sight of her younger daughter.

Gabriel looked up from the book he was reading as she approached. Despite being in full shade, his eyes were covered by a pair of sunglasses, with lenses so black they appeared to suck in the light, and he was wearing – of course he was – a black baseball cap turned around the wrong way so that the peak hung down the back of his neck. '*Kalimera*,' he said, pressing his hands together in a namaste gesture.

Oh good God.

'Actually, I'm glad to find you here,' Hazel said, after explaining why she wasn't in the spa with the others. 'The fact is . . .' She took a deep breath. How to play this? 'The fact is, I rather think you've been economical with the truth regarding who you really are.'

Economical with the truth. Where had that come from?

Gabriel didn't respond, just carried on looking at her from behind those glasses, with that infuriating benign half-smile of his.

By this time Hazel had settled herself down at the table opposite him.

'What I'm saying is I know your name isn't really Gabriel.'

She studied the moon of his face, looking for signs of shock or panic, but instead the smile grew wider, opening up that discomfiting little dent in his cheek. He raised up a hand and drew a circle in the air with his finger, then flicked his hand open and mouthed 'pow'.

Was the man on crack?

'I'm afraid I don't have a clue what you're trying to say. What was that round thing you drew with your finger?'

'Circle of trust. That you just blasted a hole right through.'

'What? Now hang on a minute. I admit I had a quick look at your passport when Jess sent me back to her room for her phone. But any parent would do the same when a complete stranger turns up at a family wedding.'

'I didn't turn up. I was invited.' Such a toneless, unmusical voice he had, so soft that one was constantly craning to hear.

'That's debatable. But perhaps you could explain to me why you're calling yourself Gabriel Kidd when your passport says your name is Vince Harris?'

Gabriel's black sunglasses remained trained on her face, and she felt her cheeks burning under his scrutiny. Then he wagged his finger at her, lazily.

Gabriel lay back on his lounger and picked up his book, which Hazel now saw was *The Power of Now*. 'Why don't you relax, Hazel? Here we are in this beautiful place, surrounded by your beautiful family. The universe is smiling on us.

'Why would you go looking for trouble when you are so blessed?'

Chapter Twenty-five

Lucy

Lucy was lying back against the stack of pillows on Jess's super-kingsize bed, wearing one of the floaty kaftans she'd ordered specifically for this week from an online Moroccan clothing boutique. She had a glass of chilled Prosecco on the bedside table next to her and her whole body was still tingling from having been encased in wet, clay-like sand taken from the shoreline at the far end of the beach down below and then vigorously rubbed into her skin with an exfoliating mitt before being rinsed off with icy water by a smiling young woman wearing thick contouring make-up.

She sighed with satisfaction, all lingering tensions, such as the scene with Cora on the boat, momentarily dismissed. It was a touchy subject, that's all. All families had them. Lucy had spent too much time and effort – she wouldn't think of the money – on this week to allow a little misunderstanding to spoil it. Cora had apologized. She'd let the heat get to her, she said. And Jason had been full of remorse when he realized how much he'd upset her. She refused to let it cast a shadow over this week. Here, now, was exactly how she'd imagined this week to go. Spending quality time with the people she loved most in the world in these gorgeous surroundings, relaxed and stress-free.

'Aren't you ready yet?'

'Good things come to those who wait,' came Jess's voice from behind the bathroom door.

Lucy took another sip of her drink and gazed around her. She was glad to see evidence that Gabriel was sleeping in the living room. Not that she had anything against him. He was certainly a lot better than some of the men Jess had brought home over the years. There had been that militant vegan who'd insisted on telling Lucy exactly how her leather jacket had been made, probably from a calf, he'd reckoned, who'd lived a life of abject misery, torn from its mother, before being slaughtered, its flesh turned into veal and its skin removed to make a fashion item she'd probably wear for a couple of years and then cast off. Well, he'd been wrong about that. She still wore it occasionally four years on, even though it had a tear in the lining and the elbows had gone baggy. Then there was that graffiti artist who was always taking mysterious calls which would have him leaping up from the dinner table to go hang off the underside of a railway bridge or scale a disused building to spray his 'tag' somewhere no one apart from other taggers would ever notice. Jess seemed to have spent most of their relationship in one A&E department or another.

Besides, it suited Lucy very well that Gabriel was getting on so well with Cora. With his mother distracted, Jason would be able to focus entirely on her. It might be selfish, but it was her wedding, after all.

A sense of wellbeing settled over her, that rare feeling of being exactly where she most wanted to be. Lucy had been working on her mindfulness over the preceding months, to avoid getting overwrought with all the wedding planning. By concentrating on the here and now – what her senses were telling her – she could override those niggling worries about things going wrong and that awful, sickening lurch in her stomach when she thought about Nina and the unpaid bill. She closed her eyes and thought about her breath passing through her body, how the sheet felt crisp on the back of her legs, the gentle wash of the waves wafting in through the open windows, and the drone of a faraway speedboat. She thought about the smell of salt water coming off Jess's wet swimsuit which she'd draped over the door handle and how it mixed with the other smells in the room – her own earthy, freshly scrubbed skin, the newly laundered sheets. She was entering a kind of trance state of being at one with everything, which was when she liked to make her gratitude list: *I'm grateful for my fiancé, who completes my world; I'm grateful for my supportive, quirky family; I'm grateful not to live in Syria or any of those other scary places, Tottenham for example, even though I've never been; I'm grateful for my healthy body and my . . .*

'AAAAAAAAARGH!'

Her scream shattered into tiny fragments the wall of calm and serenity she'd painstakingly built up around her.

'Do you like it? It's fun, isn't it? So much more "me" than any of the suggestions you sent. I got it from a Preloved shop near work. You wouldn't believe some of the fab stuff they had in there.'

Lucy couldn't breathe. The dress was awful. Tight and clingy in the bodice, with a halterneck that revealed all those awful tattoos; it flared out almost to the ground. But that wasn't even the worst of it. The worst was the pattern. Psychedelic colours swirled and clashed in a migraine-inducing riot.

'Dusky pink,' she whispered through the hand which was clamped over her mouth. 'That was literally the one thing I said. The one stipulation. Dusky pink.'

'Exactly! That's why I went for this one over the one that was really amazing. Because of the dusky pink in the pattern – see?'

Jess pointed to a swirl of indeterminate pink amidst the oranges, yellows and acid greens.

'You got your dress for my wedding from a charity shop?'

'Not charity. Preloved.'

'I don't believe you. I literally don't believe you.'

Lucy stormed out of Jess's room, unable to look at her sister a moment longer. It was all ruined. The photographs in which she'd envisioned being flanked by her bridesmaids in their rose-coloured gowns would now be replaced by group shots in which all eyes would be drawn instantly to that monstrous dress instead of to her, in the tulle and lace that had cost so much money.

'I think I'm having a panic attack,' she told Shelly a few moments later, sitting on the white armchair in Shelly's fiercely air-conditioned room with her head in her hands.

'Oh, Luce. You poor thing. Hold my hand. There. That's it. Calm. This too shall pass.'

Shelly was crouched down beside her, still wearing the towel she'd had wrapped around her when she answered the door to Lucy's frantic knocking just moments before.

'I just asked one thing from her. Just one.'

'She's selfish, Luce. I know I shouldn't say it, but she's a selfish cow who doesn't deserve you.'

Lucy stiffened. It was true Jess always put her own short-term gratification over everyone else's feelings. But on the other hand, she could be generous to a fault, showing up out of the blue with a bottle of Jim Beam and a family box of Maltesers just because she thought Lucy needed cheering up.

'She doesn't mean to be . . .'

'You don't have to defend her all the time, Luce. She's a grown-up, now. You're allowed to call her out for letting you down. Not turning up when she's supposed to, saying she'll do something and then forgetting all about it. How many second chances are you going to give her? You even made her matron of honour for your wedding, and she's shown zero interest in it.'

Shelly's cheeks were very pink. She must have been in the shower. And she was so intense, with those huge eyes of hers. Lucy started to feel awkward, wondering how she could retract her hand without giving offence.

If she was honest, Lucy suspected that Shelly was disappointed not to have been asked to be matron of honour herself. And she had a point. How many times had she proved herself to be loyal and true, always there if Lucy needed a hand? Yes, Jess could be called upon for the dramas and the crises, but it was Shelly who had given up her weekend to help Lucy wrap glasses in newspaper before she moved in with Jason, Shelly who'd dropped everything to rush over with the spare key that time Jason was away and Lucy had locked herself out.

'I know you're right, Shell. But at the end of the day, Jess is my sister.'

'That doesn't excuse her, though. It doesn't give her the right to be such a *bitch*.'

'Enough!'

Lucy yanked her hand out of Shelly's more forcefully than she'd intended.

For a moment Shelly remained where she was, crouching at Lucy's feet, staring at her own hand, which still lay in Lucy's lap, as if it belonged to someone else. She was so thin her collarbone pressed like a metal bar against her skin. Then she got to her feet and smiled, rewrapping the towel around her.

'Sorry. Don't tell me. Blood is thicker than water.'

She returned to the bathroom to finish whatever it was she'd been interrupted from doing, leaving Lucy sitting in the armchair, trying in vain to recapture her Zen feeling from earlier. Her eyes scanned Shelly's bedroom, which, in stark contrast to Jess's, was oppressively neat, all her clothes put away, no stray bottles of mosquito spray or sun cream.

In fact, the only sign anyone was staying here was an unfolded card lying face down on the bedside table where most people would have a book or an iPad or whatever else they used to distract themselves before falling asleep.

Lucy glanced at the closed bathroom door before curiosity got the better of her and she padded across the room to turn over the card, blinking when she recognized her own wedding invitation with its two photographs – one of her and Jason, and one of her with her parents and Jess. 'The Collins family requests your presence . . .'

The sound of the bathroom-door handle caused her to slam the card back down and scoot back to her chair. It was touching that the invitation clearly meant so much to Shelly, she told herself. And it was just a coincidence that the way the card had been folded, with Jess at the centre of the crease, had rubbed her sister's face clear off.

Chapter Twenty-six

Hazel

Hazel was sitting on the terrace of their suite, in a shady corner with her laptop on a small table in front of her, listening to Dom's soft snores floating out from the bedroom. The novel (still unread) was also on the table. The paper she'd hastily tucked into it now lay flattened out in front of her.

Idly, Hazel entered the number of the missed call on Dom's phone into the Google search box. When nothing came up she couldn't tell whether she was disappointed or relieved.

Ahead of her, the Ionian Sea sparkled like it had been Swarovski'd to within an inch of its life, needles of sunlight studding the still water. A schooner sailed serenely across the horizon, its sail crisp white against the cornflower blue sky. In the corner of the terrace a lavender bush burst out of a large terracotta pot, a riot of mauve and purple flowers and needle-shaped grey-green leaves, and scented the air. Life is good, she told herself. Life is beautiful.

What she should do, she decided, was go on a digital detox. No more phone or laptop. Just focus on enjoying these precious days, being here with her family to celebrate her daughter's wedding.

But now that the laptop was open . . . It was as if Hazel's fingers were working completely independently of her as she logged into Gmail and called up her inbox. She was taken aback, as she always was these days, by how few messages there were. When she'd worked on the paper she'd been deluged daily with new health and safety directives, mass emails about leaving dos and new security measures and retraining opportunities. It was like drowning slowly in a sea of ever-changing rules and regulations and events that didn't really concern you when you got right down to it. Background noise that slowly sucked you under, like quicksand. She'd never have imagined then that there might come a time when she'd miss those emails.

Her mouth turned dry as she saw a new unread message from Karen Grogan, deputy editor of the *Bristol Mail*, where Hazel had worked for the last twenty-three years. 'Touching Base', read the subject title. Karen had only been in the post for a year, promoted far beyond her capabilities after the last round of cuts, which had taken the scalps of the highest-paid staff members and replaced them with relative newcomers with half the experience who'd accept half the salary. Restructuring, they'd called it, getting around the legalities by merging the personnel of three publications and creating a central hub responsible for all three. Karen was at least twenty years younger than Hazel and ambitious in that way women sometimes are when they're newly returned from maternity leave and determined to make up for lost time. Gareth, the outgoing deputy, had been a product of the old days, where journalists would conduct interviews over long, boozy, expense-account lunches and reporters were dispatched with blank cheques to sign up the biggest stories. Karen, on the other hand, brought in her plant-based lunch in Tupperware containers and ate at her desk, endlessly querying the invoices Hazel submitted from photographers and stylists and the owners of white, light-filled studios. Really, Hazel ought to have known the writing was on the wall.

Karen's email, beginning with a generic pleasantry – *Hope you're enjoying the Greek sunshine. How could you not?* – was innocuous enough. She wanted to know whether to send on the personal post that had accumulated for Hazel, and to request the return of the work iPad which Hazel had forgotten she still had at home in her desk drawer. 'Housekeeping', she called it.

But although the email itself was harmless, it brought the fear and humiliation of the last twelve weeks rushing back, turning the lavender-scented air rancid. Even after all this time, Hazel still couldn't believe her career was over. Though she'd been telling people for years that she was hanging on by her fingernails, she hadn't actually believed it. She was good at her job, that was the thing. Of course she knew the whole industry was sliding inexorably into a black hole, but she'd still convinced herself that experience and hard work stood for something, that somehow she'd be spared. She tried not to notice how much older she was than her work colleagues or to mind when they missed her out of after-work drinks or weekend parties. 'We knew it wasn't your sort of thing,' they'd say.

When she'd got the email, though, inviting her to Melanie Alderman's office for a 'chat', Hazel had known. You didn't go to see the director of HR to talk about the weather. Karen had been there at that meeting, head cocked to the side in an attitude that was clearly meant to convey sympathy. Hazel still struggled to recall what was said. Phrases like 'Sad to see you go' and 'Wish there was another way' stuck in her head. She did recall Melanie, a woman with shiny black hair like a helmet, saying, 'At least you've had a good innings.'

The 'generous redundancy package' they'd promised turned out to be just over £16,000, which was £10,000 less than the amount Hazel and Dom had added to their mortgage the year before to pay for rewiring the house.

Hazel stopped sleeping and took up comfort eating. She felt beleaguered and let down and permanently sick. You could work all your adult life to build a career you thought was solid and the whole thing turned out to be as flimsy as a house of cards.

Melanie and Karen had assured Hazel her job was being 'phased out', so it had been mortifying to learn sometime later that her twenty-four-year-old intern had been promoted to the newly created role of Head of Visual Content. On Dom's insistence, she engaged the services of a hugely expensive employment lawyer. He'd taken up her case with gusto, firing off letters, racking up the bills. But she'd stopped using him after a few weeks. She felt so humiliated, that was the thing. All those years spent building a reputation and, in the event, it meant nothing and colleagues you'd thought were friends melted away into thin air.

So she'd accepted the redundancy package. Agreed to go quietly, without consulting Dom. 'This is so typical of you,' Dom had berated her when he found out. 'Avoid confrontation at any cost.'

So here she was, fifty-seven years old. Jobless and broke, feeling useless and obsolete, and determined to keep the whole thing from her daughters for as long as possible. Partly because she didn't want to worry them but, mostly, if she was honest, because she felt so bloody embarrassed.

Desperate to take her mind off her plight, Hazel decided that while she had her laptop out, she'd check up on Gabriel. There was something so unsettling about the man, she couldn't help thinking, with that spongy complexion of his.

She put the name Vince Harris into the search box and groaned when she saw how many entries there were. Switching to images, she started scanning the many photos of men called Vince Harris. A middle-aged man from an American insurance company with a perfect ring of white hair surrounding an impressively tanned bald pate featured strongly, as did the London director of a crisis management company for ailing corporations and a spokesman for the Scottish Tourist Board. Somewhere around page two, she started to lose the will to live and thought of giving up, but Dom was still snoring inside and she was bored with her book.

On page three, she stopped to admire a leather-jacketed Vince Harris with a trim beard and twinkly blue eyes. As she scanned to the bottom of the page her gaze was arrested by a photograph that had clearly been taken at a work function, featuring a young, formally dressed couple, he in a suit, she in a sleeveless dress, smiling self-consciously at the camera. Was that him? The same round face and that infuriating half-smile, but the hair was shorter and more abundant, the expression more open and engaged.

She clicked on the link. The photo was on the website of a tech company called Infinite Sky Solutions at a fundraiser for a local kids' cancer charity. *Deputy Head of Communications, Rosanna Silvain, with her fund manager fiancé, Vince Harris*, read the caption. *Fund manager?* She peered doubtfully at the photo, but closer inspection revealed it to be most definitely him. The date was eight years before. The chances of Rosanna Silvain still being at the company were minimal, but still Hazel tried going on to the company website and scrolling through the 'About Us' section. Nothing. Deflated, she typed the name Rosanna Silvain into the Google search box. It was an unusual name, at least. The first match was a PR company called the Rosanna Silvain Agency. The woman whose name the company bore was without doubt the same woman as the one in the photo with Vince Harris, although she was at least a stone heavier and the stark bob of the first picture had been replaced by a softer, longer style. There was a photograph of her with her husband – who was not Gabriel – and two young children, on a ski slope somewhere, looking like an advertisement for wholesome family life, and a contact email for Rosanna herself, under the heading 'Reach Out'. Hazel hesitated. Was she taking this too far? Whoever Gabriel was, he'd be out of their lives in a few days' time. And it's not as if he'd done anything wrong. And, as Jess kept saying, there was no law against calling yourself anything you wanted.

An image flashed across her mind of Gabriel and Cora, heads bent together in conversation on the fishing boat the day before. Hazel and Cora weren't close, for all Lucy's best efforts to force a friendship on them. They were too different, Hazel supposed. Cora so very self-contained, as if she already had everything she needed. But they liked each other, and Hazel felt a certain responsibility to her. Cora was a woman on her own and, after all, it was Hazel's daughter who'd introduced this stranger into the group. If there was something off about him, shouldn't she at least try to find out what it was? Be proactive, for once?

Hazel tapped out a message. *Please excuse this communication out of the blue*, she began. Then she briefly explained the circumstances, overegging them slightly. Her young, vulnerable daughter had turned up at a family wedding with a much older man who turned out not to be who he claimed to be, she said. She was sure Rosanna would understand how concerning that was and how, as a parent, you'd want to be sure there was nothing dreadful in that man's past to have prompted him to change his name. Hazel stared at the message and then deleted the word 'dreadful' and replaced it with the milder 'untoward'. After all, this Rosanna had once been engaged to Gabriel. For all she knew, the two of them could still be the best of friends.

Without stopping to read the email through, she pressed send. Then she took off her glasses – still her good pair, as she hadn't found the others – and snapped shut the laptop lid.

Out at sea, the schooner had disappeared, the horizon re-forming itself into an unbroken navy-blue line as if nothing had ever been there at all.

Chapter Twenty-seven

Lucy

When Lucy had planned a shopping day in Fiskardo as part of her wedding schedule, she'd envisaged herself and the female component of her party pottering around the sweet little shops and boutiques of the upmarket seaside resort, trying on clothes, buying souvenirs and knick-knacks to take home, reminders of this happiest of weeks in this most beautiful of places. They'd stop frequently for coffees or cold beers and spend a couple of hours having lunch at one of the harbourside restaurants, everyone taking their new purchases out of their bags to show to the group. There'd be chat and laughter and a sense of bonding. What there wouldn't be was Jess rolling her eyes over the mixed mezze while Zoe took them through every single item in the two huge carrier bags of gifts to take home to her daughter.

'I know I'm spoiling her, but I feel so guilty at leaving her at home, she was so heartbroken not to come with us,' she said pointedly.

What there also wouldn't be was her own mother questioning Jason's mum about her new-found friendship with Gabriel. It wasn't like Hazel to pass comment. Usually, she was very hands-off when it came to other people's private lives. Too hands-off, it sometimes seemed to Lucy – after all, there was a fine line between living and letting live and just not giving a fuck. Many times in the past she'd tried to involve her mum in some or other drama going on in her life, only to be met with 'That's really up to you, Lu-lu.' So it was weird that she'd chosen this moment to start showing an interest.

'I just wonder if you shouldn't be a little cautious,' her mother was saying. 'I mean, we have no clue about his background.'

'What she means is . . .'

'I don't mean anything at all, Jess.' What was that look about that passed between her mother and her sister, Lucy would like to know.

There were sharing platters of mezze in the middle of the table – golden tiger prawns coated in garlic and chillies, Greek salad topped with fat chunks of herb-dusted feta, bowls of silky tzatziki with fresh crusty bread, and small fried fish with chunks of lemon . . . Unlike the others, who were picking at salads and dips, Jess had loaded her plate with bread and battered squid and juicy meatballs and peppers dripping with oil. Zoe, who had insisted on taking her measly portion of salad before they added the oil and vinegar dressing, was gazing at Jess's plate as if it was something alive and dangerous. Lucy felt a pang of pity for the woman. Anyone could see she had some kind of eating problem, all those trips to the bathroom after a big meal. Jess was sitting at the far end of the table to Lucy, who still hadn't completely forgiven her for what she and Shelly had termed DressGate. In fact, Lucy had tried to interest her sister in various dresses in the little shops they'd visited that morning – all a million times more suitable than the swirly monstrosity she had hanging in her wardrobe – but she hadn't even agreed to try them on.

'Thanks, Hazel. I appreciate you looking out for me, but there's nothing between me and Gabriel and, anyway, I'm quite capable of looking after myself. I ought to be after all this time on my own.'

Cora was looking cool and elegant as ever, in a loose-fitting khaki linen dress that showed off her bare brown shoulders and enviably toned arms. If you leaned over the rail of Lucy and Jason's terrace, you could see on to Cora's more modest balcony, and Lucy had twice covertly observed her soon-to-be mother-in-law going through her morning yoga routine wearing a plain vest and harem pants. Working in a designer-fitness-clothing store, Lucy had a range of high-fashion exercise gear at home, mostly skin-tight leggings in geometric prints and Lycra tops with keyholes in strange places that were a workout in themselves to get on and off, but she had decided then and there to ditch those in favour of an outfit like Cora's.

Cora's phone buzzed with an incoming text and the conversation at the table briefly lulled.

'It's all right, it's not Gabriel. You don't need to worry,' she joked. 'It's just Jason checking we're having a good day.'

Lucy's chest tightened and she slid her own phone out of her bag under the table and glanced at the screen. Nothing. Shouldn't Jason be texting his fiancée to ask how things were going rather than his mother?

Maybe it was feeling hurt that made Lucy decide to have another go at digging around for information about his dad's relatives. She hadn't forgotten Cora's strange reaction when she'd brought the subject up before, but it was so rare she got to chat to her soon-to-be mother-in-law without Jason there.

'I was trying to remember the other day how long it has been since Jason's dad died,' she said, crinkling her forehead as if it were a casual, fleeting thought.

'About sixteen years.' Cora reached for her folded sunglasses and put them on, even though they were under an awning well away from the glare of the sun.

'You poor thing!' Zoe exclaimed. 'I wouldn't last two minutes on my own. But then, I'm a people person. I need that kind of human connection.'

'There must have been other men on the scene, though, in all that time,' said Jess. 'Fit bird like you.'

Cora smiled, but the fine skin around her eyes looked stretched and tight.

'You know what they say. Once bitten . . .'

'It wasn't a happy relationship, then?' Lucy felt a rush of gratitude to her mum, realizing that Hazel had asked the question on her behalf. Lucy had never made any secret of being frustrated with how little she knew of

Jason's dad. In a few days she'd be family, for God's sake. And just because Cora hadn't got on with his relatives, it shouldn't rule the whole subject out of bounds.

Cora, impossible to read behind her dark glasses, pressed her lips together.

'I thought this was a celebration,' she said. 'The last thing we need to be doing is raking up old history. How about we order another bottle of that lovely white?'

And just like that the subject was closed down.

Afterwards, as they half-heartedly browsed in some of the shops they'd missed easier, while the after-fug of lunchtime drinking settled over them, turning their limbs sluggish and making their heads throb, Lucy slipped her arm through Shelly's and the pair slowed their pace so that they hung back behind the rest of the group.

'Don't you think it was weird the way she clammed up like that, Shell? I'm not being paranoid, am I? I just wish they weren't so secretive about him. If there are any skeletons in the closet, I'd much rather know about them.'

'I don't blame you. But—'

'But?'

The two had stopped outside a shop selling beautifully packaged olives and honey and bottles of olive oil with fancy labels and little corks in their necks. Shelly paused as though carefully considering what she was about to say.

'The thing you have to remember, Luce, is that you've been really lucky with your parents, but for lots of other people family is a dark place.'

Shelly was wearing her usual wide-brimmed floppy hat, so it was impossible to see her expression. Lucy felt instantly guilty. So insensitive of her to bang on about Jason's dad to Shelly, of all people.

'Sorry, mate,' she said as they started moving again, following her sister's pink ponytail up ahead. 'I know families aren't your favourite thing. Have you heard from your uncle since you've been here?'

Lucy knew Shelly had been brought up by her uncle and aunt in Norfolk after her mum 'went mental' – as Shelly described it bluntly in one of the few conversations she and Lucy had had about her past. Thinking about everything her friend must have gone through always gave Lucy a lump in her throat. Shelly was right. How lucky was she?

'We've swapped a few messages. I might go for a visit when we get back.'

They passed a tiny pharmacy, its window stocked with expensive-looking face creams and serums. 'Can you just wait a second while I nip in here?' asked Shelly. 'My sodding eyes are killing me.'

Lucy scrunched up her face in sympathy. Shelly suffered from a condition that made her eyes extra dry. It was something to do with the shape of them, so big and curved. She even slept with them half-open, which had freaked Lucy out the first time they shared a room on a girls' weekend away. At work, she kept a little bottle of drops under the counter, and Lucy would often walk in on her in front of the big mirror in the toilets with one arm upstretched and her head thrown back.

'How are you feeling about DressGate today?' Shelly asked when she emerged, clutching a small plastic bag.

Lucy shrugged. 'Still fuming, but what can I do? Apart from cut her out of all the photos, which would serve her sodding well right.'

'You're too soft, that's your problem. You know, she reminds me a little of my mum.'

Lucy stiffened. Shelly's mum had spent years going in and out of psychiatric institutions before dying of an overdose of prescription drugs. How could she be anything like Jess?

'Don't take this the wrong way, Luce, but Mum was a narcissist, and I see some of that in Jess.'

'Don't say that. You don't even know her.'

Lucy could tell from Shelly's expression that she was hurt. But *Jesus*. For all her faults, Jess was her little sister. She wasn't some *psychopath*.

Still, when she glanced ahead again and saw that defiant pink ponytail blazing a path through the throngs of surrounding tourists, her stomach felt tight as a drum.

Therapy Journal, Week 8

You asked me what Uncle Adrian was like. Well, I loved the fact that he was an architect. It seemed such a solid sort of job. He had a kind face but a tired expression, with a perpetual vertical crease between his brows. His mousy-brown hair already had a large streak of white even though he was still in his thirties when I went to live with them, far younger than Harry was when we met. I adored him and would invent reasons to get him alone, asking for help on homework that I could do perfectly well by myself or advice on imaginary dilemmas. He'd said early on that if ever I was feeling sad about what had happened 'before' – which is how he referred to my life with Mummy – I should come to him to talk it through, so I would put on a pained expression and pretend I'd had a bad dream just so he'd give me his undivided attention and put his arm around me, awkwardly, because Uncle Adrian never did really relax around me. Every few months he'd take me to see Mummy in the private hospital where she was living in Barnet – the red-brick London house having been sold to pay for her care – and even though I hated those visits, my beautiful mother now bloated with drugs, her lovely eyes pink-veined and glassy, I loved the four-hour round trip from our house in Norfolk. Getting ready to leave, I'd make a big fuss about forgetting my book or some piece of homework I wanted to show Mummy – not that she ever reacted in any real way – just to make sure that Alex and Carl, and to an extent Julie, too, were aware that I was going to be spending the best part of the day on my own with Uncle Adrian. Looking back, I'm embarrassed at how obvious I was. But, in my defence, I had so little that was mine.

Alex and Carl resented me. Well, duh! They'd been used to being a family of four and suddenly they had an outsider in their home, vying for their parents' attention. But at the time, I'm sorry to say, I thought them selfish. They had so much and I couldn't understand why they wouldn't share it. I tried hard at first to get them to accept me. But trying too hard is as bad as not trying at all. Gradually, the lines were drawn – Alex and Carl on one side and me on the other. They shut their bedroom door to keep me out and spoke in a secret language at dinner. They told their parents I was 'weird', but only when they called me 'crazy' did I really lose my temper. Julie tried to broker the peace, but when it came down to it she was always going to choose her own children over me. It's natural, though I didn't see it like that until much later. When I was younger I still wanted to believe love was a meritocracy and preferential treatment would be given to those who deserved it, or had already suffered so much. It makes me sad now to think of how naïve I was.

I wish more than anything that I could go back in time knowing what I know now. I'd do everything differently. I know you've got a dog. I've seen photographs of it on your desk during our weekly sessions. So you'll know that when you take a dog for a walk and it runs off, you're supposed to stay where you are or walk off in the other direction. If you run after them, you'll never catch them. But the more Alex and Carl and, eventually, Julie, pulled away from me, the closer to them I tried to get. I tried on Julie's clothes and make-up, wanting to know how it felt to be her, to feel safe*. I spied on the boys to see how they talked and acted when no one else was around. I think I was looking for the magic key that would let me into the inner sanctum of family life. I didn't know until the hearing, when a social worker read out Julie's statement, how nervous my behaviour made them. It did hurt, though, that word – 'creepy'. If I could see them again, I'd try to explain how completely lost I felt. I saw a movie once where an astronaut made a wrong move and ended up spinning out into space, and the idea of it made me sick, eternally free-floating in the darkness. That's why I tried to cling to Julie and the twins despite the myriad of tiny rejections. Because the other option, the lonely free-wheeling through space option, was unbearable.*

Chapter Twenty-eight

Nina

Nina increasingly felt as if her entire life was like her little Fiat Panda, zigzagging down a steep hill with only a set of malfunctioning brakes between her and certain disaster. She had no idea where Mark was now. And she didn't care. Their row had followed its usual course. She'd gone home and demanded to know where he'd been the previous night and why Mr Angelis's nephew was now sporting a shining black eye. First there'd been the denials. 'Nothing to do with me. I went for a walk to clear my head.' Then, after she pushed and pushed, had come the concession: 'Okay. I went to talk to him. But it was only talking. I swear it.' After that the admission of a scuffle: 'It was self-defence. That's all. He came at me. I had no choice.' The righteous justification: 'I was only trying to protect you. I know how much this business means to you. Everything I do is for you.' Then the anger: 'He was bang out of order, Nina. He called you a bitch. Why do you always blame me? He was right. You *are* a bitch.'

Finally, worst of all, the self-pity phase: 'I'm useless. I'm a waste of space. I can't do anything right. You're better off without me. I'm going to find a cliff to jump off. Or maybe I'll just hang myself from a tree. No one would miss me. I'm a burden to you.' Then he'd crashed through the door out into the night.

Usually Nina caved at this phase, leaving it for an hour and then calling to make sure he was still alive, repeating the calls with increasing panic if he didn't pick up, on one occasion begging the local police to cruise around the neighbourhood to check he hadn't followed through with his threats. She'd end up leaving sobbing voicemail messages on his phone: 'Just come home. I love you. Come home.'

Well, not this time. After Mark had slammed out of the house, telling her she'd never see him again, not alive anyway, she had slid the bolts across the front door so he couldn't come back in, poured herself two fingers of neat vodka, which was all that was in the fridge, and FaceTimed her sister, Katie, back home in England. And when Katie had said, 'It's enough now, Nina,' she hadn't bothered to protest. Afterwards, she'd switched off her phone and taken one of the sleeping pills she'd bought over the internet from some pseudo pharmacy in the US and gone to sleep. And if there were bangs on the door in the night, or drunken yelling through the windows, she had ascribed it to her dream and slept on.

Now she felt groggy with the after-effects of the pill, and filled with apprehension about what would happen if she didn't get some money to the Angelis family. She'd tried to access her British bank account the previous night, but the wifi had been down (so what's new?). All she could do now was hope the payment had come through from Lucy Collins.

Heading out to her car, she stopped to double-lock the front door and when she turned around again, her heart plummeted. Mr Angelis and his two sons stood blocking her path, their expressions hard and set. Still, Mr Angelis was polite as ever when he addressed her, his large hangdog eyes with their absurdly thick black lashes brown pools of sincerity.

'We look for your husband, Mrs Foster.'

'I'm afraid he isn't here.'

Nina's mouth was dry as dust and her smile felt tight and unnatural as she gestured towards the empty space where Mark usually parked his old motorbike.

'That is a pity. I like you, Mrs Foster. You work hard, as I do. And this is why I know you will understand how important it is that bills should be paid. I have a family. People who depend on me. If it was just myself, of course, it would be different.'

Mr Angelis shrugged his slight shoulders in a 'what can you do?' gesture. The larger of his sons – Nina had occasionally wondered if he was quite all there – moved his own shoulders up and down in imitation.

'I know you work on a wedding this weekend at the Paradise View,' Mr Angelis went on. 'Such a beautiful hotel. Some members of my own family work there. It would be a pity for you and for your happy couple if something goes wrong at this wedding. Imagine how it would be for your business. These are difficult times.'

'Pardon? What are you saying?'

But Mr Angelis had already turned and headed back along the road, walking unhurriedly in his dainty leather shoes, flanked by his two silent sons. A few yards away, he stopped and turned.

'Oh, Mrs Foster? I almost forgot,' he said, slapping his head with his hand as if in frustration at his own stupidity and smiling at her complicitly. 'When your husband returns, please pass on a message to him. Please tell him that if he puts one finger on anyone in my family again, he is a dead man.'

Chapter Twenty-nine

Nina

By the time Nina arrived at the hotel, she'd just about got her breathing back under control.

It would be all right. This was Greece. One of the great ancient civilizations. Mr Angelis was just trying to scare her. And doing a pretty good job, she had to admit. But that was just what men did, wasn't it? Some men, anyway. Mark was the same, full of bluster and macho posturing, but he'd never act on it. An image of the waiter's glossy black eye flashed into her mind and she shut it down firmly. Everything would be fine. Lucy's bank transfer would have gone through to her account so she could pay Mr Angelis his first instalment. The wedding would go off without a hitch. Mark would limp home intact and contrite. The business would prosper, and sooner or later she'd have enough money to go home. She missed her sister and her friends and gathering together to watch *Bake Off* or to compare notes on how they were getting on with Couch to 5K. She missed feeling like she belonged.

She couldn't log on to the hotel wifi until she was in the lobby, so she first had to have a chat with the receptionist about the weather – so hot! – and whether the condition of the road up to the hotel was getting worse: yes! Then a guest she'd once chatted to by the pool, a middle-aged woman with a husband in tow with whom Nina had never seen her exchange two words, engaged her in conversation about how long she'd been living in Greece and how easy it had been to acclimatize. 'I wish I had the courage to do what you've done,' she said wistfully, and Nina had to bite back the words 'Be careful what you wish for.'

Finally, she managed to extricate herself. Dropping down into a white leather armchair in the corner of the lobby, she painstakingly logged into the internet banking app for her UK account. She remembered her sister trying to convince her once about the value of positive visualization, and while the account details were uploading she visualized her statement showing a healthy positive balance. An unhealthy positive balance would have been enough. But when the little wheel finally stopped whirring round, even before her brain had registered the true state of her current account, the sick feeling in her stomach told her that no money had been paid in over the last few days.

Through the plate-glass doors she saw Jason and Gil on loungers by the pool, each lost in whatever was blaring through their headphones. Normally, she'd never have approached a client so publicly to talk about money, but these were desperate times.

'I wonder if I could have a quiet word,' she said, crouching down next to Jason's lounger. Looking up she caught Gil's eye and smiled to show there was nothing wrong, hoping he couldn't see how much effort that smile cost her.

When she told the groom-to-be about the non-appearing funds, he looked aghast.

'I'm so sorry, Nina. Honestly, Lucy's brain is all over the place this week, the amount of planning she's put into everything. She must have just totally forgotten. Let me sort it out here and now.'

He sat up and swiped his phone from the table next to his sunbed.

'I hope I can remember the log-in details to the joint account. It's Lucy who's been sorting out all the wedding stuff. I've just left her to it, which was probably a bit dickish of me.'

He jabbed at the onscreen keyboard and frowned.

'Crap. Password incorrect. Let's try this one.'

Again, no success. He tried again.

'If it's not this one, it'll lock me out. Fingers crossed.'

Nina, still crouching uncomfortably, hoped her anxiety didn't show in her face.

'Eureka!'

Oh, thank God.

'Right. I'll just transf— What? That can't be right. It says we're over our overdraft, but that's not possible because we've both been putting half our salaries in for the last two months and . . . that's weird.'

Jason's always ruddy complexion had deepened into a maroon shade and his fair eyebrows were knitted together.

'Everything all right, bruv?' asked Gil, extracting his headphones from his ears.

'There's no money in the joint account to pay Nina because Lucy hasn't paid her share in.'

'Well, that's easily cleared up, isn't it?' said Gil. 'There's been some cock-up and Lucy's money didn't get transferred over. Soon as she gets back from shopping she can get online and sort it out. Happy days.'

'Yeah, you're right,' said Jason. But Nina didn't like the way he kept staring at the numbers on the screen with that puzzled expression, as if trying to figure something out.

Therapy Journal, Week 9

Harry once told me that marriage is like a car windscreen – the tiniest chink weakens the glass and can cause the whole thing to shatter. With the benefit of hindsight, I can see that Uncle Adrian was in an impossible position. Although I was his family in one sense, I was also part of a past he'd turned his back on. I was the family he'd rejected. Julie and the twins were the family he'd chosen. There was really only ever going to be one outcome. Yet at the time I really thought he might choose me. I did everything he asked of me. I worked hard at school, even though I wasn't a natural academic and had missed so much of the basics that I now lagged way behind my peers. I started learning the piano because I knew how much he liked music, and practised assiduously, even making a paper keyboard so I could carry on practising upstairs in my room when the twins complained about the noise.

So when he came to find me in my room, that day a couple of weeks after I turned fourteen, I felt a tingle of excitement. I thought he might be coming to ask me if I wanted to go on another visit to Mummy or was even just wanting a private chat away from the others. He sat down on the bed and patted the mattress next to him.

'How would you like to go on a summer camp for a couple of weeks in August?' he asked me. 'It'll be all kids your age, and you build forts and rafts and cook for yourselves and stay up till all hours singing songs around the fire. Doesn't that sound good?'

I nodded slowly – even though it didn't sound good at all – but I knew there was something he wasn't telling me. 'But I'd rather stay here with you,' I said.

Uncle Adrian looked away then. We were sitting on my duvet with its daisy-pattern cover that I'd long since outgrown and he plucked at the fabric with his strong, square hands as if he were trying to pick the flowers clean off. 'The thing is, we'll be away. We thought – your auntie Julie and I – that we'd take the boys to Disneyland while you were gone. I know that's too babyish for you, which is why we booked you into this camp.'

'But I'd much rather go to Disneyland.' My hurt feelings overcame my natural tendency to acquiesce.

Uncle Adrian's fingers stopped plucking at the duvet cover and instead came to cover my own.

'It's just that we think it will be good for you to get away on your own, have a taste of independence and . . .'

I knew what he was going to say even before he said it. In a sense, I'd always known from the very first day I set foot in the house.

'To be honest, we need a little family time on our own.'

~

I know you want me to talk about what happened next. I know you want me to own what I did. And I appreciate what you say about not judging. Hurt people hurt people. You've told me often enough. But there are some places I'm just not ready to go yet.

Chapter Thirty

Hazel

The returning shoppers were in fractious mood, everyone too hot and already regretting their impulse purchases. Hazel looked glumly at the black, floppy-brimmed hat she'd been persuaded to buy in one of the little boutiques. 'It's very Audrey Hepburn,' Cora had assured her, and Hazel had imagined wearing it to the wedding, looking sophisticated and coolly glamorous. But on the way home in the hot, sticky taxi – no air-conditioning, as Zoe insisted on having the window open, claiming that otherwise she'd be sick – she'd taken the hat out of the bag and realized that it wouldn't go with her dress at all and remembered about being unemployed and wished that she could return to the shop and get a refund.

She'd been hoping to have their suite to herself when she got back. She needed some time away from everyone else. She hadn't appreciated before they came how claustrophobic it would be, spending every waking moment in a group, every decision taken by committee, every conversation liable to be hijacked by people other than the original participants. Never mind the dynamics of the whole thing. Who wasn't getting on with whom, who had to be treated with kid gloves. It was exhausting.

So she probably was less enthusiastic than she should have been when she let herself in and saw Dom once again lounging on the bed in a towel, reading his book.

'I thought you'd be down at the beach. Weren't you the one back home going on about how you couldn't wait to be doing your two-mile swim in the sea rather than in a horrible chlorinated pool with plasters floating around in it?'

Dom looked wounded.

'I was in the sea earlier, but my ear got blocked. It's the most irritating thing, I can't seem to get the bloody water out of it.' He stuck a finger in his right ear then cocked his head to one side and shook it violently. Then he stared at the finger he'd just withdrawn. 'See,' he said. 'Nothing at all.'

Hazel, who just wanted to take off the sweaty clothes she'd been wearing all day and lie like a starfish in the exact place Dom was currently occupying, felt a fresh rush of annoyance.

'I'm going to take a walk along the cliffs,' she announced, surprising herself.

She threw down her bags crossly, pulled on the silly new hat and headed out of the door, but she hadn't gone more than two steps down the hallway when Dom appeared behind her, wearing the shorts he'd hastily scrambled into.

'Wait up, darling, I'll come with you. I've been meaning to explore along there since we arrived. What in Christ's name have you got on your head?'

Hazel glared at him but could not think of a good reason to turn back.

They descended the steps from the swimming-pool terrace in silence, setting out along the path that led around the top of the cliffs that enclosed the small bay. It was hot and Hazel was glad of her hat, taking a savage pleasure in seeing the sweat already beading on her husband's forehead. Below them, they could clearly see two of the three little coves that made up the bay, the outer ones accessible only by climbing over rocks from the middle one. Hazel saw a lone figure sitting on a towel and recognized it as Vivian. She tried to feel sorry for the woman, down there on her own, but there was something about her that made sympathy hard.

'This is lovely, isn't it?' Dom took her hand.

It *was* rather lovely, in truth. The path itself was part red dust, part stone, fringed on either side by thickets of wiry green bushes interspersed with wildflowers in all colours – sprays of yellow Spanish broom, a rich abundance of wild valerian with its clusters of tiny purply-pink flowers, blowsy red poppies and delicate white daisies. On their left was a low bank of vegetation, beyond which the cliff fell away into the sea, today a patchwork quilt of turquoise and emerald, sapphire and navy blue. On the right, once they'd skirted the hotel wall, there were trees mixed in with the undergrowth – fig and pine, and behind them the odd cypress pushing its green needles up towards the sky. And everywhere the smells of wild sage and thyme, jasmine and honeysuckle.

The path zigzagged around an ancient olive tree and Hazel dropped Dom's hand to duck under its twisted branches. The other side opened out on to a clearing covered in low, rough gorse, where the path forked. The upper fork headed inland – Hazel supposed it would eventually join the road leading to the next town – but they stayed on the lower path, curving around the bay. From here they could look back and see the three little white-shingled coves, ringed by grey rocks, and beyond them the gleaming white facade of the Paradise View.

'Shall we stay here for ever?' Dom said when they stopped to admire the view. He put his arm around her shoulders and tried to pull her in for a hug, but she resisted.

'It's too hot. Anyway, you'd go bonkers within days here. No pub. No Bristol City matches. No day trips to London to skive off with your old mates. You know, it's a good job I'm not the jealous sort.' She'd said it on purpose, to gauge his reaction, but when, still encompassed by his arm, she felt him stiffen, her first response was numb surprise. *Oh my God*, she thought. *It might actually be true.*

'Do you want to tell me about that text message from the other day? The one you deleted?'

Dom kept his arm around her, so she couldn't see his face without twisting around.

'What are you talking about, darling? What message?'

Hazel wondered if she would regret this, once Dom told her whatever perfectly reasonable explanation lay behind the text, but something made her plough on.

'The one that said, *I can explain.* First you didn't mention it. Then you deleted it.'

'Hang on a minute.' Now, finally, he did pull away. 'Did you go through my phone?'

She knew him so well. Knew his tendency to deflect guilt about one thing by fostering a sense of righteous indignation about another.

Now, in place of the numbness came a dreadful exhaustion, her limbs heavy lead pipes she was dragging around.

'Tell me,' she said, sinking down on to a low rock.

'I don't know what—'

'*Tell me!*'

'OK. There is . . . was . . . someone,' he said in a hoarse voice. 'But nothing happened. We just chatted, that's all.'

'Bollocks.'

'What's the point in me saying anything if you're not going to believe me?'

He was trying to summon his aggrieved tone, but the hollowness in his voice gave him away.

'Have you slept with her?'

'Oh, for fuck's sake, Hazel. What do you take me for?'

Still that giveaway, tinny note running through his words.

'I'll ask you again. Have you slept with her?'

'No!'

'Look at me while you say that.'

Dom glanced at her, then almost immediately away again. When he spoke next, his voice was as gravelly as the path on which they stood.

'Just once. I'm so sorry, darling. It just happened once.'

Hazel felt strangely unmoved, as if this were a scene she was watching on television, she and Dom actors performing their lines. So here's where the wife character becomes hysterical, she thought, and yet she didn't feel hysterical, rather as if she'd been encased suddenly in ice, all emotion frozen.

'Who is she?'

'No one you know. I met her at the gym. It was just once, I swear. Years ago.'

'Bollocks.'

Hazel couldn't remember the last time she'd used the word 'bollocks', but now it seemed to be the only response she had. But really, did he think she was entirely stupid?

'If it was years ago, why is she messaging you to explain something while you're *at your daughter's fucking wedding*?'

Now the anger was coming. She felt it like the rumbling of a distant volcano, her neurons and synapses tingling into life.

Dom reached out for her. The feel of his hands on her bare skin was like being branded by a scalding iron.

'Don't you dare touch me!' She jumped to her feet.

'Where are you going?'

'Away from you. I need to think.'

'It's completely over, darling. I swear it.'

Again he reached out for her, looking for that physical connection. The nerve of him.

'Just fuck off, Dom!' Hazel yelled, stepping backwards. To her horror, rather than the firm earth of the path, her foot encountered something soft and spongy that, as her weight bore down on it, seemed to be ominously giving way. Panicked, she glanced behind her, realizing too late that in her haste to evade Dom she'd come way too close to the edge of the cliff, where the wildflowers and gorse bushes into which she'd stepped disguised the sheer drop down to the beach below.

Time slowed, as if this moment of nightmare were something to be savoured. As Hazel's arms windmilled in the empty air, trying to stop herself falling backwards, she could hear the soft coo of a dove or wood pigeon in the olive tree and her nostrils were filled with the peppery, citrusy scent of sweet marjoram.

Her stomach seemed to dislodge itself, rising up to meet the scream building in her throat. She closed her eyes . . . and felt hands grasp her around her shoulders, yanking her away from the edge.

'Oh God, Hazel. Oh fuck. I thought you were . . .'

When she opened her eyes, there was Dom, panting as if he'd run a marathon, his cheeks wet with tears.

She shoved him aside, every nerve fizzing with adrenalin.

She'd almost died. Because of him.

'You complete arsehole,' she spat.

A curious thing happened then – Dom appeared to be folding in on himself, as if he'd been punctured, sinking down on to a nearby flat rock, and she turned away, only to hear him shouting after her.

'It's not easy, you know. Having to rely on your wife for handouts. I can't afford a pint unless it comes from you.'

She whirled around.

'So it's my fault, that's what you're saying?'

'I'm only trying to explain how, in the past, I've felt . . . *unmanned*.'

Once more Hazel turned her back on him in disgust. She often felt as if she experienced life too much through the filter of her thoughts, rather than directly through her senses, but as she made her way back along the path, skirting around the olive tree, a flame spread through her entire body from her feet up to the crown of her head, until she was a blazing column of red-hot rage.

Chapter Thirty-one

Lucy

'Don't yell at me.'

'I'm not yelling, babe, I'm just asking you why you didn't transfer your share into the joint account this month.'

'Yes, well, you're asking in a really aggressive way.'

The truth was, Jason was barely raising his voice, but Lucy needed to buy herself time to think up an explanation. And, until then, defensiveness seemed the best option. They were in the jacuzzi on their terrace. Or rather, Lucy was in the jacuzzi, after flopping straight into their private plunge pool on getting back from the exhausting shopping trip. Jason, who'd arrived back in the room sometime later, was standing next to her head, fully dressed in shorts and a T-shirt, which put her at a disadvantage, Lucy couldn't help feeling.

'You have no idea how much goes into planning a wedding, Jase. Not just this – the hotel, the ceremony, Nina, all those spa treatments – but also the party back home. There were so many extra things we didn't budget for. All that paperwork that needed translating so we could get married here, and authorizing Nina to register it all at the notary's office after we've gone back. It's never-ending, but I didn't want to come to you because you made it really obvious you wanted me to deal with everything.'

'That's not fair. You *wanted* to do it all. I kept offering to help, but you told me you had a vision for how this whole thing was going to go and I'd only get in the way.'

It was true. Lucy had been planning this wedding in her head for so many years she hadn't been able to relinquish control over a single detail, hadn't wanted to.

'I can't believe some of the payments that have gone out of this account,' Jason went on. 'Why the hell do we need a photographer *and* a cinematographer? What even is a wedding cinematographer?'

'Oh my God! I don't believe this. You're hands off the whole time while I'm killing myself organizing this thing. Then you wait until my wedding week, the most important week of my life, to start giving me a hard time.'

Jason looked so upset Lucy felt a hot pang of shame. She knew this was her fault. She'd overspent. Massively. She felt the weight of the money she'd paid out like a brick in her stomach. But what could she do about it now? All she'd wanted was for this week to be perfect. She'd always known there'd be a financial reckoning, but she'd just hoped it could hold off until after they got home. Was that really so selfish of her?

'Listen, babe. We've got to pay Nina, so why don't you transfer what you can from your personal account now, just to tide us over until we get back and sort it all out properly?' Jason took her nearest hand in both of his, stroking the top of it gently in the way she usually loved. 'I'm sorry. You're right, I should have shouldered more of the responsibility for organizing this wedding. I should have seen you were struggling. Transfer whatever you've got left and, as soon as we're home, I'll see about extending my overdraft. I'll put in more hours to cover it.'

'I can't.'

'What do you mean?'

'There's no money left in my account either.'

'Then you'll just have to go overdrawn.'

'I've used up all my overdraft.'

Jason dropped her hand and sat down heavily on the tiled terrace.

'Where did the money go?'

Tears stung the backs of Lucy's eyes. This was not how it was supposed to be. This week was supposed to be all about her and Jason cementing their bond in the company of their family and friends. Not arguing – about money, of all things.

'On the wedding. You've no idea how much it all costs. The dress, the shoes, the treatments.'

'Treatments?'

'Just a tiny bit of Botox and fillers. Hardly anything, really.'

Now the tears were brimming over, clumping in her eyelash extensions and running down her face. She wished she could take it back, all the money she'd lavished on things she didn't need. It was just she got so carried away. All those photographs in the bridal magazines, Jasmine and her 'helpful' suggestions.

'I'm sorry,' she sobbed wretchedly. Normally, Jason would have caved at this point of an argument and be comforting her. He hated to see her cry.

Instead, he sat back on his heels and stared at her, as if seeing her for the first time. His eyes scanned her face, from her threaded eyebrows to her chin, where the cosmetic technician had injected filler to 'give it a bit more shape'.

Then he got up to go inside, stopping at the open doors to say:

'You know, I preferred how you looked before.'

Therapy Journal, Week 10

You want me to write about my relationship history, but to me a 'relationship' is what Lucy and Jason have. Love. Trust. Connection. *What I had, looking back, was a series of encounters, some lasting longer than others.*

The first older man was a teacher at the new school where I was sent after I had to leave Uncle Adrian's house and ended up in foster care on the other side of the country, with Maeve, a sixty-three-year-old foster mother who'd seen it all before. Jamie was only twenty-six, but when you're fifteen years old, that seems a lifetime away. I was a skinny little thing, practically invisible, but Jamie saw *me. He tossed out nuggets of attention like he was throwing a ball to a dog, and I couldn't catch them fast enough. Now, we know all about grooming, but back then I was only flattered and grateful.*

Harry said I have a Father Complex, but I'll leave the labels up to you. You're the expert, after all.

The affair with Jamie petered out when I went to sixth form, but there were others to take his place. The manager of the gastropub where I worked washing dishes on Friday and Saturday nights, one of my college lecturers when I went to university in Leeds. I knew it wasn't healthy.

In my second year I went out with a boy my own age, determined to break the pattern. His real name was Simon Muggins, but everyone called him Muggsy. There was never any great spark between us, but we had fun together and didn't ask a lot of each other. He invited me to stay with his family over the Easter holidays. Well, thinking back, I probably kind of invited myself. I had nowhere else to be. They lived in a village outside Oxford, in a house made of honey-coloured stone with wisteria over the front door and two geriatric greyhounds. Muggsy was the oldest of three boys, with a headteacher mother and a father who ran a company making bespoke kitchens. When I'd asked him beforehand what his parents were like, he'd been infuriatingly vague: 'OK', and 'normal, I guess'. In real life, his mother was reserved and nervous, filling silences with a high-pitched hum, while his father was fond of the sound of his own voice. But still they were there, every day, in the kitchen, or the living room that they called the Den, or in the garden with its weeping willow tree and ornamental pond. There was never any worry that they might have gone somewhere else in the night or be completely different people at breakfast to the ones they'd been at dinner. So I couldn't understand why Muggsy was so down on them. We ate meals at the house – but then we'd be off seeing his old schoolfriends, or at the pub or the cinema. Anywhere but his house. 'I always forget how much they get on my tits,' he told me. I tried to make up for his off-handedness when we were at home by being extra attentive. I followed his mother around the garden when she was deadheading the flowers and tried to engage his father in conversation about kitchens. I suggested games of cards with his younger brothers that both made excuses to avoid. I broke up with Muggsy on the train back to Leeds. I said I couldn't be with someone who treated his family so badly. He said he wasn't fussed one way or the other.

Still, my social life was OK. Healthy, you might say, all things considered. Yet once a month I'd make the two-hour journey to Norfolk to check on Uncle Adrian and Auntie Julie and the twins. I couldn't afford to be seen, thanks to the court order, but I would take sandwiches and sit on a wall a little way down the street, wearing a baseball cap pulled low. It helped that, if I tucked my hair under, I looked like a boy. I knew it was risky, but I couldn't keep away. That's what family is, though, isn't it? That feeling of being connected, no matter what.

Only when I met Harry did I stop making those monthly pilgrimages. And I know your theory, that he could have been anyone, that I needed someone to plug that huge hole inside me and Harry was the one who happened along. But I disagree. As soon as I met Harry, he became home.

'When you know, you know.' I never understood what people meant by that until I met Harry. That's why I tried so hard to keep us together. Because when you know, you know.

Chapter Thirty-two

Hazel

Down on the terrace by the pool area, Hazel was sipping a large gin and tonic and trying to ignore the row she could hear coming from Gil and Zoe's room. 'You promised to stop,' Gil kept shouting. It sounded as if Zoe was crying, but Hazel couldn't be sure. And no sooner had they gone quiet than Lucy's raised voice came drifting down from the honeymoon suite terrace, followed by Jason's lower register, also sounding more strident than usual. Normally, Hazel would have been worrying what it meant that her daughter and soon-to-be son-in-law were arguing so close to their wedding, but she was too shaken by that scene on the cliffs and the seismic ructions within her own marriage to consider anyone else's.

Her husband – Dom! – had slept with another woman.

The Dom who went to the loo two or three times in the night, stumbling heavily, half asleep, and sneaked her tweezers from her toiletry bag to pluck the stray hairs from his nose. The Dom who always bought the first round, even now money was such a worry, and thought nothing of spending £5 on a loaf of artisan bread that cut the roof of your mouth when you tried to eat it.

This was the Dom who had slept with another woman. Not only slept with her, but quite probably had dinner with her, and gone to the movies, kissed her in the back of a taxi or on a riverbank or in a park or a lift, made arrangements and assignations. Somewhere in the world there was a woman who'd given him her number and waited for him to call, perhaps with butterflies fluttering around her ribcage when she saw his name on the screen. A woman who might have had her legs and bikini line waxed just for him, maybe bought new underwear, or dreamed of him, perhaps even imagined a future with him. What an absolute bastard. What a *cunt*.

She had that sensation of being watched, that soft tippy-tapping on the back of the neck, but when she looked up, there was no one there.

On the next table, the Other Bride, as they all now referred to her, was talking animatedly into her phone. 'Up half the night being sick,' she was saying. 'He'd better recover by tomorrow. He'd just better.' Hazel took another slug of gin.

Yet . . . this was Dom. Her Dom. The girls' father.

She'd transferred the number she'd scribbled down from Dom's phone from the paper where she'd first scrawled it to her contacts list, and now she got her phone out of her bag and stared at it. A UK mobile number. It gave nothing away.

'That looks good.'

Hazel looked up, startled. She'd been so intent on her screen she hadn't noticed Zoe approaching, barefoot and wearing a messily tied sarong as if she'd left the room in a hurry. The whites of her eyes were tinged with pink.

'Sorry?'

'The drink. I could murder a gin. Do you mind?'

Without waiting for a reply, Zoe plonked herself down next to Hazel and started looking around for a waiter. 'Excuse me,' she said loudly into the open door of the bar area, not even pausing for breath before loudly repeating: 'Excuse me!'

The waiter appeared, the lovely young man who usually smiled at all the guests. Today, though, he seemed subdued and there was a hint of purple bruising on his cheekbone.

Hazel tried to disguise how very much she *did* mind as Zoe ordered her drink and the waiter disappeared back into the bar. Usually, she was quite tolerant of Gil's wife. After years of being cast in the role of Wise Elder at work, doling out tissues to younger colleagues who felt overwhelmed or undermined or who were going through break-ups or family 'stuff', she recognized that behind Zoe's abrasive surface lay a troubled young woman.

Today, though, she just wanted to be left alone.

Luckily, Zoe turned out to be in reflective mood.

'I miss my baby,' she said sadly, taking out her phone to show Hazel her screensaver – a photograph of a smiling little girl in a fairy outfit with lots of black, curly hair and no teeth.

'She's gorgeous,' said Hazel obligingly.

'She's not just beautiful on the outside, but on the inside, too – do you know what I mean? And so advanced for her age.'

Hazel took another sip of her drink so she wouldn't have to respond.

'I know the other girls – Lucy and Jessica and Shelly – think I'm over the top. One of these tiger mothers who can't bear to be separated from her child.'

Hazel didn't bother telling her that she didn't think that's exactly what a tiger mother was.

'The thing is, though, Hazel, they haven't got kids, so they don't understand. You and me, though, we know what it's like to have a daughter and feel like you want to do everything in the world to protect her. I don't want Anastasia to go through what I went through.'

Well. Where did that come from? Hazel glanced over at Zoe in that sarong, tracing her daughter's face with one of her long, shellacked fingernails, and her heart ached at her vulnerability. *She's still a child herself*, she thought, seeing the plump curve of Zoe's cheek. At any other time, she might have probed gently to find out what Zoe was talking about, the dark secret that she was clearly wanting to confess.

But the thought of Dom with another woman was still taking up all the thinking space in her head and she found she couldn't manage more than a generic: 'Of course you want to protect her. You're her mother.'

Even as the platitude was coming out of her mouth she was ashamed of it. The girl was offering an opening, an invitation to forge some sort of intimacy, and she was choosing to ignore it. But her churning thoughts of Dom wouldn't allow for anything else.

'It isn't easy, you know,' Zoe blurted out now, the rejection clearly stinging. 'Being the outsider here. Lucy only invited me because of Gil, and Jess hates my guts. That's why, sometimes, the things I say come out wrong. It's nerves. That's all it is. But no one makes any allowances. They can be so bitchy sometimes. Sorry, I know they're your daughters. But you must have noticed.'

Hazel didn't know what to say. Should she defend Jess and Lucy, or sympathize with Zoe? The truth was, she couldn't think about any of it. As she'd been sitting here, the numb calm she'd been trying to cultivate since she came back from that hellish clifftop walk had given way to a building tsunami of feeling, and now her head and heart were full to bursting with her own as yet unexplored emotions, stuffed inside her like a sleeping bag into its case.

She stood up abruptly, her chair making a loud scraping sound on the whitewashed concrete floor.

'Sorry, Zoe, I've just remembered something I forgot to do. Will you excuse me?'

Zoe looked up, surprise giving way to hurt then ending in a kind of knowing nod, as if this was what she'd expected all along. Hurrying away, guilt wrapped itself like an unwelcome scarf around Hazel's neck. She hadn't been kind.

There was a little white chapel attached to the hotel, a basic one-room structure made from adobe with a dusty, blue-painted door and, inside, a simple white-painted moulded shelf on which a single fat candle burned in front of a gold shrine tucked into a recess.

Inside, it was cool and dark, and Hazel's eyes took a few seconds to adjust to being out of the sun. There was nowhere to sit, so she leaned against the back wall as she took out her phone. She called up the screen where she'd keyed in the number of the missed call on Dom's phone.

The number of her husband's mistress.

How unthinkable that sounded.

When she held her finger over the number a message box came up with the option to call, and she stared at it for a few moments. Through the open door, she heard the screeching of the gulls flying over the beach below and the faint clattering of the kitchen staff preparing for the dinner service. Life paused for a moment, just as it had done back there on the cliff, teetering on the edge of what had gone before – the known – and a shadowy, uncertain future.

She pressed call.

Hazel held her breath, waiting for the number to connect, the silence amplifying the pulse of blood in the ear that pressed against the cool surface of her phone. There was a fly in the chapel with her and she flapped it away with her free hand.

From somewhere in the ether came a ringtone. Hazel imagined a faceless woman glancing at her screen, seeing Dom's name flashing up there with whatever accompanying emotions that might bring.

The phone rang on, and Hazel's stomach muscles unclenched, acknowledging it was not now going to be answered, surrendering to the hypnotic rhythm of it until she was almost disappointed when a robotic voice cut in, telling her to leave a message after the tone.

She clicked end call without speaking. And stood for a moment, leaning against the wall, watching the flame of the candle flicker in the gloom.

She wondered whether the mystery woman was at this very moment studying her phone, perhaps listening to the click of the otherwise silent voicemail. And wondering what it meant that, when the phone rang, it hadn't been the double ringtones of a British phone but the long, single beeps of an international call.

Therapy Journal, Week 11

Finally, you're letting me talk about Harry. The hard part will be getting me to shut up again! Here's how we met. I was doing a lot of internet dating. It suited me to have the option to study a profile before committing to any interaction and to shut down communication instantly without feeling awkward or hanging around out of politeness or pity. I usually had three or four men who I was chatting to at any one time, but I rarely met up with them in person. Real life is so often disappointing.

I'd been talking to Harry for a month or so, online and over the phone. There was no real spark there, but I liked him and his stories about negotiating post-divorce life with his ex-wife and his three young children. I wasn't in a particularly good place. Mummy had died a few months before from an overdose of prescription drugs and, though I hadn't seen her for over a year, it still hurt more than I'd imagined. By that stage Mummy had been living on her own for six years in a rented flat that she paid for by inputting data for a pharmaceutical company three days a week. But she was broken into so many pieces she wasn't really a person any more, just a collection of dust in an envelope of skin. Also, it was coming up to the eleven-year anniversary of leaving Uncle Adrian's house for the last time, staring back through the window of the police car with my things in a black bin liner on the seat next to me.

So I agreed to meet Harry mostly to stop myself sitting at home dredging up the past rather than because I thought it might lead to anything. We'd arranged to meet in a pub near Paddington Station that had a small outside patio in the back. I always arrived early for my first meeting with a new date. I know lots of women prefer a late entrance, but I liked to be already installed. It made me feel more in control. Wherever possible, I would seat myself somewhere apart from the main area where I could watch the door unobserved. Not so that I could make a quick exit if I didn't like the look of my date – although I'm ashamed to say I did this once or twice – but so I could get the measure of him before we began talking.

It was rush hour, so the main bar was crowded, but I spotted a free table by the wall with a view of anyone crossing from the front door to the back patio. The table had a half-finished pint on it, as if the previous occupant had left in a hurry. I was leafing through the Evening Standard, *with one eye on the door, when I became conscious of someone standing by my shoulder.*

'Sorry, but you're in my seat.'

I looked up in surprise, and there he was, his nose twitching in that way it does, as if he didn't know whether to be amused or annoyed. I don't know whether it was because I was seated, but he seemed enormous, as if he filled up all the space in the room. I looked around for another table, but they were all full and so, really, what could he do but tell me to stay and then slip into the seat opposite? After that, we started chatting, and soon we were bonding over a shared loathing of cheese-and-onion crisps and exchanging raised eyebrows over a woman on a nearby table talking into her phone and ignoring her toddler, who was banging his spoon on the table as loudly as he could. 'Bring back smoking,' Harry said. 'Never any kids in pubs before the smoking ban.' I didn't mention that I couldn't remember a time when the smoking ban hadn't existed.

Did I know he was married? Of course. That was his appeal. I could never love a man who didn't have a family. Family is everything.

I'm sorry to say, when I saw my original date – the real Harry – coming through the door, late and flustered, I sank down in my seat, and when, eventually, he came over and tentatively introduced himself, I pretended I didn't know what he was talking about. 'I don't know any Michelle,' I said. I'm not proud of that. It's so important to be kind.

After that, Dom was always Harry to me. It was our private joke.

Chapter Thirty-three

Shelly

The words of the wedding invitation, which were anyway already imprinted on Shelly's brain through having read them so many times, now swam across the white card in a line of blurry black dots.

Reluctantly, she removed the glasses, blinking until the room came back into focus, and replaced the invitation on the bedside table. She lay back on the bed, smoothing down the cherry-silk sarong she'd wrapped herself in. She knew she'd taken a risk with the sarong, but it had been too tempting when Hazel left it by the pool to go and read in the shade. She turned the glasses over in her hands. Purple and surprisingly cheap-looking. Shelly had been a bit disappointed by that at first. But then she'd decided it was actually one of the things she liked most about Hazel, that she lived in a great big house but had no airs at all. She'd buy off-the-peg glasses and wear a swimming costume that had gone baggy in places and give zero fucks about it.

They were just nice people, her and Dom. Like Lucy. Just a nice family.

After getting dressed for breakfast, she folded up the sarong and hid it in the back of the wardrobe. Her heart had been in her mouth the night before when Lucy banged on her door, her lovely face a mess of snot and tears. Even as Shelly had been letting her in, she'd been panicking in case she'd left something incriminating on view, even though she knew deep down she hadn't. She'd always been neat to the point of obsession, a product of all those years of trying to please first her mother, then Adrian and Julie.

'Jason and I had the most awful row about money. God, Shell, I've never seen him so angry.' It had taken over an hour to calm Lucy down. It wasn't a crime to want your wedding to be perfect, Shelly had reassured her. Any bride would. And who could blame her for doing everything she could to look her best. Not that she wasn't gorgeous exactly as she was. As soon as Jason saw her get off the boat on Saturday, he'd forget all of this.

As Shelly talked, she'd found herself falling into a kind of contented trance. This here was everything she'd wanted. Sitting up with Lucy, talking her down. Just like a sister would do. Unless they were Jess.

Stepping out on to the restaurant terrace for breakfast this morning, Shelly felt the usual fluttering of anxiety mixed with excitement seeing Dom and Hazel already seated. When Dom had called her the day before she'd been so relieved, seeing his name on her screen. Finally, she'd have a chance to explain that he had nothing to fear from her, but he hadn't let her speak. Instead, he'd ranted at her, some garbled story about Hazel and a cliff-top. Eventually, she'd understood that Hazel had found out he'd slept with someone. 'But she must never know it's you. Understand? I think she's got your number – or whoever's number you're using to get round the fact I blocked you – so if your phone goes, don't answer. Repeat. Do. Not. Answer. I don't know what sick game you're playing, *Michelle*, but if you try to destroy my family, you will regret it. Capito?'

Capito? Shelly had only ever heard people on old films say that. Once, she might have gently teased Dom about it, but he gave her no chance, nor would he allow her to explain that she had no intention of hurting his family. That she *loved* his family or that she'd changed her number when she switched phone provider – there was no big conspiracy. When her phone rang again an hour later, she'd known instantly it was Hazel and pressed her fingers to the screen as it flashed up that unfamiliar number, wanting to feel that connection, even if she couldn't answer it.

Glancing up from the table, Hazel gave Shelly a weak smile, while Dom looked elsewhere, as he always did. It hurt, of course. But it wasn't as if she wasn't used to rejection.

Lucy wasn't looking her best. Her eyes were all puffy and her skin, which had been glowing yesterday after the clay exfoliation treatment at the spa, looked blotchy and grey.

It was the day of the wedding rehearsal. Shelly knew Lucy had planned it as a coming together after these last days of different activities. The idea was that they'd all be relaxed and happy. There'd be no pressure, as it was just the rehearsal, and they'd be joking together over breakfast – a perfectly bonded group with Lucy and Jason holding court. Yet this morning they were barely speaking to each other.

On the next table, the Other Bride was having her bridal breakfast, ahead of her wedding later that day. Even though she was wearing a dress that erred just on the wrong side of tarty, she looked incandescent with happiness, clinging on to her groom's arm and pausing every few mouthfuls of cereal to pull him towards her in a long, lingering kiss, each one greeted with loud whoops by the other members of her party. Her groom, who Shelly understood had been sick all the previous day, seemed pale but did his best to join in. It was quite touching, really, to see the effort he was making not to let his fiancée down.

The exuberance of the Other Wedding Party threw into sharp relief the heavy atmosphere that hung over their own table. Here, the only people talking were Jason and Cora, who were holding a private conversation in low murmurs that no one else could hear.

'Probably telling Mummy what a spendaholic he's about to marry.'

Lucy looked wretched as she recounted to Shelly how she'd got back to the honeymoon suite after leaving Shelly the night before and Jason had been asleep 'or pretending to be asleep', so she'd lain there staring at his back and going over all the frivolous purchases she'd made that she wished she hadn't. In the morning, he'd hardly spoken to her until, finally, she'd cracked and burst out crying, apologizing over and over, explaining that she just wanted the wedding to be special.

'And do you know what he said, Shell? Oh God, it just about killed me. He said that if we'd got married in Bath registry office on a rainy Monday afternoon with no guests at all, it would have been special to him. He said he doesn't give a shit about canapés or flower arrangements. He only cares about me. Then he went on about letting Nina down, and all the people who depend on her, like the florists and the caterers. He accused me of risking their livelihoods over champagne and injections of poison into my face.' Her voice broke on the last word and Shelly moved closer so that her arm was pressing against her friend's.

'Maybe he's asking his mum for a loan,' Shelly suggested, gazing over at Jason and Cora's bent heads.

Lucy groaned. 'That's all I need. For Cora to have another reason to think I'm not good enough for him, and for the two of them to freeze me out. And as for those two' – Shelly followed her gaze to where Dom and Hazel were standing stiffly and silently at the buffet table – 'you'd think they were at a bloody funeral, not a wedding.'

A shadow fell across the table, making the fine hairs on Shelly's arm stand up. When she looked around,

Vivian was standing behind her, far too close, blocking the early-morning sun.

'What are you lovely young ladies up to today?' Without warning, she reached out to rest her hands on Shelly's bare shoulders and Shelly gave an involuntary shudder.

'It's the wedding rehearsal,' said Lucy flatly.

'That sounds very jolly. Of course, in my day, we didn't have all this fuss. Just turn up, get hitched and have a bloody good party. When did everything get so complicated? So commercialized?'

As she spoke, her claw-like fingers were digging painfully into Shelly's soft skin. Shelly wanted to tell her to stop, but her voice seemed to have dried up in her throat. Instead, she stared mutely ahead to where the two of them were reflected in the stainless-steel coffee pot. The blood in her veins turned icy as she noticed Vivian's deep-set blue-marble eyes fixed greedily on the back of her head, as if she a live monkey at one of those Japanese feasts Shelly had once seen a clip of, and Vivian were about to slice off the top of her skull and gobble up her warm, still pulsing brain.

Chapter Thirty-four

Jess

Gabriel was starting to seriously freak Jess out. He was so vague about everything. She still had no clue what he really did for a living – though, to be fair, someone only had to mention the words 'tech' or 'finance' for her eyes to glaze over. Last night she'd heard him tell Cora he'd had a series of long-term girlfriends – 'serial monogamy is my jam'. But she was sure he'd told her at the start that he never could seem to get the hang of making relationships last. Then there was that thing when her mum had tried to pin him down on which part of Sussex he'd lived in and he'd gone all weird and mumbly.

It wasn't even the fact that he might turn out to be a pathological liar that got her, it was more about how he projected himself as being so wishy-washy and nothingy, as if you could put your hand straight through him, and yet she hadn't forgotten that scene in the bathroom. The unexpected splinter of fear. Then there was the mystery of his having a different name on his passport. When her mum had first brought it up, Jess hadn't even given it a second thought. Loads of people she knew called themselves different names to the ones they'd been given. Her non-binary friend Robyn had been born Esme, and another friend, who'd fallen out with her family, had changed her surname to Primrose, which was the road where she lived. But since Gabriel had shown himself to be so *slippery*, she'd started to wonder if he might have a more sinister motivation.

On the whole, she pretty much ignored him now, except if Gil was watching, when Jess would suddenly fake a deep interest in whatever Gabriel might be saying or doing and lean in to him, throwing her head back and roaring with laughter, whether or not he'd said anything particularly funny. He would sometimes try to talk to her, some boring comment on the weather, or come out with one of his cringeworthy expressions, like the other day, when he was just sitting there on the terrace with his mouth open and his eyes shut and she'd asked him what he was doing and he'd said, 'Oh, just listening to the universe.' She tried to be civil, at least. She did feel some sense of obligation for bringing him. But she'd never been good at hiding her feelings and, on the whole, the two of them gave each other a wide berth. If they'd been two circles in a Venn diagram, the only overlapping section would be the suite, and even there they avoided each other. Luckily, the bathroom had separate doors leading to the bedroom and the living room that could be locked from the inside, which Jess made sure she did. And yes, there were a couple of times she'd forgotten to unlock the other door, leaving Gabriel effectively locked out of the loo, and she'd felt bad about that. But really, he couldn't complain. He was getting a free holiday was the way she saw it.

But last night something else had happened to make her question whether they could go on sharing a space. For once, she'd come back to the room early after talking to one of the waiters round the back of the hotel – the handsome one with the black eye – who'd led her behind the car at the very end of the car park and rolled the fattest spliff she'd ever seen. The suite had been in darkness and she'd assumed she had it to herself, so after opening the doors to the terrace from the bedroom, keeping the light off so the mosquitoes didn't come in, she'd walked through to the living room and opened those doors, too, wanting to get a through draught. For a moment, she'd stood leaning against the doorframe, enjoying the almost cool breeze coming in from the open living-room doors and feeling pleasantly stoned. Then something had alerted her, perhaps a noise or a slight movement, and when she'd whirled around she'd made out, in the shadows in the centre of the room, the pale disc of Gabriel's face, his eyes black holes in the darkness.

'What the FUCK! You scared me.'

'Sorry.' That soft, toneless voice.

'Yeah, well. Goodnight, then.'

She'd walked unsteadily back into her own room and sat on her bed, her heart still thudding, thinking of how he'd watched her in silence without letting her know he was there.

Then she'd got up again and padded softly to the adjoining door between the bedroom and living room and, trying to make as little sound as possible, turned the metal key in the lock.

This morning, lying in bed with the sun streaming in through the slats in the shutters and the sounds of the other guests congregating by the breakfast buffet drifting up from the restaurant terrace, last night's nerves were largely forgotten.

She should write about it! This whole week was perfect fodder for the novel she'd been on the brink of writing for the last couple of years. Working in the bar, life tended to pass in a blur of night-time and booze. She'd finish her shift at 2 a.m. with the adrenalin pumping, and frequently be awake until dawn, when she'd fall asleep and then wake up mid-afternoon, just in time to prepare herself to do it all again. But on holiday in Greece with her family, there were no excuses. She glanced across to her bedside table, where the notebook she lugged around everywhere sat looking authentically battered, although in actual fact it was mostly blank, apart from a few pages where she'd scored the last game of cribbage she'd played. Very underrated, was cribbage.

The sight of the notebook, with its empty, accusing pages, gave her a pain behind her ribs.

There was no sound from the living room, but a sense of unease returned from the night before and Jess got dressed in silence, sneaking out of the suite with her sandals in her hand.

Breakfast with the others was a subdued affair. Everyone was so fucking moody all of a sudden. Her mum and dad hardly addressed two words to each other and did that thing people do who have argued with each other of being extra ingratiating with everyone else. Even Lucy and Jason, who were normally all over each other, to the point it made you puke, were sitting as far apart as possible. Jason and his mum were so deep in conversation they might as well have been on a table just by themselves, and Lucy spent the whole time whispering to sycophantic Shelly.

Jess even considered gatecrashing Gil and Zoe's table, but as she approached Zoe had leaned forward and hooked a hand behind Gil's head, pulling him towards her for an unnecessarily long kiss, and Jess ended up swerving course out of the restaurant, pretending that was what she'd been intending all along. Now she was stuck. She couldn't go back to the suite because Gabriel was still there, and she was bored of lying by the pool with all those other people basting themselves in the sun like a row of rotisserie chickens.

Instead, she decided to go down to the private beach below the hotel. You'd have thought it would have been packed – a perfect little fingernail of fine white pebbles fringed by clear water, backed by a cluster of evergreen trees – tamarisks, Gabriel had told her when they first arrived, though, obviously, you couldn't trust much of what he said. But every time Jess had been down there she'd had the place to herself. People got so lazy on holiday, that was the thing. So much happier to stay penned together on the pool terrace within reach of the bar and the umbrellas and the adjustable-backed loungers with their luxurious cushioned pads than to venture down all those stairs to take their chances with nature.

The steps were steep, she'd grant them that, and uneven, with some necessitating a long drop down and others just a shallow step. As she clomped her way down, the slap-slap of her Dr Marten sandals on the stone echoed around the cliff-enclosed bay. The air was still and hot, suspended thickly over the beach. It was only nine thirty, and already Jess could feel the sweat pooling behind her knees, dripping down the backs of her calves. She gazed longingly at the turquoise sea, its glassy surface broken only by the odd gentle swell here and there and, towards the horizon, where the water darkened to a navy blue, a few individual white-crested waves.

At the bottom of the steps, the cliff face graduated down to a series of low rocks and, when the tide was out, as now, you could easily scramble over them to another tiny cove, hidden from view, which is where Jess made her way now, having remembered halfway down that she had no swimming costume. Stripping off, she flung her clothes down on the already sun-baked rocks and charged headlong into the sea. Oh man, that felt good, the cold shock of impact bringing her sluggish nerve endings tingling back to life. She submerged her head under the water, despite Lucy having warned her that the salt water would fade her hair to a hideous washed-out peach colour.

A shoal of small dark fish passed underneath her pale feet and she watched them through the clear water with benign goodwill. She was at one with the world, as Gabriel no doubt would have said. Nature flowed through her veins, pulsing at her wrists and her temples. *Life.* That's what she was talking about! Throwing herself on to her back, she spread out her limbs in a starfish shape and floated with the sun warming her face. High up above, a single string of white clouds, wispy as lace, drifted across an otherwise unbroken blue sky and, suddenly, all of it – Lucy, Gabriel, her parents, this stupid over-the-top wedding – ceased to matter. 'I am the universe and the universe is me,' she said out loud, and laughed. Finally, she felt as if the empty space that had opened up behind her ribs since the boat trip might be closing up again.

Back on the beach, she hopped up on one of the rocks that divided this little inlet from the main beach. There was a taller rock behind shielding her from view of the steps on the other side, and she rested her back against it, savouring the absorbed warmth of the sun on her spine.

Perhaps it hadn't been such a bad idea of Lucy's to get them all out here. She closed her eyes and listened to the gentle lapping of the water on the shore and the drone of a distant jet ski. Mindfulness. She'd scoffed at that in London, but now she was starting to see how it could work. You just closed off your thoughts and tuned in to what was around you, isolating the sound of, say, the gulls screeching overhead or somewhere up behind a car engine revving to get up that steep, curving road or that buzzing that might be a fly or a wasp or . . . voices.

Jess opened her eyes and frowned. Damn. Someone was coming down the steps above her head. She could hear the slap of feet hitting stone and a man talking fast and urgently. The feet came to a stop just above Jess's head, where the steps curved to the right, creating a shaded corner that was tucked away out of sight from the top.

'This is so fucked up. You must be able to see how utterly fucked up it is?'

Jess recognized her dad's voice immediately, that particular note of outrage that crept in when one of them had done something he considered out of order. But the thin, soft voice that came next did not belong to her mother.

'I told you. It's not what you think. I love Lucy. I mean, genuinely. I wouldn't do anything to hurt her.'

Naked on her rock, Jess felt the surface of her skin rise up in tiny, frozen bumps. Why was Shelly talking to her father in that intimate way? They hardly knew each other.

'I am here with my *wife*. Are you planning to make a scene? Is that it? Expose me in front of my family?'

'No! I'd never do that.'

'Or did you think maybe we'd fall back into bed? After I told you a million times how much I regret what happened?'

'No, I didn't think . . . I didn't want . . . I didn't mean any of this to happen. It just got out of hand.'

'I love my wife. I told you that at the time. I love my wife, and I will spend the rest of my life trying to make up to her for what I did.'

'I know. And I'd never—'

'Let me make myself perfectly clear. My family mean everything to me, and I will do anything – *anything* – to protect them.'

'Why are you saying it like that, like a threat? This is me. Michelle.'

'Yes, and there's a word for people like you, *Michelle*. Stalkers.'

There came a thin cry, which was then muffled, as if someone had put their hand over their mouth, followed by the patter of light footsteps running up the steps.

Hidden on her rock, Jess hooked her arms around her shins, hugged her knees to her chest and rocked like a child. *Oh fuck. Oh fuckity fucking fuck.* Her dad. And *Shelly. Fuck fuck fuck fuck.* Her tattoos formed a dark, blurred web against her pale kneecaps as she stared at them without seeing.

She jumped as, from over the top of the rock, her father bellowed out an echoing '*Fuck!*'

For one horrible moment, she feared he might decide on a dip to cool off and discover her here, naked and eavesdropping, but after a few long seconds, and a few more '*fuck!*'s, she heard the sound of his Birkenstocks hitting the steps, his progress far more laboured than Shelly's. And then it was just her again, and the gulls and the water. But the Zen-like peace of a few minutes before was shattered.

Jess got shakily to her feet and jumped down on to the sand, picking up her clothes from the rock where she'd flung them and pulling them on as fast as she could.

Her father and Shelly. It was unthinkable. Impossible. She'd always known there was something fake about Shelly. She could spot inauthenticity a mile off. Shelly always tried to give the impression of being so friendly, so eager to help, and yet Jess had known instantly she couldn't be trusted. She put Jess in mind of that disgusting tinned white asparagus you found on the shelves of Spanish supermarkets. Pale and limp and slippery. But at the same time, Jess could tell that underneath all that sliminess was a hard, sharp edge.

Jess fiddled with the stud in her nose, which she'd nudged loose while yanking down her T-shirt over her head. Though the sun was already climbing in the sky, baking the sand and salt to her limbs and face, inside she felt cold and her legs were trembling.

Her father. Having an affair. With Shelly.

Holy shit, what would she tell her mum?

A fly that had been buzzing around a piece of rotting seaweed on the shoreline landed on Jess's arm, and she stared down at it blankly. She'd never been one of those women who flapped about when insects and wasps and bees came near. Only when it flew off did she realize it had bitten her, a red welt appearing out of nowhere on her salt-crusted skin.

She tracked its progress to a nearby rock. Then she picked up her sandal and slammed it down as hard as she could.

16/6/19, 00.52. Original English-language transcript of police interview with Mr Dominic Edward Collins. Police officers: Demitri Iraklidis and Tomaso Diakos. Interpreter: Eulalia Scala.

Threaten Michelle? No, really, I have to object to that. I would never threaten a woman. I'd never threaten anyone. I know I look like a big, ugly old bruiser, but I'm a pussycat, really. Violence isn't my bag. Oh God, who says 'my bag'? Can you wipe that off the transcript, please? I talk a load of nonsense when I'm nervous.

No! Absolutely not! I'm not nervous because I have something to hide. For fuck's sake. I hope this isn't how this interview is going to go. Twisting my words. Can you remind them about the lawyer back in London? He really is first rate. Well, he ought to be, for what he charges. He'd wipe the floor with this lot. Someone died tonight. That's why I'm nervous, OK? All right, 'nervous' probably wasn't the best choice of words. In shock. Exhausted. It's been the longest day. I'm not thinking straight.

I don't give a flying fuck what your witness saw. We weren't arguing. We were just talking animatedly. And she didn't flee, she rushed off because she'd forgotten to do something. Can you please stop with the innuendo? It's not helpful.

Chapter Thirty-five

Lucy

'It's just until I get paid next month. Well, probably the month after, since I already took unpaid leave for this week.'

Lucy had squeezed in with Hazel on her sunlounger to make this entreaty for a loan. Her mother hadn't exactly welcomed this state of affairs. 'It's too hot,' she'd protested when Lucy had told her to budge up. But Lucy had always been a tactile sort of person and she knew her parents found it hard to resist a full-on physical affection onslaught.

Except for now.

'I'd love to help you, Lu-lu, but it's just not possible at the moment.'

Lucy shifted up towards her mum, snuggling into her resisting body.

'You know I wouldn't ask unless I was desperate. And I'll pay it back the second I can, honestly.'

On the rare occasions Lucy had asked her parents for bailouts in the past, this was the point where they'd cave, usually telling her the money was a gift, just as long as she didn't make a habit of it. It wasn't that she was spoiled, but they respected the fact that, on the whole, she was self-sufficient and she didn't take the piss. Not like Jess, who was always running out of money and having bailiffs turn up on her doorstep, her parents having to transfer money on the spot to prevent her losing her laptop or her guitar.

'I'm really sorry, darling. I would if I could, but I just can't.'

Lucy pulled away, feeling the first prickling of real alarm. She'd been so sure her parents would step in. She should have waited until her dad was there, too. He was always more of a soft touch. What if she really couldn't get the money? Would that jeopardize the wedding? A tear rolled down her cheek.

'Please, Mum. I'm only asking for a short-term loan. It's not like you and Dad can't afford it.'

'We're broke.'

'Pardon?'

Lucy turned to face her mother, waiting for the qualifier that would make what she'd just said make sense, but it didn't come. From the corner of her vision, she saw Vivian sit up on her lounger directly opposite across the pool and stare at them over the top of her sunglasses, which she had pushed to the end of her nose. Her bird-like eyes were so close together across the bridge of her beaky nose that from this distance she appeared almost cross-eyed.

'I lost my job. Well, officially I was made redundant.'

Hazel went into an explanation about the slow death of print media and hubs and God knows what, until Lucy cut in.

'When did this happen?'

Hazel shrugged. 'Two months ago? Maybe three?'

'And you didn't tell me? You let me plan this whole wedding and ask you for all that money and it didn't occur to you to let me know you had no job?'

Lucy felt like a pit had opened up under her feet and everything she'd previously been certain of was falling into it. Her mum had always worked. Though she'd known for years that her dad's income was unstable, her mum's sensible, dependable job had always been a given. A monthly salary, sick pay, decent holidays, a bloody good Christmas party. And now this.

'Haven't you got a pension?'

Hazel put her arm awkwardly around her.

'A little one. But I'll lose money if I try to draw it before I'm sixty.'

'And Dad's work?' Lucy's voice had become almost childlike.

Hazel made a sour face.

'Your father hasn't earned any proper money in years.'

'But the new book idea?'

'Oh, Lucy, haven't you noticed how it's always the new ideas he talks about, always the new material that is going to be the next big thing? Never the material he has already produced? That's because no one wants his stuff any more.'

How bitter she sounded. Lucy stood up abruptly, leaving Hazel leaning awkwardly into thin air.

'Why are you being like this? Why are you having a go at him when you're the one who's lost your job? You know that I've been looking forward to getting married my whole life. You remember how you used to laugh at me for dressing my dolls up as brides and holding make-believe weddings and watching your and Dad's wedding video on a loop? You know how important this week is to me. And you're ruining it by bitching about Dad all the time.'

'Wait. Lucy—' Her mum held out a hand, but Lucy turned away. Ahead of her, Vivian stared unabashedly, her mirrored shades reflecting back to Lucy a diminished version of herself.

Back in the suite, Lucy sat on the huge kingsize bed with her head in her hands. All she'd wanted was a week with the people she loved most in the world forming memories that would stay with them for the rest of their lives. Instead, it was all disintegrating around her, all her careful planning, all her painstaking preparations. All of it falling apart.

She picked up her iPad. Looking at the wedding moodboard she'd created on Pinterest always soothed her. For a few precious minutes, she lost herself in images of fresh lavender spilling over terracotta pots, dreamy green swimming pools set into verdant terraces, a smooth brown foot in a silver-thonged sandal with a dusting of pale, powdery sand on the toes, a white smile against a cobalt sky, two hands clasped against a background of breaking surf, the sun setting through a white lace veil, delicate as a spiderweb.

Lucy's breathing slowed. Everything would be all right. The world was beautiful. Look how the vast cerulean sky stretched infinitely on through the plate-glass windows, the endless reach of the sea! How petty her troubles were, in the scheme of things. Laughable, really. Love was all that mattered, in the end.

She had a number of other tabs open on her browser and she noticed a (1) flashing on her email inbox. For a moment she hesitated. Now that she'd arrived at this tentative state of Zen, she was loath to jeopardize it by an ill-timed email from her bank or, worse, from Nina. But then, what if it was something to do with the party the week after next? What if there was an issue with the venue or one of their out-of-town friends needed help finding somewhere to stay?

Cautiously, she clicked on the tab. *Connor Kerswell.* Why was that name familiar? A sensation of fluttering unease preceded by a nanosecond the realization that this was Jason's long-lost cousin, replying at last to her wedding invitation. A few days ago, she'd have been whooping with excitement, but that was before the scene on the boat where Cora had accused her of meddling. Oh God, what if he was writing to accept? If even the mention of him had stirred up such bad feeling, just think of the damage his actual physical presence might do.

Lucy clicked on the message with trepidation and then everything inside her froze.

YOU HAVE NO IDEA WHAT YOU'RE MARRYING INTO

Chapter Thirty-six

Lucy

An hour later, shock was still reverberating weakly around the edges of Lucy's consciousness, but after a lot of reassurance from Shelly and a half-hour soak in the hot tub on the De Luxe terrace, she was daring to believe there was a sliver of a chance that her world had not, in fact, imploded with the email from Jason's cousin.

'Cora said they'd never got on, didn't she?' Shelly pointed out. They were now sitting on the edge of the little private pool, their legs dangling in the tepid water. 'So there must be something dodgy about this guy. There's obviously a family rift there and he's spotted a chance to make trouble.'

'But why would he do that? He doesn't know me. Why would he deliberately try to spoil my wedding?'

'Some people can't bear other people to be happy, Luce.' Shelly was wearing her big-brimmed hat, so Lucy couldn't see her expression, but her voice was grim.

They were both silent for a moment, and then Lucy finally got up the nerve to ask the question that had been sitting like a stone in her mouth since Shelly had arrived.

'You don't think there could be . . . I mean, there's no way there could be . . . ?'

'Any truth in it? Are you insane? This is Jason we're talking about. *Your* Jason.'

'No! Not Jason. Not in a million years. I'm talking about Cora. She's so . . . Forget it. I'm being idiotic. Ignore me.'

'Are you going to talk to him about it? Jason, I mean?'

Lucy shook her head miserably. 'Him and Cora got so worked up when I mentioned this Connor Kerswell before, God knows how they'd react if they knew he'd actually got in touch to slag them off. The wedding's tomorrow. I just don't want any bad feeling.'

Lucy knew it was the right thing to do but, still, when she was alone again, her stomach twisted at the thought of keeping something like this from the man she'd committed to spending the rest of her life with. She and Jason shared everything. Once, her mother had suggested it might be healthier in a long-term relationship to keep a few secrets from each other, and Lucy had been appalled at the idea. She'd tell him as soon as they were back home again, she decided, when they had time and space to discuss it without their families around. He'd most likely dismiss her fears in an instant: *Oh, Connor, he's always been a nutter.*

Having made this plan, she felt better. She was allowing things to get on top of her, that was all. Jasmine and she had discussed this at length, how important it was for a bride to allow herself me-time in this lead-up to the wedding, to avoid getting tied up in knots of stress. Jasmine had even hired a personal wellbeing coach to come in every day for a fortnight leading up to the big day. Lucy would have to be responsible for her own self-care.

She set up her laptop on the small table on the terrace, unrolled her yoga mat and logged into Breath-Work4Brides.com, assuming a cross-legged position. 'Imagine your head is a flower and your neck is the stem,' instructed the soporific voice. 'Now waggle your flower gently from side to side.'

Mid-waggle, Lucy became aware of a voice shouting her name. Reluctantly, she unfolded her legs and went to the railings at the edge of the terrace.

'Oh, there you are. I've been calling you for ages.'

Zoe's cross-looking face appeared over the railing of a terrace on the floor below.

'Well, here I am.' Lucy attempted a mindful smile.

'Right. Well. I just thought I should let you know that I won't make it to the wedding rehearsal this evening.'

Lucy's smile evaporated in the heat.

'What do you mean?'

'It was the only time the facial woman could fit me in. Of course, I'll come along after, if there's time. But you know how facials are – you sometimes feel a little bit out of it afterwards, so I'll play it by ear.'

A strange stasis descended on Lucy, her surroundings suddenly hushed. No birdsong, no sound of the waves far, far out at sea, no chatter rising up from the swimming-pool area. Everything was deathly still. Even internally there was an absolute numbness like that moment after you plunge your hand into boiling-hot water and for a second there is no feeling at all and you think, *Oh, OK, that's all right, then*, before the pain comes roaring in.

The brief calm while Lucy gazed down on Zoe's upturned face was shattered by a rush of outrage so powerful that Lucy found herself gripping the rail upon which she was leaning in case her suddenly shaky legs gave way underneath her.

'You have got to be kidding me.'

Zoe's disembodied face, improbably floating above the sheer drop to the terrace below, registered a surprised expression, so that Lucy found herself staring down into the open circle of Zoe's mouth, straight to her very pink tonsils.

'Look, I'm sorry if it messes up any plans, but there's no need to get stressy with me. At least I had the courtesy to tell you I can't come. Some people – your sister, for example – would have just not bothered showing up.'

'You had treatments the other day. We all did. Why do you need another facial now? It's not you who's getting married, you know. Nobody will even be looking at you.'

It wasn't the most diplomatic thing to say, but Lucy was beyond social niceties. How dare she? She'd been invited to the wedding – purely on account of who she was married to – and, literally, there were only two requirements. You show up at the wedding rehearsal and you show up at the wedding. How hard was that?

Zoe's face had turned pink.

'For your information, I have a skin condition. It's very rare and I see a private dermatologist for it. I have little flare-ups occasionally and, as you can imagine, I'm quite self-conscious about it, actually. So, if you don't mind, I'd like to have a facial, which is the *only* thing that makes me feel better. Obviously, if she'd had any other appointment, I'd have taken it, but it was this or nothing.'

Lucy closed her mouth so firmly she could feel her teeth biting through her lip. There was nothing wrong with Zoe's face – she was staring right down at it, for God's sake.

Everything was going wrong. All the work she'd put into this week – the endless comparisons of different suppliers, the trawling through brochures for this venue or that one, the bride forums she'd posted on, looking for tips on the correct wording for invitations, or whether it was unethical to put a £500 coffee machine on your gift list, or the right make-up look for a late-afternoon beach wedding so one looked glowing rather than shiny. All that preparation, and now her fiancé was hardly talking to her, her parents were broke, her wedding planner was chasing her for money. And on top of all that, Gil's *cunt* of a wife – even in the safety of her own thoughts, Lucy shocked herself by using the c-word, which she normally avoided at all costs – couldn't even be bothered to turn up to one of the only things she'd been asked to do.

Suddenly, it was all too much.

'You know what? I'm glad you're not coming.' Lucy could hardly get the words out past the hard ball of loathing lodged in her throat. 'What's the point in paying a fortune for you to have a lovely meal when we all know you're just going to throw it straight up afterwards?'

She withdrew and sat back down on the yoga mat, still shaking with anger. Lucy had never in her life been a violent sort of person, but for the first time ever she understood how the desire to inflict harm on someone could be so strong that your whole body burned with it.

Therapy Journal, Week 12

I get what you said on Tuesday about breaking 'the illusion of intimacy'. So I'll do what you say and call Harry by his real name, and you'll have to forgive me if I slip up every now and then. Dom – *God that sounds strange – wasn't the kind of man who had affairs. That's what I loved about him. He said he'd never cheated on Hazel before, and I believed him. He said family meant the world to him, and my heart just about jumped out of my chest, because that's exactly how I feel.*

Our first couple of dates were in anonymous pubs in London, like the one we met in. Except we didn't call them dates. We just chatted, as if we'd always known each other. I think he was convincing himself he wasn't doing anything wrong, that this was all perfectly innocent. I really liked the way he struggled with himself. It showed how much he loved his family – and I thought he must like me a bit to risk it all for me.

The first time we slept together he cried afterwards. He was so sweet and mortified and said he'd crossed some irreversible line. He almost backed out before we even started. When we got back to my flat and I took off my clothes, he looked pained. 'I can't do this,' he'd said. 'You're such a fragile little thing and I'm such a big clumsy old fool. I feel I could snap you in half like a twig.' I'd had to take the lead, to show him that I wanted what he wanted. It sounds corny, but it didn't feel like sex but rather a merging of two people, two lives. After that, I knew there was no going back.

'That was lovely, but I love my wife and my daughters,' he told me when we said goodbye. 'This can't happen again.' But I didn't believe him. When you know, you know.

Chapter Thirty-seven

Jess

Jess couldn't handle the immensity of her feelings. She'd always been that way. 'Try not to take everything so personally,' her mother would tell her when she was a child, her small body quivering with the emotions she was powerless to control.

Now, she sat on the edge of her bed and every particle of her, every hair follicle, every skin cell, was alive with the wrongness of everything.

Her parents were stable. Solid. Boring, even. Their role was to be the fixed point by which Jess could navigate her way home if she'd gone too far astray, the anchor above which she could float freely. That they existed independently of her was a concept she'd always struggled with. That they might cease to exist at all, at least not in the form she'd come to rely on, was simply inconceivable.

'You are such a fucking idiot, Dad,' she said out loud, taking full advantage of having the suite to herself for once, Gabriel having left a note to say that he and Cora were heading out for a walk. He'd signed off, 'love and peace', which made her want to scream.

It was such an embarrassing cliché. Middle-aged man has affair with far younger woman to boost his ego. The oldest story in the book. Only she'd never in a million years imagined it would apply to her own father. God knew her mum could be annoying – one day grilling you about every detail of your life as if she was going to be tested on you, and the next, if you were having a crisis and needed her help, not answering your calls because she was too busy with work. Like work was more important than her own family!

But she was clever and reassuring and, when you did manage to pin her down, you realized she'd noticed things you thought you'd kept hidden and, more than all that, she was part of their family unit, and now her dad was in danger of tearing that unit to shreds.

No, not her dad. *Her.* Shelly.

Whenever Jess thought of Shelly a pressure built up in her head, as if her brain was too big for her skull. If her dad had been going to have an affair – and she wished to *fuck* he hadn't – why did it have to be her? Jess loved women. *Adored* women. All of them. Old, young, thin, fat, gay, straight, trans, black, Asian, Latin, Inuit. She was a woman's woman. That's what she proudly told people. But the one type of woman she couldn't abide was Shelly's type. Superficially insipid and *so* pass-agg. She was the type who'd say, 'Oh my God, I don't mind at *all* having the smallest, pokiest suite. If my claustrophobia gets bad, there's that little balcony, isn't there?'

Somehow, she'd managed to burrow into Lucy like a quiet, colourless tick, and now there was no dislodging her. Jess loved Lucy to bits, but she was a pushover when it came to lost causes like Shelly who'd had a shitty life and had no family and about as much charisma as a paper bag.

Jess threw herself back on the bed and tried to work out how it could have happened. As far as she'd been aware, Lucy had never introduced Shelly to her dad. He'd been away that time Lucy had brought her to that pizza place in Bath. But then, she acknowledged, she wasn't very good at keeping up with the day-to-day goings-on of her family. Sometimes, weeks would go past with her forgetting to reply to their calls and emails. Maybe her dad had dropped into Lucy's shop unannounced, and found only Shelly there. He'd called her Michelle. Perhaps that's how she'd introduced herself, to make herself seem more sophisticated.

If she forced herself to look objectively, Jess could see how Shelly could be attractive – tall and willowy, with that wide, wonky smile that split her face in two. She was intelligent, too. Lucy was always saying how much cleverer Shelly was than her. And plenty of men went for that 'pale but interesting' vibe, didn't they, even if, underneath it all, the person was a manipulative bitch.

Jess had definitely got the feeling it hadn't happened often and it was Shelly who'd done the running. What had he called her? *Stalker?*

Her eye once again fell on the notebook on her bedside table. She snatched it up and opened it on her lap. This thing with Shelly and her dad was surely a rich mine of material for a novel. Weak middle-aged has-been confronting own mortality falls victim to . . . well, *who* exactly? Was Shelly this quietly loyal friend who'd triumphed over a difficult past, as Lucy seemed to think, or was she a parasite who'd latched on to Jess's family because she didn't have one of her own and had set her sights on Jess's dad without any thought for what it would do to her mum – to *all* of them?

All of a sudden, Jess felt furious. Her parents were paying for this week, paying for that bitch's luxury suite, paying for her to dunk her long dishcloth of a body in the pool. And what that really meant, of course, was that her *mum* was paying, as everyone knew her dad hadn't earned a penny in years. So, basically, her mother was treating her father's former *mistress* – such a passionate word for such a passionless person – to a week at a luxury hotel.

It was unendurable.

Jess jumped to her feet and stormed through the door and down the corridor, powered by the force of her rage. Everything – from her fingertips to the fine blonde hairs on her shins, which she'd refused to wax off, despite Lucy's attempts to persuade her – vibrated with her righteous fury.

Without pausing to think or take stock, she pounded on Shelly's door. And when it didn't immediately open, she put her mouth to the wood and shouted through it. 'Oi!'

Finally, the door swung open and Shelly appeared. Her eyes were red, as if she'd been crying, which put Jess in mind of the white mouse she'd once bought with her pocket money, bringing it home from the pet shop as a fait accompli, despite the protests of her family.

'I want to talk to you.' Jess didn't even wait for a response before pushing her way past Shelly into the room. Well, her mother was paying for it, wasn't she? So Jess had every right to make herself at home.

Shelly's suite was modest in contrast with Lucy's and her parents', but it was immaculate.

Where was the clutter? Jess wanted to know. Where was Shelly's handbag, her fey floppy hat, those ugly white sandals she wore? What kind of a person left no trace of themselves in the room in which they were the only occupant?

A non-person, that's who.

Or a person with something to hide.

Jess led the way through the living room, past the open door to the bedroom and on to the modest terrace, which was half the size of Jess's own and mostly in shade.

'What's all this about? Why did you come barging in here like that?' Shelly was standing in the doorway, leaning against the metal doorframe. She was wearing a tatty old sarong that looked vaguely familiar in a red colour that made her appear even more washed out than usual.

'You've been crying.'

'What? No, I haven't. Anyway, it's none of your business.'

'Isn't it?'

'What?'

'See, I think it *is* my business when you've been fucking my dad.'

Jess was gratified to see that Shelly's always pallid complexion blanched to the colour of skimmed milk. She hadn't been expecting *that*! But then, like a shutter coming down, Shelly's face once again returned to its usual state, as featureless as soap.

'I don't know what you're talking about.'

'Don't give me that shit. I heard the two of you down there on the steps.'

Jess kept her eyes on Shelly, greedy for a reaction, but the other woman stepped back inside the room so that her face was in shadow. There was a long silence and, despite herself, Jess started to feel uncomfortable. Shelly was so unnaturally still, that was the problem, and now there was that disconcerting dark void where her face should be. Where was her conscience? She ought to be losing her shit right now, begging Jess not to tell anyone. Begging her forgiveness, for fuck's sake. Yet there she stood, as motionless as if she were carved out of the same white stone as that wall down there behind the swimming pool. No sharp intake of breath, no sobs, no pleading.

Her earlier rage, which had started to ebb away in the face of Shelly's resolute calm, now came whooshing back, flooding Jess's veins with a boiling energy that she welcomed. She had the moral high ground here. This woman – this *leech* – had seduced her father and now threatened to break up their family.

'Just wait till Lucy finds out what her so-called friend has been doing behind her back. In fact, that's the one positive thing about this whole shitty situation. That you won't be hanging around my sister all the time any more, like a bad smell.'

'And you'd do that, would you? Ruin your own sister's wedding?'

'She has a right to know. We're family. Not that you'd have the first clue what that means.'

Shelly remained in shadow, but there was a crackle of electricity in the air around her that told Jess she'd scored a direct hit. But her satisfaction was short-lived.

'I don't know what you think you heard, Jessica. But you've got the wrong end of the stick. Not that you're the type to let the truth get in the way of a good scene. You know, I really wanted to like you, for Lucy's sake, but the truth is you're a drama queen who can't bear for anyone else to have the spotlight, even for a minute. But this is a new low, even for you. To willingly wreck your own sister's wedding, that she's been planning for years, over something you know nothing about, just so you can make it all about you, yet again.'

For a moment, Jess wavered, taken back uncomfortably to the scene on the boat when Gil had accused her of making a pass at him out of sheer boredom. Then Shelly added: 'That is next-level narcissism.'

Narcissism? Jess was the most selfless person she knew! She was always doing things for her mates – throwing them surprise parties, sending them expensive bunches of flowers on a whim. Only the week before, she'd turned up at her friend Amy's house with a bin liner full of clothes she thought would suit her. And yes, OK, she'd been about to chuck them out anyway, but the point was, she'd thought about her and taken the trouble to go around there and persuade Amy to try them on there and then. She'd had guests round, which had been a bit awkward at the beginning, but they'd all got into it in the end – it'd been kind of like a private fashion show. And there was no one who got behind causes like Jess did. She was always sitting herself down next to homeless people to chat to them, for hours, sometimes. So many others just pretended they didn't exist, as if they weren't even human. She went on all the marches, glued herself to things, even. Just look at how generous she'd been to Gabriel. Inviting him here, just because she wanted to do something nice for him. And now the selfish bitch who'd slept with her father without any thought for what it would do to his family was accusing *her* of being self-absorbed. It was just a joke.

Jess felt a pain in her hands and realized she was clenching her fists so hard the nails, jagged through biting, were digging into her palms. It was true, though, Shelly had her over a barrel. If she told Lucy what she'd just learned, the whole week would be ruined, after all the planning, all the expense. Could she really break her sister's heart like that?

Yet, equally, how could she sit across from her dad and pretend nothing was wrong? *You see*, she felt like saying to Shelly now, *how I consider everyone's feelings except my own?*

Shelly stepped forward out of the shadow, her pale brows knitted in mock concern.

'Look,' she said, gesturing limply in the air with her long fingers. 'I'm just trying to think about Lucy in all this. She's a good, good person. She deserves her perfect wedding.'

'I don't need you to tell me what kind of person my sister is, thank you very much.'

Still, Jess privately conceded, she was right. It would be beyond cruel to spring this on Lucy on the eve of her wedding. The unfairness of the situation made her want to scream. She strode back through the suite and flung open the door to the corridor, pausing in the doorway.

'You think you've won something, but you just wait,' she told Shelly, her voice thick with emotion. 'You'll pay for what you've done to my family.'

'Are you threatening me, Jessica?'

'I'm just warning you to be careful, that's all. I'm a live-and-let-live type of person normally. Chilled as fuck. Ask anyone. But if you mess with my family, I promise you'll regret it.'

Chapter Thirty-eight

Nina

Normally, the lush beauty of her surroundings was guaranteed to lift Nina's mood. Even at her most homesick, her heart still swelled at the sight of the pine-covered hillsides where she and Mark would go walking out of season, every now and then stumbling across the ruins of villages left abandoned after the earthquake in 1953, or a herd of curious goats, their approach heralded by the tinkling of the bells they wore around their necks.

But today, as she drove up to Club Panorama, on the neighbouring clifftop to the Paradise View, the splendour of the scenery around her felt like a sick cosmic joke. When she was still living in Leicester and working as a school administrator and driving to work every day on the outer ring road around all those interminable roundabouts, she'd convinced herself that all she needed to be happy was to see the ocean, or the mountains, or to feel the morning sunshine on her face. And while she never took these things for granted, she now knew that you also needed a partner you didn't want to strangle, and old friends to meet for a glass of wine when you had to let off steam, and family to support you, and to be able to make jokes that people understood without you having to explain them in halting Greek, by the end of which they'd been drained of every ounce of humour. On days like today, when her stomach was churning and her nerves were grated like Parmesan, the low golden sun reflecting on the Ionian Sea and the wide ultramarine sky against which the pale ghost moon was starting to materialize only seemed to mock the mess she'd made of her life here and the current blackness of her mood.

The wedding-rehearsal dinner had been meticulously planned. Cocktails from 7 p.m. out on the Sundowner Terrace, where there were wide, double loungers with calico-covered mattresses and Moroccan scatter cushions, and low tables in between where one could rest one's mojito or negroni and watch the sun set over a small bay perfectly framed by two plunging cliff faces on either side to a soundtrack of cool ambient tunes. Then dinner in the pretty cobbled restaurant courtyard, where olive trees were threaded through with multicoloured fairy lights and a three-piece band played an eclectic mix of jazz and pop classics from a discreet distance and the waiting staff were chosen as much for their looks as their aptitude. The courtyard was open on one side to make the most of the breathtaking view and, on clear nights, the lights from the fishing boats gave the impression that the stars themselves were floating on the surface of the sea. There, the family and friends would go through the order of ceremony for tomorrow and make sure everyone knew their roles. Maybe there'd be a couple of speeches.

It was customary for the groom's family to pay for this segment of the wedding. Nina's heart went out to Cora Beazant, who was footing the bill on her own. Club Panorama was not a cheap night out, by any means. Nina had made the mistake of asking Jason whether his father would be contributing and had felt awful when he told her he'd been dead many years, in a tone that very much didn't invite further questions.

Nina had sent many wedding parties to Club Panorama over the three years it had been open and, as a result, was on very friendly terms with Darius, the restaurant's owner, who was one of the new breed of young entrepreneurs on the island who had left to make money overseas during the bad years and had now returned to try to resurrect family fortunes back home, bringing new, sophisticated ideas with them. But this night, when she parked up at seven o'clock and made her way into the covered section of the restaurant where Darius stood behind the lectern which held the bookings register, waiting to swoop out to greet guests as they arrived, there was none of the usual fuss: no smiles, no embrace, no shouting out of her name when she walked through the doorway. Usually, Darius spoke to her in Greek, enunciating each word slowly and clearly and greeting each sentence Nina spoke with rhapsodies of delight, insisting that she had improved immeasurably since the last time they had spoken, indeed was practically fluent. But today all business was conducted in English, which Darius spoke perfectly.

'Everything is prepared for your group.' Darius ran a finger down the register and Nina found herself transfixed by the enormous gold watch that shone out against the dark skin of his arm. He was wearing a black linen shirt with the sleeves rolled up to the elbows, generously unbuttoned at the front. Nina happened to know that he had his chest hair waxed, because he used the same salon she did in the main town.

She waited for him to look up at her, but instead he walked straight past her to the Sundowner Terrace, leaving her to follow, the knot in her stomach growing tighter with each step. This was because of the money they owed, she was sure of it. The perils of living in such a small community where everyone knew everyone else, and most people were related in some complicated way. Now she remembered that Darius's star chef was indeed a brother of the cook at the Paradise View. Which meant he was also an Angelis. Her heart grew heavy and again she cursed Mark for getting them into this position, destroying the relationships they – *she* – had worked so hard to build.

She only hoped Darius's new frostiness wouldn't extend to Lucy and Jason's wedding party. Her intimacy with the locals was one of the things her clients seemed to appreciate most, feeling as if it conferred on them a special connection not available to the regular tourists who made the journey up here.

The wedding party arrived in dribs and drabs. First Mr and Mrs Collins and Lucy's sister, Jess, and that strange man she'd brought along. They walked on to the terrace in silence, bringing with them a leaden atmosphere that thickened the glorious late-afternoon heat, turning it oppressive and stuffy. It was one of the traits Nina most despaired of in herself, that she always felt the need to fill in gaps in conversation, overcompensating wildly for any shortfalls in her companions' contributions, and now she found herself talking too fast and too loud, about the club and Darius and the beauty of the day, until she could hardly bear the sound of her own voice.

She was relieved when the rest of the party arrived – Jason and Lucy, with Jason's mum and handsome Gil and that nice red-headed friend of Lucy's whose name Nina kept forgetting. Sally? No, Shelly, that was it. Here at least there was more animation, and Nina felt calmer hearing their exclamations about the view and the sleek terrace with its outside bar. But when she took a closer look at Lucy, her misgivings returned. Not that she wasn't gorgeous, with that heart-shaped face now sun-kissed and glowing and her blonde-streaked hair swept up in a complicated chignon that Nina immediately recognized as the handiwork of the Paradise View's resident hairdresser. She was wearing an eye-catching sleeveless dress with a low neckline in a pretty lemon colour that fitted her as if it had been sewn to her shape. Nina knew, because Lucy had told her in a breathless whisper, making her swear she wouldn't tell Jason, that it was by an up-and-coming British designer and she'd bought it in Selfridges. At the time Lucy had confided this, Nina had been quite charmed and told her that if you couldn't splash out on your wedding, when could you, but now she found herself wondering exactly how much that designer dress had cost, and how much of Lucy and Jason's unpaid bill it accounted for.

It was Lucy's eyes that gave Nina pause for thought, beautifully made up with those eyelash extensions all the young women seemed to be wearing these days but surrounded by puffy pink skin. Had Jason given her a hard time about the missing money? For a moment, Nina felt guilty. Then she felt cross with herself for feeling guilty. It wasn't her fault.

The sun was already very low by the time the guests were all assembled, and it was shaping up to be a stunner of a sunset, the sky streaked with orange and pink. A black-T-shirted waitress with cheekbones that could cut glass glided around with a tray, passing out flutes of chilled champagne. The tension that had wound itself tightly around the group started to loosen as the sinking sun coated them all with tones of honey and rose gold, turning their Northern European pallor radiant and glowing until . . .

'What the *fuck?*'

A long black cloud, emerging from behind one of the dark cliffs that framed the view, had drifted slowly across the face of the sun, plunging the terrace into shade and causing Jess, who'd been sprawled on a lounger to Nina's right, to exclaim crossly, as if someone had placed the cloud there deliberately to annoy her.

Robbed of their view, the guests glanced sideways at each other as they sipped their drinks. The only two who seemed lost in deep conversation were Cora and Gabriel, side by side on a double daybed.

The heaviness returned, and though Nina did her best to chivvy everyone along and raise spirits, her heart wasn't really in it and the jovial tone she was aiming for sounded fake. In her bag, her phone vibrated with an incoming call, but when she glanced down at the screen and saw Mark's name, she zipped up the bag to hide it from view.

By the time they all trooped dutifully into the restaurant courtyard for dinner, following the waitress's very neat behind, energy levels had dipped dramatically and Nina was fast running out of chirpy chatter. Usually, Darius would have come over to the table to welcome Nina's guests – that personal touch made all the difference – but tonight he stayed behind his podium and sent his head waiter, Lukas, to greet them and take their drinks order, even though the restaurant wasn't yet busy and he could easily have slipped away for a moment or two. When she thought about what his reticence could mean, Nina felt like someone was pressing hard on her chest.

Still, the food was excellent, as always. There was crumbly Kefalonian feta with honey and fat ripe figs to start, followed by lobster linguine and grilled sea bream, which Lukas brought to their table before it was cooked so they could see how it was fresh from the sea. There were lamb chops from the restaurant's own farm and almond cake dripping with syrup. And, once the solitary black cloud that had disrupted the sunset drifted away, the night was clear, the moon a perfect curve of silver gazing impassively at itself in the mirror of the sea. Gradually, the awkwardness eased, the crisp white locally grown Robola and an imported Provençal rosé helping to oil the conversation so that it no longer creaked and groaned. Lukas was attentive without being intrusive and, when Nina stood up to talk everyone through the schedule of events for the following day, they all cheered good-heartedly.

As Nina talked, she was conscious again of her phone buzzing. She knew it would be Mark, calling and calling, refusing to accept that she wasn't going to pick up. He'd be drunk, she already knew that. It was a pattern she was all too familiar with. Argument, booze, relentless phone calls to justify himself or tell her why it was all her fault. Then tomorrow would be the self-recriminations and the promises that things would be different from now on. It was so sad and so predictable and she couldn't do it any more.

Then it was time for Cora's speech. Nina was curious to know whether she'd refer to Jason's missing father, but in the end it was all about the happy couple. Well, to be completely accurate, apart from a heartfelt mention of how Lucy was the daughter she never had and a joke about getting a better class of birthday gift since Lucy had been on the scene, it was all about Jason. Nina had listened to a lot of these kinds of speeches over the years. Parents growing dewy-eyed over the thought of their children moving on. Some were entirely jokey, others became paeans to their offspring, lists of their attributes to ensure that their soon-to-be son- or daughter-in-law knew what a prize they were getting. She never judged. It must be hard letting go of your children, and not just of your children but of the family unit you'd built with those children and the version of you contained within that unit. Now that unit would splinter, the newly-weds becoming a unit of their own. It was a little death in a way, she supposed, even while it was also life-affirming and natural and celebratory.

But there was something about Cora's speech that made Nina uncomfortable. She didn't always stay around for this part of the evening, but Lucy had insisted, and now she wished she had made some excuse. She struggled to analyse the source of her discomfort. It wasn't the words themselves, which were the usual mixture of anecdote and homily. Rather, it was the way she was saying them. Addressing her son directly, as if they were the only two people present. 'We've been through things that no one else could possibly understand,' she was saying. 'I've done things I haven't always been proud of, but he's never lost faith in me. And that's given us an unshakeable bond.'

There was a noise across the table, and Nina saw that Lucy had knocked over her wineglass and was dabbing frantically at the tablecloth, where rosé was bleeding into starched linen. 'Sorry,' she mouthed to the rest of the group, her cheeks as pink as the spilled wine.

Nina's phone was ringing almost constantly now, and she surreptitiously unzipped her bag to take a look at the screen. To her surprise, the caller wasn't Mark, although a notification of thirteen missed calls from her husband's phone flashed up along the top of the screen. It was Eulalia, the receptionist from the Paradise View.

Worried, Nina made an 'excuse me' gesture to her companions and crept away from the table as unobtrusively as she could.

'Nina. I'm so happy to catch you.' There was a note of tension underpinning Eulalia's almost unaccented English. 'Your husband has been here. I'm afraid he was a little bit . . .'

'. . . drunk?' suggested Nina weakly.

'Exactly so. He was demanding to know where you were. He was making a big scene, you know?'

Nina stood stock-still, leaning against the outside wall of the courtyard. She squeezed her eyes shut.

'You didn't tell him, did—' But now she heard it, the sound of a motorbike roaring and spluttering up the hill. *Please don't let this be happening.* There was a crunching of gravel and, now, the engine stopped. A moment later came the sound of raised voices. Nina rushed back to the table just as Mark arrived, wearing a faded red T-shirt with sweat stains under the arms and jeans that used to be loose but now strained across the waist because of the weight he'd put on recently. He'd always been a big man, broad and bear-like, and she'd loved that about him, but now the brawn was tipping into fat. His hair, which badly needed a cut, was plastered to his head from the bike helmet, and the skin of his face that wasn't covered by the moustache and beard she'd begged him to shave appeared clammy and waxy.

'Which one is Jason Beazant?' Nina could hear in his voice every single one of the beers he'd drained at Constantin's bar and the bottle of Greek Metaxa he'd have worked his way through before he got there. His unfocused eyes swung between Jason and Gil, having narrowed it down to those two. Jason tried to stand, only for his mother to pull him back down again. Mark lunged towards him, but Nina managed to get there first, interjecting herself between the two men. Behind her husband's head, she saw Darius approaching. Stripped of its usual smile, his face was all tight angles and almost unrecognizable.

'You need to pay your bill,' Mark yelled over Nina's shoulder. A drop of spittle flew into her eye. 'You're killing us, dude. Just pay the fuck up.'

Nina was glad her back was to the table so she couldn't see Jason's face, glad none of the guests could see her own contorted in anger at her husband. She stepped forward to steer Mark away, just as Darius put a hand on his shoulder. Mark stiffened and, for a horrible moment, Nina thought he was going to lash out. But then the fight went out of him, his shoulders slumped and he allowed himself to be docilely led from the table and out through the restaurant to the car park, with Nina following behind.

'This is the last party you bring here, Nina,' said Darius, giving Mark one more withering look before turning on his heel. Then she and Mark were alone.

'I can't believe this,' Nina said, her voice breaking.

'Well, someone had to do something.' Mark used the self-pitying, self-justifying tone that was like nails down a blackboard to Nina's ears.

'We're finished, Mark,' she said flatly. She knew he wouldn't believe her, not after all the other times she'd said it, but as she walked back to rejoin the others, too ashamed to look Darius in the eyes, a sense of finality settled over her. And when she heard the motorbike engine kicking into life and the thought jumped automatically into her head that Mark was in no state to be driving, it was in passing, as if he were a stranger and nothing to do with her at all.

15/6/19, 23.40. Original English language transcript of police interview with Mrs Nina Caroline Foster. Police officers: Demitri Iraklidis and Tomaso Diakos. Interpreter: Eulalia Scala.

Business is good, thanks. Well, you know, a few ups and downs, like anyone. But ticking over. I can't complain.

I'm sorry, can you please ask them why they're looking at me like that? Like they don't believe me? What is it they know?

OK, there were some financial issues. My husband borrowed some money against my wishes. I'd rather not say where from.

Mr Angelis? How do they know . . . ? Hang on, is he related? That younger one? Is that why he looks so familiar?

Yes, all right, there was a bit of a scene last night, if you want to put it like that. My husband has a drink problem. I don't think that's a secret any more. But that has absolutely no bearing on what happened here tonight. Mark is harmless. 'All mouth and no trousers,' we say in England. No, please don't try to translate that.

What a funny question! Yes, I believe in marriage. With all my heart. I'm a romantic.

Chapter Thirty-nine

Hazel

Back at the hotel, Hazel was still feeling jittery. The scene at the restaurant hadn't lasted more than a minute or two, but it had left a bad taste in the mouth, even though Nina had done her best to smooth it over afterwards, with the help of a free round of espresso Martinis. Hazel felt sorry for the wedding organizer, if truth be known. She seemed like a genuinely nice woman, just trying to make a living, as they all were. It wasn't her fault if her husband was a thuggish git. That's just how husbands were, Hazel felt. All of them gits.

She and Dom had hardly spoken since the confrontation over the missed call when he'd admitted being unfaithful, except when she'd tersely told him she wouldn't discuss it until they were back home so as not to ruin Lucy's wedding. She knew this would be torture for Dom, who was a big fan of clearing the air, even on those occasions where, as far as Hazel was concerned, the air was tolerably clear already. 'But, darling, we have to—' he'd begun, only for her to shut him down. '*We* don't have to do anything, and anyway, there *is* no we. And don't call me darling.'

Only once had she weakened. 'She must have been some fuck,' she'd said as they exited their suite, the rarely used word sounding foreign to her own ears, 'for you to risk your family over.'

Predictably, Dom's eyes had filmed over. 'Darling, you make it sound like this was something I set out to do, something I actively wanted, but it wasn't like that at all.'

'So she forced you?'

'Of course not. Oh, I'm not explaining it very well, but it was like it just happened, without me really having much agency over it.'

'Oh, please, spare me. I'd have more respect if you had the decency to own your actions.'

All evening, she'd ignored his little pleading glances. Did he really think that would work? Really, she had two children. She didn't need another. At dinner, he'd been virtually silent, sticking to her side as if she hadn't made it quite clear where they stood.

Only on returning to the hotel had he seemed to relax, agreeing readily to join Jess in the bar for a nightcap, leaving Hazel to go back to the suite, finally alone.

Now that the numbness was wearing off, she was starting to explore her feelings gingerly, as if pressing a bruise. She began to think about the specifics of it – all the lies Dom must have told about where he was and who he was with, the money he might have spent. Did they go to a hotel? Who paid for the room? Because if it was Dom, it meant that she, Hazel, had indirectly funded his extramarital shag, which made her see red, especially after that scene back there in Club Panorama.

'We have to bail them out,' Dom had whispered as Nina apologized again and again for her husband's behaviour. 'He'd had way too much to drink. Please just forget that scene ever happened.'

'How many times do I have to say it?' Hazel had hissed at her husband. 'There. Is. No. Money. Unless you're sitting on some news you haven't told me about. A six-figure advance for your new book? Five figures, even. A tenner? I'm not fussy.'

That'd shut him up. But now the thought that Dom's tawdry affair might have used up money they could have spent helping their daughter out made the breath catch in Hazel's throat.

She wandered out on to the terrace. The night was clear and still, the creamy moon sharply defined against the black velvet sky. Looking out over the railings, she watched a bat swoop low over the swimming pool while the sound of Jess's raucous laughter drifted up from the bar area. Hazel's heart contracted with worry for her younger daughter, with this need she had to be the last person standing, to drink the hardest and shout the loudest. Why did ordinariness hold such fear for her? How far would she go to avoid it?

While Hazel was standing there, her hands on the cool metal railing, she became aware once again of that prickling on the back of the neck as if she was being observed, and swung her head around, her breath catching when she saw the pale saucer of a face looking down at her from a neighbouring balcony before melting back into the darkness.

For a split second, she was afraid, until her head caught up and she realized it was Shelly's balcony and the girl must just have been taking one last look out at the silver reflection of the moon on the water, just as Hazel was herself. She probably hadn't even noticed there was anyone else around.

Still, the mood was broken, and Hazel went back inside. She tried to think again about the timeline of Dom's infidelity. She was regretting having closed down the conversation so decisively now that she realized how few details she had in her possession. She thought about the last few months. How consumed she'd been with losing her job. If she was brutally honest with herself, it was true that she'd pulled away from Dom because, at some level, she blamed him for the lack of a safety net, that constant nausea she'd suffered, knowing that without her salary there was no one to take up the slack. No one to step in to cover the bills for that big, rambling house, or the mortgage that still had seven years to run or the expensive lawyer's bills. She'd cried on her way home after that awful meeting in Melanie Alderman's office, but her resentment as she walked back from the station, her eyes sore from weeping, was directed at her financially dependent husband rather than the people who'd driven her out. They might have forced her to jump, but it was Dom who would fail to catch her.

So yes, objectively, she'd withdrawn from him. She knew he'd been hurt that she hadn't consulted him before getting rid of the lawyer and dropping the idea of challenging her redundancy. Had it been during this time that he'd looked elsewhere for validation?

Not that it in any way excused him. She'd read an account once in a Sunday supplement, a woman talking about her husband's affair and saying, 'I acknowledge fifty per cent of the responsibility for the state of our relationship, but the decision to cheat was one hundred per cent his.'

Hazel kicked off her shoes – two-inch wedges that had been a nightmare in the gravel of the restaurant car park. Really, why did she bother? Who had it all been *for*, in the end? The shoes that pinched her toes together, the underwired bras that dug into her ribcage, the trousers she took off the second she got home from work because they compressed her around the middle. Not for Dom, that was for sure. Not for years. But then who? Her workmates, to whom she was just another middle-aged woman, bleeding seamlessly into all the others? Herself?

She lay back on the bed, resting her laptop on her stomach, keeping to her own side out of habit, even though she'd had to walk all around the mattress to get there.

The usual depressing list of unread marketing emails – Netflix, Wickes, Waitrose. LinkedIn, for God's sake, even though she hadn't been able to remember her password since 2014. Scanning down, her attention was caught by a name that seemed familiar, although she couldn't work out why. Rosanna Silvain. Then it came back to her. Gabriel's former fiancée.

Hazel sat up straighter. For some reason, she felt nervous, her palms clammy as she clicked on the message.

Dear Mrs Collins

I can't say it wasn't a surprise to get your message. Equally, I can't pretend it was a pleasant one. Yes, I was engaged to Vince Harris, but that was a different life and one I was quite happy to say goodbye to after Vince went to prison and everything he'd ever told me turned out to be a lie.

If your daughter is involved with Vince, or whatever he's calling himself now, I'd suggest you tell her to run.

Please don't contact me again. I have a new life now, and these kinds of reminders take me back to a dark time I'd far rather forget.

Best,
Rosanna Silvain

Hazel snapped shut the laptop lid, her heart galloping as if it might race clear of her chest. *Prison.* It was so much worse than she'd imagined. The fact that she'd been right to be suspicious of Gabriel was scant consolation for finding out there was an ex-con in their midst. And he was sharing a suite with her very vulnerable daughter.

Suddenly, it felt freezing cold in the room. When she looked down at her arms, they were covered with little bumps, as if someone had turned the air-con up way too high.

Chapter Forty

Shelly

Shelly was slowly counting backwards, something she'd first learned to do in that basement room, back when the biggest number she knew was ten. By her last stay there, she was starting on five hundred, which is what she was doing now. It steadied her mind, keeping her thoughts from shooting off in all directions. Keeping the panic at bay.

But still the old jitters were creeping in, every muscle tensed as if thousands of tiny needles were pressed up against her, ready to pierce her skin if she relaxed the tiniest fraction. Everything was falling apart, and she didn't understand why. Dom's anger. Jess's threats. And now she was going to lose Lucy. She couldn't bear it. Surely, she reasoned with herself, Lucy would see that she meant well, however things might look from the outside. She'd remember all the myriad little kindnesses Shelly had shown her. One time, Lucy's favourite necklace had broken, scattering tiny beads all over the shop floor, and Shelly had picked them up and taken them home and spent days painstakingly threading them all again. When Lucy had period pain at work, it was Shelly who made her up a bed in the back office and brought her a hot-water bottle and Nurofen, Shelly who'd bought her flowers after she failed her driving test for the third time. Surely all those things counted for something? Of course, Lucy would be upset that Shelly had slept with her dad, but wouldn't she weigh that up against all those other acts of selflessness?

Shelly had once watched a documentary about a nun who visited prisoners on Death Row. 'How would you like to have your whole life judged on the single worst thing you ever did?' she'd asked the interviewer. Surely Lucy would see that their friendship was worth more than those two brief encounters with her dad?

Yet the heaviness of her heart told a different story. It was all happening again. Just like with Uncle Adrian and Auntie Julie. She kept trying her best and trying her best, and it was never, ever enough.

Shelly wished she could just go to bed and lose herself in sleep, but last night, after things started to go wrong, she'd had that dream again. Walls closing in – that awful peeling, stained wallpaper with the faded green stripes. Damp creeping into her bones until she felt there were mushrooms growing out of her skin.

She could hear the others' voices coming from the bar and she made up her mind to join them, even though it meant facing Dom and Jess. It had been Jess's idea to have a nightcap and unwind after the drama of the dinner, with that awful drunk man. Shelly had said no, following the lead of Hazel and Cora, assuming Lucy would be going straight to bed on the night before her wedding. But instead, Lucy had decided to join her sister and her dad and the others, and now there they were all together, with Jess dripping God knows what poison into her sister's ear. Shelly knew Dom had only gone to the bar because she'd said she wasn't, but she couldn't help thinking this might be a chance for her to explain things properly to him and make him understand she was a *friend* to his marriage, not a threat.

And she couldn't stay here on her own with the walls pressing in.

It was a relief, when she entered the bar, that Lucy was clearly so pleased to see her. 'You came! And this is why you're my bestie.'

Shelly didn't dare look in the direction of Dom or Jess, but she felt their animosity.

Gil was in the middle of telling a story about how he'd taken Anastasia out somewhere on his own and she'd insisted on going to the women's toilets, not the men's. 'I had to lurk outside like some pervert, accosting random women until someone agreed to take her in with them.'

Lucy had told Shelly about her row with Zoe earlier, and how she wished she hadn't said that thing about her making herself sick, but that she'd seen red. She'd wondered if Gil might mention it at dinner, but he hadn't said anything. In fact, he'd seemed more relaxed without his wife there. Shelly had spent too much of her life walking on eggshells around the people closest to her not to be able to recognize the signs in someone else.

A sickly-sweet strawberry smell wafted from the doorway.

'Vivian! Oi! Over here!'

'Don't you dare,' Lucy hissed at her sister. But it was too late.

'Just look at all you gorgeous people,' Vivian said when she pulled up a chair at their table, forcing Shelly to squash up next to Gil. 'If it wasn't cannibalism, I would just eat you all up.'

When she laughed, it was like someone dragging a metal table across a wooden floor, and Shelly's mouth felt dry.

Zoe appeared in the doorway, wearing a white vest and a pair of white cotton pyjama trousers pulled low over her hips. Her hair was tied up with a white scarf and her face was pink and scrubbed. She had a champagne flute in one hand and was carrying the bottle in the other.

'If I'd known you were all going to be gone so long, I'd have come to join you at the restaurant,' she said petulantly. She was ignoring Lucy completely. Then she went to stand behind Gil and put her hands on his shoulders. 'Babes, you should have called me. Didn't you see I'd been trying to get hold of you?'

Her voice was high and thick. *Pissed!* Shelly realized.

'Budge up,' said Zoe, climbing over Shelly's legs so she could plonk herself down on Gil's lap.

'Was it a good meal? I love Darius. Isn't he just divine?' Vivian asked them.

Next to Shelly, Zoe wriggled on Gil's lap so she was facing him. 'There was a guy here on a motorbike, shouting and yelling. Did he find you? Was there a scene? Tell me all the goss!'

The goss! The insensitivity of it! With Lucy sitting right there as well!

'It was nothing,' said Gil, clearly embarrassed. 'We had a great time. The food was out of this world.'

'Oh, you're such a bore,' Zoe slurred. She turned to appeal to the rest of the table. 'Come on. I've been stuck here on my own all night. The least you can do is tell me what happened. Was there a fight?'

'You chose to stay here, if you remember,' said Lucy, her earlier remorse over what she'd said on the balcony seemingly forgotten. 'Not that it's exactly a hardship to be in this gorgeous hotel with this gorgeous view. And I notice you're taking full advantage of the minibar too.' She nodded to the champagne.

Despite the dimness of the bar, Shelly saw Zoe's face darken.

'I told you why I needed that facial.'

'Yeah, yeah, your "stress-related skin condition".' Lucy made rabbit ears in the air with her fingers.

'You clearly don't know the first thing about mental health issues. If you must know, I've spent the evening curled up on my bed looking at photos of my daughter and sobbing my eyes out.'

'You know, I can't understand this younger generation,' Vivian interrupted, aiming her comment at Dom, who sat mutely at the far end of the table. 'No one gets miserable any more, they *have depression*, and if you're royally pissed off, you have *anger issues*. You're not allowed to be worried any more, you have to *suffer from anxiety*. Why do they insist on slapping labels all over themselves? Who wants to be put in a little box? I want to be free to have whatever emotions I feel like, thank you very much.'

Zoe twisted around in Gil's lap. 'Aren't you going to stick up for me? You're my *husband*!'

Gil abruptly pushed his chair back so that Zoe all but fell off his lap.

'I think it's probably time we turned in,' he said, getting to his feet. 'Big day tomorrow, and all that.'

'That's nice. I've been stuck here all night waiting for you lot to come back because no one had the decency to call and tell me where you all were. And as soon as I come to join you for a drink you decide to bugger off.'

Zoe, leaning on the back of the chair Gil had just vacated, was pulsating with rage. Shelly could feel the vibrations through her own seat.

'If you'd stuck to the itinerary, we wouldn't have needed to tell you where we were,' snapped Lucy, sounding on the verge of tears.

'I've already told you why I needed that facial. Why are you being such a *bitch*?'

Gil stepped forward, taking Zoe by the arm. 'That's enough,' he hissed at his wife, who was trying to pour another glass of champagne, blind to the fact that the bottle was already empty. Zoe resisted.

'I'm just sick of her being so condescending all the time, like she has this perfect life and the rest of us should be so in awe, when, actually, her sister is a massive fuck-up and she doesn't even know that her own mother-in-law was accused of murdering her husband.'

Chapter Forty-one

Jess

By the time she left the bar, Jess had reached that stage of drunkenness where she could hear someone talking and laughing far too loud but, though she knew on some level it was her, she was also strangely disassociated from it, concentrating only on the physical tasks like staying upright and not missing the table when she put her glass down.

The tequila shots had been a bad idea.

The thing was, they'd all needed that release in the wake of Zoe's bombshell and the clusterfuck that followed it. Gil started yelling at his wife for sharing something he'd told her in confidence. Jason was yelling at Gil for the same thing. Lucy had an expression on her face as if she'd just been shot. Then Zoe was crying and Jason was telling everyone it was a misunderstanding – something that had happened years ago. 'I'll explain everything when we're not all pissed out of our heads and it's not the eve of our wedding,' he'd said. Then Gil had bundled Zoe out, and Lucy had slipped away without saying anything to anyone, and Dom, looking shell-shocked, had taken himself off without meeting Jess's eye, and it had occurred to her belatedly that Shelly might have told him that Jess knew about the two of them. The thought that her dad might be actively avoiding her had given her a strange, empty feeling.

For her own part, she'd decided to put the whole disgusting idea of her dad and Shelly on hold until after the wedding, for Lucy's sake. Jess had always been good at compartmentalizing, something she was quite proud of. 'Men do it all the time. It's what gives them the advantage,' she was fond of telling people. Since her confrontation with Shelly, when she'd realized she was going to have to keep quiet about what she knew until they got home, she'd successfully squished it right to the back of her mind.

She'd ordered tequilas for all of them, but in the end it had been only her and Vivian and Jason left. And Jason's heart hadn't really been in it. He was still upset about the scene with Zoe. 'She made it sound worse than it was. Mum did nothing wrong. It was just a misunderstanding. The police laughed when they turned up, it was so ridiculous. I didn't mention it to Lucy because it wasn't important. I should never have told Gil.' At the same time, he kept looking at the doorway Lucy had gone through and Jess could tell he was itching to go after her. She told herself she couldn't imagine living like that, in someone's pocket, but that didn't stop her feeling a hollow regret for what she'd never had, like pain in a phantom limb.

Once Jason had gone, it was just her and Vivian. The bar staff wanted to close up and had pointedly turned most of the lights off, so Vivian's beady eyes were just pinpricks of reflected moonlight.

Up until then, Jess had enjoyed Vivian's company. She knew the old woman wound people up, but then Jess wound people up, too. She didn't get this whole thing of needing to be liked. She would far rather stir up a strong reaction – positive or negative – than coast through life trying not to upset people and living at a constant level of 'meh'. At least, that's what she told herself. And she admired Vivian's give-zero-fucks attitude. The woman did what she wanted when she wanted. Lucy had told her about Vivian washing her tits in the sink at the airport, the first time Shelly had seen her. Legend! And so what if she demanded attention? Life was all about survival of the fittest, dog eat dog. That was human nature. Not that Jess didn't champion the weak and unrepresented. Fuck, she was VOCAL about giving voice to the voiceless. It's just that she had little time for people who dithered about in the background then complained about someone else stealing the limelight.

But tonight, at some point after the second round of tequilas, Jess had become uncomfortably aware that she was really just going through the motions of having a good time, laughing uproariously at Vivian's endless anecdotes, most of them involving famous people she claimed to have known over the years, and her denigrating put-downs of everyone she'd ever met. But inside her the thin fabric of her bonhomie was tearing, revealing that terrible empty cavity.

If only she had some drugs, now would be when she'd be racking out a huge line, or swallowing another pill, desperate to keep at bay the awful slump she knew was coming.

In the absence of pharmaceuticals, she'd tried her best to keep the evening going, but when she looked out at the stars and they seemed to be moving around in the sky in a sort of centrifugal spiral, she'd had to admit defeat.

If she was honest, she was also finding Vivian a little . . . *much*. Jess was used to holding court herself, and Vivian's domination of the conversation, her seeming lack of awareness of anyone else, was grating. And then there were the quite rude questions, firstly about Cora: 'Do you think she did away with her husband, then? She seems such a *beige* sort of woman,' then, while Jess was still repeating what Jason had said about a misunderstanding, she'd moved on to Shelly, seemingly her favourite subject. 'What do you know about her? Is she always such a *mouse*? Life's too short, don't you think, Jess, to fade into the background?' The month before flying to Greece, Jess had finally got around to fixing the hole her last boyfriend had made in the wall of her rented flat – now *that* was a story. The man in the hardware shop had sold her this foam stuff you squirted in and then it expanded to fill the cavity. As Vivian's monologue progressed, it occurred to Jess's drunken mind that Vivian was like that foam, growing bigger and bigger, expanding into every corner of the space until Jess felt like she was squashed into a tiny corner of the terrace. Vivian was a vampire, sucking out the oxygen, leaving Jess gasping for breath.

In the end, Jess had had to leave. She couldn't remember the last time she hadn't been the last one standing, begging her companions not to go. Vivian hadn't been happy. 'Stay,' she'd commanded, putting a claw-like hand on Jess's arm to detain her. When Jess had refused, the older woman's attitude had changed from the expansive jollity of a few moments before as abruptly as if someone had flicked a switch. 'I thought you were different,' she'd said in a hard voice, bringing her sun-coarsened face right up to Jess's, her fingers pinching Jess's skin. 'But underneath all those tattoos, you're just as dull as the rest of them. Run back to your room like a good little girl.'

For a few moments after she stumbled out of the bar, Jess had felt chilled, almost to the point of sobriety. *What was* that *all about?* she'd thought, rubbing her arm where the skin still smarted. But a few seconds later, she'd convinced herself she'd misread the situation. Or misheard. It wouldn't be the first time she'd got things completely wrong while drunk. And she was *very* drunk, she realized. There was a hairy moment on the way back to her suite where Jess managed to fall *up* the stairs, hitting her forehead in just the same spot where she still had a cut from the night before she'd come here. Bugger, now it was bleeding again. Stumbling into her room, she saw a note on the floor addressed to her in her mother's writing. When she tore it open, it simply said in thick capitals. LOCK YOUR BEDROOM DOOR! What the actual *fuck* was going on tonight?

In her bathroom, Jess tried to dab at the cut on her head with a square of wet toilet paper. God, she looked like shit. And felt like shit, too. When she tried to get the toothpaste on her toothbrush she missed and had to try again. And now she looked more closely, she wasn't sure it *was* her toothbrush. Which would be a bit rich after the argument the other night. The hollow feeling was back, as if all her internal organs were basically free-floating in thin air inside her. Fuck. Why did it always end up like this? She could be in a club having the most brilliant time, on top of the frigging world, and she'd still end up here at the end of the night, staring at her own ragged reflection and thinking, *Who the fuck are you?*

As she sat on the loo, the white robe hanging on the back of the bathroom door facing her seemed to be swaying from side to side as if it was dancing, and when she tried to get up, the movement was beyond her and she had to haul herself up by clinging on to the side of the basin. Whoops.

In her bedroom, she managed to unbuckle her heavy Dr Marten sandals, but her dress, with its crossover straps and back zip, defeated her. She lay back, the room lurching around her while the feeling grew inside her of having said something she shouldn't. Had she told Vivian about Shelly and Dom? She rather thought she might have. Shit. That wasn't cool. At least the wedding was tomorrow, so they had an excuse to avoid her. The last image that crossed her mind before she passed out was of Vivian throwing back her head in laughter, so her throat was an endless red tunnel.

Sometime in the night, Jess awoke. The inside of her mouth felt as if it had been coated in felt and she was struggling to free herself from her dress, which had become bunched up around her waist. The hairs on her arm stood up as she made out, through the darkness, a figure standing by her bed. Almost simultaneously, she realized that it wasn't her dress she was struggling with but a hand, soft but insistent, that she was trying to push away.

'What the *fuck*?' She sat up so quickly she thought for a moment she might be sick.

'*Tranquila, chica.* You were shouting in your sleep, and when I came in you'd got tangled up in your sheet and were getting upset, so I was liberating you.' Gabriel's voice was toneless, as ever, but there was a gap between his words as if he couldn't catch his breath.

'Fuck off out of my room.' But the shape that was Gabriel was already moving towards the doorway.

'No problemo. Sleep well.'

After he'd gone, Jess lay for a moment, willing her heart to stop pounding. Was she having a fucking coronary on top of everything else? Then, drawing on her reserves of willpower, she dragged herself to the bedroom door and turned the key.

Returning to bed, she fell asleep almost instantly, only to dream that her sheet was being wrapped around her over and over until she was fully mummified.

Therapy Journal, Week 13

I'm sorry I got upset on Tuesday. It's just that sometimes it gets to me – how much other people take for granted. Like Jess Collins. She has everything and, instead of being grateful, she just seems to feel entitled to more and more. I sensed that the second I met her.

Sorry, I'm getting ahead of myself. I know you want me to set out the whole story from start to finish. Leave nothing out, you said. You're hoping I'll start spotting patterns of destructive behaviour. I'm trying. I really am.

After our first night together, I studied Dom like I was revising for an exam – methodically, forensically. He'd been practically famous at one point in the 1990s when a book he'd illustrated called Wrong Position of the Week *– a parody of the long-running sex feature in a well-known women's magazine – became that Christmas's fun stocking-filler, staying at the top of the bestseller lists for more than two months. He must have made a fortune from that, and from the two follow-ups, along with all the merchandise – T-shirts, tea towels, that kind of stuff. But the books soon went out of fashion, and he never had another hit. I liked that about him. That he'd known both success and* *failure. I couldn't love someone who'd had everything easy. What would we have in common?*

It was his home life I was most interested in, though. I scoured the internet, looking for clues. Don't tell me you wouldn't have done the same. I found a magazine feature called 'A Room of One's Own', where various creatives talked about their work spaces. His was a room at the top of their semi-detached Georgian home in the Redland area of Bristol with a shabby chic sofa piled high with books and papers and a white desk in front of the back window. In the photo you could just make out a trampoline at the end of the long garden. At the time the article came out, Lucy and Jess would have been in their teens and have probably considered themselves too old for it. But I sat looking at that trampoline for a good long time.

Dom didn't have a social media profile, but Hazel had a Facebook page and, though her posts were set to private, I could still access her photographs, which wasn't as exciting as it sounds, as most were of sunsets on holiday beaches and work events. A couple, though, were of the girls and there was one of the whole family, standing on a lawn, dressed up for a wedding or a posh party.

Hazel was wearing a mid-calf dark sea-green dress, a little bit on the shapeless side, with lots of chunky jewellery. Her brown hair was that middling length, as if she was growing out a short crop, and she'd tried to tuck it behind her ears, even though it wasn't quite long enough. She had a wide, shallow face that was attractive but not pretty and the tops of her arms were soft and pillowy. I liked her.

The girls were a few years younger than they are now, but the difference between them was still just as striking. Lucy, with her blonde, gleaming hair and her 'isn't life amazing?*' expression, wearing a pale blue fitted trouser suit and high heels, clinging on to her father's arm. Jess, scowling at the camera, her arm with all those tacky tattoos held out as if to stop the photo being taken, her hair short then and bleached white, clashing with her pale, up-all-night skin.*

Dom stood in the middle of all his women, and it gave me a thrill to see him like that, as if he were a wild animal I was viewing in his natural habitat. He wore a loose-fitting suit jacket over a white T-shirt and I studied the bit where the T-shirt disappeared into the waistband of his trousers. I know you, *I thought to myself,* I know every inch of you. *His handsome, craggy face beamed with pride and it occurred to me I'd never seen him like that, truly relaxed.*

After I'd absorbed every detail of the photo – giveaway body language, clues as to where they were – I sat back and placed the forefinger of my right hand over each of the four faces in turn, imagining myself in their place. Then I went back to Jess and held my finger over her so that she was completely obliterated and I stared at the picture as if I might burn a hole right through the screen.

Chapter Forty-two

Lucy

The first thing Lucy did when she woke up on the morning of her wedding was take an inventory of how she was feeling. Anxiety had woken her in the early hours, her stomach cramping horribly, her head full of the events of the previous night. The second thing she did, once she'd made sure that – thank God – the cramps were gone, was run to the window to raise the shutters and check on the weather. For the eighteen months that she'd been planning this wedding, the thing that had been keeping her awake at night, the tiny loose thread that threatened to snag all her best-laid plans and had her consulting long-range weather forecasts from as far back as they would go, was the possibility of rain.

Ever since she'd first had a vision of herself walking along a golden beach at sunset, her blonde hair rippling around her like a Botticelli painting, towards her admiring loved ones and the misty-eyed groom – the initial vision had preceded her meeting with Jason, so he'd taken various guises, including Tom Hardy and the manager of a nearby gastropub she'd spoken to only a handful of times – she'd known that her dream was entirely weather dependent.

She scanned the clear blue sky anxiously. Was it slightly hazier over there towards the horizon? Stepping out on to the terrace, she felt sure she could feel a drop in temperature. It was still warm, thank God. But was it *as* warm?

She unrolled her yoga mat to do some morning exercises, hoping to clear her busy mind, but last night's scene with Zoe was a sour taste in the back of her mouth that wouldn't go away.

Cora – self-contained Cora, with her soft mohair throws and scented diffusers – had been accused of murdering Jason's dad. And Jason had kept it secret from her.

The night before, when he'd come stumbling into bed, he'd started again with that 'misunderstanding, nothing in it, but if you want me to, I'll explain . . .' and she'd held up her hand to stop him. 'One question. Did your dad die of cancer?' 'No, not exactly but . . .' Again she'd held up her hand. 'I can't deal with this now. I just can't. We're getting married tomorrow. Just let me have that one, perfect day before I have to face all this shit, please.'

She couldn't think about it. Wouldn't think about it. Nor that horrible message from the cousin she wished to God she'd never tracked down. There'd be time to thrash this all out once they got back to England. She'd spent too much time and money on today to let it be ruined by something that happened decades ago.

Today was about her and Jason and love and family and enjoying being in this beautiful place.

Lucy lay on her back for her stomach crunches. A tiny lizard scuttled across the white-rendered ceiling above her and she tracked its progress while she contracted her abdominals and forced herself up and down: *5, 6, 7, 8*. Think of that dress, she told herself: *29, 30, 31, 32*. Think of that collective gasp as she approached along the sand: *42, 43, 44*.

At least Jason had forgiven her about the money. After she'd said that thing about wanting one perfect day, he'd put his arms around her and she'd started crying about the scene in the restaurant with Nina's drunk husband, and how guilty she felt for overspending. She'd promised to work overtime and cut corners on the wedding party they were throwing for all their mates to make up for it and pay Nina back. When he'd told her Cora was going to lend them the money, just as soon as they got back to England, Lucy had sobbed even harder, and that had melted any last reservations Jason might have had. He never could bear to see her cry.

Finishing her crunches, Lucy swivelled on the mat so that she was facing into the room, rather than looking out at the view. From here she could see Jason's strawberry-blond curls spilling out over the pillow and her heart softened with love as she performed her seated side bends. In all the drama of the last couple of days, it was easy to forget that the most important thing about all of this was she got to marry this man, and spend the rest of her life with him. Jess didn't believe in all that kind of stuff. 'Yeah, but how do you know?' she'd asked the last time Lucy had talked to her about finding love. 'Fifteen years ago, when you were going out with Martin Martin Centre Parting, you swore you'd be with him for ever. Do you remember, you even scratched his name in your arm with the end of a compass? And now you don't even know where he is.' That wasn't quite true. Lucy had looked Martin Isaacs up on Facebook not that long ago and had been quietly gratified to see that he was already losing his hair and was still working at the same bank he'd joined when they left school.

Jason was waking up. She saw him stretch his freckled, muscly arms up to the ceiling, as he did each morning. He was bathed in a slant of early-morning sunlight that turned his normally ruddy skin a lovely honey gold and Lucy reminded herself how lucky she was to have found him. She felt sorry for Jess, really, that she'd never known this absolute conviction of being in the right relationship, of finding The One.

She wished Jason hadn't had to ask Cora to bail them out. It would be another thing binding them to Jason's mum, just at the point where Cora ought to be stepping aside. After today, there should be no question who was the top priority in Jason's life. A wife – God, how she loved that word – trumped a mother. Everyone knew that. Not that she'd ever be anything less than gracious to Cora, and she'd always encourage Jason to be close to his mother. Just on Lucy's terms.

Murderer. The word flashed unbidden into her head, causing her to wobble in her one-legged Vrksasana pose and stumble forward. When she righted herself, the light had changed, so suddenly Jason no longer looked sun-kissed but washed out and grey. Whipping her head around, she watched with an ice-cold feeling of dread as a single thick white cloud inched its way across the face of the sun.

16/6/19, 12.15. Original English-language transcript of police interview with Mrs Vivian Cassandra Kaffel. Police officers: Theodoros Christakis and Kostas Stephanides. Interpreter: Xanthe Liourdis.

I was able to keep tabs on Michelle while she was at Adrian's. Keep tabs: that must be tricky to translate, but it's important you keep the nuance. I don't want you to say I spied or snooped. There's a distinction. I'm not going to give away my methods, as I still keep tabs on Adrian to this day and I wouldn't want him to find out how. Keep your enemies close, and your family closer. Ha!

But after she was absorbed into the care system, I lost track. Every few months I tried to run a search on her, but nothing came out. I guessed she wouldn't be advertising herself on social media. Not after what she'd done, but I thought she must come up sooner or later. I've never had any time for it myself. Social media, that is. I like to live my life, not take photos of it. But young people put it all out there, don't they?

In the end, I found her by using one of

those DNA ancestry kits. I hadn't considered it before, but now I've met her it's obvious that someone so needy for family would be straight on to those. She was looking for her father, I think. Fat chance. That man couldn't get away fast enough.

Sending that swab off went against my better judgement. My DNA on a database somewhere, used for God knows what? Sold to the Russians, most likely. No thank you. But needs must. I don't mind telling you, I shed a tear when the results came and there was a match in the 'Immediate Family' box, 'Predicted Relationship: Grandchild'. She'd changed her surname. That's why I hadn't been able to find her. Even so, it took a while to track her down. She'd switched to Shelly by then. It doesn't suit her.

It was lucky for me that Shelly/Michelle's new best friend Lucy was so prolific on Instagram. I do think there's something broken about women – and let's face it, they usually are women – who live their whole lives on social media, don't you? On *The Gram*? Good grief, could these two possibly look any blanker?

Lucy obligingly committed every detail of her forthcoming wedding plans to Instagram – the party in the garden of a hotel in Somerset for two hundred and fifty of their closest friends. The boutique family wedding in Kefalonia. She'd even provided helpful pictures of all the guests, annotated with their roles at the wedding. Shelly Madden: Bridesmaid and Champagne Pourer. It was emotional, seeing my granddaughter for the first time. She hadn't inherited her mother's looks, I'll say that. But there was a certain something around those bug eyes of hers – an astuteness, if you like – that reminded me of myself.

Once I knew where they were going and when – Lucy not only posted photos of every single room in her chosen hotel but also hashtagged every post with a countdown of how many sleeps till the Paradise View Hotel and Spa – I realized the wedding would make the perfect opportunity for a reconciliation. I've always been a romantic. I make no apology for it. And I was long overdue a jaunt to Greece. I have an affinity with the place. It feeds my soul. Make sure you translate that exactly. The Greeks love to feel appreciated.

Chapter Forty-three

Jess

'Oh my actual *God.* What happened to your head?'

Jess, who'd made what she regarded as Herculean efforts to get up for this wedding breakfast, even though every part of her body had protested, made a face at her sister and dropped heavily into an empty chair at the table.

'Oi, that's where Shelly is sitting.'

'She'll just have to find somewhere else.'

A shadow fell across the table and Jess turned her head – setting off a tsunami of nausea – just enough to clock Shelly hovering by her shoulder, holding a bowl of grey sludge in one hand and a plate of fruit in the other.

'Do you mind, Jess? Only my juice is here and everything.'

Shelly smiled that goofy smile, and Jess looked at her mouth that seemed too wide for her delicate face and imagined her kissing her dad, and *worse.*

'Sorry, computer says no.'

She put her head in her hands so she didn't have to see the turquoise sea, or the gorse-topped cliffs or the high white clouds scudding across a blue-silk sky. It was as if nature in all its beauty was mocking her roiling guts and throbbing head and the thick, yeasty smell of her own breath. She could sense Shelly still lurking at her shoulder. Fucksake, was the woman going to choose now, of all times, to stand up for herself? Just at the point where Jess was at her weakest and only wanting to be left alone to wallow in her own filth and misery? But no, Shelly moved away and deposited her breakfast at the far end before going in search of a chair, which she dragged showily across the floor.

'I apologize for my rude sister,' Lucy shouted down the length of the table.

'No worries. It's your wedding day. You don't have to apologize for a thing.' Surely Lucy could hear the tight thread of insincerity running through Shelly's words? But her sister was scanning the sky and frowning.

'What do those clouds mean up there? Anyone study biology?'

'Don't you mean meteorology, sweetheart?' asked Dom, who was sitting across from Jess and studiously avoiding her eyes. 'And I don't think those clouds are anything to worry about.'

'Has anyone seen Mum this morning?' Jason asked. 'She's normally one of the earliest up.'

'Gabriel's not here either,' said Lucy.

'What's that supposed to mean?'

'Nothing. God, chill out. It's supposed to be our wedding day.'

A strange feeling had come over Jess when Lucy said her roommate's name, an involuntary constricting of the abdominal muscles, one by one, until her navel felt pressed up against her spine. She had a flashback to waking up in the night, a shadowy figure by her bed. Gabriel's voice. She'd been angry. Kicking. But no sooner had the memory zipped through her mind than it was gone again.

The door to the lobby area opened to admit Gil and Zoe, both wearing dark glasses and identical tight-lipped expressions. Reflexively, Jess covered the cut on her head with her fingers. The newcomers glanced over and Gil raised his hand before they headed to a table for two at the far side of the terrace. Normally, Jess would have felt compelled to say something, but she was battling a fresh wave of nausea and thought if she opened her mouth there was a fair chance some vomit would come out.

Lucy insisted they had Buck's Fizz for breakfast. 'It's my wedding day. It's compulsory.'

'Are you literally trying to kill me?'

'Nobody forced you to drink those tequilas with your *new best friend*. Anyway, hair of the dog.'

The handsome waiter appeared with a bottle of fizz. The purple bruising around his eye had faded to that kind of weird green-yellow. Even through her hangover, Jess tried to muster a smile. That need to establish a mateyness with waiters and bar staff, to show that no matter that she was the one being served and they were the servers, she was still one of them, was deeply ingrained. But the waiter didn't even glance at her. At the next table, the bride who'd had her wedding the previous day was looking clammy and pale, her breakfast untouched in front of her.

Zoe, who'd been sitting in uncharacteristic silence while Gil talked to her in a low, urgent voice, now walked hesitantly over to them. Her shoulders sloped and even her hair, pulled back into a ponytail, seemed more subdued than usual.

'I just wanted to apologize for last night,' she said quietly, directing her words to Lucy's plate. 'I was drunk and still upset about what you had said earlier, but I was out of order sharing stuff Gil told me in confidence. I hope it didn't spoil your night, Lucy.'

Now Jess wanted to know what Lucy had said to Zoe to make her upset, as well as the truth behind Zoe's bizarre outburst last night. But before her mush-filled brain had a chance to grind slowly into gear, Zoe had gone back to her table.

'Now let's draw a line under it,' said Jason gruffly.

Jess looked at him more closely. He seemed tired and a little out of sorts, but then again, maybe that was normal on your wedding day. Otherwise, everything was the same. He still glanced at Lucy all the time, as if checking she was still there, as he always did, and asked if anyone else needed anything whenever he went to the buffet table. He definitely did not, no matter what Zoe had said, look like a man with a shameful, dark secret in his past.

Jess turned her attention to the sea, where a white speedboat pulling a water-skier behind it was making a lazy figure of eight. Gradually, the pressure in her head eased and she stopped feeling as if she were stuck in an aeroplane flying through turbulence. The missing members of the group joined in dribs and drabs. First Cora, looking cool and unruffled in a charcoal-grey linen vest and chino shorts. For a split second after she appeared, there was a pause in conversation as everyone recalibrated what they saw in light of the previous night's revelations before deciding, after all, she was just the same woman as twenty-four hours earlier. Whatever Zoe had been talking about, it had been a misunderstanding, as Jason said.

Jess saw Jason eyeing his mother sharply, but whatever he was thinking, he kept it to himself. Five minutes after Cora, Jess's mother arrived, sweeping Lucy into an awkward embrace. 'How's the beautiful bride?' She turned down the Buck's Fizz. 'Bit of a dodgy tummy.' Come to think of it, she did look drained. Probably picked up on all the tension. Anger blazed a path through Jess's still-sensitive gut as her gaze swung to Shelly at the other end of the table. How could that *bitch* sit there sipping her drink as if she didn't have a care in the world while her lover's wife was just a few feet away? What a *psycho*!

Jess got abruptly to her feet and headed for the buffet. From the corner of her eye, she saw Gabriel arriving, wearing his usual black T-shirt and jeans, and once again she had that same physical reaction, that feeling of everything tightening up inside her. The dark figure by the bed in the night. Her legs kicking out.

'Are you OK, Jess? You've gone very pale.'

Gil was next to her, clutching his own plate.

'What? Oh, yeah. Tidy, mate. You know me. Could murder a fry-up, though.'

Jess shakily reached out for a mini Danish, ignoring the dainty metal tongs and grabbing a couple off the tray with her fingers.

'You seen Vivian this morning? Fuck, we had a skinful last night. I thought I was hardcore, but that woman could drink me under the table.'

'Do you like her, though?'

'What?'

'I mean, don't you find her a bit . . . *extra*? The way she talks over the top of you and kind of takes over everything. I know she's a character and everything and, you know me, live and let live, but I just don't think she's very . . . *nice*.'

Jess had an uncomfortable flashback to that moment last night, Vivian gripping on to her arm. Hadn't she said something weird? Jess remembered feeling desperate to get away. Feeling scared, even. But she wouldn't think about that now. Just as she couldn't let on to the others how much Gabriel was freaking her out, as that would be like admitting she'd been wrong to bring him, so she couldn't now turn on the woman she'd insisted on introducing into the group.

'No, she's jokes. She's her own person, you know. That's what I like about her.'

'Oh. Right.'

Gil looked so miserable and forlorn standing there with his empty plate that Jess's heart hurt for him, despite everything. Impulsively, she reached out and put a hand on his shoulder.

'Don't feel bad about telling Zoe Jason's big secret. It's not your fault she basically told the whole world.'

Gil's face crumpled as if he were fighting off tears and she pulled him awkwardly in for a half-hug, trying not to tip her pastries on to the floor.

Jess was always at her most emotional when hungover, so it was no great surprise that her own eyes instantly blurred with tears. When they cleared, she found herself staring, over Gil's left shoulder, straight at Zoe, whose face was twisted into an expression of such undisguised hatred that, even from that distance, Jess shuddered.

Chapter Forty-four

Hazel

Ever since Hazel discovered that her husband of nearly thirty years had cheated on her, she'd entered a strange, surreal state where nothing seemed quite real, and the low-level nausea she'd been experiencing off and on for hours now, on top of the effects of last night's alcohol intake, had only increased that sense of being alienated from her own life.

Down by the swimming pool, she stretched out on a lounger. As it was still relatively early and the sun hadn't reached maximum strength, she decided to risk exposing her face to it, in the hope of acquiring some last-minute colour before they began the long process of getting ready for the wedding. Lucy had wanted the preparations to start right after breakfast – a whole day of exfoliating and buffing and moisturizing and plumping, even before the make-up artist and hairdresser arrived. 'We'll banish the boys and hole up in my suite with champagne and music, and we'll try on clothes and sit in the jacuzzi, and it will be so special.' But Hazel had managed to persuade her that they'd all be falling over drunk by the time the ceremony came, and their dresses would look like crumpled rags. So she'd agreed to start after lunch, giving them the morning off. Thank God.

Hazel draped the borrowed sarong over her face half-heartedly. If the sun was really so damaging, how come it felt so good, as if her skin was crying out for it? Cora's smooth, sculpted face came into her mind and Hazel tried to remember if she'd ever seen her expose it to the sun, though she supposed if Cora really had shelled out hundreds on Botox, she probably wouldn't be doing something that instantly wiped out the benefits.

She found herself thinking about Dom's mystery woman. Up until this moment, she'd been an abstract concept. But now, lying in the sun with the gauzy fabric of the sarong turning everything orange and green, she forced herself to picture her. She'd be in her early forties, Hazel decided, probably someone he'd met at the gym, a newly divorced yummy mummy with muscular thighs and plenty of free time during the day. And no droopy eyelids.

A giggle alerted her to the fact that she was no longer alone on the terrace. Surreptitiously peeping out around the edge of the sarong, she saw that Gabriel and Cora had taken up the loungers directly opposite across the dazzling surface of the pool. Could there be something romantic between the two of them? Hazel was taken aback by the jolt of envy that passed through her at the thought. Not that she wanted anything to do with

Gabriel herself. It was the idea that Cora might be enjoying the fizzing anticipation that comes with a new relationship, a clean slate, with someone who hadn't yet let her down.

Cora was wearing a plain sage-coloured bikini and a straw cowboy-style hat, and her stomach muscles moved like piano keys against her taut skin. As she watched, Gabriel said something that made Cora throw back her head and laugh, and Hazel couldn't help noticing the lack of jowls and was reminded of that humiliating consultation with the Botox-giving GP. She'd bet Cora had never been told she had a perfectly ordinary middle-aged face.

Now Hazel's gaze switched to Gabriel. She tried to see him through Cora's eyes. He wasn't bad-looking, really, in that bland kind of way. His body, divested of the usual black T-shirt, was more toned than his round face would suggest, his chest broad, with whorls of surprisingly dark hair. So many men of Hazel's own generation seemed to have held on to their youthful vigour way past what could be reasonably expected, only to pitch overnight directly into old age, without passing through that middle ground women tended to get stuck in. But Gabriel was still incontrovertibly fit and healthy.

With everything that had been going on with Dom, Gabriel's murky past had almost slipped her mind, but looking at him now it all came back to her – Vince Harris, Rosanna Silvain's stark warning. That word: 'prison'. As Hazel watched, Cora sat up cross-legged on her lounger and turned her back, holding up her hair while Gabriel sprayed her shoulders and back with sun cream before using his fingers to gently rub it into the bow of her spine.

She should tell her, Hazel thought now. She should warn Cora about this man. She gazed at the points where his pale fingers dug into Cora's skin and shuddered. What might those fingers have done?

'Wish he'd back off a little.'

Jason had arrived without her noticing and was sitting stiffly on the lounger next to hers. For a man embarking on what was supposed to be the happiest day of his life, he looked decidedly stony-faced. Hazel wondered if it had anything to do with what Zoe had said the night before. Dom had come back to their suite with some garbled story about Cora having been mistakenly accused of having something to do with her husband's death. But that couldn't be true. He'd died of cancer. But because she wasn't talking to Dom more than necessary, and because she'd already started feeling a bit sick, she hadn't bothered correcting him.

Hazel knew she ought to tell Jason what she'd discovered about Gabriel, was on the point of saying it. Only the thought of Lucy stopped her, knowing how much store her elder daughter had set on this day and how much any hint of a scene would upset her.

'I expect your mum is just enjoying a little bit of male attention,' she said instead, meaning to be placatory, and tried not to notice how the fingers of Jason's left hand were pressed so tightly against his other forearm they formed four perfect, bloodless circles.

Chapter Forty-five

Nina

I could kill him. I wanted the floor to swallow me up. Honest to God.

The reply from her sister Katie came instantly.

Do you still love him?

Hunched over the steering wheel of her little car outside her house, Nina hesitated, her fingers hovering over the keyboard.

Truth? I feel sorry for him.

This time, there was a longer gap before the response.

Pity is Kiss of Death for love. Come home.

She was right, Nina thought, turning the key repeatedly until the engine finally spluttered into life. A relationship could withstand anger, hatred even, but once you felt sorry for a man, that was the end of it.

She hadn't spoken to Mark since that mortifying scene the night before. He'd been in the house when she got home and had jumped to his feet, hands outstretched, ready with his self-justifications for why he'd acted as he had, how you couldn't let people walk all over you, that wasn't the way it was done here.

She hadn't even looked at him, just gone straight up the stairs into what had been their bedroom and was now hers, and locked the door. This morning, he hadn't emerged from the spare room while she'd been in the kitchen making breakfast. Probably sleeping it off. The anger and then the self-flagellation would come later. He had left her a note, though, scrawled on the back of one of her own welcome letters that she always gave to new couples when they arrived. 'Bugs has got out again. In case you're interested.'

Nina rolled her eyes. As if today wasn't shitty enough already. Well, the AWOL rabbit would just have to wait.

Before leaving, she took the keys to Mark's motorbike from his jacket, which had been flung down on the sofa. She couldn't risk him coming up to the hotel and making another scene. Not on Lucy and Jason's wedding day. Jason had texted her sometime in the night to tell her his mum would transfer half the money as soon as she got back to the UK and they would get the other half to her the second they got paid. She hadn't had the heart to tell him that it might be too little too late.

She was nervous as she approached her car, half expecting to see Mr Angelis or one of his many relatives heading her way, wielding baseball bats or hunting rifles. But all was quiet, apart from a fly that flew in as soon as the car door opened. As she turned off the main road and started winding up the hill towards the hotel, leaving the town far behind, she found herself growing lighter with every metre the little car ascended. She loved wedding days, when all those months of planning and organizing came together. The endless phone calls and trips out to meet this supplier or that photographer, the emails about floral arrangements and gazebos and fairy lights, the bureaucratic nightmare of getting all the legal documents translated and registered – all of that ceased to matter once she had her first glimpse of the bride, glowing and gorgeous as they all were in their own way, walking towards her groom, hesitant and hopeful and self-conscious and achingly proud all at once.

The truth was, no matter what had gone wrong in her own relationship or how many times life showed her that love was a commodity like any other, whose value went up and down, or ceased altogether, that could be traded or withheld or just be left on a shelf in the dark to grow stagnant and stale, Nina still believed in the transformative power of marriage. She believed that two people could be stronger together than apart, could put each other's wellbeing before their own, could want to be better, try harder, because of the other. And when she saw her couples turning to each other in front of all their most-loved people, and holding each other's hands and looking into each other's eyes and smiling their shy, hopeful smiles, she still believed that it was possible – the enduring, selfless, mutually empowering kind of love everyone dreamed of.

Apart from a few high white clouds, the day was clear and beautiful, not like some of the wedding days she'd had, when a storm had arisen from nowhere, rain lashing on hastily erected canvas canopies, wind blowing veils off heads and decimating meticulously constructed hairstyles.

When the buzzing of the fly, which had settled somewhere behind her, grew too irritating, Nina turned off the air-con and opened the window wide to breathe in the smell of jasmine and wild thyme on the warm air. Everything would be all right, she told herself. She would make sure Lucy and Jason had the wedding of their dreams, and the same with the other couples whose nuptials she was contracted to oversee over what remained of the season. She'd go to see Mr Angelis and explain the situation, and they'd agree on a sensible repayment plan, and then, when all the loose ends were tied up, she'd go home. Start again. She was only thirty-five. Still time to rebuild her life. Despite what her sister said, she did still love Mark in a way. But it was the kind of love that came from a shared history. The kind of love that kept you rooted in the past instead of allowing you to forge a new future. He would always be a part – the most important part – of this adventure they'd been on together. But that adventure was ending.

Nina slowed to admire a demoiselle damselfly that had alighted on a low rock by the side of the crumbling road, its delicate, iridescent wings shimmering from emerald green to sapphire blue. She held her breath, watching the creature's long, slender abdomen quiver in the clear morning. It was a sign, she decided. From now on, everything would fall into place, because she was taking back control. Even the car was behaving itself, barely protesting around those steep hairpin bends.

By the time she pulled into the car park, she was feeling almost buoyant. Everything happens for a reason, she reminded herself.

She leaned over to pick up her bags from the passenger-seat footwell. Always so much extra *stuff* needed on wedding days. Printed itineraries, various official forms, beta blockers, painkillers, sunscreen, a pashmina just in case, spare fuses, batteries.

The buzzing from the back of the car had intensified, as if the original fly had been joined by a friend. Lots of friends. As Nina straightened up, she turned her head to check it out – and screamed at the sight of the rabbit, skinned and bloody, stretched daintily out along the back seat.

Therapy Journal, Week 14

We only slept together twice, Dom and I, but those times were spaced apart so I prefer to think of our relationship lasting nearly a year. After that first time, he sent me a sweet email that I printed out and still read when I'm having a bad day. He said he'd acted out of character and was ashamed, and I deserved so much better. That was the first time I think it occurred to me that I might deserve anything just because of who I was, rather than anything I did.

I was upset when Dom tried to break up after that first time. I'd already fantasized about the new life we'd have together. That's normal, isn't it? But at the same time I liked how hard he was fighting for his family. I said I understood but asked if we could meet to say goodbye properly. I told him I was bored at work and wanted his advice on next steps. I already knew he couldn't resist feeling needed. We met for lunch. We drank. Plenty. He had come into town on the pretext of buying a new suit for some awards ceremony he'd been invited to. We spilled out of the pub and ended up in a menswear boutique around the back of Covent Garden, giggling as I pulled out suits for him to try, overruling him when he protested they were too young for him. 'I can't possibly pay this,' he'd said on the third one, but after he'd studied his reflection for a long time, he got his wallet out, and I felt a small thrill of pleasure, knowing that whenever he wore it, he'd think of me. We ended up in a Travelodge near Paddington Station. He didn't cry this time, but when we'd finished he sat silently on the edge of the bed for a full ten minutes with his head in his hands.

After that second time, I wasn't so surprised when Dom again told me he felt ashamed and it had to end. I knew how much he wanted to do the right thing, though I thought he'd buckle eventually. There's a cliché, isn't there, about how something that feels so right can't be wrong. But gradually his emails and texts slowed to a trickle, becoming shorter and more abrupt. The more he pulled back, the more I tried to remind him of everything we'd been to each other. I tried to make him understand that I'd never hurt his family, that I was as invested in them as he was. In the end, he blocked me. Now, I understand, but at the time I thought I would go crazy. It felt like being back there again in that windowless basement room, alone, while out there in the world Dom went about his family life as if nothing had happened, just like Uncle Adrian and Auntie Julie had done after I left. And the nothing that had happened to all of them was me.

Chapter Forty-six

Lucy

Now the big day was finally here, Lucy couldn't believe how quickly it was passing. She wanted to slow down time, take the individual seconds and press them like flowers between the pages of a book so that when she was back home in Oldfield Park on a rainy Monday morning in November, she could take them out and there they'd be, perfectly preserved. The particular quality of the light here, the smell of pine in the warm air, the eagle circling way up high over the far clifftop, Jason's face, so dear to her – how could she ever have thought him plain?

Stepping out of the shower, she stood for a moment, gazing down at her body in unashamed appreciation. She'd always taken care of herself, always exercised, but she had lost ten pounds to get in shape for this wedding. Well, to get in shape for the dress, more accurately. She'd had laser hair removal on her bikini line and upper lip, and had waxed every other part, including the fine hairs on her toes, which she hadn't even noticed until the beautician pointed them out. She was tanned and toned and smooth, and her hip bones jutted pleasingly. Lucy knew for a fact she would never look so good again. Sure, there'd be other sun-kissed holidays and, obviously, when she got pregnant she'd be radiant and glowing and all the rest of it, but there'd never be another time when her body would be subject to such a sustained and costly programme of improvements.

My last shower as an unmarried woman. She'd been doing that a lot today, dismantling her single life piece by piece, ready for the next stage. *The last breakfast, the last time I'll get dressed in the morning.* She couldn't wait to be Mrs Beazant, even though every time she whispered the phrase to herself it conjured up Cora's face, with that unfathomable smile of hers.

But she wouldn't think of Cora now. Or what Zoe had said last night in the bar. Or Connor Kerswell's shit-stirring email. She *did* know exactly what she was marrying into, thank you very much. She was marrying into Jason Beazant, the kindest man she'd ever met, and that was all she needed to know.

There was a knock at the door. Jason had long been dispatched to Gil's suite with strict instructions that he was not to return, under pain of death. As soon as he'd gone, Lucy had liberated her dress from the wardrobe, as if it had been held captive there against its will. When it came tumbling out of the dress bag, the rush of pure joy she experienced eclipsed anything she'd ever felt for a lover from whom she'd been parted for any length of time. Now, it was hanging up on the wardrobe door, and, wrapped in the brand-new ivory silk sarong she'd been saving for today, she brushed her hand gently against it as she passed.

'Oh my God, I can't believe this is actually happening,' said Shelly when Lucy opened the door. She threw her arms around her friend, and Lucy was touched. Normally, Shelly was quite guarded about her own personal space. It was Lucy who was the tactile one.

'I know!' Lucy squealed.

She was delighted to see Shelly. She knew some people – like Jess, for example – questioned their friendship, but Lucy found something very grounding in Shelly. She was one of the very few people Lucy knew who really focused on you, rather than on what you reflected back to them. And she was unswervingly loyal. Out of all her friends, Lucy knew Shelly was the one who would drop everything if she needed help. And, in return, she gave Shelly a sense of fun in her life, and a sense of family.

'Now you're here I can open this!' Lucy picked up the bottle of champagne that had been sweating in an ice bucket. The truth was, she didn't much feel like drinking after the excesses of the night before and the Buck's Fizz at breakfast, plus her stomach was still tender after the overnight anxiety cramps. But sipping champagne with her bridesmaids while they fussed around getting her ready was a scene she'd pictured so many times she couldn't bear to depart from it now.

Once the drinks were poured, they headed out on to the terrace. They had plenty of time before the make-up artist and hair stylist arrived. Come to think of it, Shelly had turned up a little earlier than the itinerary suggested, but Lucy didn't mind. She was too excited to be on her own.

'I'm glad you're not letting last night get to you – that scene at dinner,' said Shelly as they took their seats at the small glass-topped table.

Lucy felt that tightening in her chest, remembering Nina's horrible drunken husband and how she'd thought for a moment that he was actually going to hit Jason. Then she deliberately shut the memory down. When she was a hormonal teenager and unable to sleep because she'd fallen out with one friend or another, or was stressing about schoolwork or some slight from a boy she liked, her mum had told her to imagine herself putting her worries in a drawer and then closing the drawer. The next day, she could open up the drawer again, her mum said, and nine times out of ten, whatever had been worrying her would have resolved itself overnight.

That's what she did now with the whole issue of the outstanding payment and the ugly scene at the restaurant and Jason's cousin's email and the business of Jason's dad's death. There'd be time enough to open up those particular drawers when they got home.

'You know how long I've been planning today, Shell. I'm not about to let some drunken *wanker* in a motorbike helmet ruin it.'

'Good for you.' Shelly took a sip of champagne and moved her chair further into the shade. It must be awful having to shield your skin from the sun all the time, Lucy thought. She took a closer look at Shelly's face.

Why did she look so tense? Surely Lucy was supposed to be the one having nerves, and it was Shelly's job to calm her down.

'You OK?'

Shelly looked stricken, although she swiftly covered it up with a smile.

'I'm fine. Oh my God, Luce, I'm so excited about today. I just . . .'

'Just what?'

'Look, I don't want to make a big thing of this, and honestly, it's nothing, but I'm worried Jess might try to stir up trouble between you and me today. I just wanted to flag it up to you.'

Shelly was still wearing the loose-fitting cotton dress she'd had on at breakfast, and she wound the hem around her finger as she talked. A cold, hard lump formed at the base of Lucy's stomach. Not today. Of all days. She knew Jess and Shelly didn't get on, but they needed to park their hostilities for the next twelve hours.

'I'm sorry, Shelly, but I can't be hearing this. I've worked so hard to get myself into a place of positivity.'

Shelly nodded.

'I know, and I feel like shit bringing it up, but I just wanted to warn you, so you can head it off if she starts. I don't want anything to spoil your day.'

Come to think of it, Shelly really did look like she was suffering. Her pale, freckled face was marked by a lattice of red, blotchy lines and the whites of her eyes looked pink and irritated.

'What's happened?' asked Lucy flatly.

'Oh God, it's just stupid stuff. Nothing for you to worry about *at all*. I think, deep down, maybe she resents me being a bridesmaid. I made the mistake of suggesting she lay off the booze until tonight, just so we can really appreciate the effort you've put into today. Anyway, she didn't take it well. You know how she is. Sorry, Luce. I know it's not what you want to hear right now.'

Shelly looked so wretched, Lucy found her anger dissolving into the hot afternoon air. The truth was, she was relieved, that's all it was. Shelly's expression had been so solemn, but Jess throwing a strop was nothing she couldn't cope with.

'Don't worry. I won't let her get to me. Or slag you off when all you were doing was trying to help me. Come on, put it out of your head. There's champagne to be drunk.'

Shelly smiled gratefully, her face slackening with relief. She picked up her glass and held it out.

'Here's to the bride.'

Lucy clinked her own glass against her friend's.

'Here's to all of us. One big, happy family.'

Chapter Forty-seven

Jess

Jess was glad she'd stuck to her guns about the dress. No way would she want to be decked out like a stick of pink candyfloss in this heat. She admired her reflection in the mirror, swirling the psychedelic fabric this way and that. What a find! She'd teamed it with the chunky silver and leather cuff she'd borrowed from a friend and conveniently forgotten to give back, and fitted a garland of fake flowers around her head that she'd bought at some festival or other. She'd dabbed concealer on the cut on her head and applied a bright pink lipstick to match Lucy's precious colour scheme. At least no one could accuse her of not entering into the spirit of things!

She was feeling better since the Buck's Fizz and no longer thought she was going to vomit every time she looked up too suddenly. And she'd managed to arrange her thoughts into a narrative she could live with. For now. Her father was a prize dick, but he was vulnerable. Everyone knew middle-aged men, like teenaged boys, were basically genetically programmed to be sex addicts, given half a chance. He'd been weak, not evil, and Shelly had taken advantage. Not that Jess was letting him off the hook.

Jess didn't hold with rug-sweeping, or secrets. As soon as this was over, she would head straight to her parents' house and have it out with both of them. And once Lucy was back from honeymoon, she'd tell her exactly what kind of sneaky bitch her so-called best friend really was. Obviously, they worked together, so that might complicate things, but there must be a way to get Shelly out.

Jess still felt seismically shaken by the threat to her family, but at the same time weirdly energized. It was as if the cracks in other people's lives made her own more palatable. Having shit to deal with didn't make you a fuck-up, she decided philosophically. It just made you normal.

Jess firmly believed that her parents would weather this crisis. The thing was, even though she was all for personal freedom and everything, they had to understand that this was about more than just the two of them. Lucy and Jess's emotional wellbeing, their entire identity really, was also at stake. They wouldn't break up their family over a meaningless fling with a nothing like Shelly Madden.

She headed down to the main terrace, where, already, Gil and Jason were waiting, unfamiliar in their sharp lightweight suits. The two men looked uncomfortable and, though, ordinarily, Jess disapproved of suits as a concept, regarding them as just as subjugating of men as high heels were of women, she had to admit Gil looked pretty hot in his, with the crisp white shirt perfectly setting off his smooth, brown skin.

'Smokin', guys,' she said, giving Jason a hug. He looked so anxious, standing there, glancing up towards the terrace of his suite where his bride was getting ready, but at the same time excited, like a child about to take part in a school concert desperately scanning the audience for their parents. For the first time, Jess felt a glimmer of understanding. So this was why people put themselves through this – for this sense of holding another person's hand and jumping off together into the unknown, with all the terror and the exhilaration that entailed.

'How come you're not with Lucy?' he asked, hugging her back. He smelled of citrus-toned aftershave and light perspiration.

Shit. She'd forgotten all about Lucy's instructions that she and Hazel and Shelly should convene in the De Luxe suite to get ready together.

Well, she *was* ready. And no way was she letting some make-up artist loose on her face. What if she tried some of that contouring shit? Standing in the sweltering heat with an inch thick of foundation melting down your cheeks? No, thank you. Jess was half tempted to ignore the itinerary, but then she thought about Shelly being there alone with Lucy, filling her ear with God knows what lies.

'Right. I'm offski.'

Jess was expecting to be in trouble with her sister. Outside the door, she braced herself for the usual judgemental looks and comments about being late and whatever was she wearing. It didn't upset her. It was part of their long-running sibling pantomime.

But Lucy was in no mood to fall into tired old patterns.

'I'm nearly finished having my hair done. Oh God, I'm so excited, I might wet myself!'

Until now, Jess hadn't set much store on that tired cliché about radiant brides, but now she totally got it. Lucy was so alive with joy and nerves and anticipation, she was practically levitating.

'Drink!' It was a command rather than an offer, but Jess wasn't about to object to having a glass of champagne thrust upon her.

Lucy was wrapped in some kind of sheet, but her make-up was perfect, courtesy of the make-up artist – a chubby young woman with surprisingly bad skin – who was out on the terrace, applying eyelash curlers to their mother's lashes.

'Oh, hello, darling,' said Hazel, and it occurred to Jess just how little time she'd spent with her mum over these days and how preoccupied she'd seemed. Now, it all made sense. Hazel wasn't an idiot. She might not know that her husband had *fucked* – even within the privacy of her own head, applying that verb to her own father made Jess feel a little sick – a psychopath half his age, but she'd be aware on some deeper level that something was very out of place.

'Are you OK?' Her mum was looking decidedly pale – unless the make-up artist had used a foundation several shades too light.

'Yes, fine. Well, I've had a little bit of a dodgy stomach, but that's probably just excitement.'

Or emotional trauma, more likely, Jess decided. She looked around, only now noticing Shelly, sitting at the little table in the corner wearing a soft-pink sleeveless dress that did nothing for her colouring, although Jess did concede that her red hair looked better than usual, swept back off her face and held up in one of those hairdos where a lock of the hair itself is wound around whatever elastic has been used to make the ponytail. Their eyes met. Shelly had obviously succumbed earlier to the make-up artist's ministrations and her usually fair eyelashes were dark and defined, her freckles blurred into a healthy glow. A look of animosity passed between them so intense Jess couldn't believe the others didn't sense it sizzling through the hot air.

'As soon as Olympia finishes my hair' – Lucy gestured to a statuesque woman in a tight white shirt and black skirt holding aloft a set of steaming curling tongs – 'I'll put on my dress, and then Dad and I and Shelly will go to the harbour, and the rest of you head down to the beach to wait.'

'Er, hang on, back up. How come *she*' – Jess jerked her head in Shelly's direction – 'gets to go with you and Dad?'

'Only as far as the harbour, then Nina has arranged for her to get a lift back to the hotel. I needed someone to come with me in case of last-minute adjustments to my dress or hair or make-up. And I know you'd rather stick pins in your eyes than do that.'

In ordinary circumstances, this would be true. Jess was not a girly girl in that way, but the thought of Shelly and Dom being together was agonizing. Jess glanced at Shelly and thought she saw a faint smile.

'But I'm your matron of honour.'

Lucy, hair springing back from the tongs in a perfect curl, looked astonished.

'Well, yes. Technically. But you've never paid any attention to that before. You said you hated that kind of crap.'

'Don't listen to anything I say. Seriously, I wanna come with you.'

'Are you sure?'

'Abso-fucking-lutely.'

'It'll be nice for you sisters to be together for a change,' said Hazel. 'I'm sure Shelly won't mind.'

They all turned to look at Shelly, who had flushed the same colour as her dress.

'Would you be upset, Shell?' asked Lucy. 'Only I get to spend so little time with Jess. And actually, it *is* supposed to be the matron of honour's role . . .'

''Course not,' said Shelly, getting to her feet and blinking in a sudden shaft of sunlight. 'It's your wedding day. You make the rules.'

She smiled. Where the light hit them, her huge, rounded eyes, starkly framed by those unfamiliar dark lashes, appeared completely white, like the membrane of an egg.

Chapter Forty-eight

Shelly

It was happening all over again. Just the same as before. Right now, Shelly should be crammed into the back seat of the white Mercedes Nina had booked, heading down to the nearest port with Lucy and Dom, drinking champagne with Lucy's veil looped over her lap so it didn't get tangled up. Laughing, clinking glasses. At the beating heart of everything.

Instead, here she was, picking her way down to the beach on her own in the shoes Lucy had picked out for her, which were already giving her blisters.

Was this to be her life? Always on the outside? While people like Jess, heedless and self-absorbed, blithely assumed intimacies they'd done nothing to earn?

She heard her name being called and turned around. Hazel was approaching from the swimming-pool deck, wearing a blue knee-length dress. Her hair, which had been blow-dried and sprayed by the stylist until it had the properties of a motorbike helmet, was already wilting, and her face was clammy under the thick make-up.

Shelly's pulse quickened and her fingers crept to the garish purple glasses she carried in her handbag. It had been a risk bringing them, but they had become a kind of talisman.

'Thank God I found you. We can go down together.'

Hazel looped her arm through Shelly's, and the warmth of her touch spread out along Shelly's veins and nerves and sinews until her body hummed with it. Surely, after everything she'd been through, after the basement room, and being exiled from Adrian and Julie's and everything that had happened since, she would be allowed to keep this? Just this. Her place on the edge of this little group of people. She wouldn't ask for anything more. Only what everyone else had. Only that. Hazel and Dom and Lucy would understand she meant no harm. She would be forgiven. Just as Jess was always forgiven.

That's what families did.

15/6/19, 23.24. Original English-language transcript of police interview with Mr Gilberto Victor Rodriguez. Police officers: Demitri Iraklidis and Tomaso Diakos. Interpreter: Eulalia Scala.

Describe Shelly? Oh, wow. Let's see. Quiet. Smart. Kind. Just a nice person, you get me? Doesn't like to talk about her childhood, but that's cool. We all have our hang-ups, right? I think it was pretty chaotic, though. Perhaps that's why she ended up so calm. I'm no psychiatrist, but sometimes you grow up in diametric opposition to your upbringing. Yin and yang, you know?

The first time I met her I went in for a hug, like I always do – I'm a hugger, what can I say? – and she went like this. What's that? Oh, in words. Got you. Well, she kind of flinched. We had a rescue dog once when I was a kid and when we first brought him home he used to do the same thing. No, I'm not saying she'd been maltreated, but she was definitely wary, you know? I thought, 'I'm gonna have to win your trust.' Nothing wrong with that.

You could see she loved Lucy. I mean *Loved* with a capital L. It was touching to see, actually. No, there was never anything weird about it. It was nice.

Chapter Forty-nine

Nina

Nina couldn't concentrate. Normally, she would already be getting tearful around this point, swept up in the emotion of the occasion, while still keeping one eye out for any last-minute hiccups that might need sorting out.

But today she was dry-eyed and preoccupied. As she descended the petal-strewn stone steps to the beach below the hotel, all she could think about was that dead rabbit lying across the back seat of her car. The missing Bugs. It had to be. Even though it was Mark who'd found the injured animal all those months before and brought it home and looked after it, Nina had been fond of him in her way, sometimes finding unexpected solace in reaching into the hutch to stroke the creature's smooth fur.

When she'd fished the carcass out from the car, balancing it between thick sticks she'd found by the side of the road that she used like big chopsticks, the creature was already stiff, the blood congealed around the slit that ran from its head to its tail. For a moment after she'd hurled it into the undergrowth, her entire body had heaved, as if she might be sick. You couldn't live in Greece without seeing plenty of dead animals, and many of the locals owned hunting rifles, often piling into dusty old four-wheel drives at the weekend to head up into the mountains and shoot rabbits or boar, arriving home at the end of the day with bloody corpses roped to the roof. But this was different. Someone had gone over the side gate and taken the rabbit from its hutch. Then taken it away and done unspeakable things to it – that lovely soft fur. She rarely locked her car, so it would have been easy to position the carcass along the back seat. How much would you have to hate someone to do that?

The little cove was already set up for the wedding. The white chairs were arranged in rows towards the back of the beach, where the fine white stones gave way to compacted sand, and faced the white-canopied pergola carefully positioned to frame the rustic wooden jetty where Lucy would be arriving. The chairs had been used just the day before by Hayley, the wedding planner who'd been hired by the other bride at the hotel. She and Nina had done a deal rather than have to do two set-ups and two packings-away. There were several wedding planners on the island, and Nina knew them all, and while there was inevitable competition, and two of them refused to talk to each other after one accused the other of posting bogus negative reviews on Tripadvisor, on the whole they supported each other when they could. God knows they all understood how tough it could be. Nina felt sorry for Hayley, who'd had to cope with a feverish, vomiting groom. Sometimes it happened that way – the combination of booze and heat proving too much.

A makeshift bar had been set up in the shade right at the back, where a bartender in a white jacket – a local lad called Georgio Nina used quite often; nothing to do with Mr Angelis, thank God – was already in place. The cool boxes of champagne were hidden out of sight. The only thing on the bar was the ice bucket and the crystal glasses laid out in neat lines. 'Everything all right?' Nina asked Georgio in Greek. He gave her a thumbs-up but didn't quite meet her eyes, and her mouth felt dry as she tried not to think about what that might mean. She sent up a mental prayer. *Please, God, don't let them spoil Lucy and Jason's wedding*. She knew now that her business wouldn't survive past this season, but she still felt a duty to these remaining couples who'd entrusted her with the most special day of their lives. Ordinary life was stacked against romantics – the drudgery of work and the routines of domesticity took their toll on even the most hardcore daydreamer. It was so vital to cram in enough shiny memories from days like this to see you through the greyer times ahead.

Nina scanned the beach, alert for any signs of trouble. On the far side, an older woman sat on a towel, drying off from a swim. She had long hair which she'd wound up into some sort of turban made from a turquoise sarong, and her skin was conker brown. Nina recognized her from the hotel and smiled, hoping she would soon leave. The beach was theoretically still open to guests who weren't included in the wedding party, but most people took the hint and stayed away.

She heard voices at the top of the cliff. The wedding party was arriving.

Nina got herself into position at the bottom of the steps, ready to greet them. She had a basket of individual white roses to hand to each of them as they arrived. When she'd first started doing weddings, she'd bought dresses she thought made her look professional – fitted and structured with cinched waists and narrow skirts. But she'd soon realized that, though they looked great with heels, they went less well with the flat gold sandals she needed to navigate the stony beach, and they were utterly impractical for some of the other tasks she might be called upon to execute, like clambering up rocks or wading into water to rescue errant gazebo canopies and umbrellas blown about by strong winds. So, these days, her wedding-day uniform was a smart but loose-fitting ice-blue linen sheath dress that came to her knees and could be adapted to most circumstances.

Taking one last look around the beach, she frowned when she noticed that the woman on the towel hadn't moved. Nothing to be done about that now. Shoulders back. Smile on.

First to arrive at the bottom of the steps were Jason and his best man, Gil. 'Nina, I'm so sorry about the mix-up over the payment,' Jason began, but she quickly shut him down. 'We don't talk money on wedding days.'

His pleasant, open face registered such relief she felt a rush of warmth that momentarily melted the lump of dread that had been sitting in her throat since she had found the rabbit that morning.

Behind them came Gabriel, wearing a dark jacket over his usual black T-shirt that Nina knew immediately belonged to one of the hotel staff because of the discreet logo on the pocket. His hair, already bleached in the sun, had been pulled back into a neat ponytail, emphasizing the exaggerated points of his receding hairline. When he shook her hand the lenses of his dark glasses were so matt they reflected nothing back, as if Nina didn't exist at all. As he neared the bottom step, he turned to help Jason's mother, who was following behind, only to be elbowed out of the way by Jason himself.

'I love your dress,' Nina gushed on autopilot as she registered Cora's outfit. But the truth was, she was unsettled by the mother of the groom's choice of outfit. Not that it wasn't lovely – a lightweight crêpe cut on the bias and reaching halfway down her toned calves with narrow spaghetti straps over the shoulders. It was just . . .

'. . . white!' exclaimed Shelly, who arrived just seconds later with Hazel.

Cora looked down at her dress as if she were only now becoming aware of it. 'Not white. Bone. It's one of my colours. I showed it to Jason back home and he said it was fine.'

'Oh. Right.'

Shelly was one of those people, Nina reflected, who could look plain one minute and utterly beautiful the next, as now, with her red hair pulled back, showing off her long, pale neck, and her skin, often so sallow, glowing pink in the reflection of the early-evening sun, to match her pale peachy-pink dress. As she reached the bottom and accepted her rose, Nina saw her gaze flick to the woman on the towel further along the sand, and a crease appeared in her forehead, rendering her momentarily plain again.

Hazel was next, in a blue garden-party-style knee-length dress. She looked off-colour.

'Are you OK?'

'Me? Oh, fine. Well, maybe not fine. I've been feeling a little sick. You don't expect the bride's mother to get pre-wedding nerves, do you?'

A thunder of footsteps announced the arrival of Jess in her clumpy Dr Marten sandals, fresh from seeing off her sister and father from the harbour of the next town a few twisty-turny miles down the coast. Nina had been surprised by the sudden switch in arrangements – as far as she'd known, it was always going to be the steadier Shelly who carried out those last-minute adjustments and settled those eleventh-hour nerves, rather than Lucy's loud and volatile younger sister.

'Let's get this fucking party started!'

Nina noticed that Shelly separated herself off from the group on Jess's arrival, turning her back to gaze out at the sea.

'Are we missing someone?' Nina asked.

'Zoe. My wife,' said Gil.

Nina glanced at her watch surreptitiously. Lucy's boat would be arriving in ten minutes, by which time they all needed to be gathered around the jetty with a drink in hand. What was it with some women, that they always had to be late, arriving with a 'sorry' and a smile, as if them being there made up for all those minutes of waiting, as if their time was somehow more important than everyone else's?

'She had to wait while Jason and I got ready in our room, so that's probably held her up,' Gil said with a wry 'what can you do?' smile. Nina got the impression he was well accustomed to apologizing for his wife.

'Why don't we grab a drink and then get in place, ready to meet Jason's gorgeous bride? Our official photographer is on the boat with Lucy and her dad, but I expect you'll all want to take your own pictures as she arrives.'

As they drifted off to the bar, Jess stopped still so suddenly that Nina almost walked right into her.

'What the *shitting fuck* is she wearing?'

Cora Beazant was just ahead, and Nina guessed Jess was only noticing her dress for the first time.

'What do you mean? What's wrong with it?' Gil was squinting at Jason's mother with a puzzled look on his face.

'It's the bride who wears the fucking wedding dress, Gil. That's what's wrong with it. Lucy is going to do her nut.'

'You've gone so conventional in your old age, Jess.'

'Oi, who are you calling conventional?' Jess leapt on to Gil's back, and he grabbed her legs, setting off in a piggyback, the two of them giggling, just as Gil's wife, unmistakeable with her cloud of black hair, arrived at the foot of the steps, wearing a silver sequinned dress and a pair of vertiginous shoes that would never make it across the sand unaided.

Nina found herself feeling sorry for the woman, who'd clearly been hoping to make some sort of an entrance, and hurried over to hand her a flower.

'You look beautiful,' she said sincerely. Zoe wasn't model thin, but she possessed a kind of blowsy attractiveness, with her smooth, flawless skin and her ample curves, like a creamy pudding that you knew wouldn't be good for you but tossed in your basket anyway.

'Thank you,' said Zoe quietly, her gaze still fixed on the two laughing figures on the sand. Up close, her face appeared swollen, like she had allergies – or she'd been crying. Nina was about to turn away when Zoe started talking again. 'She's doing it on purpose, you know. Trying to prove something to me. She doesn't give a shit about him. Women like her don't care about anyone except themselves.'

Minutes later, the guests gathered around the foot of the picturesquely weathered wooden jetty, scanning the gently swelling sea for the first sighting of the bride, while Nina stood with her back to the guests, answering last-minute questions from the newly arrived string quartet, and from Nikolaos, whom she often hired to officiate at her weddings.

A cry went up from Jason. 'They're here!'

Nina turned back towards the shore, but something caught her eye. Twisting her head, she saw a dark figure standing at the top of the cliff just below the hotel. It was too far away to make out features or even to tell if it was a man or a woman, but something about the person's utter stillness and the way her own skin was rising up in tiny, frozen bumps told Nina that, whoever it was, they were staring directly at her.

Chapter Fifty

Hazel

Hazel wished to God she could stop feeling sick. She knew what was behind it. She wasn't stupid. The knowledge of Dom's infidelity was like a virus slowly working its way through her body. The Buck's Fizz at breakfast, followed by the champagne she'd drunk with Lucy while getting ready, hadn't helped, nor had it eased that jittery feeling she had of being under observation.

She'd cried, of course, when she'd watched the gleaming white speedboat drop anchor and drift into the jetty just as the sun started to streak the sky behind with tints of rose and pale orange, her elder daughter never so beautiful with her hair and veil fluttering gently behind her, and her face so full of pride and wonder and pure, unadulterated joy. Even when the photographer who'd been documenting Lucy's journey jumped out on to the jetty and made the boat circle around again so he could get a shot of them arriving, Hazel found it just as moving second time around. She glanced at Jason, and the adoring smile on his wide, honest face made her well up all over again.

This was what it was all about. *This*. Love. Hope. Faith in the future.

Hazel took a large gulp of her champagne as Dom descended from the boat, looking unfamiliar in his sharp, well-fitting suit, tanned from the preceding days' sunbathing, suave almost in his Ray-Bans, and stretched out his hand to help his daughter disembark. They would get over this, Hazel decided suddenly. No one else would ever love her daughters the same way she and Dom did. That was enough, wasn't it, to bind a couple together – the knowledge that the most important thing in your life was also the most important thing in theirs? Relationships were built and sustained on far more spurious grounds.

'Right. Shall we take our seats?' Nina was ushering them back towards the pergola at the back of the beach. Hazel noticed, to her surprise, that a string quartet had taken up positions under one of the trees while their backs had been turned. There was also a man with a video camera who'd apparently been filming the boat's arrival, while a second man Hazel couldn't identify stood smoking by the bar. 'Lucy and Dad will walk towards us from the jetty and join the groom and the officiant.' The wedding planner – who seemed a little on edge today – nodded towards the man by the bar, who stubbed out his cigarette in the sand and began shrugging on a jacket that had been hanging from a low branch nearby.

Seated, Hazel had to admit Lucy had been right when she said this would be the perfect wedding setting. Ahead, to the right of the white canopy that fluttered softly in the gentle early-evening breeze, Jason and Gil stood shoulder to shoulder, Jason's eyes fixed on the jetty, where Lucy posed for photographs in a deceptively simple column dress with an appliqué bodice that gave the illusion that the white fleur-de-lis pattern was etched directly on to her smooth, tanned shoulders. The musicians had started playing the opening chords to 'Somewhere Over the Rainbow', the violin notes soaring into the air and rebounding off the cliffs that surrounded the bay, their sheer rock faces giving off an orange glow, reflecting back the lazily setting sun. From the bushes at the back of the beach the evening chorus of cicadas had started up, giving accompaniment to the stirring strings. Hazel drank in the scene: the smell of jasmine and oleander and salt in the air, the rose-tinted rocks, the pink-tinged pebbles. *Oh.* Hazel noticed Vivian for the first time, sitting there on the towel. How very odd. Why would you gatecrash someone else's wedding like that? It wasn't as if she was about to go for another swim, not now the sun was on its way down.

But there wasn't time to reflect further because Lucy and Dom had begun their advance, perfectly framed by the wooden pergola so it seemed to Hazel as if they were characters in a film she was watching, rather than two of the people she loved most in the world. *There. See. She did still love him.* All around them the golden day was melting into a molten dusk, the sun bleeding rust and pink across the sky and the sea until the white of Lucy's dress was like a beam of rose-gold light coming towards them, transfixing them. As Lucy reached the pergola, her face a rapture of pure happiness, Dom bent to kiss her, and Hazel knew he would be crying. He was such an old softie when it came to anything emotional. Once, she'd come in from an evening out and found him and Lucy side by side on the sofa sobbing in front of *Love Island*, of all things. 'He just asked her to be exclusive,' Dom had explained, tears tracking down his face.

Now Dom stepped aside, circling the chairs to join the end of Hazel's row. As he found his seat, his eye seemed to be caught by something behind her and his mouth set in that way it did and he made a head-shaking gesture so slight and brief she wondered if she might have imagined it. When she twisted her head, there was nothing to see, only Shelly sitting on her own, fiddling with something in her handbag, her red hair a brazier in the light of the setting sun.

Here came Jason, stepping forward to claim his bride. The two of them stood facing each other, their hands entwined, their profiles, defined by the perfect sharpness of youth, silhouetted against the fiery sky.

'I, Jason Matthew Beazant . . .' In front of Hazel, Cora made a strangled noise and buried her head in Gabriel's shoulder. A tiny pinprick of unease pierced the bubble of wellbeing and harmony Hazel had been floating in.

She ought to have warned Cora. God knows, if the woman was easier to get close to, she might have done so by now, but there was always that sense with Cora of being kept at arm's length. Not that she wasn't always perfectly friendly, but she certainly never invited intimacy. And wasn't there something perversely odd in wearing a longish white dress to your son's wedding, even if Jason *had* approved the dress before they came? Still, she had a right to know what kind of man Gabriel was. How many lies he'd told. Hazel studied the back of his shoulders, where the material of the borrowed jacket strained. He was broader than he seemed, more powerful. Because of that doughy, amorphous face and the softness of his voice, one ascribed a lack of substance to him that his physical reality belied. People didn't get sent to prison for no reason. What might this man be capable of? What might he have done?

'I pronounce you man and wife.'

The little orchestra behind broke into a string rendition of 'I Will Always Love You', and up ahead, Jess, who was standing in the wings to the side of Lucy, turned to Hazel, her eyes theatrically wide.

'You have got to be fucking kidding,' she mouthed.

Hazel shot her a warning look and hoped to God she wasn't about to be sick.

Therapy Journal, Week 15

I didn't move to Bristol because of Dom. I just want to be clear about that. I was working in the marketing department of a hotel chain based in a stuffy office in Holborn. I'd hoped it might be glamorous, but I was the bottom of the food chain, answering phones, inputting data from the relentless 'how are we doing?' questionnaires. And all for a salary that only just covered the rent on my studio flat in Greenford. I realized early on that the others in the company on my level were living rent-free with parents in zones 2 and 3 who kept the fridge stocked and the broadband speed fast.

There were still pockets of Bristol that were affordable. For two thirds of my London rent I got a one-bedroom flat with a balcony in a new-build in Totterdown, just outside the city centre. And, OK, my maître d' job in an upmarket Asian fusion restaurant down by the harbourside paid less than I had been earning, but I saved a fortune on travel.

Though I hadn't met any of Dom's family by this point, I still checked in with Hazel and Lucy on social media. Jess posted such random stuff – angry political rants, clips from foul-mouthed comedians I didn't find funny – I hardly bothered to look at her pages.

Hazel, as I said, was an unsatisfactory subject, with weeks passing between posts and, even then, they were mostly to do with work. But Lucy was a dream. There wasn't one aspect of her life she didn't commit to Instagram. Her journey to work #nature #spring, her lunchtime smoothie #TastesBetterThanItLooks, her midweek happy-hour cocktail #Cheeky. If she couldn't decide which outfit to wear, she would post photos of herself in all of them and get her 834 Instagram followers to choose. When she and Jason went to Majorca on holiday, there wasn't a single beach or bar or sunset that wasn't artfully filtered and posted. #Paradise #DontMakeMeGoHome. Though I socialized with the people from work, it was Lucy I came to feel closest to.

Chapter Fifty-one

Jess

Jess was feeling particularly mellow as she stood with the others around the makeshift bar while the swollen blood orange of a sun descended magisterially into the inky sea, and they raised glass after glass to the happy couple, who were busy posing for photographs in the pergola. She glanced across at Gil, whose cheekbones gleamed like polished oak. There had been a moment back there on the sand when she was clinging on to his back when she'd felt a buzzing all along her various nerves and nerve endings, and she had felt sure it wasn't finished between them.

She didn't want a wedding of her own. *No way*. But when she thought about how nice it would be to have *someone* of her own to look at her the way Jason had looked at Lucy, she felt such a pang of longing her stomach hurt.

Her mother, on the other hand, seemed to be in an odd mood, sipping her drink slightly apart from everyone else. Normally, in a situation like this, she would have been friendly if detached, watching everything, making sure everyone seemed OK. At first, Jess worried she must have found out about her dad and Shelly, but then she'd seen her dad put his arm around her mum, and just for a moment she'd leaned into him before pulling away. She was definitely acting weird, though. Every time Gabriel spoke, she rolled her eyes like a teenager. It gave Jess an odd, tight feeling, as if her mum might know something she didn't. Jess still daren't think about that scene in the middle of the night when she'd woken up with him next to the bed, about his hands fumbling at her dress.

Now Lucy and Jason were approaching hand in hand, and Jess put her thumb and middle finger into her mouth to whistle loudly. The sky above was now a deep navy blue, apart from the residual orange glow hovering over the horizon, courtesy of the recently departed sun. 'Come on, you lot, time to get your photos taken.' Jess didn't think she'd ever seen her sister look so serene, or so blissfully happy. Until, all of a sudden, she froze, her smile sliding off her face as if melted by what heat remained of the day.

'Oh my God. I literally don't believe this.'

Lucy was staring at her new mother-in-law, who was deep in conversation with Gabriel and Dom. *Oops.* Jess had known the minute she set eyes on Cora's white – sorry, *bone* – dress that her sister was going to lose her shit.

'What the fuck is she playing at?'

'Apparently, she showed it to Jason back in England and he gave it the thumbs-up.'

'But who wears white to someone else's wedding? I spelled out the colour theme, didn't I?'

'There's not a lot you can do now,' said Hazel, coming to join them, looking washed out and sweaty. 'Don't let it spoil your day.'

'But the photographs!' Lucy was almost wailing. 'The whole point is that I stand out. I'm the bride. That's only fair, isn't it – to have one day where all the attention is on you?'

Jason came to see what the fuss was about.

'Don't tell me you're getting het up about a dress. Come on, babe. This is our wedding day.'

'Why didn't you tell her it wasn't appropriate?'

He looked at her helplessly.

'Because it didn't occur to me. It's just a nice, simple dress. Classy, like all of Mum's clothes are. Come here.' He opened his arms. 'I want to give my wife a kiss.'

Lucy stepped forward into his embrace, but the blissful look of earlier had gone.

'Hello, you beautiful people. I hope you don't mind me coming over to congratulate you. So many blessings to you both.'

Jess had spotted Vivian earlier, sitting there on her towel. Well, you couldn't very well miss her, seeing as she was the only other person on the bloody beach. But she'd tried not to catch her eye. She hadn't forgotten how she'd turned on her in the bar, could still feel the pinch of the woman's fingers on her arm. But now here she was, and, of course, what could Jason and Lucy do except offer her a glass of champagne?

'Lovely wedding,' Vivian remarked. 'Of course, it's all a big industry nowadays. So many rules and regulations. I remember going to a wedding on a beach in Mykonos that went on for five days and nights. We were all tripping on acid, including the bride and groom, and all these yachts kept dropping anchor and coming to join the party. Joan Collins was there, and Elton John.'

Jess rolled her eyes behind Vivian's back. Who was she trying to impress with these stories? Anyone could see half of them were made up.

'You could do what you liked in those days, do you see?' Vivian continued. 'Be as wild as you liked. Not like today, with health and safety this and that. And all these restrictions! Two allocated hours on the beach then two hours in the restaurant. These kinds of flowers in this kind of arrangement. Conveyor-belt weddings, that's what they are now. Not that yours isn't adorable in its way.' She rested her hand on Lucy's shoulder, showing off a chunky silver ring that wound itself up her finger like a snake.

Chapter Fifty-two

Lucy

They had taken over half the hotel restaurant with a long table that stretched the entire length of the terrace, from where they could see the sparkling dots of light that were the fishing boats bobbing out on the water. This was where they'd be having cocktails and canapés and making speeches. The main meal would come later. Lucy just hoped the nerves that had been making her stomach roil all afternoon would have eased off by then.

The plan was to go around the table, with each person making a short speech. Of course, when she'd written this into the itinerary Lucy had reckoned without the presence of Gabriel, who she still hardly knew at all, but that couldn't be helped.

As Jess got to her feet, Lucy glanced again at her satin clutch bag sitting on the table, in which was a lipstick, a room key and her phone. Lucy had already got the photographer to send her a few preliminary photos he'd taken earlier in the day, arty shots of her getting ready, the sun catching her lace veil and creating a delicate pattern of white lights, a grainy black-and-white portrait of her leaning over the railing of the speedboat gazing pensively out to sea, and another of Lucy and her dad laughing, their faces close together, teeth white and gleaming, thanks to whatever filter the photographer had applied. These, she had posted to Insta, with a breathless message involving plenty of hashtags. #blessed #family #bigfatgreekwedding had been just a few.

She'd had to make sure Jason didn't catch her posting, though. He'd made her promise that their wedding day would be a social-media-free zone. And it had been. Until half an hour ago. Lucy got it, she really did. She knew the buzz she got from a hundred likes on a picture or a list of empty compliments with multiple exclamation marks on the end wasn't healthy. But sometimes it felt like a thing hadn't actually happened until she saw it reflected back through the eyes of the 834 friends and complete strangers who followed her account. When she'd nipped to the loo earlier – in as much as you could nip in a dress that was practically sewn on to your body – she'd been determined she would just post the pictures and then forget about it. Her gorgeous dress had no pockets, of course, and she couldn't retrieve her phone from her bag without Jason noticing. But now the urge to find out how many people had responded to her photographs was like a persistent itch that, despite the joyous food and company, she was desperate to scratch. She glanced over to the cinematographer to make sure he was capturing every moment of this evening. She planned to release short clips three times a day over the next week or so.

'To Lucy and Jason – poor sod!' Jess was winding up her short speech with a toast. Lucy smiled and shook her fist affectionately, relaxing the part of her that automatically tensed up when her unpredictable younger sister was given a platform of any kind. Despite Shelly's warnings, Jess had been on her best behaviour all day – well, apart from that cut on her head, which would now need to be airbrushed out of all the photos.

For the first time, Lucy wondered whether it might be Shelly rather than Jess who was the problem. She and Jess hadn't hit it off the one time they'd met and, while that was disappointing, in a way it was also flattering – as if neither wanted to share her with the other. On the way from the hotel to the harbour, Jess had ramped up the digs and the not-so-subtle hints that Shelly wasn't everything she seemed. Lucy had expected Dom to step in to object, but he hadn't said a word – didn't even seem to have heard. Lucy had told herself it was just Jess being Jess, but now, as she watched her best friend sitting across the table from her, self-contained and inscrutable, sipping her drink without ever seeming to get drunk, a sliver of doubt worked its way into her mind like a splinter.

Cora's turn now. 'I made my speech last night, so I won't inflict another one on you,' she said. Well, thank God for that. Lucy still couldn't get over the fact that Jason's mum had turned up to their wedding wearing white. And Cora could ramble on until she was blue in the face about it being bone, not white, but as far as Lucy was concerned, she was just splitting hairs. Lucy'd had to take the photographer aside and ask him to position Cora towards the back of the group as much as possible, but in the obligatory photos with her and Jason and their two mothers there was no hiding it, and Lucy had been mortified.

Lucy knew deep down that half the reason she was fixating on Cora's dress was to keep her mind from probing where it must not go – at least not until they were safely back home. But though she had tried to block out the question marks hanging over Jason's dad's death, Zoe's phrase 'arrested for murdering her husband' was a black slick of oil on the surface of her thoughts.

Now her mum was getting to her feet and, *oh my God*, was she drunk? She'd seemed not quite herself all day. In fact, Lucy strongly suspected she'd actually been sick earlier, but Hazel had assured her it was only nerves, nothing that a few drinks wouldn't sort out. Since then, Lucy had noticed her knocking it back, but when she'd suggested to her dad – half joking and half not really – that he keep a check on his wife, he'd just shrugged and said, 'She's her own boss,' as if it was nothing to do with him.

'I want to start by saying that if there's ever been a more beautiful bride in the history of the world than my daughter, I should like to see her.' A whoop went up from the table, and Lucy relaxed. It would be all right. Next to her, Jason put his arm around her and squeezed. She leaned into him and that thought came to her: *This is my husband*, as it had a hundred times in the last couple of hours, injecting her with a warm shot of contentment. She put her face up to his for a kiss as her mother went around the table, thanking each guest in turn for coming to the wedding, as she'd told Lucy she was going to do, but when Lucy next turned to face the others, it was immediately clear the atmosphere around the table had changed.

'I'd rather you didn't call me that.' Gabriel, normally so serene, looked unhappy.

'I'm sorry. I thought that was your name.'

Lucy wanted to laugh at her mother's drunken attempt to style out her mistake.

'You're losing it, Mum,' she said. 'If his name had been Vince, Jess would never have brought him. There are literally no cool Vinces. End of.'

'As I've told Jess before, he's not who he says he is. His real name is Vince Harris. And what's more, he's an ex-con. Ask him.'

Lucy had that feeling as if she'd walked into the wrong screening room at the multiplex, that growing, panicky awareness that she was seeing the wrong film and couldn't now get back to the right one, the one she'd wanted all along. This was not how her wedding was supposed to go. This was not on the itinerary.

Now Jess had stopped laughing.

'What the *fuck*?' she said, turning to Gabriel, and her whole demeanour was different. 'I woke up with you by my bed last night. You were doing something with my clothes. Are you a fucking *pervert*? Is that why you were put away?'

'No. Let's be cool about this.' Gabriel was making a pressing-down motion in the air with both hands, as if appealing for calm. 'I wasn't . . .'

'If you've laid a finger on my daughter . . .' Dom was standing up, and Lucy felt everything lurching away from her, like a magician pulling away the tablecloth in slow motion and all the plates and glasses on it perilously teetering.

'Oh, for goodness' sake, he wasn't doing anything. You're totally overreacting, Jess, as usual.'

Cora, normally so cool and measured, had virulent pink blotches blooming on her chest and neck under the white – *bone* – straps of her dress.

Jess gripped the edge of the table. 'And how the fuck would you know? Were you there?'

'Yes.'

The short word was a blunt needle puncturing the swell of violence in the air.

'What do you mean?' Next to her, Jason had dropped his arm from Lucy's shoulders and was leaning across the table. 'What are you saying, Mum?'

'Not that it's anyone's business, but I was in Gabriel's – *his* – room. We were just talking, that's all. I didn't want to go back to mine in case you came in to say goodnight and got the wrong idea. Then Jess started screaming blue murder and I went to the door and saw she'd passed out in all her clothes and got tangled up in her sheet. She was just thrashing about, yelling in her sleep. I didn't want to risk her waking up and asking why I was there and so I asked Gabriel – *him* – to go and sort her out. I was watching the whole time. So you can all stand down. No defiling was done.'

Lucy could feel the tension thrumming in Jason's body. She put her hand on his arm to steady him, but he shook it off.

'So you spent the night there? With him? I honestly don't believe this. I suppose you knew he was an ex-con, did you?'

'No, of course I didn't know.' Cora got to her feet and pushed back her chair. 'I'm just going to get some air,' she muttered, as if they weren't surrounded by the stuff. After a second or two's delay, Gabriel – *Vince* – got up to follow her out and down the stairs to the swimming-pool deck. This prompted Jason to get to his feet, but Lucy grabbed hold of his shirtsleeve to detain him.

'Where are you going? Let them sort it out.'

'But we don't know who he is or what he's done.'

'Cora's a grown-up.'

'She's my mum.'

'And I'm your *wife*.'

The word hung in the air, solid enough to cut with a knife.

16/6/19, 00.24. Original English-language transcript of police interview with Mr Jason Matthew Beazant. Police officers: Demitri Iraklidis and Tomaso Diakos. Interpreter: Eulalia Scala.

I'm not sure I get what that has to do with anything. It was a misunderstanding, that's all. It was all sorted and dealt with. Yeah, maybe it stirred up a bit of tension, but that didn't have any bearing on what happened.

My dad wasn't a nice man. That's the truth of it. I hid that from Lucy because I didn't want her asking too many questions or wondering if the apple fell far enough from the tree. I didn't want to risk losing her. Yeah, he was violent. To my mum, mostly. She did everything she could to keep me safe, but occasionally I'd catch a kick or a punch if I was in the wrong place or looked at him the wrong way. He was a drunk, basically. Like I say, not a nice man.

There's no mystery to how he died. I told people he died of cancer because that's easier, but the truth was he was drunk. He fell down the stairs, hit his head on the edge of the hall table and died from a bleed to the brain. Yeah, I was upset. What do you think? He was my dad. You only get one. And there were good memories, too, alongside the bad. But I won't lie, it was a relief not to have to walk on eggshells, or to see bruises on my mum's arms or hear shouting in the night.

It's easy to ask why she didn't leave, but like I say, there were good times, too. He could be charming. If you'd met him, you'd have thought he was a top bloke. Also, he'd got her isolated by the end. She didn't work then – he'd made her give up when she had me – so she had no workmates. And she hardly saw her friends and family any more because she was embarrassed about what state he'd be in. That's why it's so amazing to see the life she made for herself. She's an incredible person. My idol, really.

But he fell. That's the God's honest truth of it. Of course, Dad's family wouldn't have it. They knew the relationship was rocky and made out like she pushed him. Refused to believe he was a drunk. If you talk to them, he was some sort of saint. It was because of them Mum was investigated, but she was never charged. I just want to make that crystal clear. She was never charged, because there was no evidence. The police even said they were embarrassed that they had to go through the motions of bringing her in.

Yeah, I guess that made us close. There's no law against that, is there? It happens all the time here in Greece, doesn't it? Mums and sons having a special bond.

No way! There was no animosity between Lucy and Mum. Or between Mum and the Collinses. Look, mate, I know you're just doing your job, trying to find the cracks, but you really just need to leave us alone to grieve now. We're all in shock. I know I am. One hundred per cent. It hasn't hit me yet, to be honest. It's too massive. Every time I think about it, I feel like I'm going to throw up.

Can I be done now? Please?

Chapter Fifty-three

Jess

Jess was all over the place. She couldn't believe she'd fucked up. Again. She'd brought this man into their lives, and now he was going to turn out to be an axe murderer or something and everyone would blame her. She'd only wanted to inject a little fun and spontaneity into the whole thing. What was it about her that she kept on making these shitty, shitty choices?

Anxiety tugged at her. Despite what Cora had said, she couldn't get the image of that figure by her bed last night out of her head, or that earlier occasion when she'd thought she was alone in the suite and, all the time, he'd been sitting there in the dark, completely still.

She'd picked up a complete stranger.

She could have been murdered in her bed.

Any of them could have been murdered in their beds. And it would have been all her fault.

'Can we please get back to my wedding now?' asked Lucy, who still had her hand on Jason's – sorry, her *husband's* – arm, as if she were holding him in place. For a horrible moment it seemed as if Jason might go after his mum regardless, and Jess found herself mentally urging him to stay. Her sister looked so vulnerable – very beautiful, but oh so vulnerable – that Jess was overcome by a wave of protectiveness that made her feel she would fight anyone who tried to hurt her.

They started to go around the table again, making speeches. Jess had to dig her fingernails into her leg when Shelly stood up. She shot a look at her dad, whose attention was suddenly trained on his drink.

How could he? Her poor mum. Jess's feelings towards her mum were so complicated, so *big*, she couldn't make sense of them. On one hand, she was cross that Hazel had so little trust in her she'd gone snooping in her room, checking up on someone who'd come as Jess's guest. That her mum had been right to be suspicious of Gabriel wasn't the point. She wouldn't have done it if it was Lucy who'd brought him. But, on the other hand, she felt consumed by a wild and ungovernable pity that she didn't know what to do with. Even Hazel's obvious inebriation only made Jess feel more sorry for her. Her mum had confided that she'd been sick earlier, and she still wasn't well, from the look of her. No wonder she was drinking too much, just to get through the day. Jess, too, had been experiencing spasms of gut rot that surely couldn't still be down to the effects of last night's tequila?

'You're the best friend I ever had,' Shelly was saying, holding up her glass to Lucy. Her rounded eyes, like fat snooker balls sitting in her sockets, were blurry with tears. 'And I'm so happy you've found your person. I think that's the most important thing in the world. Finding the person, or the people, who are made for you. And when you know, you know. You'd better treat her well.' She turned to Jason now. 'Or I'll hunt you down.'

There was a ripple of laughter. The idea of Shelly with her long, twig arms and her lopsided smile and that friendly, eager-to-please manner of hers hunting anyone down. Even Jess's dad seemed to be smiling – or was he grimacing?

Only Jess remained stony-faced and apparently unmoved, while her anger swelled and crystallized into a hard ball of hatred in the pit of her stomach.

Chapter Fifty-four

Nina

'It's not paranoia, Mark. I wish to God it was. People are dropping like flies. Nausea. Stomach cramps. The mother-of-the-bride vomited into the bloody ice bucket. It's got to be them – Mr Angelis's nephews, putting something in the food or the drinks. They warned us they'd discredit us, and now they have. Oh my God, this is a nightmare.'

Nina was out on the swimming-pool deck, with her back to the sheer white wall at the base of the hotel. The wall still gave off residual heat from a long day's exposure to the sun, but Nina hardly registered it. She'd started off whispering, but she now grew uncomfortably aware that her voice had risen to a point that it could easily be heard from balconies above. Oh, what did it matter? Her reputation was ruined. She might as well pack up and go home.

But first she had to pay off her debts, otherwise they'd lose even what little equity remained on their all but unsellable house.

Then again, if Lucy and Jason found out what was going on, would they even honour their final payment? Might they even sue for the return of the money they'd paid up till now? Nina gazed down towards the cliffs and felt her own future crumbling beneath her feet. What would happen to her if she went bankrupt here, owing money to the bank? Might she end up in jail? If she fled to England, would Interpol find her and send her back?

'You mustn't tell *anyone* about this,' Mark was saying, as if he could read her thoughts.

He'd always been decisive in a crisis. That's one of the things she'd loved about him. When things went wrong, he'd quietly and calmly tell her what they should do. He'd been so authoritative, it had taken her years to realize how often his instructions had turned out to be wrong. And yet still it remained an ingrained reflex, to turn to him like this when things were slipping out of control, even though she knew he'd take it as proof she still needed him. It didn't alter the fact she was leaving him, but old habits die hard.

'But surely I have to warn them? People are still eating and drinking God knows what. What if someone gets seriously ill? What if someone dies?'

'No one is going to die, Nina. If this really is Angelis's doing, he's just trying to scare us, flexing his muscles. He wouldn't risk his Neanderthal nephews' jobs over this.'

The stress of the day was a tight band around Nina's head and she slid down the wall until she was crouching near the tiled floor. She couldn't think straight. If she said anything, they would almost certainly be ruined.

But if she allowed them to carry on eating and drinking, it was on her head if anything really bad happened. On the other hand, what evidence did she have that it wasn't just a coincidence, everyone coming down with stomach upsets? It could happen.

'Look, sweetheart, be rational about this. Can you work out what exactly is making people ill? Is everyone affected?'

Nina thought about it. 'No, just a few of the women so far.'

'Right. Exactly. So find out what they all had last night or earlier today.'

Nina thought about how the chef here at the Paradise View and the one at Club Panorama were both related to Mr Angelis, as well as the handsome waiter, and how easy it would have been for any one of them to add a few of the poisonous mushrooms that grew up in the hills to a stuffed-pepper starter or a drop of something to the cocktails. She thought of Georgio pouring champagne down there on the beach and how he wouldn't meet her eye.

'You can do this, Nina. Be alert, but for fuck's sake don't say a word or we're completely screwed. You've got this, sweetheart.'

After she'd hung up, Nina stayed where she was, her head bent, as if it was entirely too heavy for her neck to support. In her early twenties, she'd had so many dreams of how her life would go, and all of them had seemed possible. When you're just starting out, potential paths radiate from you like the rays of a sun and all seem yours for the taking. But the minute you make your first choice – of career, or mate – you start shutting off all the others. And while there's a certain amount of wiggle room, there are only so many U-turns you can make, and the further you get along one path, the harder it is to return back there, to the point where life fanned out around you like a box of chocolates from which you could pluck whichever you chose. And sooner or later, you find yourself too far down one path to turn around, and when you get to the end you find it's led you here, to a place that's never felt like home, married to a man who lets you down, trying to justify to yourself keeping quiet about something that might cause other people harm.

She stood up. Composed herself. Tipped back her head to run a fingertip under each eye to wipe away any mascara that might have smudged there from the tears she hadn't even registered crying. Looking up, she was shocked to see a face staring down on her from one of the terraces above. It was the woman from the beach earlier, the one who hadn't moved, even when the wedding was going on. Nina swallowed painfully. Had she overheard her conversation with Mark?

In the underwater light from the pool, the woman's face was indistinct, only that scarf wrapped around her head and the sharpness of her features, those tiny close-together eyes like dark studs on either side of her pronounced nose, making her recognizable. But still, as Nina walked away, she felt the intensity of her gaze through the rippling shadows.

Chapter Fifty-five

Jess

She knew Lucy wasn't going to be happy about her walking off from the table, but the truth was, Jess was really not feeling good. She'd been OK until the speeches resumed, but then her stomach had started groaning and she'd had to hotfoot it to the toilets – now *that* hadn't been pretty. It had eased up a little now, but she was desperate for fresh air. More to the point, she wanted to have it out with Gabriel once and for all. The more she thought about it – the fact she'd invited him here to this amazing place and he'd repaid her by lying to her about who he was – the more incensed she became.

Obviously, she was glad to hear Cora say that nothing terrible had happened last night when she'd woken up with him by her bed, his hand fiddling with her dress, but then after what Zoe had told them, could Cora herself be trusted? Plus, Jess couldn't forget the sheer panic she'd felt kicking out to free herself, or the icy fear from the night she'd thought she was alone, only to see Gabriel's shadowy figure sitting silently in the living room. She'd even go so far as to admit that this whole thing might be a wake-up call for her to stop getting so off her head that she ended up making these shitty decisions. She was sick of waking up in the mornings with the lurching dread that something had been done to her – or by her – in the night, that she'd lost something important. She knew she'd become expert at burying things she didn't want to see under the thickest layers of herself.

From now on she was going to take control of her life. Starting with Gabriel. Just who was he, anyway? And what had he done to end up behind bars?

She guessed the missing pair would have made their way back down to the beach and, sure enough, when she reached the top of the steep steps and stopped to look over the rail, she spotted the two moonlit figures walking along the shore below.

'I need to talk to you,' she said, when she finally caught up with them. She'd descended the stairs too fast and now her stomach was hurting again. When she realized Cora and Gabriel were holding hands, she found herself looking away, embarrassed.

Gabriel gazed at her, passive as ever, but Cora was defensive.

'Go back to your sister, Jess. We can do without any of your drama. We've come down to escape from that.'

Jess tried to summon outrage, but it was thin and unconvincing even to her. Was this really how people saw her. A drama queen?

'I've just found out the man I invited to my sister's wedding is an ex-con. I think that gives me the right to ask questions, don't you?'

She was addressing herself squarely to Cora, so it was a surprise when Gabriel answered in his flat voice.

'I'm afraid this will come as a disappointment to you, Jess, but I was inside for fraud.'

Jess registered her own flickering sense of deflation.

'Fraud?'

'I'm sorry it's not more glamorous.'

Jess winced as her stomach cramped. 'How do I know you're telling the truth? For all we know, you could be a kidnapper or an arsonist or a child murderer.'

Gabriel continued to gaze at her steadily.

'Sit down and I'll tell you.' He indicated the beach, where the shingle was threaded with silvery moonlight.

Jess's instinct was to refuse. Who did he think he was? But her stomach hurt and she felt, all of a sudden, unsure of everything. Usually, her burning conviction of being fundamentally right propelled her through the world, but now that it had begun to dissolve, she was starting to suspect it had been masking the fact that she didn't have the first fucking clue who she really was. Or *why* she was.

She sat. And Cora sat down beside her. Not touching, but near enough that she felt a kind of comfort from her, which was confusing.

Gabriel began. He came from a modest background, he said, but had started mingling with far wealthier boys when he won a music scholarship to a private boarding school.

'I was too insecure in myself to be who I was, so I reinvented myself as a rich kid, someone whose father owned oilfields, and that started it all off.'

'Started what off?'

'The lifelong habit of pretending to be someone I wasn't.'

In order to finance his deception, Gabriel had first offered his services forging essays for his lazier classmates, studying their previous form and tailoring his style to make sure not to raise suspicion. He also had a side hustle in making fake IDs. He prided himself on his work, and turned out to be very good at it. He garnered a reputation at school and later at university in Edinburgh as someone who knew how to make money. As a result, people started lending him their money to 'invest' in his many schemes. Everyone knew he came from money. And money breeds money.

'So you just wanted to be loaded,' Jess scoffed.

Gabriel shook his head. Still that infuriating smile.

'I wanted to be *someone*. And since the age of eleven, I'd forgotten how to be me.'

Jess had an uncomfortable twinge of recognition. Might that be her problem, too? That, in her determination to be uncompromising and 'authentic', she'd stopped being herself?

Inevitably, Gabriel got in way over his head. He was living a lavish lifestyle he had no hope of affording, he said. He started an investment fund and persuaded his wealthy friends to invest, doctoring the accounts so it appeared to be thriving. In reality, he was gambling all the funds on an algorithm he'd developed for judging the fluctuations of the Volatility market, whatever that might be.

'I was sure I'd be able to pay them back double.'

Jess knew that feeling, too – that conviction that the favours she demanded of other people weren't really favours, they were investments – in her – that would be repaid tenfold. Instead, after a promising start, the algorithm failed. Leaving Gabriel – or Vince Harris, as he was then – owing £1.3 million to friends and family, including the parents of his then fiancée, Rosanna. His investors fully expected Vince's wealthy family to step in and bail him out. Except they didn't exist.

'They found out I was a fraud. I was sent to jail for five and a half years, came out after three.'

'And then made a fortune for real,' said Cora, proudly, as if she'd had a hand in it herself.

Gabriel shrugged. 'What can I say? Prison gives you a lot of time to hone algorithms. I paid back my debts.'

Jess wasn't often lost for words, but now she found herself floundering. She knew she was too quick to write people off as boring. She needed to work on that. But the notion that people might wear their unconventionality so much on the inside that they could still go about their daily lives as quietly as little mice, without any outward indication, was something that stopped her in her tracks.

'So you don't mind?' she asked Cora now. 'That your *new boyfriend* has a criminal record?'

She knew she sounded petty and silly, but there was a pain in her stomach and her head had started throbbing and she was finding it harder and harder to work out exactly what was going on.

'Grow up, Jess,' said Cora. 'Life isn't theatre, much though you might like it to be. It doesn't follow a script. It's messy and sometimes you end up on the wrong side of the law and have no idea how you got there.'

Cora's face was in shadow, so Jess couldn't see her expression, just her disembodied white dress floating in the darkness.

Therapy Journal, Week 16

Do you believe in fate? I'm undecided, but I do think it's funny how things happen in your life without you really having much say in them, as if they were waiting in store for you the whole time.

It wasn't hard to find out where Lucy worked. She posted photographs of the window display to Instagram every time it changed. A high-end leisurewear boutique in Bath for women who spent more on a vest that was fifty per cent holes than I did on my weekly food shop. It was part of an exclusive franchise with outlets in Knightsbridge, Covent Garden and Harrogate, those kinds of places.

Bath was only half an hour away by bus and, working in the evenings, I had daytimes to myself, so it was perfectly natural that I would spend time there. It's a stunning city, full of beautiful buildings and gorgeous shops selling things I couldn't afford. The first time I went into Lucy's store, she was behind the counter. I browsed the rails for quite a while, trying to stop my heart from racing, looking for something that wouldn't take me over my overdraft limit. I settled on a sports bra with a complicated arrangement of straps that criss-crossed over the back. 'Do you think this would fit me?' I asked her, hoping my voice didn't give away how nervous I was. She smiled – she really does have the loveliest smile. 'You're probably one of the very few people who could get away with that size. You're so petite. I'm an elephant in comparison.' Hardly.

*We got chatting, and clicked. You know how that can happen? And I know what you're going to say, but the clicking would have happened even if I hadn't swotted up on the boxsets she and Jason enjoyed (*Ozark, Walking Dead*) and her favourite singer (Laura Marling) and found out that she'd once dreamed of singing in West End musicals and still belted out a winning 'I Know Him So Well' at karaoke nights.*

After that first time, I dropped into the shop in Bath as often as I could afford to buy something, and Lucy would come bustling out of the back room or turn from packing something away on the shelves and her face would light up when she saw me. She called me Shelly right from the start. That's just what she's like. Straight to nicknames. I told her I was fed up with my job. Working late hours didn't suit me, and people were so rude. They didn't like the table they'd been given; what did I mean, we'd given their table away, when they were only twenty-five minutes late? Then one day when I arrived at the shop I saw a typed notice in the window. 'Wanted: Senior Sales Associate'. That was the kind of company it was. 'Sales assistant' was too common.

Lucy had been promoted to Deputy Manager, she told me breathlessly. 'So there's a vacancy?' I asked.

'Oh my God!' She clapped her hand to her mouth. 'Why didn't I think of that? You'd be perfect*!'*

So, you see, I didn't go looking for this. It wasn't something I engineered or manipulated. It wasn't even to do with Dom by that stage. Sometimes, things just happen for a reason.

Chapter Fifty-six

Shelly

She wasn't imagining it. Shelly was so attuned to Lucy's moods – anticipating almost before Lucy herself what was going to upset her, or make her angry or sad, or bring on one of her rare bouts of introspection – that she felt her detachment like a physical ache. Had someone said something to her? Had Jess blabbed about her and Dom, after all?

Now, Shelly regretted not having been proactive in putting her case first. She hadn't wanted to spoil Lucy's day, but she should have known Jess wouldn't have similar qualms. On the other hand, if Lucy had found out about the affair, would she be sitting here so calmly next to her?

Of course not. She couldn't know. And so it had to be nerves causing Lucy to look at her with that quizzical expression, as if she were recalibrating something in her head.

Still, Shelly was all too aware that the stay of execution was temporary. As soon as the wedding was over, Dom and Jess would make sure Shelly was banished. She'd lose them all. Dom, Lucy, Hazel. Just like she'd lost everyone else in her life who meant something to her.

What if there was something she could say to make Jess keep quiet? Dom wouldn't take much persuading, she was sure of it. He'd give anything for Lucy and Hazel not to find out. It was Jess who was the loose cannon. If Shelly could just appeal to her somehow. She could tell her the truth. Jess liked an underdog. Surely if she knew about Mummy and that basement room and Adrian and Julie, she'd take Shelly up like she was one of her lost causes? She'd want her to be given a second chance. Wasn't it worth a shot?

'Just off to the loo,' she whispered to Lucy. But Jason was saying something in her other ear, and Lucy hardly registered her leaving.

Shelly knew Jess had gone to the beach because she'd seen her crossing the swimming-pool deck, heading for the steps. Suddenly, she felt aflame with purpose. It was imperative that she make Jess see things her way. And this might be her only opportunity to get her on her own. But as she hurried out of the restaurant, ready to follow in Jess's footsteps, she found her path blocked.

'Just the person I've been looking for!'

Vivian was standing at the top of the staircase that led to the bar area below. Shelly felt the usual sense of suffocation the older woman's presence invoked, as if she couldn't catch her breath.

'I'm afraid I'm in a bit of a rush.'

'Buzz, buzz, buzz. What a busy little bee you are. Buzzing about doing the Collinses' bidding.'

Shelly swallowed painfully. 'The Collinses have been very kind to me. I'm happy to do what I can to help.'

Vivian cocked her head to the side so that the little silver discs sewn on to the scarf she wore wrapped around her head tinkled in unison.

'Is it all of them you're so helpful to, or Mr Collins in particular?'

'I don't know what you mean.' Shelly could feel how the blood had rushed to her face, knew how pink she would be.

How did she know? Who else knew?

Vivian approached, closing the gap between them until Shelly could smell the woman's sour hangover breath.

'I've been trying all week to get you on your own. We need to have a chat, you and me. Don't you think?'

'About what?' Shelly's voice was barely audible.

Vivian let out one of her mirthless barks of laughter.

'You know perfectly well. Don't dissemble. I can't bear it when women dissemble. It's a deeply unattractive habit.'

All the time Vivian was talking, Shelly's windpipe was closing up segment by segment, starting from the lungs, until she felt as if she might pass out from lack of oxygen.

'I'm sorry. I have to go now.' She lunged past Vivian, taking her by surprise, and clattered down the stairs, tracking through the bar area and across the swimming-pool deck, her pulse thundering at her throat.

Was she coming? Were those footsteps she could hear? Shelly sagged with relief when she reached the arch leading to the clifftop steps. Then she heard it:

'Michelle!'

The name stopped her dead in her tracks, and she whirled around.

Vivian's turbanned head was poking over the railings the next floor up, just outside the entrance to the restaurant.

'I thought that might get your attention.'

Shelly's throat was fully constricted now. No one from her new life called her Michelle apart from Dom.

'What did you call me?' Her words came out in an almost soundless croak that was absorbed into the airless night.

'Have you done it again?'

It was such a strange question, coming out of left field like that. At first, Shelly thought she'd misunderstood.

'What?'

'Was it the food this time, or the drink? It's very important that you tell me.'

She couldn't know about Adrian and Julie. There was no way she could have found out.

'You're mad,' Shelly whispered, turning away to hurry down the steps and out of sight.

But still, as she made her way to the clifftop, her breath tore from her in ragged, burning strips.

Chapter Fifty-seven

Jess

The steps stretched up above her like the sheer face of a mountain. Despite the cool breeze coming off the sea, Jess found herself sweating as she forced her wobbly legs to keep climbing. Surely this couldn't still be the dregs of this morning's hangover?

She stopped to get her breath and glanced back down towards the beach, where Gabriel and Cora were still sitting on the shingle, facing out to sea, their heads bent so close together they seemed from here to be conjoined twins. Her thoughts raced. How could she have got everything so wrong? She had happily condemned other people for leading their quiet, boring lives, without even bothering to dig beneath the surface. Now, here, it turned out that Gabriel's blandness masked a more colourful past than she could have imagined.

She looked up to the top of the steps. Still so far to go. Jess forced herself to start moving again, this time putting her hands on the next step but one to steady herself as she climbed. Her body felt heavy and cumbersome, bloated and gassy. The swirly dress was getting in the way, so she tucked it into her knickers. She glanced up again and thought she saw a movement where the steps opened out on to the clifftop, a dark blur against the sky. Her heart juddered. Were there wild animals here? Foxes? Wolves, even?

Uncertain, she looked back again to the two figures on the beach. Would they hear her if she screamed? Funny how she never gave a second thought to walking around Brixton or Peckham at two o'clock in the morning, and yet here she was, scared of something that would turn out to be a stray dog or even nothing at all. How ridiculous she was.

She turned her attention and efforts once again to the steps. Now, there were definitely more behind her than in front, though when she turned to see she felt dizzy at the sight of them dropping away into darkness. Up one more. And another. That's right. Establish a rhythm.

Finally, she reached the top and stood clutching the rail. From here, there was a peculiar perspective. The hotel was above, lit up against the slate of the sky, while behind her lay the inky sea with its silvery frosting of moonlight. To her left lay the beach upon which Cora and Gabriel sat, and beyond it sat the next little cove, walled up by the rocks that divided the two. And curving around them both, the steep bank of cliff face and the yawning chasm of empty air that stretched from the gorse bushes at the top to the hard sand below.

The sweat dried on her skin and, now, tiny bumps were prickling on her arms. What the fuck was *wrong* with her? There was a noise off to her left in the darkness across the clifftop, a crackling of twigs, and she froze, her mouth bone dry.

'Who's there?' Her voice sounded reed thin in the clear night air.

There was another crackle, and the whisper of movement up ahead. Jess's stomach roiled, even while the rest of her body remained still, suspended in a thick jelly of fear.

Now a shape detached itself from the darkness ahead, rearing up so suddenly Jess cried out.

'Sorry. Did I startle you?'

Shelly's face was ghostly against the black sky.

'Fuck!' Jess put a hand to her chest to calm her racing heart. 'What were you doing, creeping around like that?'

'I came to find you, actually. I wanted to have a chat.'

Shelly's weak and breathless voice grated against Jess's already raw nerves and fear turned quickly to anger, in that way it often did.

'I have exactly nothing to say to you.' Jess straightened up so quickly she felt dizzy and clung on to the rail.

Shelly advanced towards her, the ugly pink dress shimmering when she passed through a beam of light from a point high up on one of the hotel walls.

'Are you OK? You don't look good.'

'I'm fine. Thanks for your concern. Not.' Jess had no intention of showing weakness in front of Shelly Madden. 'What did you want to talk about, anyway?'

'I just wanted to explain a little about what happened. Between me and your father.'

And while Jess was quite sure she didn't really want to know, still she knew she *should* find out. She felt so strange tonight, and the thought of anything bad happening to her little family – Lucy and her parents – sitting up there on the terrace, so safe and so intrinsically *good*, no matter what her dad had done – made her heart ache. She knew she wasn't always nice to them, but she loved them with an intensity that took her by surprise.

'Five minutes,' she said.

Behind her, the sound of laughter carried on the breeze, and she saw that Cora and Gabriel were beginning the long climb up from the beach.

'Not here,' said Shelly, who'd spotted them at the same time. 'Can we take a little walk?'

She moved off along the cliff path, and Jess weighed up her options. She had no wish for another encounter with Cora and Gabriel. And she really did need to make sure Shelly wasn't planning to spring any horrible surprises on her mum or on Lucy. By now, Shelly was a pearl-pink column in the distance being slowly eaten up by darker shadows. Jess ran a hand across her clammy forehead, willing her head to clear, before finally coming to a decision.

'Wait up, then, for fuck's sake.'

Therapy Journal, Week 17

I knew there was little chance of Dom walking into the shop, seeing as he lived all the way over in Bristol, but still it took weeks before I stopped glancing at the door every time the bell sounded.

Lucy and I got along like we'd known each other our whole lives. There are no sides to her, you know. She isn't a do-gooder, but she always made sure the man who begged outside our shop had a cup of tea whenever we did. Just decent, you know. Once, during the first week we worked together, she came in upset because her mum had said she lacked ambition. 'Isn't being a nice person, being a good *person, ambition enough?' she asked. Soon we were sharing confidences. I told her a whitewashed version of my history – that my mum had been in and out of psychiatric care since I was young, and that I'd been brought up by my uncle and aunt. I brushed over the years in foster care, for fear she'd ask me why I'd had to leave Norfolk, and why I wasn't allowed back. By this time, it had been over a year since I'd last sat on the wall outside Uncle Adrian's house, but I didn't like being reminded of that period in my life. She told me how desperate she was for Jason to ask her to marry him. 'When you know, you know, right?' I said.*

Lucy lived with Jason in a small garden flat in Oldfield Park, the studenty part of Bath. I've never seen anyone happier than Lucy the morning after Jason proposed. She floated into the shop in a kind of blissful glow and, later, she bought a bottle of fizz to celebrate, typically insisting on giving a glass to the beggar outside.

You've suggested before that I was jealous of Lucy, but I really wasn't. I liked Jason. Who couldn't? I'd been out with Lucy and Jason several times and met their friends, and I introduced her to some of my old workmates from the restaurant. It wasn't all one way.

One time, I even met Hazel and Jess! Lucy was having dinner with them in Bath and she asked me along. She said her father was away for a week at a literary festival in France where his Wrong Position *book was still popular, so she'd suggested a girls' night out. I was more nervous than before any date I've ever been on. By the time I left the flat in the morning, my bed was piled with rejected clothes. I knew what to wear to attract a man, but what do you wear to attract a family?*

All through that day I rehearsed excuses not to go. I'm not an idiot. I knew it was messed up to spend an evening with the wife and daughters of a man I'd slept with. Except, by that stage, it wasn't about Dom any more, it was about Lucy. Please believe that. In spite of my gene pool, I'm not a monster. Anyway, I knew that even if Hazel mentioned she'd met me, there'd be nothing to set alarm bells ringing that Lucy's friend Shelly was the same Michelle he'd known in London.

So at six thirty I found myself sitting with Lucy in a posh pizza place, opposite her mum. And it didn't feel weird. It felt right. Natural. I watched Lucy and Hazel bantering back and forth and gently teasing each other and occasionally annoying each other while, internally, I tried to memorize the tone of their voices, the rhythm of their speech, the unfamiliar language of mothers and daughters.

Jess came late, obviously. Making a big entrance with her bleached backcombed hair and a guitar strapped to her back. 'You don't even play,' said Lucy. 'Shows what you know. I'm in a band, actually. We played a gig just last weekend in a pub in Camden. The two old men and their dog in the audience rocked out.'

We were introduced and took a long look at each other, and I saw her assess and dismiss me in a matter of seconds. Until that point, the chatter had been fairly even-handed, but now it was as if Hazel and Lucy sat back and ceded the floor to Jess without any resistance. She dominated every conversation, holding forth on the subjects she cared about and shutting down the ones she didn't.

I couldn't understand it. Why did no one say no to her? Jess changed the energy in the room in a way that felt oppressive and yet familiar. Only later on when I was at home did I remember that Mummy had done that, too.

Chapter Fifty-eight

Lucy

It wasn't turning out quite how she'd expected, but Lucy was still determined to wring the last drop of pleasure from the wedding in which she'd invested so much money and time and sheer emotion. And though she was upset that Cora and the others had gone off like that, she was also experiencing a quiet euphoria at having won that first battle as a married woman. The presence of Jason, her husband, here by her side, rather than off somewhere chasing after his mother, felt like a small but important victory. This was how it would be from now on. She had drawn her line in the sand.

In many ways, Lucy saw this unlikely liaison between Cora and Gabriel as a good thing. She wanted Cora to be happy, and since love was the thing that made Lucy happiest, she fervently wished it for the people closest to her. And yes, it had occurred to her that a new man on the scene might lessen the intensity of Jason's relationship with his mum, loosen the hold of whatever secret they shared with each other. The dark shadow of that word 'murderer' crept across her thoughts, and she wilfully shut it out.

All that was in the past now.

Also, now the party was reduced, it was more intimate somehow. Cosier. Jess had been good as gold, really, all day, after all Lucy's worrying. But with her sister, there was always that potential that something might set her off, so it was only now she wasn't here that Lucy found herself able to fully relax. She was vaguely aware that Shelly had been in the loo longer than expected. Lucy hoped *she* wasn't feeling sick. There was definitely some sort of bug doing the rounds. It had been touch and go with her mum earlier, and the more Lucy thought about her own early-morning stomach cramps on her yoga mat, the more she wondered if it really had been nerves after all. If Nina had been around, she might have asked her if there was something going around, but the wedding planner had seemed distracted all day and Lucy hadn't seen her since they sat down to eat.

So they were down to six around the table, as the waiter brought out platters of dainty little pastries with a cheese-and-mushroom topping. Besides Lucy and Jason, there were her parents and Gil and Zoe. The latter had been quite mellow, not her usual prickly self at all, and Lucy had found herself warming to her, as they all leaned in over the candles, forming an intimate circle.

They were talking about families, and Hazel was making them laugh about the outrageous things Jess used to do as a teenager and how Lucy would be torn between not wanting to snitch on her sister but, equally, not wanting to lie to her parents, especially if, as often happened, Jess was doing something risky. 'I couldn't bear the idea that something bad would happen to her and it would all be my fault because I hadn't warned anyone.'

Jason leaned over to drop a kiss on her shoulder. 'You're such a soft touch, Mrs Beazant. And that's why I adore you.'

Gil had already told them about the time he and his younger brother had had a party in the house when his mum was away for the night and it had got so out of hand Gil's brother had ended up sitting at the top of the stairs, sobbing, 'Please make them all go away.'

'What about you, Zoe?' Lucy asked. 'I bet you were a teenage rebel.'

Lucy was coming to suspect that Zoe's brash manner masked a monumental insecurity. And she could relate to that. Before meeting Jason, Lucy had often felt out of her depth in a big group, conscious of the fact she hadn't gone to uni or travelled or done any of the things her more ambitious peers seemed to take for granted a person should want to do, and now she recognized in Zoe's defensiveness something of the same sense of floundering. So she fed her the line as a kind of gift so that she could launch into one of her usual anecdotes, paint herself as a wild child if she wanted. She was taken aback when Zoe replied, quietly:

'Not exactly.'

Gil, who had his arm around his wife, looked nervous, and Lucy felt for him. How tiring it must be to be always on edge about what your partner might say next.

'I don't think it's much of a secret that I have . . . um . . .' She took a deep breath. 'That I have an eating disorder.'

Next to her, Gil's face registered shock.

'God, that's the first time I've admitted it out loud since having Anastasia. It was awful when I was in my teens. In and out of hospital. My poor parents were worried sick. That's probably why they spoil me. Then, when Gil came along, he helped me get it under control. And by the time Anastasia came along, I was so sure I had it beaten. But it's been creeping up again, only I haven't wanted to admit it. Then yesterday . . . Oh, I'm so sorry about the dinner, Lucy. It was just stressing me out so much, because I'd promised Gil I wouldn't . . . but I knew it would be so hard with everyone watching and everything . . .'

Impulsively, Lucy stretched her hand across the table to cover Zoe's.

'It's fine. Honestly. Don't give it a moment's thought.'

Now, it all fell into place. The way Zoe's parents treated her like she was made of eggshell and could shatter at the slightest harsh word. Her wariness about what people thought of her. Lucy felt a rush of pity. Poor Zoe.

'Anyway,' said Gil. 'Let's move on to happier things. This is a wedding, don't forget. How about another toast? Raise your glasses while I read you out the text Jason sent me after he met Lucy the very first time.'

And though Lucy had heard this before, her stomach still melted into a happy, sticky mess, and she leaned her head on Jason's shoulder, determinedly ignoring the fleeting wooziness that came over her at the sudden movement. Mind over matter.

Chapter Fifty-nine

Nina

Nina couldn't remember the last time she'd craved a cigarette, yet here she was, leaning against the front wall of the hotel, dragging on a Marlboro Light she'd cadged from the photographer. The unfamiliar smoke went straight to her head, and for a moment she forgot her fears and the acid burn of guilt that had been eating its way through her digestive system ever since bumping into Jess ten minutes before. Jess had been on her way down to the beach, and Nina could see instantly that she looked pale and waxy. 'Yeah, I do feel a bit shit,' the girl had admitted. But she'd brushed off Nina's attempts to help. 'It's just an extension of my hangover from last night. All my own bloody fault.'

Whatever Mark said, Nina knew without question that she had to confess everything to Lucy and Jason. The only question was when. It had to be done before the dinner was served, but she was painfully aware that the minute she did, the wedding would be ruined. The least she could do was give the poor couple as many minutes of blissful ignorance as possible, even though she now just wanted to get it over with. Her business wouldn't recover. That much was sure. Oh, there had been incidents in the past, of course. Things going missing from one hotel she'd used at the beginning, the odd dodgy oyster or undercooked chicken. But this – a deliberate sabotaging because of mistakes *she* had made . . . Well, there was no coming back from it.

The only saving grace was that no one had so far seemed seriously affected. Nina was sure the Angelis family were just trying to scare her, not to hurt anyone else. But then, what if it was a cumulative thing? What if the Angelis boy was systematically adding tiny amounts of whatever he was using to whatever they were eating or drinking so it was building up in their systems?

There was a movement by the kitchen entrance to the hotel, on the other side of the main doors to where Nina stood, and a figure emerged. *Him.* The Angelis boy himself. Coming out to smoke a cigarette, leaning coolly against the wall in his white apron. As if he'd done nothing wrong. The nerve of him. The absolute nerve.

'I know it was you at the top of the cliff earlier, while the wedding was going on. Trying to intimidate me.'

Nina said it in English first, her rage propelling her forward until she was standing merely feet away from him.

He shrugged lazily. 'I come to watch. Is not a crime.'

'No? Well, the other stuff is. Deliberately making the guests ill. I know what you're doing.'

He didn't bother straightening up, just took a long drag on his cigarette, hollowing out his smooth cheeks. His dark eyes met hers and, as he exhaled, he released a plume of smoke that danced in the weak beam coming from the light at the top of the wall. The corners of his mouth twitched. Was he *smirking*?

Outraged, Nina repeated herself in shaky Greek, though she wasn't exactly sure she'd said it right. Now his smirk stretched into a full smile. He threw his cigarette to the floor, grinding it under his foot, and finally, languorously, he stood up to his full height and, without taking his eyes from hers, he put a finger to his temple and made a turning gesture in the air. Then he disappeared back inside the hotel.

Crazy. He was calling *her* crazy. After what he'd done? The Angelis family thought they were untouchable, that was the thing. They obviously assumed Nina would never go to the authorities because it would mean the destruction of her business and possibly charges being brought against her husband. Nina hadn't forgotten the black bruise blooming underneath the waiter's eye the morning after Mark went storming off.

Well, they'd underestimated her. She may have made mistakes. Huge mistakes. And she was well aware that it was Lucy and Jason's failure to pay on time that had tipped this whole situation into a nightmare. But that didn't mean they deserved this. They were just a young couple too caught up in the romance of being in love to consider other people. She'd been like that herself at one time. Nina knew what was right. And standing by while her clients and their guests were put at risk definitely wasn't right, whatever her husband might think.

She looked at her phone, judging the time. She knew Lucy and Jason's itinerary off by heart. After all, she had designed it.

She could afford to give them ten minutes more happiness. That was her secret wedding present to them.

Chapter Sixty

Hazel

Despite everything, it was turning out to be a rather lovely evening, Hazel thought. The sickness from earlier seemed to have gone, and it was actually far less stressful now they were down to six.

She never felt completely relaxed around Cora, and knowing what she knew about Gabriel and having to keep it secret had been a strain, she realized now. Also, if she was honest, without Jess, everything felt calmer, less unpredictable. Lord knew she loved her headstrong daughter, but that didn't mean she couldn't appreciate having a break from her. Hazel had even managed to put her fury with Dom on ice for the time being. And while a part of her worried what it said about her that she was able to compartmentalize her feelings like that, she was resolved to have it out the second they got back to England. For now, though, it was enough to see Lucy so happy with the man she loved.

Zoe's confession about her eating disorder could have made the atmosphere awkward, but instead it seemed to have had the opposite effect of bringing the six of them closer together, as if they'd shared in something quite special. Hazel had always had reservations about Zoe, but now she could see how vulnerable she really was. She felt for her parents. It was so hard raising children, trying to find that balance between keeping watch on them and allowing them space to become their own people. Whatever you did, it seemed to Hazel, you were bound to get it wrong. All you could hope was that your kids knew that whatever mistakes you made, you always had their best interests at heart.

Gil was talking, one arm draped across Zoe's shoulders, his face soft in the glow of the candle. Hazel could see how it functioned now, Jason's best friend's peculiar relationship dynamic. He was someone who liked to give, while she needed constant affirmation. Would it last? Who knew? But there seemed to be a rationale behind it, a binding thread that had eluded her until now. At one stage, years back, Hazel had hoped Jess might stick with Gil, but Jess wasn't ready then for a steady relationship, still equating volatility with passion. And really, wasn't passion itself overrated? All that upping and downing and all-consuming, when really one just wanted the straightest, simplest, *easiest* route?

While Gil told them about the hard time he and his brother had given their stepfather, Hazel watched Lucy, so beautiful in her white dress that shimmered almost silver where it caught the light. She was leaning into her new husband so that the top of her head nestled under his chin, and every so often he would bend his face down to brush her hair with his lips, and each time that happened, Hazel's eyes blurred with tears. Happy tears, of course, seeing Lucy shining like this, but also, if she was completely honest, tears for herself, remembering her own wedding day and how she'd struggled to believe it was real, what was happening to her, and not something she was watching in a film. She remembered talking to Dom about it a long time afterwards and trying to explain to him how she never really felt happy in the moment, how happiness for her was always in retrospect, how it came from looking at photos, examining memories and realizing *yes! That was a truly magical day.* Wouldn't it be wonderful, she thought now, to be like this daughter of hers, living completely in the now rather than always at a remove, always a *looker,* as Jess had described her all those years ago?

Hazel was vaguely aware of someone stepping out on to the terrace and standing still, as if surveying the room, and now her heart sank as she saw Vivian heading towards them, coming to a halt behind Lucy and Jason. Wasn't it enough that she'd virtually gatecrashed the wedding itself, sat there unmoving on her towel? Now she wanted to insinuate herself into the reception as well? It was really too much.

'I'm so sorry to interrupt.' Vivian's tone was sombre, but her gimlet eyes danced around the table like fireflies. 'I'm afraid I have some . . . *information* that might come as a bit of a shock.'

A hush fell over the table as they gazed at her blankly, all movement stilled.

'Have any of you been feeling peculiar today? Tummy aches, sickness, that sort of thing?' Hazel caught Lucy's eye across the table and made a shrugging gesture that meant 'What is this woman talking about?' but also 'Isn't it odd that she should say that?'

Vivian saw the look and nodded.

'I can see I've hit a nerve.'

'Look, I don't mean to be rude, but we're in the middle of a very special family gathering here.' Hazel could tell Dom was angry by the steel in his voice but, even so, his smile stayed in place. Charm was a hard habit to break. 'Can you just tell us what it is you want to say?'

Vivian, who had her stringy hair wound up in a turquoise scarf, nodded again, and there was a sound like tiny bells tinkling.

'Of course. Well, this isn't easy. But just now, I overheard your wedding planner on the phone, sounding very upset. She said she thought the staff here were deliberately putting something in the food or the drinks to make you feel ill. Destroying her business, you know, because she'd borrowed money and hadn't paid it back.'

'*What?*' The word came from both Hazel and Dom in unison. The others were silent, their mouths fallen open.

'Not seriously ill,' Vivian qualified. 'At least, I don't think so.'

'You can't be serious,' said Jason, who had swivelled in his chair to look up at her.

'Oh, I'm afraid I am. But what I wanted to tell you is that I don't think it's the staff who are doing it.'

'Oh, so now there's someone else here going around poisoning people? Is that what you're saying?'

Vivian turned her attention to Dom, who had posed the question, and there seemed to be something hidden in the way she was looking at him, some special knowledge.

'Yes, I believe there is.'

'Oh, this is ridiculous. Go on, then. Who?'

'Michelle. Shelly.'

Lucy, who until now had been frozen in position and looking as if she might cry, came to life, shaking her head.

'You're crazy. Jase, can you go find the manager and tell him to get rid of her? This is my wedding, for Chris-sakes.'

Vivian reached one of her taloned hands out and rested it on Lucy's bare shoulder, and Hazel saw her daughter visibly shudder.

'I know this is painful to hear, but I'm sorry to tell you Michelle has form for this.'

'Form?'

'Fourteen years ago, she was removed from her uncle's house for putting tetrahydrozoline in the family's food. That's a chemical found in eyedrops, in case you didn't know. Oh, she didn't use much. Otherwise, she would have been sent to some sort of facility, wouldn't she? Just enough to give them all whopping great tummy aches.'

Hazel shook her head, as if the woman's words could be dislodged, like swimming-pool water after a swim. She was mad, clearly. They'd all thought so, even before this. This stuff she was saying about Shelly – and why was she calling her Michelle? – was inconceivable. Preposterous. She refused to let herself think about the shopping trip to Fiskardo, Lucy teasing Shelly on the way back because all she'd bought were drops for her eye condition. Lots of people used them. There was nothing wrong with that.

Hazel caught sight of Lucy's stricken expression, and her resolve hardened. This horrible woman had to be stopped from talking, before she ruined the whole night.

'Shelly would never do that. She adores Lucy. Why would she want to hurt us? There's no reason for her to bear a grudge against any of us.'

Vivian angled her head to the side, fixing her eyes on Hazel like a bird of prey. There was an accompanying jingling and Hazel noticed the damn scarf was strewn with hundreds of tiny silver discs.

'Isn't there?'

She shifted her unsettling gaze to Hazel's left, where Dom sat, and when Hazel turned to look at her husband, a hole opened up inside her through which everything she thought she knew, every fixed point of her world, was sucked out like water through a plughole.

16/6/19, 12.45. Original English-language transcript of police interview with Mrs Vivian Cassandra Kaffel. Police officers: Theodoros Christakis and Kostas Stephanides. Interpreter: Xanthe Liourdis.

I know what they're getting at here, but the truth is, I didn't feel the need to warn them at the start what she was capable of, no. For starters, that thing with Adrian and his family happened more than a decade ago now. And let's not forget there were no charges brought. She was never found guilty of a crime in a court of law. And secondly, she is not my responsibility. Mea non culpa.

She pulled the same stunt with Adrian as she did here – which I hope you're investigating thoroughly, by the way – a few eyedrops in the tea she was always making them. So terribly helpful. She had that eye condition. Adrian had it, too. A weakness in the genetic make-up. Well, they didn't get it from me, that's for sure. Not too many drops, I should add. I don't think she ever meant to hurt them, just to affect them. What do I mean? I should think it's self-explanatory. She'd been living with Adrian's family for a few years and she still felt an outsider. Passed over. She wanted to have an effect on them. To make her mark. She'd tried being good, and that hadn't worked. So, really, what option did she have? That's not what I think, you understand. I'm just putting myself in her shoes. Shoes. Papoutsia.

Adrian and his wife were sick, but one of the boys ended up in the hospital. They're not the most physically robust children, from all accounts. Quite runty. So they didn't have the strength to fight it off. But he was right as rain in the end. Really, I think they overreacted. But that's my son for you, I'm afraid. He always was a prissy type. And he holds a grudge for ever – as I can testify!

Chapter Sixty-one

Lucy

Oh my God. This literally couldn't be happening. Lucy's gaze swung like a pendulum from one parent to the other and then back again, trying to find an explanation for what was going on. But there was no misinterpreting the look that had passed between her mum and dad just now, after that awful old woman had said her bit.

'Well? You'd better begin talking,' said her mother now, in a voice so flat and expressionless that Lucy, still struggling to work out what it all meant, suppressed a shiver of dread. She turned to her father, channelling in his direction the unspoken plea that he put an end to all this, shut down this unpleasantness with the perfectly obvious explanation that would allow them to return to where they'd been just a few moments before. The warm glow of the candles. The intimacy of the chat. *Come on,* she urged him silently, *make this all right. Please.*

'It was only a couple of times, and it was over years ago.' Her father's voice sounded strangled. Not like him at all.

'I don't understand,' said Lucy, and her own voice, too, sounded strange, like a child's. 'What only happened a couple of times?'

'Your father's affair,' said her mum, as emotionless as if she was commenting on the weather. 'Your father's affair with Shelly.'

'You have to believe that I had no idea she would be here,' said Dom. 'I haven't had anything to do with her for well over two years. I blocked her calls and her emails. Everything.'

'Hold on.' Lucy felt she was coming back to life slowly, as if emerging from a coma, nerves popping one by one in her brain. 'Are you saying you slept with *Shelly*? *Our Shelly?*'

Her dad nodded, mute.

'*Before* I met her?'

Another nod. His eyes were fixed on the tablecloth in front of him.

'And then, what, she coincidentally ended up working with me in the shop?'

'I'm sorry to say it's more likely she targeted you deliberately, dear,' said Vivian, who was standing behind Lucy, watching the scene unfold, as if they were some sort of entertainment. 'She has separation issues, you see. Not surprising, after what her poor mother put her through. She was mad, you know. Her mother. She didn't know any better.'

'And you'd know because . . . ?' Jason had finally jolted himself out of whatever trance he'd been in for the last few minutes and had twisted around in his seat to face the woman in the turquoise turban.

'Because I'm Michelle's grandmother, dear.'

Slowly, Lucy got to her feet.

'This isn't making any sense,' she appealed to her dad, as if what was going on was a maths problem that might yet be put right. 'You're saying you slept with Shelly?'

'I'm so sorry . . .'

'And she was never really my friend? That's what you're saying? She only used me to get close to you again? Did it never occur to you, when I used to talk about her over dinner or whatever, that it could be the same person?'

'You have to understand, Lu-lu, I had no idea. She called herself Michelle. I never thought in a million years your Shelly might be the same person. Why would I? Oh God, what a mess. What a hideous fucking mess. I'm so sorry, sweetheart.' He turned now to include Hazel in this abject apology, but Lucy's mum's gaze was still trained on Vivian.

'Shelly didn't have a clue who you were when we came here. How can you claim to be her grandmother?'

Vivian sighed theatrically. 'I'd never been allowed to meet her. I wasn't officially told I had a granddaughter until they carted her mother off to the loony bin. She used to hide the girl from me, down in the cellar. And then I lost track of her. It's a long story.'

'And now you're saying Shelly has been putting something in our drinks to make us ill?' Sometimes, it infuriated Lucy, this detachment of her mother's, as if she were outside the action in which the rest of them all flailed around. Why wasn't she raging?

Vivian nodded, solemnly. That unbearable tinkling sound. 'I'm afraid so.'

Lucy glanced at the table, all those empty and half-empty glasses. Had there been some poison contained in those drinks that was even now making its way towards their guts, ready to twist? She shook her head, not even caring what it would do to her hair, those perfectly tousled waves.

'This isn't happening,' she said to Jason. 'Please tell me this isn't happening.'

'Where is Shelly now?' Gil was asking. 'I don't have a clue what's going on here, but the first thing we need to do is find her.'

'She went off after Jess,' Zoe piped up. 'I bumped into her when I was on my way to the loo, and she told me they needed a chat, to clear the air.'

Zoe made quote marks in the air with her fingers.

Now something was occurring to Lucy, a thought forming, dark and heavy, in the neuropathways of her brain.

'But why was she looking for Jess? She hates Jess.'

There was a whooshing in her head, and her stomach lurched in a recurrence of the cramps from this morning. Now her thoughts crystallized into one repetitive loop. *Shelly is dangerous. Shelly is with Jess.*

She looked at her mother without speaking, and it was like she was a child again, begging her to make all this disappear.

As if she understood without needing to be told, Hazel stood up, so abruptly her chair crashed backwards on to the floor. 'I'll be back,' she said to Lucy. 'Please try not to worry.' And then she was off, even as Lucy's dad leaned out to detain her, his hand grasping at empty air.

From the other side of the terrace came a flash of light that lit up the table, causing the occupants to blink, as if startled out of a deep trance, as the photographer, now back from his break, pressed down the shutter.

Chapter Sixty-two

Hazel

Hazel couldn't remember the last time she had felt this way. The blood shooting around her body, her nerve endings buzzing with electricity, energy pulsing in every atom, every cell. Yes, she felt scared, and there was a rage pushing at the edges of her brain that she knew would consume her whole if she allowed it in, but also she felt *alive*. Imbued with purpose. Her daughters were in danger, and it was up to her to protect them. How disturbed would a person have to be to do what Shelly had done? Sleep with a married man. Stalk his family. Put eyedrops in their drinks, for goodness' sake. What else might such a disturbed person be capable of?

She couldn't think about Dom. Couldn't allow herself to go there. Still, her instinct was to believe him. That it hadn't lasted long, that he hadn't spoken to her in years. He had been stripped back to the bone back there at the table, with nowhere to hide. She knew how he reacted under pressure, how hot and bothered he became, his brain seizing up, not capable of dissembling or fabricating, not with any degree of credibility. Now, she remembered his strange behaviour that first day when they arrived and they'd been outside by the pool walking towards Lucy and Shelly and he'd stopped still, pretended to have forgotten something, gone back to the room and never returned.

Idiot.

The swimming-pool deck was deserted, and Hazel threaded her way through the empty loungers, ghostly in the anaemic glow from the underwater pool lights. Then through the bougainvillea-crowned archway and down the steps that led to the clifftop. She hesitated for a moment while her eyes adjusted to the darkness. Ahead, an uneven line divided the dark clifftop with its fringe of gorse from the clear, midnight-blue sky, studded with pinpricks of stars and lit by a silver crescent of moon. To the left, a single dim solar lamp marked the top of the stairs leading to the beach. As Hazel watched, two figures materialized in the circle of weak light thrown out by the lamp, head and shoulders first and then the rest of their bodies seemingly growing up out of the shadows.

Jess.

Hazel set off along the stony, dusty path, stumbling in her uncomfortable wedge shoes. Her mind, which so often these days seemed to be fogged and out of focus, was now sharpened into a single point of thought – to warn Jess and get her away from Shelly.

'Oh my God, Hazel. You made me jump.'

Panting from a mixture of exertion, adrenalin and fear, Hazel drew up short at the sound of Cora's voice. Jason's mum and Gabriel looked pale and jaundiced in the yellow light at the top of the steps, their open mouths black holes of surprise.

'Have you seen Jess?'

'Sure,' said Gabriel, nodding as if pleased to be of service. 'She was down here about ten minutes ago. We were . . . chatting, you know.'

'Chatting?'

'Clearing the air.'

Hazel moved to the edge of the steps and looked down. The shoreline was visible in the silvery moonlight, but the back of the beach was a mass of dense shadow.

'She's not down there any more,' said Cora. 'She came up before us. I saw her at the top, talking to someone. I think they went off in that direction.' She pointed off along to where the clifftop path that skirted the bottom of the hotel plunged into darkness on its way around to the next bay.

'I did think it was odd that . . .' But Hazel didn't stay to hear what Cora had thought odd. Instead, she set off along the path that, even in daylight, was hard going, with its uneven terrain of sand and grit and stone, and the gorse that scratched at one's ankles and shins. In the darkness, wearing inappropriate shoes, it was doubly tough, even using her phone as a torch, and twice Hazel stumbled, cursing her dress, which seemed to catch on every bush she passed.

Only the thought of Jess kept her going, somewhere out there with Shelly – this alien Shelly with the backstory that had shifted her in one fell swoop from Lucy's slightly goofy new friend to someone entirely unknown and disturbed and dangerous. Someone who had slept with Hazel's husband. As soon as the thought came into her head, Hazel slammed down the shutters. She couldn't deal with that now. She needed all her focus for finding Jess.

Up ahead, the path climbed as it bent to the right around the trunk of an old olive tree. Hazel remembered, from when she and Dom had taken a walk here a couple of days before, that it divided in two on the other side of the bend, with an upper path steering gradually inland on an upward slope and a lower one following the curve of the shoreline around to the left. She hesitated, her breath coming in rasps. *Come on. Choose. Act.* Unable to see beyond a few feet ahead, she opted for the upper path, panic pressing on her ribs and her lungs. What if she was wrong? What if this path was taking her away from where she needed to be? She pressed on for about thirty yards, then stopped short. What was that?

For a second, all she could hear was the rushing in her own ears. Then it came to her, clear as anything: her younger daughter's voice. The first few words were unintelligible, but there was no mistaking the last one, cast out on the hot breeze: 'crazy'.

She ran.

From that point, it all happened so fast. When she tried to reconstruct it all later for the others, and then the police, Hazel would describe the scene that followed as a blur of shadows and movements and sounds and shapes. Running towards her daughter's voice and seeing her silhouetted there against the night sky. A second voice saying something she couldn't hear. A split second of hesitation – *Choose. Act.* – and then Hazel's feet moving towards Jess even before her mind had properly caught up. Only at the last second becoming conscious of that other figure – Shelly – emerging out of the darkness to her right, set on the same course, aiming for Jess.

By the time the two collided, the laws of physics had taken over, and then it was too late. There was only the impact of a full-grown, slightly overweight woman moving at speed and crashing into an eight-stone wraith. A scream. A cry. A flurry of limbs windmilling through horribly empty air.

And then nothing.

Much later, Hazel would swear she'd heard the thud of a body hitting the sand below. Would re-create it in her nightmares, and wake up with a sickening jolt, even though logic told her she couldn't have. Not with the breeze blowing the other way.

Hazel teetered on the edge of the cliff, her arms still outstretched.

'Oh God, oh fuck,' said Jess to her left. But Hazel hardly heard her. When asked to describe this moment at the inquest, she'd say she felt sickened, she felt shocked, she felt horrified. And all those would be true.

What she wouldn't say, not to anyone and not ever, was that she also felt euphoric.

Therapy Journal, Week 18

I've done the homework you set me the last time. I've read through this journal, looking for patterns, as you asked. I know my history worries you. But I'm not the same person I was at fifteen. I need you to understand that when I look back on what I did then it seems like a completely different person. I've grown so much, and I'm still growing. Lucy has helped me. And, you, too, of course. I know now what healthy choices look like. I'm starting to believe in myself. Honestly.

The official wedding invitation came this morning. Relax, I won't be going. Although it might be worth it, just to see Dom's face. Only kidding. I'm touched at being invited, though. 'It's only really for family, but that's how I think of you now, Shelly. As family.' I had a lump in my throat the size of my fist when Lucy said that. It kills me that, without me there, she'll be left with Jess, who will take over, as she always does.

My little flat doesn't have a mantelpiece so I propped the invitation up on the shelf, where I can see it from the sofa. Every time I catch sight of my name on the front my heart swells up like a balloon and I wonder if this is what belonging feels like.

Chapter Sixty-three

Jess

'I'd been feeling ill most of the evening, and then Shelly and I were walking together, talking, and I suddenly felt really dizzy, like I was about to faint, you know. So I stopped. And she . . . Shelly . . . she went on a few steps without realizing and then turned back and . . . Oh my God, you know, just what the *fuck*?'

Eulalia, the receptionist who had been translating for the two policemen, stopped to gaze at Jess, her perfectly plucked eyebrows knitted in confusion.

The younger policeman, who Jess might have considered pretty hot if she hadn't been meeting him like this, having just watched someone she knew plummet to her death, said something, and Eulalia nodded.

'What had you been talking about until then?'

Jess shifted in her seat. They were inside the hotel restaurant, where she'd never sat before. The lights were fully lit, rendering the small space sterile and clinical. Jess and the receptionist, who seemed to be relishing her responsibilities, sat on one side of the table, and the two uniformed policemen on the other, paperwork spread out on the surface in front of them, forms and notebooks and even some kind of official stamp. She'd had to spell out her own name, and her parents' names, including their middle names. She couldn't even remember whether Fenella had one 'n' or two.

The more she thought about it, the more inconceivable it seemed to her that, just a few short hours ago, she and her family had been sitting just a few feet away, celebrating her sister's wedding, and now this *thing* had happened that was so massive, so gargantuan, that life would never ever be the same and *fuck fuck fuck* how could this be real? How could Shelly be dead? Jess had never liked her, she wasn't a hypocrite like that, but that didn't mean she wanted her to *die*.

She took a deep breath. *Count to three*, her mum was always instructing her. *Her mum.* What was going to happen to her now?

'Can you ask them what's happening to my mum?' she begged Eulalia. 'Where have they taken her? Tell them it was an accident.'

'She is at the police station in Argostoli, but it is only a formality,' the receptionist reassured her, after conferring with the policemen. 'She will give a formal statement and then come back here. Now, can you respond to the question? What were you discussing with Miss Madden before she . . . fell.'

'She came to find me. She said she wanted to clear the air.' Eulalia frowned again, and Jess added, 'You know, to make sure everything was OK between us. There'd been a . . . misunderstanding earlier and she wanted to sort it out.'

This was the line the family had agreed on during that horrible, tense hour while the police were talking to Gil and Zoe and they were waiting in Lucy and Jason's suite for it to be their turn. Not that they had anything to hide, they were all quick to qualify, just that they didn't want anything to be more complicated or unpleasant than it already was. So there would be no mention of the relationship between her dad and Shelly. Already, the very idea of it was seeming impossible, anyway, a ludicrous dream. Especially what Lucy had told her about the affair coming *before* Lucy and Shelly met. Jess still hadn't been able to work out what she meant. Had Shelly deliberately tracked Lucy down because she was Dom's daughter? Surely that had to be full-on psycho behaviour?

'What kind of misunderstanding?' The older policeman was scrupulously polite, but Jess didn't like the way his eyes lingered on her pink hair and her sleeve of tattoos, as if he were drawing assumptions from them, about her, about the kind of person she was, the kind of witness.

'Shelly didn't like the fact that my sister made me her matron of honour. I don't give a shit about all that kind of stuff, but Shelly thought she'd been a better friend, and she was more reliable.'

The older policeman nodded, as if he understood absolutely the nuances of female friendship.

'Was she right?' he asked.

Jess was taken aback.

'Yeah. I suppose so. Shelly was loyal. The kind of loyal that sends flowers when you're having a bad day, and bakes cakes for your birthday and texts you to make sure you got home OK. You know.'

Now, for the first time, Jess realized that Shelly was gone. She had been alive, breathing, and OK, not always Jess's cup of tea, but still, a presence, a personality, a *force* – of sorts. And now – pffff – just like that, she had been wiped out. Like most young people, Jess only considered her own mortality when death invaded her peer group, and it shook her to her foundations to realize that she, too, might one day cease to exist. That the world could go on without her in it. And Shelly hadn't been all bad, despite everything. She had been running back to help her when . . .

'They want to know what you think about what Mrs Kaffel told you all. That Shelly did something to make you feel ill.'

'Mrs Kaffel? Is that Vivian? Look, I wasn't actually there when she said all that. My parents and my sister told me afterwards. But, you know, Vivian is a bit bonkers.'

Once again, Eulalia stopped mid-sentence and gave Jess a questioning look.

'Bonkers. You know. Crazy. Harmless, obviously, but a bit crazy. You know she never let on she was Shelly's grandmother – can you believe that? When my mum told me, I was just, like, oh man that is completely wild. You spend all these years trying to track down your granddaughter and there she is and you don't even let on to her. I mean, what is that about?'

She was talking too much, she realized. Opening her mouth and letting the words fall out. Eulalia pressed her suspiciously plumped lips together, as if weighing up how best to translate what Jess had just said. After she'd finished speaking and the younger policeman had written it down, the two men conferred in low voices.

'What happened after you started to feel ill, up there on the cliff? After you stopped?'

In the unforgiving overhead light, Jess could see that the receptionist had a raised spot on her chin that she had covered over with a thick layer of peach-coloured concealer.

'Like I say, Shelly turned around and asked me if I was OK, and then she must have seen I wasn't because she started running towards me. And then . . . and then . . .'

And then. Her mother coming out of nowhere, having seen her wobbling there on the cliff edge, rushing to save her. Meeting Shelly coming from the other direction. A sickening thud of bodies colliding, a scream. An *accident.* That's how it was. That's how it happened. A stream of bile shot into Jess's mouth and she swallowed it down.

'Neither of them saw each other. They were both so focused on getting to me. It was a horrible, horrible accident.'

'And a miracle you weren't knocked over, too,' said the younger policeman. He had one of those hard faces, so it was impossible to tell if he was genuinely sympathizing or accusing her of something.

'It all happened so fast. I closed my eyes right at the end, when I realized it was coming. I think I was waiting for the impact. They must have missed me by inches. My mum was so lucky not to go over herself.'

Her voice wavered on the last word, tears coming now, hot and fast. The older policeman made a sympathetic tsking noise and reached over to pass her a white, starched napkin from a neighbouring table. Jess buried her nose in it, giving in to the wave of emotion that finally broke through the remains of the numbness and shock that had been shielding her this far.

The older policeman looked discreetly away, while the younger one stared. Finally, the older one spoke. The receptionist turned to Jess and, for the first time, gave her a small smile. 'He says this matches what the others told him. Mrs Beazant and Mr Harris.'

Cora and Gabriel had been interviewed first, having witnessed the scene from the beach, where they'd returned after Cora had realized she'd forgotten her pashmina. Jess had seen them only briefly in passing, coming out of the restaurant as she was going in. Cora, normally so self-contained, had been badly shaken. They'd seen Shelly fall, she told Jess breathlessly, though she landed in the next cove along, so, thankfully, they didn't see her body. They'd looked up in front of them when they heard raised voices and seen one figure stopped ahead of another at the top of the cliff that curved around the hotel beach and the next little cove. Because of the direction of the breeze, they'd clearly heard, 'Are you OK?' and then seen the second figure moving towards the first and heard that awful scream when a third arrived out of nowhere, the three seeming to collide in one indistinguishable mass that sent one flying, a horrible dark shape twisting in thin air. When Cora had described this, she'd used her hands to demonstrate, and Jess had felt her still-tender stomach contract with every flick of the older woman's wrists.

By now Jess was openly sobbing in a way she hadn't done for years. Normally, she had little truck with women who burst into tears at the drop of a hat, but the events of the evening had taken their toll. The older policeman got to his feet, holding out his hand to Jess.

'He says you are free to go now. And he is sorry for the loss of your friend.'

At this, Jess cried even harder, because, really, Shelly hadn't been her friend, even before the whole thing with her dad, and now she was gone and, no matter what Jess thought of her, she didn't deserve that.

She stood up, feeling weak with relief that it was over, and said goodbye to the policemen, but she didn't meet their eyes in case they asked her to go over it again. And she couldn't face that. Not now she'd got it straight in her head. The two women coming to help her, the accidental collision right in front of her.

That's how it had happened. Cora had confirmed it.

'You don't expect something like that to happen, do you?' she blurted out now, as she reached the doorway. 'Not at a wedding.'

She left before the receptionist had finished translating what she'd said.

Chapter Sixty-four

Hazel

The night had taken on the unreal quality of a dream. Someone else's dream, in fact, related in short, disjointed bursts. The wedding. Drinks around the table. Vivian's crazy story. Dom's face caving in on itself. That stumbling walk in the dark. Voices. The shadowy blur that was Shelly moving towards Jess. The collision. The scream. Jess's face, pale in the sliver of moonlight. Then people arriving, almost instantly, it seemed. Hazel would later learn that Cora had called Jason from the beach as soon as she saw Shelly fall.

And after that the police, scrupulously polite, asking her to go with them to the station. Crossing paths with Cora and Gabriel on the way. Cora's reassuring, 'Don't worry. We saw it all. Both of you reaching for Jess at the same moment. Just a terrible, tragic accident.'

All through the two hours in the police station answering questions – they'd wanted her parents' full names, even though they were both dead, Hazel plucking them from the mists of memory – Cora's words had lodged in Hazel's mind, calming her whenever she thought too long about what had happened and the flood of panic and horror threatened to overwhelm her. If Cora and Gabriel saw it happen, then their account must be true. A catastrophic misjudgement in the dark while both Hazel and Shelly were running to get to Jess before she wobbled and fell. A tragic accident. They'd seen it, so that's how it was.

Now, finally, Hazel had arrived back at the hotel. What she really wanted, more than anything, was to go up to her suite and take off this stupid dress with its terrible smear of dust and grass and have a long, hot shower and crawl into that vast clean bed with its crisp white sheets and close her eyes and make her mind blank. Not to have to see Lucy's lovely face slacken and her chin pucker, as it always did when she was upset. Not to have to confront her own husband with whatever it was he'd done with that strange, pale young woman. Or to face her younger daughter, who'd seen what happened and who knew what she knew.

But instead, she was met at the door by a tall, thin man with silver hair that curled back from a high, domed forehead, and large, sad eyes that sagged at the bottom, as if gravity was pulling the lower lids down, revealing livid pink crescents. He introduced himself as the hotel owner and explained that the normal receptionist was off translating for the police as they gathered witness statements. His handshake was dry and rough, and he shook his head with vigour. 'Is a tragedy what happen,' he said. 'Such a young woman.'

Hazel nodded, not trusting herself to speak. The truth of the man's statement was a splinter in her heart. Shelly *had* been young. But no. She shut that thought down before it could take root.

'Your family is in the De Luxe suite. They wait for you there.'

So now she must take the steps, her feet heavy, as if she was wearing those dreadful steel-toecap boots Jess used to be so fond of. Outside the door of the suite, she paused, trying to collect herself. She was the wronged party here, she reminded herself.

The door burst open. 'Oh my God!' Lucy flung herself at her mother, as if she'd sensed her through the hard wood. Her elder daughter's painstakingly curated hair, with its soft waves and sun-kissed streaks, now hung limp and flat, and grief had melted her professionally applied mascara so that it glooped black around her eyes, clumping her eyelash extensions together.

'Oh my God, Mum. I just can't believe it. I just can't. Oh my *God*.'

Lucy stepped back, and Hazel saw where the red dust of the path had scored lines of rust that criss-crossed the exquisite wedding dress. The hem was black with dirt.

Inside the living room of the suite, the remainder of the wedding party perched on sofas and armchairs. Gil had dragged in a stool from the dressing table in the bedroom and sat leaning forward with his hands under his thighs. Dom got up from the armchair where he'd been sprawled and came towards her, but Hazel held up her hand like a traffic policeman, and he stopped.

'I was going to tell you when we got home,' he said. 'About her. About . . . *us.* I didn't want to spoil the wedding.'

'Yeah, great job,' snorted Jess.

Hazel looked around. 'Where's Zoe?' she asked Gil.

'Lying on the bed in there. She doesn't feel well.'

Hazel felt a tingling in the base of her stomach, a spark igniting, like the pilot light of a boiler. *This.* This was Shelly's doing. Stomach aches. Nausea. The girl had been unhinged.

Just look at them all. Jess's skin was yellow and waxy as cheese. Who knew where Shelly would have stopped. *If* she would have stopped.

'What did the police ask you?' Jason wanted to know.

'Just to go through what happened.'

'But they know it was an accident, right?' In the room's bright electric light, Lucy's face was puffy under the thick, claggy make-up.

Hazel's gaze shot to Jess, their eyes locking.

'Mum. I said, they know it was an accident? You were both running to help Jess and you crashed into each other and Shelly fell? You told them that, didn't you, that you didn't mean it to happen?' Lucy's voice was shrill and ragged, as if it were clinging on by its very fingertips to stop itself tipping into a wail.

'Yes, of course I told them that.' Hazel bent her head to rub at a mark on her dress, so that she didn't have to meet anyone's eyes. 'There'll be a post-mortem and an inquest.' She didn't add the rest – that depending on the results of the inquest, there was a chance she might have to return to Greece to face trial for manslaughter, or even murder. She told herself she was keeping quiet because she didn't want to cause any more upset but, really, she didn't know if she could say those 'm' words out loud.

There was a loud moan from the bedroom and Gil got to his feet. 'I'm going to take Zoe back to our room now. We only waited to make sure you were OK, Hazel. I still can't believe Shelly is gone. I mean, I know she behaved really badly' – he shot an embarrassed glance at Dom, who stared stonily ahead – 'but she was a friend, you know?'

'A friend who was trying to kill us,' said Jess, but Hazel could tell her heart wasn't in it. It was just something to say.

'Do you really believe all that stuff she was saying? Vivian?' asked Jason now. Her son-in-law. Hazel kept having to remind herself there had been a wedding here today. 'I mean, didn't she say she'd overheard Nina talking about how it was a local with a grudge against her who was doing something to the food? Wouldn't that make more sense?'

Gil rubbed his eyes. 'Oh, man. Nothing about this whole scene makes sense.'

'What do you think, Mum?' asked Lucy, scooting along the sofa, where Hazel had sat herself down, to lay her head on her mother's shoulder. Hazel stroked her daughter's hair automatically, but the truth was, she was too hot and sticky and wished Lucy wasn't quite so close. The doors to the terrace were wide open and the air-conditioning was off, so the air in the room was thick and warm. *What about mosquitoes?* Hazel was just about to ask Jason to shut the doors when she remembered that someone had died and she had made that happen and, really, what did a few insect bites matter, in the scheme of things? What did anything really matter after that? But Lucy's question was still hanging in the turgid air, and everyone was looking at her expectantly.

'I think . . . I think Shelly was a very troubled young woman. And yes, I think that made her dangerous.'

Later that night, she and Dom clung together in their very large bed. By unspoken agreement, they would not talk about what had happened that day. When they got home, there would begin the long agony of unpicking the tight, knotted rope of events that had led them here. He had fucked someone. She had killed someone. Those two immutable facts would be with them every step of their lives from this point on, whether together or apart.

But, for tonight, they were only two human souls who had got themselves so lost and untethered that the only way to stop themselves from spinning off the edge of the world into the vast emptiness of space was to hold tight to each other and to the thirty years they'd shared.

'You must know,' Dom whispered in the darkness, 'I had no idea how damaged she was. I would never have . . .'

She pressed a finger firmly against his lips to stop him saying more.

Eventually, Dom dropped off to sleep, his breath slowing and deepening so that his chest, upon which Hazel's left cheek rested, rose and fell with a kind of hypnotic languor. In the darkness, the night's developments came back to her in a series of disjointed sequences, like snatches of a film. Jess standing there. Hazel running. Shelly running. That awful scream.

Hazel squeezed her eyes shut. Shelly had been a threat, she reminded herself. Of course it was a tragedy she was dead, but at least Hazel's family was safe.

Even so, when she fell asleep, it was Jess's face she dreamed of, her eyes wide with the horror of the thing she was powerless to prevent.

Chapter Sixty-five

Lucy

The wedding dress was zipped up in its bag, and Lucy hoped she never had to see it again. That stained and ruined thing that had cost so much money.

The bag was draped over all the other bags and cases, all heaped up outside the hotel entrance.

It was not how she'd envisaged their departure: being waved off by smiling staff and other guests. Home to England to show off her tan at the party for all their friends, followed by a few days in a boutique hotel in Dorset to recover from it all. A long, drawn-out programme of bliss, starting with this triumphant taking of leave. She'd pictured them all on the flight home. Hungover, obviously, but then someone would say, 'Glass of fizz? Come on, hair of the dog. It is a wedding, after all.'

Instead, for the thirty-six hours since it had happened, they'd tiptoed around each other. Deliberately not speaking about anything to do with Shelly or Dom or the accident. Only the odd 'Can you believe . . . ?', 'It hasn't sunk in . . .', 'This time yesterday . . .' or 'This time two days ago . . .' had made reference to the fact that this was not at all how it was supposed to have gone. Even Jess had been subdued, unlike herself. Unbelievably, she had already been packed and ready when Lucy came down earlier, ahead of all the others.

'You know we don't have to be here until quarter to, don't you?' said Lucy, leaning against the white facade of the hotel. In place of the new tight white jeans and white chambray blouse outfit she'd set aside for the trip home, she was wearing an old dress she'd slung into her case at the last minute for slobbing about in. Now, she couldn't imagine what she'd been thinking of, wanting to spend a whole day wearing restrictive clothes. Really, what was the point?

'I know. I just couldn't bear to spend another second in my room.'

Jess was sitting on her rucksack, hugging her knees. If Lucy half closed her eyes, Jess turned once again into a younger version of herself. She'd always been such a mucky child, so that now her sleeve of tattoos appeared to be just more grime she'd brought home from the garden or the playground.

'You don't think anything bad will happen to Mum, do you?' Lucy asked. 'I mean, they'll see it was just a hideous accident, won't they, no matter what that mad old woman says?'

The police had taken Hazel in for questioning a second time the previous day, after they'd spoken to Vivian and she'd repeated her allegations about Shelly and suggested that Hazel had followed her to the cliffs and deliberately pushed her off in a fit of rage because she'd been sleeping with her husband. Lucy's mum had returned from Argostoli exhausted but insisting there was nothing to worry about. The police could see Vivian was nuts, Hazel had said. They didn't believe a word she said. They were just going through the motions. But still Lucy looked to Jess for reassurance, in a reversal of their usual dynamic.

Jess chewed on the side of her fingernail and, for once, Lucy couldn't be bothered to point out what a disgusting habit it was.

'Have you had it out with Jason yet?' she said, and Lucy felt wrongfooted, as if she'd been jerked out of one conversation and into a quite different one without any warning. Only much later would it occur to her that maybe Jess had changed the subject on purpose. 'About why he never let on that his mum had been accused of murder?'

Lucy stiffened. 'Why do you always have to be so dramatic? His dad fell down the stairs and some of his hideous relatives tried to pin it on Cora. They let her go almost immediately once it was obvious she had nothing to do with it.'

'So why didn't he tell you?'

This was the question Lucy had been grappling with ever since she found out. Why had he shut her out like that, making out his dad had died of cancer? He claimed that he hated talking about this dark period in his life and didn't want to risk putting her off him, yet if only he'd told her the truth, it would have explained so much. Why he was always so tight-lipped about his dad. Why he and Cora were so close. Who knew what Jason must have witnessed as a child, how he might have considered himself, even at an early age, his mum's protector? How terrifying it must have been to lose one parent – even if that parent had been a bit shit – and then be faced with the prospect of losing the other.

Until a few days ago, Lucy would have sworn that she and Jason knew each other inside out. Soulmates, she always told people. Now, it was beginning to dawn on her how much there was about this man she'd married that she didn't know.

But then, maybe that was all right, she realized with surprise. Wasn't that what marriage was all about, in the end, finding out bit by bit who this other person really was, like unwrapping layer after layer of tissue paper to get to the thing itself – only sometimes the unwrapping was the best part?

The others arrived in dribs and drabs. With bags and hats and passports and sunglasses and hastily printed boarding passes. Zoe was pale and hunched over, and Lucy felt a pang of pity. Travelling with an upset stomach was the worst, let alone on top of everything else that had happened. Next came Jason, with Gabriel and Cora. Lucy could tell instantly that Jason was using his polite voice, which lacked the warmth and richness of his usual one. But at least they were talking. That was something.

When her mum and dad stepped through the doorway, Lucy's heart constricted. Her dad had aged overnight, as if someone had put him in one of those phone apps that show you how you'll look in twenty years' time. His skin was grey and his spine was curved over like a letter 'c'. Her mum, on the other hand, seemed swollen with resolve, leading the way outside. They weren't talking to each other, and yet they weren't entirely separate from each other either, brushing arms at one point, another time her father putting his hand on the small of his wife's back, a habitual gesture he must have done thousands of times over the course of their marriage. Lucy was both surprised and, she found, hopeful, when her mum didn't instantly pull away.

A taxi pulled up in the hotel car park. At first, Lucy thought the taxi company must have made a mistake and sent them this saloon instead of the minibus they'd ordered, but then the back door opened and a man climbed out with a British winter pallor as if he hadn't seen the sun since last year and clothes that were far too heavy for the weather – jeans and a shirt with full-length sleeves with a T-shirt underneath. His hair was almost completely white, although closer examination of his face put him at under fifty.

She took in the eyes, which were familiar – large and peculiarly convex, fringed with sandy lashes – and her heart stopped in her chest. As the taxi drove away, the man turned to face them all. His expression was one of utter, abject weariness, as if life had coiled itself around him like a python and squeezed him dry, leaving just this husk of skin and bone.

'I expect you must be the wedding party.'

16/6/19, 13.23. Original English-language transcript of police interview with Mrs Vivian Cassandra Kaffel. Police officers: Theodoros Christakis and Kostas Stephanides. Interpreter: Xanthe Liourdis.

They're quite a stand-offish bunch, the Collinses. Not terribly friendly. I think I'm a little bit too out there for them. Too outré. They can't work me out. Like I say, Jess is the best of them. The others are quite conventional types. What's he saying? Yes, OK, I suppose I do mean dull. I couldn't really see the appeal of them, to be honest, but you know, Michelle wanted to attach herself to a family like a virus attaches itself to a healthy cell of a living organism. I don't suppose it mattered which family.

Even though I was outside the group, I could sense the tensions building as the week wore on. I know what you're going to ask, and the answer is yes, I did suspect there had been something between Michelle and Dominic Collins. I'm very sensitive to emotional currents. Currents. No, not like tides. Like electricity.

The thing you have to understand about girls like Michelle – damaged girls – is that they crave stability above everything, but they have no concept of how to establish it themselves. From scratch. Well, how could she? A mother like that? So they have to steal it wholesale. I imagine she had a pattern of older boyfriends who gave the impression of having stability already hardwired into them. And by stability, I mean family. So I could see right away Dominic Collins would have been her type.

And let's face it, she didn't have much competition. The wife – Hazel – is a very beta sort. Hanging back all the time, not really saying much. As I say – dull. Which makes what she did last night all the more surprising!

By the end of the week, I'd noticed a change in the energy of the group. The atmosphere was quite toxic, really. I had to keep them at arm's length for my own wellbeing. I suspected Michelle might have worked out who I was, but I was holding back, trying to decide if she posed a risk. There was just one moment where we had a . . . connection. We were outside the hotel restaurant, and she looked at me as if she was begging me to save her. Classic rescue fantasy, I'm afraid. Of course, I regret it now. Not having stepped in. Perhaps I might have averted what happened. I have a knack of knowing the right thing to say.

Look, will you tell him to stop staring at me like that. The young one. Like he's judging me. I'm sure, in his culture, it's all happy families sitting around the dinner table smashing plates, or whatever it is they do, but we're a bit more complicated where I come from. And yes, maybe I made mistakes, but no more than anyone else. What's that line from *Lear*? I was more sinned against than sinning. Don't tell me they haven't heard of *King Lear* either?

Look, I know it may not look like it, but I'm grieving. She was my granddaughter. Let's not forget that. I've suffered a loss. I've suffered a series of losses, actually. First my son, then her mother, then her. It's hard to be alone at my age.

I'm only human.

Chapter Sixty-six

Hazel

The silence had that itchy, crawling-with-ants quality, and Hazel felt compelled to break it.

'That's right. And you must be Shelly's uncle.' Her voice cracked on the girl's name. 'We're so sorry . . . I'm so sorry.'

The man ran a hand over his eyes. His skin seemed so pasty compared to the rest of them, as if he was ill.

'It was an accident. That's what the bloke from the consulate said.'

'That's right,' said Jason, stepping forward to shake the man's hand. 'I'm very sorry for your loss.'

'Thank you, but the truth is, as you all probably know, I hadn't seen Michelle in several years. I feel bad about that now but . . . anyway, I'm all there is.'

'Apart from your mother,' said Hazel. She hadn't meant to put that knowing inflection on the end of the sentence, but there was something about Vivian's greedy self-absorption that made her claims to motherhood – *grand*motherhood, even – seem impossible.

'So it's true, then?' It was hard to imagine Shelly's uncle could get any paler, but Hazel could swear he had. 'The man from the consulate said there was someone claiming to be Michelle's grandmother, but she had no proof, no documentation, so I was still Shelly's next of kin. I thought he was confused. *Hoped*, probably. I haven't laid eyes on my mother in thirty years. As you can probably tell, ours wasn't a particularly happy family.' He cleared his throat. 'Is she here?'

He looked suddenly like a child, standing there, those large eyes of his full of fear but also a kind of hopeful excitement, and Hazel's own eyes blurred with tears.

'No, she buggered off yesterday,' said Jess. 'You're saved.'

It was Nina who'd broken it to them last night as they sat down for dinner in the hotel restaurant. Nina, who had been wafting around the place like a ghost since the wedding. Dom had wanted to confront the wedding planner about Vivian's claim – that she'd overheard Nina saying someone at the hotel had been tampering with the food or the drinks, deliberately sabotaging the wedding. But Hazel had said absolutely not. Shelly was the one who'd been making them all ill. Her own grandmother had told them that. Lucy had watched her buy the eyedrops, for goodness' sake. It was no coincidence that there'd been no new outbreaks of illness in the last twenty-four hours, or that the men had remained entirely unaffected, she'd said. Shelly had chosen her victims well. Dom had gone quiet after that.

When Nina had approached them at dinner, they'd all been seated around one table on the terrace, barely speaking, the other diners giving them a wide berth, as if death might be catching.

Nina had glanced at their food and, for one awful moment, Hazel had thought she'd come to repeat the tampering allegations, but instead she said:

'I've been talking to the police, and I thought I should let you know that Vivian has done a runner.'

It seemed that after spending most of the morning questioning her at the station, the Greek police had been sufficiently concerned about Vivian's credibility to start investigating her background. They'd soon discovered that she was well known to the Greek authorities, having left over the years a trail of unpaid bills and fines criss-crossing the Aegean and the Adriatic in her wake. But by the time they arrived back at the hotel late that afternoon to take her to the station for questioning, she'd already checked out. The taxi driver who took her said he'd dropped her by the ferry port, but there was no record of any onward journey. When the hotel checked the credit card she had been using, it was found to be stolen.

The pale man with Shelly's eyes looked both relieved and deflated. How much unearned power women had over their children, it occurred to Hazel suddenly. Even when they were entirely absent from their lives.

'That sounds like my mother, I'm afraid.'

Now Dom spoke, as he had done so rarely since guilt had hollowed him out.

'If you need an account of what happened . . .'

He saw it as his penance, Hazel could tell. To offer up confessional to this man who was as close to family as Shelly had ever known. Dom wanted to hold himself responsible for everything that had happened, not understanding that Hazel needed that not to be the case, needed Shelly to have had agency.

Shelly's uncle held up his hand, and Hazel saw he had an ink stain on his palm, as if a biro had burst while he was writing something down.

'It can wait. I don't think I could take it in properly at the moment. It's all been quite a shock.'

He bent to pick up the bag he'd dropped by his feet, and something pinched Hazel's stomach hard when she realized he was leaving so she stepped in front of him.

'Your mother said Shelly did it to you too,' she blurted out. 'Put something in your tea to make you ill. Eyedrops.'

She needed him to confirm what they already knew. That Shelly had been a threat.

The man blinked in surprise. This close, Hazel could see threads of red capillaries like hairline cracks in his right cheek.

'Shelly was damaged by her childhood,' he said eventually. 'It's not her fault.'

And then he was gone, but Hazel felt a flare of relief that subsided into a new sense of security that allowed her finally to feel proper pity for the dead girl. What kind of miserable upbringing must she have had, to react so extremely to rejection? How desperate must she have been to belong somewhere to be driven to hurt the very people to whom she wanted to belong?

There was a low buzzing noise, which gradually increased in volume, the sound of an engine revving up the steep hill towards them. And now, a navy-blue minibus appeared, its tyres sending up a spray of small grey stones, its windscreen blurred with dust.

The driver jumped out and set about opening up the back doors and the boot, and the wedding party started picking up bags and cases, hats and jackets which, in the white-hot glare of the late-morning Greek sun, they couldn't for the life of them imagine ever wearing again. Already Hazel felt lighter, just at the thought of getting away from this hotel, this island. She'd decided that when she got back, she would get in touch with the National Union of Journalists, even retain that expensive lawyer if they had to. See if there was a case for challenging her redundancy. They could remortgage the house again. Downsize, even. Looking back on it all, she couldn't believe she'd just accepted being basically replaced by someone younger and cheaper. Why hadn't she fought it?

Things were going to be different from now on. She and Dom would stop skirting around each other and get it all out in the open. His affair, her dissatisfaction. Pull all that tangled mess out of the cupboards where they'd shoved it over the years and sort through it. She'd had enough of feeling like she was scrutinizing her own life through that plastic eyepiece she used to use, always observing and studying, filtering her own feelings through other people's.

Hazel picked up her handbag and did a last-minute check. Passport. Boarding card. Glasses.

'Wait! Just a moment!'

Nina came flying out from the hotel lobby, looking utterly transformed from the crushed figure she'd cut the previous evening.

'Lucy. Jason. I'm so glad I caught you. Listen, once again, I'm so terribly sorry how this turned out. Such a total tragedy. I've just seen Shelly's uncle inside. That poor, poor man. But I did want to tell you some good news. Well, not good, that's the wrong word. But comforting, hopefully.'

Even her voice sounded different today. Stronger. More assured.

'As you know, the police have been investigating Mrs Kaffel's claims of deliberate food poisoning. The samples they took from the hotel kitchen have all tested normal so far, but the health and safety people were here yesterday, checking out everything, and guess what they found?'

Her eyes flashed around the group as if she expected an answer. When none came, she rushed on, her words tumbling over each other. 'It's the jacuzzi in the hotel spa! There's something in it. Some kind of bacteria that has been making people ill. Apparently, other guests have also complained of tummy aches and feeling sick, but no one put two and two together.'

'So it wasn't Shelly?' asked Lucy. And she, too, looked brighter suddenly, her world recalibrating itself

– obviously not back to the sunny place it had been before Shelly died and she found out about her and Dom, but at least to a place where people didn't go around trying to harm other people, particularly not people they were supposed to love.

'So that's why none of the blokes have had it,' said Jason. 'Because we skipped the spa day?'

'Exactly. To be honest, I had a couple of dark nights of the soul, wondering if it might have been something to do with me. There's a local man with links to the hotel who has a grudge against me. Well, against my husband, really. My soon-to-be-ex-husband, to be completely accurate. I can tell you now, because I'm giving up the wedding business and moving back home, so it doesn't matter any more. My husband – my ex-husband – is going to stay here and try to sell the house – well, after he's taken the original seller to court.'

'Because of us?' Lucy looked as if she was about to cry.

'No. God, no. It was just time. That's all.'

Lucy stepped forward and threw her arms around the wedding planner, who seemed surprised, but pleased. 'Thanks so much for everything you've done, Nina,' she said, stepping back and wiping away a tear that was tracking down her cheek. 'And thank you for setting our minds at rest. It's all still shit, obviously, but I do feel a little bit better, knowing what Vivian said was a load of bollocks. I mean, I knew it was, deep down. Shelly was a lot of things, but she wasn't a psychopath. She'd never have hurt us. So, in that way, it's a huge relief that it was all just a terrible accident, isn't it, Mum? Mum?'

The sun was now at its highest point, and Hazel, caught in its full glare, found herself swaying, the contents of her still-open handbag spilling to the floor.

'She's going to faint,' shouted Gil, just as Dom stepped forward to put his arm around her waist.

'I've got her,' he said.

Hazel was bundled into the middle row of the car while the others collected up the remaining bags and said their subdued goodbyes to Nina and the hotel staff. As they drove off, the gravel crunching underneath the minibus wheels, the air-conditioning blasted into life, flooding the car with freezing-cold air that sent the bare skin on Hazel's arms popping up into tiny pinpricks of ice.

'Poor old thing,' said Dom. 'It's probably the germs from the hot tub, making you sick again.'

She nodded and leaned her head against the window. She closed her eyes, only to find herself back on that clifftop again, running towards the voices, her feet moving, in those stupid, stupid shoes, even before her brain had properly processed the situation, crossing the rough ground that separated the two paths, noticing the two figures walking slowly near the edge, silhouetted against the sky. Again, she saw in her mind the sturdier figure slow to a halt, while her taller, thinner companion continued onwards. Again, Hazel felt her heart surge – *That's right, Jess. Get away from her* – only to constrict again when Shelly turned around, saying something, a question, judging by the upward inflexion at the end. Now she was coming back. No, she was *running* back.

Shouting. But Jess wasn't moving, as if she was rooted to the spot.

Shelly intended to push her.

Hazel felt it in the very bones of her. This girl who had harmed her own family and then tried to harm Hazel's. This girl who had inveigled her way into her ex-lover's world.

Hazel had to do something. She must not, for once in her life, stand back and let events unfold. All these thoughts had flashed through her mind before she was even aware that she was in motion, propelled forward by rage. This girl. *This girl.* This girl had slept with her husband, had destroyed one daughter's wedding. Was now trying to hurt the other. It was up to Hazel to save her. To *act.* Only as she ran to intercept the moving figure of Shelly had Hazel noticed something strange out of the corner of her eye – that Jess was not, after all, standing still, but was wobbling there on the edge of the cliff path. There'd been a split second when they'd looked at each other, mother and daughter – could she have diverted course then? Had there been time? – before the momentum of Hazel's fury carried her onwards, barrelling into Shelly a foot or two from where Jess stood, sending her skidding the yard or so over the edge. A scream, a flapping of arms in thin air, a thud, followed by a dreadful silence. She and Jess gazing at each other through the darkness. Then: 'She was going to hurt you,' Hazel had said, her voice breathless, but energized even to her own ears. 'No. No. She was coming to *help* me.'

Hazel's eyes snapped open. Glancing up into the driver's rear-view mirror, her gaze locked on to Jess, staring at her from the row behind as, in the background, the gleaming white hotel grew smaller and smaller until they turned the first bend and it disappeared. She shivered.

Up in front, the driver leaned over and turned the air-conditioning down.

'No problem,' he said, smiling at Hazel. 'You sit. Relax. Don't do nothing. Soon warm again. No problem at all.'

Therapy Journal, Week 19

You've asked me loads of times to write about my dreams. And I haven't been avoiding it, honestly, I just don't remember them. Haha! I know exactly what you'll be thinking – that I don't want *to remember them. But this morning something woke me at five, and when I fell back to sleep I had one of those super-vivid dreams you sometimes get when your sleep has been disturbed.*

I was back in the basement. In that horrible room with the stripy wallpaper. I'd been there for days. Weeks, even – although in real life it never was that long. I'd been writing on the wall under the loose strip of wallpaper. I had that dull, sick feeling in my stomach. I knew beyond doubt that no one was coming this time and I'd be stuck in there for ever. I'd given up. I remember that very clearly. The feeling of having surrendered all hope.

And then, suddenly, Dom and Lucy and Hazel were all there in the room. I don't remember how they got there, but I do remember them standing in front of that horrible mattress, holding out their hands. And this tremendous surge of joy. And when I woke up, I felt this overwhelming sense of relief. You know how you do when you realize a nightmare is over, and that's all it was, a nightmare. Just dissolving in relief.

And that's it. Dream over. But it was a sign, don't you think? That I should go to the wedding and things will work out OK? I don't know how. I just know they will.

And when you know, you know.

Author's Note

In 2016 I went to Kefalonia with two dear friends on a yoga holiday (there was far more holiday than yoga) and fell instantly in love. The lush hillsides, the crystal sea lapping at hidden coves. When I came up with the idea of writing a novel about a destination wedding on a Greek island, Kefalonia was the obvious choice. It has cliffs, an airport with toilets where a woman who so wished could wash her breasts in the sink, a burgeoning wedding industry, aromatic herbs and flowers that scent the warm early-summer breeze. But this is fiction and certain liberties have been taken, particularly in terms of geography and police procedure. For these I apologize, and I entreat those of you who have never been to visit Kefalonia, to see for yourselves what's real and what's figment. Just be warned, there's a strong risk you might never want to return.

Acknowledgements

Heartfelt thanks go to:

Roma Cartwright and Rikki Finegold, who joined me in saluting the sun at an uncivilized hour of the morning on a platform overlooking the Ionian Sea in magical Kefalonia. Roma, you are always missed.

Travel consultant and long-term Greek resident Diane Steger Koranaki (www.dianas-travel.com), who patiently answered all my random questions about Kefalonia and Greek life in general, and my dear friend Jo Lockwood for introducing us. It goes without saying that any mistakes or downright liberties are completely down to me.

Felicity Blunt, the best agent who ever was, and her brilliant assistant Rosie Pierce. Sarah Harvey, who chats up foreign publishers on my behalf, and the whole crew at Curtis Brown. Also the wonderful Deborah Schneider, my American agent, who works tirelessly for me in the States.

The Transworld team. Frankie Gray – editor, encourager, champion – this book wouldn't be the same without you. And Natasha Barsby and Imogen Nelson for their time and invaluable input. Kate Samano and Sarah Day for catching my mistakes, Rich Shailer for the striking cover, and the peerless Alison Barrow, not just for her unrivalled publicity know-how but for her support and her friendship and the best bookish recommendations.

Amanda Jennings and the North London Writers, who all read rough (very rough!) early drafts and suggested changes that made this a far better book.

Vince Harris, who bid generously in the CLIC Sargent charity auction to have a character named after him and whom I first met outside the library at Manchester University when we were both considerably younger. Hope you enjoy being the alter ego of the enigmatic Gabriel Kidd. BTW, neither of us has changed a bit.

The book editors and book bloggers who make my Twitter timeline a gentler, more enriching place – Sarra Manning, Nina Pottell, Lisa Howells, Anne Cater, Tracy Fenton, Sumaira Wilson and so many others. Also my Killer Women pals, plus the Prime Writers and the crime writers (you know who you are).

All the booksellers who have suffered so much throughout 2020 and whose knowledge and dedication are needed now, more than ever. I urge everyone to visit your local bookshop or order from them online. Similarly, all the librarians who, in addition to being custodians and champions of books, have turned out to be the unsung heroes of lockdown, keeping vital community services running, often at risk to themselves.

My friends and family. Never before in my life have I been more grateful to you lot than over the past difficult year. Michael, Otis, Jake, Billie, Phoebe, Sara, Colin, Ed, Alfie, Simon, Emma, Paul, Ben, Margaret, Nathalie, Andrew, Rikki, Mike, Maxine, Juliet, Mark, Fiona, Richard, Jo, Ed, Steve, Sally, Dill, Helen, Shirley, Cathy, Nick, Maria, Xanthe, Barbara, Paula, Steph, Renata, Mel, Rupert, Philippa, Desmond, Amanda, Marnie, Lisa, Colette, Clare, Anna. I know I'll have missed people out and I apologize profusely – 2020 has turned my brain to mush.

My mum, Gaynor Cohen, who like so many has spent the last year confined to her care home, unsure when she will next get to go out, to hug her family, to sit in the garden in the sunshine with a cat on her lap or drink pink wine in her local pub, but who has never wavered in her optimism that things will get better.

Finally, all you readers. I wouldn't be getting to write my thirteenth set of acknowledgements if it wasn't for you. I'm more grateful than you can ever know. Please stay in touch.

Twitter: @MsTamarCohen
Facebook: www.facebook.com/MsTamarCohen
Instagram: tammycohenwriter
www.tammycohen.co.uk

Also by Tammy Cohen

STOP AT NOTHING

A mother's job is to keep her children safe.

Tess has always tried to be a good mother. Of course, there are things she wishes she'd done differently, but doesn't everyone feel that way?

Then Emma, her youngest, is attacked on her way home from a party, plunging them into a living nightmare which only gets worse when the man responsible is set free.

But what if she fails?

So when Tess sees the attacker in the street near their home, she is forced to take matters into her own hands. But blinded by her need to protect her daughter at any cost, might she end up putting her family in even greater danger?

There's nothing she wouldn't do to make it right ...

'Chillingly believable and absolutely addictive. I read it in three days flat.' LISA JEWELL

OUT NOW

Also by Tammy Cohen

WHEN SHE WAS BAD

You see the people you work with every day. But what can't you see?

Amira, Sarah, Paula, Ewan and Charlie have worked together for years. They know how each one likes their coffee, whose love life is a mess, whose children keep them up at night…But their comfortable routine life is suddenly shattered when an aggressive new boss walks in.

Now, there's something chilling in the air.

Who secretly hates everyone?

Who is tortured by their past?

Who is capable of murder?

'A fresh, clever psychological thriller. I loved it!' CLARE MACKINTOSH

OUT NOW